ᴅy ᴛom Adair

ISBN-13: 978-1480266506
ISBN-10: 1480266507

To my loving wife Cindy…
Words alone can not express the depth of my love for you.
Loyal au mort.

DEDICATIONS

To Gary; an unconventional warrior whose full contribution to the security of our nation is known only to a few men with stars on their shoulders.

From the founding of this Republic to this very day, members of the DeFrance family have defended our freedoms from all enemies; foreign and domestic.

May the light of divine providence forever shine upon them.

ACKNOWLEDGMENTS

Many people (and one dog) were instrumental in providing advice, encouragement, and support to me while writing this novel. If I have forgotten anyone, I sincerely apologize. First to my family, for always supporting me. To Karin Field, Ivanie Stene, and Charles T. DeFrance for reading an early draft and providing invaluable feedback. To Charles S. DeFrance for his continued friendship and technical assistance. To Darrin Kadel and David Larson for their technical insight. For all of their encouragement and support, I want to thank Sadie, Bernard Vonfeldt, Steven & Becky Vonfeldt, Kathy Harding, Mike Langley, Erik & Angie Murphy, Joan and Dan Dolan, Mike and Paula Dorle, Pat Adair, Alan and Linda Sprigg, Mark & Lucy (Sprigg) Fisher, Mike & Stacy Matte, Sandra Wiese, Jerri & Andreas McKee, Dave Maloney, Karen Pearson, Bruce Adams, Carol Agnew, Lee Horsley, Debbie O'Laughlin, Stacy Tingle, Grif, Silvia Pettem, C.J. West, and Andrew E. Kaufman.

To my brethren who strive to make good men better.

To all of those who still chase monsters. Thank you for standing squarely between us and them. You have my undying admiration.

Finally, to the men and women of the Army, Navy, Air Force, Marines, Coast Guard, and National Guard. Your sacrifice makes it possible to live in a country with the freedoms to write this novel.

1

August 2nd, 2013 Denver, Colorado

"Governor…your four o'clock appointment is here."

Barclay checked his watch and rolled his eyes before hitting the intercom on his desk phone. "Send him in."

He had a standing rule with his assistant. Be back in less than ten minutes with some excuse to end the meeting.

His secretary opened the large cherry doors leading to his office and motioned for the guest to enter. Barclay got up from behind his cluttered desk and came around to greet him. He sized up the visitor before he made it half-way across the large office. It was his gift; appraising people.

The man coming towards him looked pale and nervous. He wore tan trousers with a blue shirt and red sweater vest, with a satchel on a strap over his shoulder. He stood a good six inches shorter than Barclay, and fifty pounds heavier.

"Mister…" Barclay asked extending his hand.

"Adiago; Seaton Adiago Mr. Governor," the man said. His hands were clammy and Barclay released his grip quickly.

"Please, Aaron is fine. Can I get you something to drink, Seaton?"

"No…thank you, sir."

"Don't mind if I do," Barclay said as he plucked a heavy glass from the bar and poured two fingers of eighteen year old Scotch.

"So Seaton…my campaign manager said you have something of great importance to show me. Normally I don't make time for such things but he mentioned something about my family's involvement with the Revolutionary war?"

"Yes, Governor."

"Aaron," he corrected the man.

"Yes, well…"

"I understand that you're a researcher, a genealogist of some sort?" Barclay said, trying to pry the information out of him.

The man was sweating profusely now. Barclay noticed the large ring of perspiration under his arm as the man smoothed out his hair.

"Seaton…I don't mean to be rude, but I have a very busy schedule. So if you don't mind cutting to the chase."

"Yes sir," he said pushing his glasses to the bridge of his nose. "It's about the campaign commercial…the one about your family defeating the British."

"Yes," Barclay said. "A bit dramatic I'll agree, but the polling shows the numbers are off the charts. It's the highest rated campaign commercial in modern history. And it's all true of course!" he added with his trademark smile honed from a dozen focus groups.

"Well, that's the thing Governor…" Seaton said. He opened his mouth to speak but nothing came out. Barclay was starting to grow impatient.

"Spit it out, Seaton. I don't have all day."

"Your ad mentioned a relative that fought alongside General Washington to defeat the British. I don't know if you're aware but over half the officers in the Continental Army were Masons. When I saw the ad, I got curious about your relative and did some digging."

"So my great-great- great grandfather was a Mason?" Barclay said with indifference as he took a drink.

"No sir…and he didn't fight the British."

"Come again?" Barclay said as he sat on the edge of his desk.

"Sir, I didn't set out to find this…I voted for you!" the man said.

"What are you talking about?"

"Sir, Taylor Barclay didn't fight against the British…he was in league with them."

Barclay smirked as he set his drink down on the desk. "Is this supposed to be some kind of joke?"

"I'm afraid not sir," Seaton said avoiding his gaze.

"How exactly did you come to this delusion?" Barclay asked in a firm voice.

Seaton handed him a tri-folded letter which Barclay opened and read through, mouthing the words throughout.

Bloodlines

"This is preposterous! This letter is supposed to prove your claim?" Barclay said tossing the letter on his desk.

"Sir, I found three separate sources. I've chronicled all my data in my journal here," he said pulling the leather bound journal from his shoulder bag. "Academically speaking the data is solid. I'd be happy to provide a copy for verification."

"*Bullshit*. You expect me to believe that my family tried to kill General George Washington...and spied for the British!?" his said, his voice coming to a crescendo.

"Sir, I...I came to you with this to spare you any embarrassment. If I found this evidence, someone else might, too. I very much want to see you become President," he said.

Barclay narrowed his gaze and laid his index finger over his mouth. A second later he was smiling and wagging his finger at Seaton.

"I see what's going on here. Alright...what will it take?"

"Sir?" Seaton asked.

"You've got yourself a chip in the big game now. Frankly, I don't believe a word of this shit but that's not the point is it? My opponent will have a field day with this allegation. Perception is reality as they say, so...what will it take to buy your silence?"

"Sir...I'm not here for extortion, I want to help."

"And just how the *fuck* are you helping me Seaton?" Barclay snapped before regaining his composure. He saw Seaton flinch as the words spat from his mouth. Barclay looked down and took a deep breath before adjusting the knot in his tie. He walked around behind his seated guest and placed both hands firmly on his shoulders. Barclay felt the man flinch and his muscles tighten.

"Seaton...I apologize. The stress of this campaign has been, well...substantial. And this news, well...it's unexpected to say the least," he said squeezing lightly.

"Yes sir," Seaton said not turning around.

"Have you told anyone about this research?"

Now the man turned in his seat to look at Barclay. "No sir, I haven't told a soul; I swear," he said holding up his right hand.

"Good...good." Barclay said as his mind formulated a strategy.

"Seaton...I can tell you're a man of honor. You could have gone to the press but you came here instead. That tells me I can trust you."

"Yes sir," Seaton said with a slight tremble in his voice.

"Let's do this. Why don't you leave your journal here for my chief of staff to review for a few days and we can all figure out a way through this."

The man raised an eyebrow and looked confused. "Sir, I...I can't leave my journal. This is all of my research."

"Seaton..."

Barclay was cut off as his assistant knocked three times and opened the door.

"Governor, I'm sorry but the Attorney General is here and says he needs to talk to you right away." Much to Barclay's dismay, the tension in her voice was believable.

Before he could shoo her away Seaton jumped from his chair like it was a spring.

"Uh, you're clearly busy sir. I'll get out of your hair and maybe we can talk in a few days," he said as he crossed the floor and brushed past the smiling assistant.

Barclay was about to stop him but in an unfortunate turn of fate the Attorney General actually came through the door. The man wasn't an ally. Barclay offered his best smile, and a handshake, as he cursed his bad luck.

The meeting lasted less than ten minutes, but the damage was done. Barclay cursed the attorney general as he showed him out the door. Once the door was latched Barclay returned to his desk and tapped the intercom button on his desk phone.

"I don't want to be disturbed for the next thirty minutes," he said.

"Yes, Mr. Governor," his secretary replied.

Barclay stopped at the bar and refilled his scotch before heading to the wall safe. He punched in the six digit code and placed his thumb on the biometric scanner until he heard the distinctive clank of the bolt opening. He swung open the door and eyed the black satellite phone on the top shelf as he took a sip of scotch.

It had been several months since he had used this phone. After his predecessor's assassination, he had kept their conversations brief and infrequent. It wasn't uncommon for powerful men to employ mercenaries. There were advantages to employing an elite group of men willing to take enormous risks for money. In this case…a lot of money.

Barclay's family had used men like these since the Hessians. Private American 'security' groups were cheaper, but these men had been raised with certain patriotic values. They could never be trusted to engage in activities against their own government; no matter how much money was thrown at them. Barclay preferred the Russians for such matters.

The Gerovit team specialized in the impossible. Comprised of former Vyemple members of the FSB, GRU and Spetznas, the former Russian soldiers were some of the most dangerous killers in the world.

After the fall of communism, the newly appointed business-like czars needed protection and muscle as they carved up the natural resources of the motherland and formed their consortiums into powerful criminal enterprises. The Gerovit was only too happy to offer their services to those who could afford them. The fees were excessive but they had never failed to complete an assignment. Barclay had only one contact; a man code-named Reaper.

He took the phone and dialed the only number programmed into it. Three rings later a familiar voice answered.

"Hello Aaron…or should I say Mr. Governor?"

Barclay got right to the point. "We have a problem."

"I'm listening," the man said.

"A man came to my office today. He's in possession of some damaging information that could derail our future plans."

"You mean your future plans," the man said.

Barclay set his drink down and shifted the phone to his other ear. "I would think you'd be happy to soon have the ear of the President of the United States," he whispered.

The silence on the other end of the line was deafening.

"Go on," the man said.

Barclay spent the next few minutes describing his encounter with Seaton Adiago.

"I need you to get the journal and clean up this mess as soon as possible," Barclay said.

"We can make it all disappear," the man said. The icy tone of his words sent a shiver through Barclay. He swallowed hard before speaking.

"I don't want him to disappear. Someone might get suspicious and start poking around. I need you to make it look like an accident or suicide."

"*Da.* Send me as much personal information as you can about this man."

"When can you be here?" Barclay asked.

"It may take me a day or two."

"*Jesus,*" Barclay snapped. "I'll pay to get you here as soon as possible."

"I need time to assemble the intelligence and make arrangements. The last assignment took months to prepare." Reaper said.

"Just get here," Barclay said before he tapped the end call button. He stared at the satellite phone and replaced it on the shelf before closing the wall safe. He grabbed his glass and walked to one of the large office windows as he peered out towards the Rocky Mountains. The sun was two fingers above the horizon and setting fast.

By Monday, he thought, *everything will be back on track.*

2

August 4th; The Denver Consistory

The Gerovit jet touched down at Denver International Airport a little after one in the afternoon. Reaper had brought along a new man to shadow him for the assignment. He was young, but the former Spetnaz sniper showed great promise. His military performance and evaluation reports scored him high in intelligence but warned of sociopathic tendencies coupled with a lack of empathy. He was *perfect* for Gerovit.

A dark SUV and driver were waiting for them at the bottom of the air stairs.

"Welcome," the muscular driver said in a heavy Russian accent as he opened the back door.

"*Spahseeba*," Reaper said as he and his teammate, Marat, stowed their bags and climbed in the back seat. The driver was a member of the local Russian mafia whom Reaper employed from time to time for simple tasks. It was much safer than hiring a local driving service. These men didn't ask a lot of questions, and, if necessary, could be counted on to kill.

As expected, the driver wasn't talkative which suited Reaper. He thumbed the window control and cracked it open a few inches to take in the mile-high air. For a moment, it reminded him of his boyhood home in the Urals. It took them forty-five minutes to reach downtown from the airport on the eastern plains. Reaper had the driver circle the block around the Consistory as he checked for potential threats.

After spotting Seaton's vehicle in the parking lot, he started searching for a suitable surveillance position. About a block past the objective Reaper saw an opening.

"Pull over," Reaper said as he pointed to a street side parking space. The driver complied but rolled one tire onto the curb before over-correcting it. The tire came back down on the road with a thud as Reaper shot a disapproving gaze at the man in the rearview mirror.

Reaper retrieved a pair of compact binoculars from his bag, turned to face the back window, and surveyed the street. A similar looking black SUV was parked on the street directly across from the consistory.

Stupid, Reaper thought.

He had instructed the mafia men to pick a discrete spot to watch the target. To his way of thinking, that wasn't directly across the street.

"Did you bring what I asked for?" Reaper said to the driver.

"*Da,*" the man replied as he dug a portable police radio out of a bag on the passenger seat and handed it back to Reaper.

Reaper powered it on and tuned it to channel one of the Denver police. Radio traffic began squawking and he turned the volume down so pedestrians didn't hear it outside the vehicle.

"Now what?" the driver asked.

"Now…we wait," Reaper said bringing the binoculars back up. "Keep your eyes out for anyone paying too much attention to us," Reaper said to Marat.

"Will we be here all night?" the driver asked.

"*Nyet.* Once night falls I'll be on my way."

The driver looked satisfied by the answer and pulled out his smart phone.

"No calls, no texting; just watch the street." Reaper said.

The man gave an annoyed sigh as he shoved the phone back in his jacket pocket and settled into his chair.

Reaper exchanged a brief glance with Marat. The younger soldier looked annoyed with the driver.

The next few hours were uneventful. Reaper monitored the radio traffic and had seen only two police cruisers come down the street in the last hour. It had been an hour since the sun had set and darkness was setting in on the city. Then he heard a troubling call over the radio.

"David fifty-five."

"Go for David fifty-five," the officer replied to dispatch.

"Check out a suspicious vehicle in the thirteen-hundred block of Grant Street. Reporting party is calling from the Denver Consistory and says two white males have been watching the building for a while. Vehicle is a black SUV with unknown plates."

"Copy that," the officer said. "En route from Ogden and Colfax."

"Call the other men...*now!*" Reaper snapped at the driver. The man called the other car and Reaper snapped his fingers for the phone which the driver handed back over the seat.

"Timur here," the man answered.

"The police are on their way. Have one man get out and watch the target vehicle. Keep this phone on you in case I need you. Tell the other to drive away and come back in two hours. Go now." Reaper said.

There was silence for a split second before the man responded.

"*Da*," he said before ending the call.

Reaper watched as the lights came on and the SUV pulled out into the street. It traveled a half block before turning west onto a side street. He watched a heavy built man cross the street towards the parking lot but couldn't tell if he was the man he spoke to. It didn't matter. Less than thirty seconds later, he watched the police car turn onto Grant from Colfax and begin heading his way.

"I'm leaving," he said as he opened the door and got out onto the sidewalk. "You stay with the driver. Wait for further instructions." Reaper said to Marat.

"I'm not coming with you?" Marat asked.

"*Nyet*; too risky now. I'll re-evaluate and let you know if I need backup."

"What about my phone?"

"Get a new one," Reaper said as he hoisted his pack over his shoulder and slammed the door. He started walking south when the driver rolled down the passenger window.

"You're walking the wrong way," the man said.

Annoyed, Reaper shot the driver a penetrating gaze that would stop a charging grizzly.

"Go!" was all he said.

The driver checked his mirror and pulled out onto the street and turned east onto the next side street.

Reaper stood by a bus stop as he watched as the slow moving police cruiser rolled by without paying him any attention. He watched the tail lights disappear before circling back towards his target.

***

9

Reaper spent several hours on foot in the neighborhood studying pedestrian flow, scouting for security cameras, and evaluating emergency escape routes. His man, Marat had kept an eye on the target vehicle and reported every half hour that it hadn't moved. The target was still in the building.

It was nearly midnight before he entered the Denver Consistory through the basement. His movements were slow and deliberate. Insertion to an unknown building, especially large ones, was a dangerous activity for men in his line of work. You never knew who, or what, you might run into before reaching your target.

As he hoped, the building was dark and quiet save a soft glow of light spilling down the hallway. Reaper had changed into all dark clothing from his bag before entering the building. Palms flat against the wall, he inched his way step by step towards the lighted room. As he got closer, Reaper caught a glimpse of the man in the reflection of a framed picture on the opposite wall. The dim light made it difficult for him to see details, but it was clear that a man was sitting at a large desk in some kind of office or library. Reaper froze as he studied the man.

The man appeared to be studying at a desk. Reaper could make out a number of opened books on the desk and hoped one was the journal. He watched for several minutes as the man turned pages and made notations. Reaper felt his heart rate jump a little as he realized the end was near. Then he heard the man muttering to himself. Reaper couldn't make out what he was saying so he took another step along the wall. His body stiffened as one of the floor boards moaned in protest and he saw the man's head turn towards the hallway.

Shit, he thought. The next thirty seconds seemed like an hour as Reaper didn't allow himself to as much as breathe. He didn't even shift his gaze for fear any movement might be seen in the same reflection he was using to spy on his target. It was a ridiculous thought, but at the moment it seemed prudent. Then the man rose from his chair.

Reaper mentally walked through the steps required to draw his knife, advance on the room, and dispatch the man as he came into the hallway but the man turned and walked through a door behind him inside the room. Reaper strained to hear the sound of footsteps, and elevator...anything. Thirty seconds...nothing.

He was just about to advance on the room when he heard the distinctive sound of a toilet flushing. Reaper felt his muscles relax a bit and he allowed himself to take a breath. Then he heard the man washing his hands followed by a paper towel dispenser handle being ratcheted. A few seconds later the man came back into the room and sat back down at the desk.

At that moment it dawned on Reaper that he could have used the moment to get into the room and surprise the old man as he came back in. He cursed himself for the oversight and continued moving slowly down the hall.

Ten feet away...then five; his fingers crawled along the wall like tarantulas as he advanced. When he was just outside the doorway he could peer into one corner of the room without being seen. It was a library.

Every inch of shelf space was stuffed with old leather bound books. They looked dusty and worn from days long gone. A single Tiffany style desk light cast a dim glow over the cherry wood furniture and shelving in the room. Reaper saw a large wooden grandfather clock keeping watch like the Queen's guard outside Buckingham palace. A large beehive was carved into the front panel.

Reaper slowly poked his head around the corner and laid eyes on the man who was reading a book. It took only a second to recognize him. The man looked old and tired; hardly a challenge. It was times like these that Reaper questioned the need for *his* services. Surely this old man could have been dealt with by one of Barclay's local thugs.

Then he remembered something. People don't hire you to kill...they hire you to be *invisible*. Any street thug could shoot a man on the street but a professional...he killed with no one being the wiser.

Reaper had two choices. He could enter the room and advance on the man, but what if the target was armed? This was Colorado after all. He was confident of his ability to take the man out with his knife but the sound of a gunshot might alert the authorities. Not to mention a bullet hole in the wall...or worse...in him. The second option was to lure the man to him. It was riskier but, given the circumstances, he decided to try it.

Using his left index finger, Reaper lightly tapped on the wall.

One...two...three...four...

He kept the tapping soft and rhythmic. He counted eight taps before the man slowly looked up from his book and stared at the darkened hallway. Reaper could see the man cock his head in the reflection of another painting on the opposite wall and hoped it was working. The man could just as easily call nine-one-one or run to the bathroom but Reaper kept up the soft tapping.

The man gently closed the book in front of him and stood. The man took a step to the edge of the desk and stopped, resting his hand on the edge. Reaper kept up the rhythmic tapping. The man took slow, deliberate steps towards the hallway. It was clear he was afraid, but he kept coming closer. Reaper inched his right hand into his pocket and drew out a custom garrote. As the target turned into the hallway, Reaper slipped the thin cord over his head and tightened it across his neck in the blink of an eye.

Reaper felt the man's body tighten as he slipped in behind him for better leverage. Then the unexpected happened. The man thrust his head backward. Reaper felt his nose crack and his grip relax as they stumbled backwards and fell onto the floor of the library.

Reaper grabbed the man under his arms and flipped him up and over before spinning around and coming to his feet. He wanted to keep himself between the target and the doorway.

The target was on all fours catching his breath when he looked up at Reaper.

"Mr. Adiago, I presume." The man held out an open hand as if to keep him at bay.

"I haven't said a word to anyone," Seaton said. "I...I won't."

"Unfortunately, that's the problem. We don't believe you. Scandals like these bring empires down. We simply can't take the risk."

The man looked around the room in a panic.

"It's over Seaton," Reaper said.

The older man grabbed a book from the desk and clumsily threw it at Reaper. He side-stepped it and shot him a disapproving look. Then Seaton grabbed the chair. He wound up and threw the chair like an Olympic discus thrower. As Reaper moved to the right, Seaton ran full steam to the left. Twenty years and forty pounds earlier and he might have made it to the hallway.

Reaper spun his right arm in a back-handed swing connecting with Seaton's head. The librarian collapsed to the floor in a heap. His let out a loud groan from the sledgehammer-like hit before looking up from the floor. Reaper grabbed him by the collar and jerked him to his feet.

"Wait…Wait…I… I have money," Seaton pleaded.

"Money isn't as valuable to us as secrecy."

Reaper's left hand cupped the older librarian's forehead and he pulled back, exposing his neck to his tactical fighting knife. With one smooth stroke he severed the major arteries in the neck causing a geyser of blood to arch ahead of him and out into the hallway.

The older man's body slumped against Reaper's as the assassin dragged him back to his desk. He propped him in the chair and laid his head on the open volumes scattered across the table. Searching the man's pockets he found what he had hoped for--an old pocket knife.

Smearing the knife with blood, he placed it in the man's hand on the desk top. He had brought a folding knife just in case, but it was always better to use one the victim's family would identify.

Blood seeped from the neck wound and coursed over the desk like a red tide as Reaper scanned the desk for the journal, but he didn't see it. Barclay had described it to him as a small, leather bound book. Seaton must have hidden it at his home.

Ignoring the journal, Reaper pulled a tri-folded letter from his pocket. He had paid a hefty fee to a world class forger in his employ to write the suicide note based on the published writings and e-mails they could find from the target on short notice. That had been the trickiest part of the whole operation.

Since Reaper couldn't guarantee that Seaton had told others of his findings, the letter contained the perfect blend of remorse and paranoia regarding his flawed research. The Gerovit psychologist who drafted the language made sure to add the proper key words to convince any police expert of its authenticity.

Reaper glanced at his watch. *Damn.* He was running five minutes behind schedule. The dim hallway made finding the blood spatter difficult and he couldn't afford to leave any trace of the murder. The police would need to conclude it was a suicide by a desperate and crazy man if his mission were to succeed.

In Reaper's experience, most cops looked for easy conclusions to a case, and he was planning on denying them any evidence to suggest foul play.

The aging librarian had showed surprising speed and strength for a man in his seventies. After thirty minutes of staging and cleaning, Reaper took one last look around, listened for any sounds in the building, then crept back through the dark hallway to his secret entry point.

The tunnel connecting the Masonic Center's kitchen to the basement of the Capitol building was known only to a select few. Barclay had seemed pleased to be able to finally put the family secret to good use.

Seeing the dank cavernous stone walls for himself reminded him of a medieval dungeon. Taking a knee, he washed the black face paint from his skin with a towelette and tucked it in his pocket. He could leave no trace of his presence behind. He steadied himself against the wall as he stood. Rough and dirty, he wondered about who the last man was to walk down this tunnel.

Once at the end, he carefully examined the door for any signs of disturbance. He pressed his ear against the cold, iron door and listened for any sounds. Hearing nothing, he applied another ample coating of lubricant to the hinges and slid the door open an inch at a time until his body would fit through. After closing the hidden door and replacing the false wall, he darted past the stairwell leading to the main floor of the Capitol. He checked his watch. Security wouldn't make their rounds for another ten minutes.

Reaper followed the narrow-gauge railroad tracks along the concrete floor to the boiler room a block away. Once used to haul coal, they now served as his guide through the labyrinth of passageways in the dim light. The only other souls in his path were the two technicians monitoring the power plant. Barclay's security team assured him they would be lounging in an office doing paperwork, or watching television. He covered the last fifty yards of the tracks with ease.

Crouching at the entry to the boiler room, he retrieved a small circular telescoping mirror from his cargo pants and eased it into the room. Reaper listened hard for any sign of the two technicians. Muffled voices were barely audible over the hum of the burners as he angled his mirror for a better look. Up in the window of the second floor office was the unmistakable flicker of light from a television. No doubt the two were watching the Rockies baseball game.

Reaper gave one final look around the room and snaked his way through the large boilers keeping out of sight from the office windows above. Reaching the rear loading dock door, he pressed his ear against the cold metal listening for any sounds of people in the adjoining parking structure. Confident no one was around, he eased the door open just enough to get his fingers out.

The hinges felt stiff so he applied a fresh coating of lubricant and tried again. Something was blocking it on the other side. *Probably a set of pallets.* The hinges were silent so he put his shoulder into the heavy metal door with all his strength. Then he felt a hand grip his ankle.

The drunken woman was not pleased to have been awoken from her slumber. Wrapped in a dirty blanket, she staggered to her feet and wagged a boney finger at him while offering a slurred scolding. A cloud of stale beer and bile enveloped his face before he took hold of her. Her death was quick and efficient. He hated killing without compensation, but sometimes it had to be done. His orders were clear. No witnesses. After wiping the blade on the woman's blanket, he lowered her back against the door on her side and wiped his hands on his pants.

Seeing no one in the parking lot, he took a knee next to a large dumpster and punched a number into his burn phone. There was no voice on the other end when it connected.

"It's done," was all he had to say.

The line went dead a second later.

Reaper took one look around for witnesses before tossing the phone in the dumpster.

Then, like any other person downtown that evening, he strolled out onto Lincoln Street and faded into the city.

***

15

Governor Barclay massaged his temples as he stared into the glass of twenty-year-old Scotch. His leather bound chair in his study at the Governor's Mansion had become his sanctuary over the last twenty-four hours. Between planning his political campaign for the Presidency, and tying up loose ends with this potential scandal, his nerves were raw.

Politics was war, he reminded himself. Barclay's family history during the Civil War was tumultuous to be sure, but he never imagined his forefathers capable of such devious plans. The thought curled the edge of his lips.

Sitting in his darkened study alone, with only the light from the fireplace to keep him company, Barclay allowed his mind to wander. *What would America look like if the plan had succeeded?*

Reclining in his chair, he closed his eyes and imagined the cascading effects from Europe through the Colonies had the plan worked. Would he now serve as the present day patriarch of the movement? *One step at a time.*

Barclay opened his eyes, took a deep breath, and got up from his chair. He couldn't afford such fantasies right now.

With one last look into the flames, he took a sip of Scotch and turned on his foot towards the door. He didn't make it to the next step before running into a shadowy figure. The man was solid as a brick wall.

"Jesus!" Barclay said.

"Hardly," Reaper said.

"How in the hell did you get in here? You gave me a heart attack," Barclay said, brushing spilled alcohol from his trousers.

***

Reaper raised an eyebrow at Barclay. The stupidity of the question was mind-numbing. Did the man forget what he did for a living?

"Did you get the journal?" Barclay asked.

"It wasn't there."

"What? It has to be there. You searched carefully?"

Reaper's lips pursed as his face grew tight with annoyance. "Obviously, the old man found another hiding place," Reaper said.

Bloodlines

"*Goddamnit*, this is the last thing I need. Do you understand how fragile this house of cards is, my friend? If this scandal breaks, we're done for. Me, you, all your boys and toys; you can kiss all that goodbye. You and me will be swapping food trays at Super Max," Barclay said pointing a finger at him.

Reaper wanted to snap his boney finger back but stopped short of doing so. As much as he despised his employer, the Governor had a point. Besides, Barclay was their best client and, as President, soon to be the most powerful.

"Do you think he hid it somewhere else?" Reaper asked.

Barclay's eyes darted around as he bit his lower lip. "There is only one man this clown would trust with his precious journal."

"Who is that?"

"My head of security discovered that one of Seaton's oldest friends is Art Von Hollen."

Reaper remembered the man and his meddling nephew from his previous assignment in the city.

"If you want me to take care of it, the fee would be double," Reaper replied.

"*Double?* He's an old man!" Barclay yelled.

"It's the nephew. He presents certain...*challenges,*" Reaper said.

"Well, it doesn't matter. My man at the post office has been monitoring packages to that address and the only thing sent from Mr. Adiago was a postcard."

"When did he send it?" Reaper asked.

"This morning, next day delivery."

"What did the postcard say?" Reaper asked, not wanting to leave any stone unturned.

"Some gibberish about an upcoming Masonic performance; it's nothing."

"Then why did he send it express?"

"Stay focused," Barclay said.

"It could be a code," Reaper offered.

Barclay looked at him in disbelief.

"*A code?* The old man wasn't some spy, you fool. If he wanted this man to have the journal he would have sent it. The journal is probably stashed in his house some place."

Tom Adair

Reaper didn't like being dressed down by a sniveling politician but he couldn't afford to alienate the Governor at this moment, so he stood ramrod straight letting the man's criticism wash over him. Barclay sized him up and down.

"Here's what I want you to do. Tomorrow, they'll discover the old man's body at the Consistory. You go sit on the house. I'm sure the police will call the wife to come down to identify the body. Once she leaves, you'll have plenty of time to find that journal."

"And what of Mr. Von Hollen?" Reaper asked.

"What of him?"

"Governor, there are other ways of sending a message. If Adiago really trusted this man, he may have told him of his findings. He *nearly* derailed our plans last time. Do you really want him digging around after the death of his friend?"

"You're assuming he knows of the plot," Barclay countered.

"You're willing to risk that he doesn't?"

***

Barclay turned away and looked out the window toward the city lights. He rubbed his chin as he contemplated the rising cost of keeping this scandal buried. It wasn't as if he didn't have blood on his hands already. There was no sense in turning back now.

He made eye contact with Reaper in the reflection of the window and nodded his head.

"I'll head up there after I'm done with the Adiago residence," Reaper said.

"No, I want this all tied off tomorrow. Send that new kid...what's his name? Marat?"

"I think I should go."

Barclay turned and glared at the assassin. He didn't tolerate insubordination, especially from someone in his employ. "*I* don't pay you to think. I need you close in case there are any problems with the police. Send the kid."

18

3

August 5th; Steamboat Springs, Colorado: The Rocky Mountain Forensic Center

Dr. Art Von Hollen entered his outer office just as the sun crested the mountains east of Steamboat Springs, Colorado. Dragging his feet, Art stopped, rolled back on his heel, and squinted as the bright morning sunlight hit him in the face like a spotlight.

He hated Mondays.

As Director of the "Facility," an internationally acclaimed forensic research and training center, he found an early start to the day was essential in order to run an efficient workplace.

At fifty-six, Art maintained an athletic build to his six foot frame, despite avoiding the gym like it was a leper colony. He changed course and stopped at the small coffee bar. He grabbed his favorite "I'm an elk-a-holic" mug and poured the steaming dark coffee to the brim. After taking a sip, he wiped a dribble from his graying goatee before heading towards his office.

As usual, his personal assistant and childhood friend, Tilly Helton was already in her office typing schedules with robotic actions. An expert in organization and business, Tilly managed the enormous operations and staff like a military general. Together they had created a world renowned research and training center that rivaled the finest resorts.

Art had used his family fortune to spare no expense in creating the five-star surroundings. He thought of it as a reward for the gruesome work experienced by most forensic scientists. He believed students, who were expected to solve impossible puzzles, needed a stimulating environment as opposed to the dreary, dull government training centers. When the students weren't in the classroom they could be found hiking the numerous forested trails or sunning themselves in a canoe on the main lake.

"Good morning, sunshine," Tilly said not looking up.

"Do you ever sleep, young lady?"

"And miss the joy of your morning demeanor?"

It was a playful exchange the two practiced each morning. Art appreciated it for what it was, a way for his morning routine to begin on the right foot.

"There's a postcard waiting for you on your desk," she said.

"And? Anything else you'd like to share?"

"See for yourself," she said with a grin. It was Tilly's way of saying it was a personal delivery.

Peering over the rims of his reading glasses, Art offered a wink and quick smile as he passed her desk. Last night had been a long night, and he wasn't in the mood for any urgent messages. As Director, Art couldn't make time to attend every experiment conducted on the grounds, but the experiment last night had been irresistible.

Several students and faculty were out late testing a new blood reagent developed in the lab. The prototype solution made blood glow in the dark like the popular Luminol reagent, but was ten times more sensitive.

Art called it Sirius, a reference to the brightest star in the night sky. The reagent glowed an intense blue color even with blood diluted to less than one part per ten million. The project had the potential to invigorate thousands of cold homicides by giving investigators a tool to find blood over a century in age. He had been very pleased with the results of the experiment.

Art dropped into his worn leather chair, powered up his computer, and grabbed the stack of mail Tilly had neatly arranged on the corner of his desk. The postcard she had mentioned from his old friend Seaton was on top of the pile. The image on the card was just what Art would have expected; an array of Masonic imagery replicating a historic tapestry. The scene was a popular motif from 19th Century Masonic lore signifying a long journey ahead. It was entitled *From Darkness to Light*.

Art smiled as he flipped the postcard over. His eyes were drawn to the stamp. The American Flag was common enough as a stamp, but on the postcard it had been placed upside down. In the military, it was a signal of distress. Art reflected for a moment before reading the message.

Looking forward to our 14th Degree. I am sorry to burden you with extra work. Remember to relieve yourself and give the ancient adoration after lustration.

Bloodlines

Art leaned back in his chair and read the message again. The annual reunion was forthcoming but Art was not scheduled to take part this year. He had told Seaton of his conflict a few weeks earlier. Art flipped the card over again and looked at the upside down stamp. What was Seaton trying to tell him?

***

Marat settled the crosshairs of the rifle scope on the older man's head. Less than two weeks after joining the mysterious Gerovit group, he had landed his first assignment. It was a chance to prove his worth and skill. He would have preferred more time to study the target, but the operational window was short.

Marat's orders were to kill the target and evac on foot thirty miles north through the mountains into Wyoming where he would rendezvous with his handler. He had spent several hours moving into position under the cover of darkness. He broke radio silence only twice. Once to report his arrival at the objective, and once more when he was settled into the sniper nest. He selected a spot to watch the target from on top of a small rock outcrop between two thick bushes.

The forest was dense and provided good cover from the buildings on the campus. He had made good time skirting the edge of the trees and several small clearings. It was against protocol, but only the elk would be in a position to see him. He thought it was a good plan.

Marat preferred to take the shot at night. Daytime shots increased his risk of being caught. He was confident of his abilities to dispatch his target and the man's secretary without causing too much alarm. Rifle shots were common in the mountains, and at this early hour most students would still be in bed.

Marat checked his watch. Intelligence reports indicated that classes wouldn't begin for at least two more hours. By the time anyone came looking for the bodies, he would be well on his way to Wyoming.

Pressing his right cheek firmly against the composite stock of the Steyr Mannlicher SSG 04 A1 rifle, he gazed through the powerful scope. His legs were spread behind him as he lay on the ground. Using his toes, he nudged his position forward a few inches. At just over 300 meters with a twenty percent down angle, Marat made some quick mental adjustments as he aligned the crosshairs.

His target was several feet back from the window, but the deflection of the bullet through the glass should be minimal, he thought. Slowly, he eased his right thumb up and rested it upon the safety lever. Just as his thumb touched the small ribbed lever, Marat felt the unmistakable cold metal of a rifle muzzle pin his left earlobe to his head.

"Now...*who* might you be?" a voice asked him.

4

Marat froze. Panic coursed through his body as the bush man to his left spoke. He calculated the time needed to thumb off the safety and take the shot mentally running through the motions.

As if reading his mind, the muzzle backed off a half-inch then jabbed him again in the ear.

"Slowly...take your right hand off that weapon and lay it flat on the ground." The voice was calm and deliberate, as if the man had said the words many times before. Then, the bush man repeated the command in perfect Russian.

That was the moment Marat knew he was dealing with a professional and removed his hand from the rifle one finger at a time.

With both hands firmly planted on the forest floor, the rifle muzzle pressed his head to the right. Marat's left eye stretched to its limits in order to catch a glimpse of the man beside him.

He was a bush man with a SCAR rifle. Marat was amazed at the man's field craft. Donning a Ghillie suit fitted with local vegetation, Marat could only make out the man's eyes; that is, until his porcelain white teeth emerged from a broad smile.

"Don't you just hate it when a plan turns to shit?" the man asked.

Marat exhaled as he dared a single question, "How?"

"Luck," he replied.

Marat's left eye darted back to the stranger.

"I saw you sneaking down the ridgeline a few hours ago; pretty sloppy approach. I figured you were headed for this outcropping so I just got ready and waited. You're kind of new at this, aren't you?" the bush man said, light sarcasm in his voice.

Marat felt a surge of anger rising in his chest but dowsed it. He needed a clear mind to act. Being captured was not an option, not with *his* employer.

"Get up," the bush man said.

As the bush man rocked forward from his kneeling position, Marat made his move. He kicked his left arm back against the rifle and rolled to his right. His hands snatched the barrel and pulled. It *almost* worked.

Instead of resisting the pull, the bush man rolled forward slamming his left elbow into the assassin's solar plexus, arching his body through the roll, and landing his right elbow across the man's cheek.

A half-second later the bush man rolled to his knees on the other side of Marat. Reeling with pain, Marat yanked his tactical knife from his upper arm sheath and swung the blade at the bush man.

Marat knew the second his arm swung, it was too slow. The bush man's fingers dug into the pit between Marat's thumb and index finger. The pressure point popped his hand open like a spring trap. His knife tumbled free and stuck into the ground. Marat tried striking out with his left fist but the bush man's right hook caught him first. The last thing he remembered was the man's forearm wrapped around his neck as his mind was overcome with darkness.

***

One nice thing about a world renowned forensic science center, there was always a cop around when you needed one, Art thought.

The local sheriff's office had the suspect handcuffed and on his way to the local jail within the hour. None of the students were even aware of the danger. Art, Tilly, and Art's nephew Daniel were all gathered in Art's office. Much to Tilly's chagrin, Daniel had not bothered to remove his Ghillie suit before entering Art's office.

"Do you have to wear that thing in here?" she asked.

"Sorry Tilly, I'll clean up the mess," he said looking at the dirt and leaves littering the floor.

"That, my dear, is a given," she said, lecturing him like an annoyed parent before her expression changed to one of concern.

"How did you happen to find this man?" Tilly asked.

"I was just getting some air."

"In the woods before the sun came up?" Tilly asked, folding her arms.

Bloodlines

Daniel shrugged his shoulders.

"You're still having trouble sleeping, Daniel?" Tilly asked. Art could hear the concern in her voice.

"I'm fine."

"Of course," Art said with a disapproving look. He looked at Tilly and gave a nod to the door. "You two can discuss that later. Tell me about our mystery guest." Art said, as Tilly closed the door behind her.

Art folded his hands behind his head and leaned back, gazing at the ceiling, as Daniel laid out the details from the morning. When Daniel finished, Art waited a full minute in silence before speaking.

"Do you think he's the same one?"

Daniel knew Art was referring to a serial sniper that had plagued Denver almost a year before. The serial killings had become a national news story that nearly cost Daniel his life. The same couldn't be said for Art's friend, Governor Hoines. Daniel worried that Art's continued pursuit of the killer might lead to retribution one day.

"No," Daniel said.

"How can you be sure?" Art asked.

"This guy was too green. Don't get me wrong, he's had military training but he's not the sniper we've been looking for. Honestly Uncle Art, it was pure luck I saw him in the first place."

"Nightmares?" Art asked.

"I'm handling it," Daniel said dismissing the question.

Art stood and walked to the window. He stared across the meadow to the spot on the hillside where Daniel had explained he had caught the sniper.

"I suppose I've generated a number of 'fans' over the years. Death threats come with the territory."

"This guy understood Russian," Daniel said.

Art turned back to his nephew and pinched the bridge of his nose between his eyebrows as he sat against the window sill, thinking.

Almost a year earlier, Governor Hoines had been the final victim in a series of horrific sniper killings that rocked the city of Denver and its suburbs; Art had failed to stop it. The only clues left behind had implicated a group of well-funded and highly trained former Russian Vyemple members of the FSB, GRU and Spetznas known as the Gerovit. He and Daniel had nearly stopped them but, Art could have pushed harder. He should have known that Governor Hoines was the real target. He had missed some crucial piece of evidence and that just wasn't something he could accept.

Since then, Art had burdened himself with unending questions and second guessing his actions during the investigation. He had spent the better part of the past year analyzing evidence of the sniper killings looking for something—anything—to identify the killer. The DNA and ballistic evidence they had gathered didn't turn up a match in any federal database.

"And then there's this," Daniel said as he extended a closed hand to his uncle.

He dropped the unfired bullet into Art's open palm. Art pinched it with two fingers and turned it as he examined it closely. He was all too familiar with the orange colored coating on the bullet. It was an advanced polyvinylsiliconcarbide that prevented rifling marks on fired bullets. The previous assassin had used the same type of bullet to kill the Governor. It was a perfect tool for an assassin.

Art turned the bullet over and examined the base with a magnifying glass from his desk. There on the base of the bullet was the distinctive lightning bolt engraving. An identical engraving had been found on the bullet that killed Governor Hoines.

"I pried that bullet off the cartridge in his rifle," Daniel said.

"So, he *is* from the Gerovit group," Art said. It was a statement, not a question.

"That marking leaves no doubt. I had one of your lab rats take fingerprints and a cheek swabbing from the guy before the deputy hooked him up. Maybe we'll get lucky and this guy is in Tech-fed."

The TECFD is a highly classified Terrorist/Enemy Combatant Forensic Database run jointly by the CIA and Joint Special Operations Command. It stored everything from fingerprints and DNA, to bomb making signatures, to psychological profiles.

Bloodlines

Unlike the civilian databases run by the FBI, this system was not burdened by legalities and bureaucratic red tape. The profiles weren't used to prosecute terrorists like common criminals. It was used to hunt them down before they could carry out another attack.

Art set the items down and rubbed his eyes. Shock was a common reaction to nearly being shot, but Art hadn't felt this defeated for a long time.

"Why here...why now?" Art asked.

"Maybe you got close to something in your investigation," Daniel said.

"We haven't got squat, you know that."

"Maybe you do, and you don't know it."

Art smirked in reply. He shook his head as he seemed to gaze upon the floor for answers.

"Aren't you always saying that it's not what the cops know, but what the suspect *thinks* you know?" Daniel said folding his arms and crossing his feet as he leaned against the wall.

Art inhaled deeply as he looked from the floor and up at the ceiling running his fingers through his thick, graying hair.

"Think Uncle Art. Something brought these guys to your doorstep. It had to be something recent," Daniel said.

Daniel watched the far-off stare in his Uncle's eyes evaporate as he snapped his fingers.

"The postcard."

"What postcard?" Daniel asked.

Art snatched a card from his desktop and handed it to Daniel.

Daniel read the message, looked at the address, then read the message again. "I thought you couldn't make it to the reunion this year."

"I can't," Art said.

"Is Seaton getting senile, or what?" Daniel asked.

"Seaton? Hardly. Did you notice the stamp?"

Daniel turned the card over again and saw the upside down flag. "An upside down flag is a symbol of distress, or imminent death." Daniel said.

"Exactly. Seaton is a former Marine and a stickler for details. He would never have put that flag stamp upside down unless he meant to send a message."

"What message? I mean, what could your 14th degree ritual possibly have to do with the assassins?"

"I'm not sure, but we're going to find out."

5

Art snatched the phone from his desk and dialed Seaton's cell phone. The call went to voicemail.

"Hey Brother Seaton, this is Art. I wanted to talk to you about our 14th degree ritual for the reunion. Give me a call."

No sooner had Art hung up than Tilly buzzed him from the outer office.

"Art? Paul Whittier is on line one for you."

Judge Paul Whittier was the executive officer of the Denver Masonic Consistory and a long time friend of Art's.

"Brother Paul, how are *you* this fine morning?"

"Not too well, Art. I see you're trying to get a hold of Seaton."

"Yes, how did you know that?" Art asked, surprised.

"Because I'm holding his phone at the moment."

"I see. I suppose he left it under a stack of books in the library again," Art joked.

"Art, I think it best if you sit down to hear what I have to say."

"What's going on, Paul?" He sat on the corner of his desk.

"I'm here with the police. It appears Brother Seaton took his own life last night in the library. The caretaker found him this morning and called me after notifying the authorities."

"Suicide? You can't be serious?" Art said.

Art noticed Daniel move a little closer and he put Paul's call on speakerphone.

"I'm afraid I am," Paul said.

"Paul, there is no way Seaton would take his own life. You know him as well as I do. He was full of passion, and he would never do that to Barbara." Art said.

"I agree with you, Art, but the police are telling me there is no evidence of foul play. They also tell me that Barbara indicated he has been under a lot of stress lately. He was apparently obsessed with some new research project he was working on."

"What new research project?" Art asked.

29

"She couldn't be specific, but he's been acting very out of character the past few days." Paul said.

Art placed his hand over his mouth as he took the postcard and read the message again.

"Paul, would this project have anything to do with the 14th Degree?"

"Honestly, I have no idea. I got here about an hour ago and haven't had a chance to talk to anyone else. If you hadn't called…"

Art gave his nephew a hard look.

"Paul, don't touch anything. We're coming to you."

"I can't stop the police from processing the scene."

"I'm not asking you to. Just don't touch anything after they're done. I want to see this for myself. Use your charm and persuasion to get the CSIs to leave you a copy of the crime scene photos, too."

"And just how am I supposed to do that?" Paul asked, his tone a bit annoyed.

"You're a federal judge. Tell them I'm coming down for a consult. If that doesn't work, scare the shit out of them with threats of a subpoena."

Art knew it would never come to that.

"How soon can you be down here?"

"I'll fly into Denver and be there in less than two hours."

"Okay, see you then."

Art disconnected the line and punched the intercom.

"Tilly, call out to Dave at the airport and get the jet ready to go to Denver ASAP."

"Is everything all right?" she asked.

"No. Clear my schedule for the next few days. Daniel and I will be leaving as soon as we throw some things together."

"I'm always packed," Daniel reminded him.

"Tilly, did you get that?"

Hearing no response from Tilly, Art looked up to see his childhood friend standing squarely in the door.

"You mind telling me what is so important that you have to jet off to Denver?" Tilly asked, her hands on her hips.

Art had hoped to spare her the details but Tilly was practically his wife, without the marriage certificate. There had never been a sexual component to their relationship, but their friendship had grown considerably since his wife's death four years earlier. He had known Tilly all his life. Art often joked that Tilly was more protective than any wife would ever be.

"Come here and sit for a moment," Art said.

She took a few steps toward his desk. "Art...you're scaring me. What's wrong?"

He took her by the shoulders and leaned into her. "It's Seaton. They found his body in the library this morning."

"Oh my God!" Tilly screamed just before her hand cupped over her mouth.

"The police think its suicide," Art said.

Tilly's brow furrowed. "Suicide? But..."

"I know, I know...that's why we're heading down there."

Tilly sat motionless, a blank stare in her eyes.

"Can you call Dave and tell him to get the plane ready? I want to get down there before the scene gets cold."

"Certainly," she said. Tilly stood, took a deep breath, and straightened her blouse before returning to her desk.

Art looked over at his nephew who was still wearing his Ghillie suit. "You'd better change outfits. We can't have you walking around Denver looking like a bush. Some dog is gonna piss all over you."

"Anything else?" Daniel asked.

It was an odd question but Art knew what Daniel meant. He didn't mince words.

"I'll take care of the forensic stuff, but given the events of this morning, I'd feel better if you made sure we were covered on the tactical side." Art said as he slid open his top drawer and placed the holstered Colt forty-five on the desktop.

"Wilco, uncle."

6

The pilot was wheels up in just under forty-five minutes. The Gulfstream G150 was Art's preferred method of travel. It was an expensive luxury, but he relished the convenience private air travel offered him. He didn't miss the TSA pat downs either.

Daniel carried in two large black gear bags with a rifle case as a spry Belgian Malinois pranced into the cabin and curled up on an empty chair.

"Ranger is coming along for the trip?" Art asked.

"I thought Sarah might like to meet him, spend some time with him."

Sarah Richards was like family to Art. He had promised her grandfather before he died that he would mentor her both professionally and personally. Above all, he promised to watch over her. It was a promise he was all too happy to keep.

The day she became a senior criminalist for his old employer, the Arapahoe County Sheriff's Office, was one of the proudest days of his life. He was convinced she would become a magnificent criminalist.

Art glanced back at the two large duffle bags and rifle case Daniel stowed in the rear compartment.

"That's a lot of gear for a day or two," Art said.

"You know me; hope for the best...plan for the worst." Daniel said patting Ranger on the head.

Art smiled. Daniel was the spitting image of his father. Dark wavy hair, chiseled olive skinned physique, and dark brown eyes forever scanning his surroundings. He shared the same fighting spirit, too. Like his father, Daniel had been an elite special operations soldier.

Art's brother Max had died a hero during the Tet-offensive in the Vietnam War, and Daniel was committed to carrying on the warrior creed. His nephew had come to work for him after an administrative discharge from the Army the previous year.

Daniel carried the shame of that discharge like a half-ton rucksack. Art knew some of the details of Daniel's former life, but Daniel wisely kept him in the dark about the specifics, especially those surrounding his unexpected discharge.

Daniel had once told him that he wanted to save men like his father so other children wouldn't have to grow up without a dad. Art knew Daniel had been an elite Air Force PJ, or Parajumper, until the morning of September 11th, 2001. Everything changed with the terrorist attacks that killed over three thousand innocent Americans.

Like every red-blooded American on September 12th, Daniel wanted to take the fight to the enemy. Shortly after, Art lost contact with his nephew until the day he received a phone call from an Army base in North Carolina.

The transition to civilian life had been difficult for Daniel. Like a racehorse that was put to pasture in his prime. He never complained, but Art could see it in his eyes. The civilian world just didn't have much need for professional soldiers. Art gave him a job as a hunting guide and repairman at the Facility, but he knew it was not enough to give Daniel a purpose.

Sarah had been the one bright light that gave Daniel hope for a normal life after the Army. Almost a decade his junior, Art could see Sarah invigorated Daniel like no one else had. Unfortunately, distance and her hectic work schedule had stymied their romance. It wasn't dead; it just couldn't gain much traction.

Art sensed Daniel wanted to change that but Sarah was not one to be suffocated. She was young and enthusiastic about her career. Daniel would have to wait.

***

Littleton, Colorado

It was a typical Monday morning for criminalist Sarah Richards. Despite repeated pleas from her alarm clock Sarah woke late, threw on her wrinkled uniform shirt, and holstered her Glock pistol. She tied her chestnut red hair in a simple ponytail before dashing from her house on Sterne Park. Like most Mondays, she sacrificed a shower and breakfast to make up time. She imagined her neighbors being jolted from sleep as the diesel engine of her Ford F-350 King Ranch pickup thundered to life.

With one hand on the wheel and one eye on the road, Sarah rummaged through her duty bag for something to eat. Under her

ballistic vest she fingered an energy bar of such antiquity she had
no memory of purchasing that brand.

How bad could it be?

Clenching the corner of the packaging in her teeth, she tore
it open and bit off a sizeable piece. Ten seconds later a shower of
stale oatmeal and rock hard fruit chunks erupted from her open
window as she spat it out.

Sarah plotted a route to work that would avoid predictable
speed traps and schizophrenic traffic lights she was convinced
were programmed more for entertainment of the city planners
than efficient traffic flow. Twenty-five minutes later, she pulled
up to the security gate and swiped her credentials over the card
reader. She noted the time as she pulled into her parking slot.
Fifteen minutes past six; it could have been much worse.

Grabbing her backpack, Sarah pointed her key fob over her
shoulder and chirped the alarm as she snaked her way between
the parked cars. Just as she was about to clear the last row, a
rotund man in a cheap grey tweed suit stepped out and blocked
her path. His dark brown eyes gave her a once over as he made
an exaggerated effort to shake his head after assessing her
appearance.

"Miss Richards. I'm glad to see you could join us this
morning."

Lieutenant Bart Manilow was head of the internal affairs
bureau and self-appointed president of the 'I hate Sarah
Richards' fan club. He could cite policy and procedure like a
southern Baptist preacher quotes the bible.

"How do you know I'm not coming in from a crime scene?"
Sarah asked as she tried to side step around him.

"Are you?" he asked, extending the open hand gesture he
had perfected after years in the traffic division.

"I guess that wasn't my point," she said.

"Richards, we expect our employees to arrive on time for
work. This isn't a sorority house; it's a sheriff's office." His
words were dripping with condescension.

Lt. Manilow made no effort to hide his displeasure with
women in law enforcement. It was well known in the department
that Manilow thought women were better suited for dispatch,
secretarial duties, or more disgraceful positions under his desk.

Bloodlines

Manilow had set his sights on Sarah from the very first day she arrived for work. That day she even arrived on time. But she had disregarded his advancements. Simply put, she wasn't going to be a pawn in his fantasy world. Since then, it had only gotten worse. He looked for any and every opportunity to make her time there unpleasant.

At first she tried complaining to her supervisors, but Manilow was careful to keep his actions grounded in policy; petty as some were.

During her involvement in stopping a brutal rapist and murderer the year before, Manilow had reached new lows. He tried several times to get her fired. But like an annoying pebble in his shoe, she managed to keep her job.

"Sorry sir, obviously I'll stay late tonight to make up for it."

She really wanted to tell him to shove it. She wasn't in his chain of command. But with the high turnover rate of supervisors in the crime lab recently, she figured it was only a matter of time before she was under his command.

"That wouldn't be necessary if you took a little more personal responsibility." Manilow said.

The truth of the matter—Sarah packed sixteen hours of work into a ten hour work day. Her two short years at the crime lab seemed like seven as her colleagues marveled at her ability to find trouble. The last four weeks had been pretty mild though, and she used the time to catch up on her backlog of casework.

"I appreciate the advice, Sir," she said as she squirmed past him exposing her back. It was the best way to avoid an 'accidental' brushing of her anatomy he was famous for with other female employees.

Thankfully Manilow let her go without another comment.

Sarah managed to make it to her cubicle without seeing her supervisor, but the stack of lab requests resting on her chair made it clear he knew she was late. She was sure she'd hear about it later.

Sarah powered up her computer and was checking e-mails when her phone rang. The little red light indicated the call was coming from the video room upstairs in the interrogation suite.

"This is Sarah."

"Hey, kiddo."

It was Detective Manny Lopez. Manny was her favorite detective and unofficial big brother. She could handle herself but it was nice to know someone had your back.

"What's up, Manny?"

"We're on our last DVD up here. Do you guys have any we can use?"

"Sure, I'll run some up."

Sarah grabbed a stack and made her way up to the third floor to find Manny sitting in the interrogation room with a pimple-faced boy and his parents. The boy hung his head low with an occasional glance up towards Manny when answering a question. His father slumped in his chair and stared at the floor as if in a trance. The mother sat ramrod straight, her purse resting in her lap, as she kept a hawkish eye fixed on her son.

Seated in front of a bank of monitors was Manny's partner, Detective Sal Vargas, nicknamed 'Vegas'. Vargas was a twenty-five year veteran of the sheriff's office and an expert in doing the least amount of work possible. That's one reason Sarah was so surprised to see him scribbling notes on a notepad as he observed the interrogation. He was regarded as the J. Edgar Hoover of the office and was rumored to have dirt on everyone from the sheriff to the county commissioners. His secret files managed to keep him employed after a number of major screw-ups.

Vargas was a waif of a man and Sarah doubted his wiry frame topped a hundred-fifty pounds. She entered the room behind him and hoped she could drop off the stack of DVDs without being noticed. It was then that she heard the pen stop writing and the distinctive squeak of the old chair as it turned.

"Stop staring at my ass, Vegas."

"Hey…how did you…"

Sarah turned around and offered a sly smile. "Caught you."

Vargas held up his hands. "Can't blame me being a man."

"That last part's debatable," she said.

He flashed a smile, smoothed out his few remaining wisps of bleach blond hair before interlacing his fingers behind his head, and leaned back in his chair.

Sarah couldn't pull her eyes away from the powder blue polyester suit he was wearing when she noticed something absolutely horrible.

"Jesus Vegas," she said pointing to his open zipper.

"What?" He looked down. "Oh, that." He zipped it closed. "Kinda hard to keep your eyes off the old barn door, huh?"

Sarah glared at him with narrowed eyes and a pinched face.

"Remind me again why you've never been fired for sexual harassment?"

"Well, good morning to you, too, kitten. What's got your tampon in a twist?"

Sarah had devised several fool-proof methods for disposing of Vargas' dead body and she mentally ran through the options as she slowed her breathing and tamped the anger rising inside her. In truth, she didn't mind Vargas. He had saved her life the year before; a fact he reminded her of whenever she got angry with him.

But Vargas was a walking, talking, embodiment of political incorrectness. He lived on the edge of inappropriateness and managed to stumble over that edge on a daily basis. He was an insatiable flirt but he would never do her harm, never betray their friendship. He rewarded his few friends with a loyalty that defied his personality, and like Manny, she could see the goodness in him that he so desperately tried to hide.

"Never mind," she said. "What's with the kid?"

"Who him?" He said turning his chair back around. "Meet Jeffrey, the newest sex offender in Arapahoe County."

"I would have thought he was a murderer by the way you were scribbling notes. What did he do?"

"The kid's a frickin' genius. He sets up a website called St. Catherine's College of Medicine advertising free mammograms over the internet; very professional looking."

"You're kidding?"

"Scout's honor," he said holding up three fingers. "The webpage directs you to download free software that opens a video portal. The woman exposes her breasts and he takes a picture with a *special camera*," Vargas said using finger quotes.

"Oh my god," Sarah said.

"Yeah, I know. Then, the instructions tell her to turn left, right, squeeze 'em together, the whole nine yards."

"And he actually found some woman gullible enough to do this?"

"Not one…we have over 200 victims so far."

37

"No way!" Sarah said squinting at the innocent looking teenager on the video monitor.

"Like I said...kid's a genius."

"How did you catch him?"

"Classmate turned him in. Apparently he made arrangements to sell DVD copies of the exams at school today for ten bucks a pop. Kids were asking their parents for an advance on their allowance, I guess."

"How many copies did you buy?"

Vegas held up a DVD and waved it back and forth.

"I get mine for free," he said with a devilish smile.

Sarah rolled her eyes as her cell began vibrating. Snatching it from the cradle on her belt, her eyes lit up when she read Daniel's name on the caller ID.

"Excuse me," she said as she ducked out of the room and into the hallway.

"Hey there," she said trying not to sound like an excited teenager on prom night.

"Hey yourself. Do you have any plans tonight?" Daniel's voice came over the line.

"You're in town?"

"Inbound as we speak. Unfortunately one of Uncle Art's friends was found dead at the Consistory this morning and they asked him to come by and take a look."

"Seriously, how awful. Do they suspect foul play?"

"Denver PD thinks it's a suicide, but you know Art."

"Do you guys need any help?"

"I think we're good. Listen, I don't know how long we'll be there but I thought I could come by tonight for dinner?"

"Definitely, do you have any requests of the chef?"

"Totally open," Daniel said.

"No worries, I'll figure something out. How long will you be in town?"

"Not sure at this point, but I think I can safely say probably a few days."

Sarah was dancing with joy.

"Oh, and I have a surprise for you," Daniel said.

"A surprise, huh?"

"Well two, actually."

"Ohhhh, I'm intrigued."

"How about we plan for five o'clock?"

Sarah was just about to agree when she remembered her late arrival. Manilow would no doubt be keeping an eye on how late she left the office.

"Let's make it six. I have a few things in the hopper today that need to get cleared up."

"Six it is. See you then."

"See you then, bye."

Sarah closed her eyes and leaned her head back against the wall. Her relationship with Daniel had been a roller coaster ride.

When they first met at the Facility, there was a real spark. She had dated plenty of men, but none of them effected her like Daniel. When he was around, she was filled with joy and when he wasn't; well, there was a feeling of emptiness. His greatest flaw was secrecy. Sarah hated keeping secrets. She accepted the fact he couldn't tell her everything about his former military career. Men in his unit had died from loose lips in the past, but not knowing everything about him made her hesitant to commit one hundred percent to the relationship.

It didn't help that they lived on opposite sides of the state either. Bounding down the stairs to the crime lab on the first floor, Sarah convinced herself the day might not be so bad after all. Coming through the door she eyed her friend and colleague, Andy Vaughn, looking over enlarged photographs of shoes in the conference room.

More than any other criminalist, Andy had taken a special interest in Sarah. Most of her colleagues saw her as young and impulsive, and didn't take her seriously. Several thought her constant riling of management actually hurt the reputation of the crime lab. Not Andy. He made her feel like an equal when others didn't.

"Whatcha got there?" she said looking in from the doorway.

"A pretty cool case actually, come take a look," he said.

Sarah took one of the large photos in hand and stared at the image.

"Looks like a skater shoe," she said dismissively.

"Yep. Notice anything unusual?"

Sarah looked at the photo for several long seconds before answering. "It's ugly?"

Andy smirked. "Yeah well, it is that, but look at the tongue," he said.

Sarah looked again but shrugged her shoulders. "I don't see anything."

"Neither did patrol. Check this out."

Andy grabbed an evidence bag from the chair and pulled out the shoe from in the photograph. He turned the tongue flap towards Sarah and pried open a Velcro sealed pouch.

"No way; a hidden compartment?" Sarah asked.

"Pretty cool, huh? Little punks were hiding ecstasy pills in here and doling them out to buyers at the skate park. Patrol picked them up on a vandalism charge and wanted me to compare the shoeprints to the crime scene impressions."

"So the photos are for court?"

"Naw, they already plead out. I wanted to frame them for display in here. I thought it would be cool to show the tour group coming next week." He said holding his arms up as if framing them for the wall.

"That's awesome!" said Sarah.

"Oh, before I forget. The sarge is looking for you," he said.

"Great," she said, biting her lip.

"Don't sweat it. You just need to make an effort to get here on time; especially on Mondays. You can't keep serving up underhanded pitches Sarah, okay?"

"I know, but I do stay late to make up for it."

"They don't care. It's all about impressions; I keep telling you that."

Sarah let her shoulder length chestnut hair out and fingered it loose. She wasn't one to dwell on appearance. It wasn't that she tried to look drab, she just never liked painted nails, a pearl necklace, and evening dresses like her mother. "Manilow has it in for me," she said.

"Manilow has it in for everyone. Just do your best to stay under the radar. Sooner or later he'll shift his focus to someone else."

Sarah was still so confused by the lack of common sense in the police culture, but she knew she couldn't change it. *At least I have friends looking out for me.*

"Thanks Andy, I'll do better."

"Remember, bad sergeants are like kidney stones...sooner or later they'll pass."

***

It was just after 1PM when Art and Daniel arrived at the Consistory. Two marked police cars were still parked on Grant Street outside the main entrance on the west side of the building. They met Paul and an older Mason in the lobby. Daniel was the first to offer his hand to the familiar face.

"Alan Sprigg, it's been a while," Daniel said.

"I heard you were coming down so I figured I'd stop by." He tipped his white colored Masonic hat to him. Alan had been instrumental in solving a key piece of evidence in the sniper killings the year before.

"How are you, young fella?" Alan asked Art.

"I could be better," Art confessed.

"You and me both," Alan said.

"I hate to ask, but can you watch Ranger while we're down there?" Daniel asked Alan.

"Love to," Alan said. He looked the dog over and winked at Daniel.

"He from the same outfit you served with?"

The old man didn't miss a thing. Alan Sprigg had been part of government black ops before the phrase was even coined. He was one of the few men who knew Daniel's file inside and out. Daniel nodded.

"He and I sure chewed a lot of the same mud, that's for sure."

"Well then, it would be my pleasure. We'll just sit here and swap old war stories." He ruffled Ranger's fur.

Paul, Art, and Daniel slipped under the yellow crime scene tape strung across the marble stairs and descended to the lower level. A man in a dark blue suit was waiting for them at the bottom of the stairs.

"Art, I'd like to introduce you to Detective Thomas Lew. Brother Tom is with Liberty Lodge #134. He wanted to stick around to meet you."

"It's a real pleasure, Dr. Von Hollen. I've read all your books," Lew said giving the customary handshake.

"Art, please. Would you mind giving us the tour and brief us on your findings, Tom?"

"Of course."

Paul stayed back by the stairwell while the others turned right and walked to the library. Art and Daniel dropped their gear bags just outside the doorway to the library. Detective Lew spent the next fifteen minutes going over the crime scene photos, statements, and evidence found. He didn't miss a detail.

"Do you have a time of death?" Art asked.

"The coroner estimated sometime between midnight and one a.m.," Lew said.

Art was studying a close-up photo of Seaton's thighs seated in a chair when Lew pointed to the screen.

"I'm no expert in bloodstains but these here on his leg just don't look right to me."

Art agreed with Lew, but the teacher in him pressed further. "Why is that?"

"They look horizontal to me."

"And why is that strange?"

Lew suddenly acted like a child caught in a lie. "Uh, I don't know...like I said, I'm no expert."

"No, I agree with you. Forgive me, Tom, sometimes I play the role of teacher a little too much. Walk me through it."

Lew's lips curled up in a smile before explaining.

"To me, these stains are traveling horizontally towards the knee. Now, if he was sitting like this when he cut his throat then I would think the stains would be traveling down towards the floor. I mean, how does blood fall down from his throat turn sideways?"

It was a statement rather than a question.

"So what does that tell you?" Art asked.

"Looks to me like he was standing up when those stains hit his legs." Lew said.

Art studied the photo for several moments before agreeing.

"What did your crime scene folks think?" Art asked.

"They said it didn't prove murder. They said he could have just been standing when he cut his throat and then slid down into the chair."

"But you're not buying that, are you?"

"Well, if he was standing, wouldn't we see more blood spatter on the desk? I mean, further out?"

Art nodded while stroking his gray goatee.

"What else?" Art asked.

"The chair," Lew said.

"What about the chair?"

"If he was standing at the table then the chair would have to be scooted out more. How did he pull it back in?"

"Can you prove this photo shows exactly where the chair was when the first responders found him?" Art asked.

"That's just what my guys said," Lew said with a hint of disappointment.

"Well, let's not dismiss your theory yet. It's good to keep an open mind," Art said patting the man on the shoulder.

"Hey, Art?" Daniel called from the hallway.

Art and Tom found Daniel crouched on the floor with a small flashlight. Art could see the blue-grey colored tile floor outside the library was coated in black fingerprint powder.

"The techs were searching for shoe prints." Lew explained.

"Your idea?" Art asked as he took a knee to get a better look.

"I thought it couldn't hurt."

Art watched Daniel as he studied the wipe marks on the floor intently.

"The Consistory staff mops that floor three times a week, I already checked." Lew said expecting the next question.

"What are you thinking?" Art asked Daniel.

"You remember that mop study your grad students did a few months back?"

Art nodded his head.

"I agree," Art said.

"Wait…you guys have a multi-million dollar facility filled with lasers and cutting edge stuff, and you study mop marks?" Lew asked.

Daniel looked up at the detective and smiled.

"It kind of started as a joke," Daniel said.

Lew raised his hands and eyebrows begging for more information.

"You see, I found these grad students late one night playing Luke Skywalker with their mops instead of cleaning." Daniel

43

explained. "They told me they were bored so I told them that instead of screwing around, they should make a positive experience out of it. You know, make lemonade with lemons. So I asked them if they could tell the difference between someone mopping a floor and someone cleaning up bloodstains. The idea just popped in my head. I didn't plan for them to *actually* do a study on it."

"But they did." Lew said.

"Did they ever. It would have made for a nice little thesis if they didn't already have ones they were working on. It never got published. It was a great reminder to them though." Art said.

"Reminder?" Lew asked.

"You have to understand the normal before you can identify the abnormal."

"So, what did they find out?" Lew asked.

"Picture a man mopping a floor," Art said closing his eyes. Lew did the same.

"He's generally going to swing that mop head back and forth in big wide arcs, right?"

"Yeah," Lew said without opening his eyes.

"Now look at these marks."

Lew got down while Daniel shined the bright light at an oblique angle to highlight the wipe marks.

"You see how these marks, highlighted by the fingerprint powder, are in a tight circular pattern?"

"Yeah."

"That's something that we typically see when a person gets down on their hands and knees and wipes up a liquid with a cloth. If you look real close, you don't see the 'hair-like' strands or marks you expect from a typical mop head."

"Shit…you're saying someone cleaned up blood?"

"Hold on, it's just an observation. We're nowhere near the zip code of murder yet," Art explained.

"We're still going to look though, right?" Daniel asked.

Art smiled and gave a short huff. "You bet. Seaton wouldn't expect any less out of me."

7

Art pulled a bottle of distilled water and a small vial of white powder with green colored flecks in it from his crime scene kit.

"Luminol?" Lew asked.

"Better," Art said as he began mixing the solution in a spray bottle.

"It's an experimental blood reagent I call Sirius. It's ten times as sensitive as Luminol," Art said.

"So you think you can find blood spatter out here in the hallway?" Lew asked.

"I doubt we'd see any specific blood droplets. The blood spatter would likely be destroyed by the cleaning. I'm more interested in any footwear impressions that may have been made by a person walking through this area while it was still wet." Art said.

"Paul, can we turn off the lights in the hallway?" Daniel called out.

Paul came down the hall, flipped the appropriate switches, and the team was enveloped in near-darkness.

With Paul, Daniel, and Tom standing by the wall, Art began methodically spraying the reagent across the tile floor. In an instant, the four men felt a surge of excitement coursing through their veins. Blue-colored boot impressions seeped up from the black floor as if summoned by magic.

"Unbelievable. I can't believe my guys missed this," Lew said.

"Better late than never," Daniel said.

Lew held out a closed fist to Daniel which he touched with his own. Lew then extended his fist to Art. Art had seen many of the younger students at the Facility touch fists and he returned the gesture.

"I've never actually fisted anyone before," Art exclaimed.

"Fist *bumped*," Daniel exclaimed.

"Big difference," Lew added.

"Yes, of course, fist bumped," Art said mimicking the jargon.

Art watched the two men exchange smiles and wondered what faux pas he had committed. Art brushed the thought from his mind as he continued to spray the reagent.

Within seconds, a trail of glowing boot prints led them down the stairs, through the dining hall, and into the kitchen before abruptly stopping at a large wire rack of drinking glasses and plates. Art sprayed around the cart but no other boot prints appeared.

"So, what…he got a glass or something? Why did he stop here?" Lew asked.

"Maybe he didn't stop," Daniel said as he studied the cart.

"Do it," Art said.

Daniel moved the large wheeled cart out of the way while Art sprayed the floor underneath. Half of a blue-colored boot print seemed to vanish under the wall.

"False wall," Daniel said.

"A false wall, you gotta be shittin' me," Lew said.

"Look for a release," Daniel said as he ran his hands over the wall. The three men split up and began examining the area for a way to get through. After several minutes, Daniel called out.

"Over here."

Art and Lew crouched down to see Daniel sticking his finger in a small hole in the wall about six feet away from the boot impression.

"Looks like a trip wire back there," Daniel said as he shone his light down the hole.

"We need a long metal rid with a hook," Art explained. He couldn't hide the excitement in his voice.

"What are you thinking?" Daniel asked.

"I've seen door releases like this in speakeasy clubs from the prohibition era."

"How old are you Art?" Lew asked.

Art frowned. "Funny. I *mean* I've read about them. You insert a long rod and pull on a wire back in there. Tripping the wire releases the locking mechanism and the door should open."

"Will this work?" Lew said, producing a broom handle.

"Yes, I think so. Take the end off. Daniel, I need the duct tape out of my crime scene kit."

Within minutes Art had the broom converted into a key using a shish kabob skewer as a hook. He carefully inserted it into the hole several feet while Daniel illuminated the way with his flashlight.

"I think I have it," Art said as he carefully twisted the handle before pulling back.

The men heard a metal clank and whoosh of air as a four foot section of the wall dropped back an inch. Art and Daniel exchanged looks of satisfaction as the three men muscled the door back a few inches and slid it sideways into a pocket in the wall.

"It's like a huge pocket door," Lew said.

"Did you know about this Uncle Art?"

Art studied the passageway like an archaeologist.

"No," Art said running his hand over the rough tunnel walls. "I doubt anyone here knows this exists."

"Where the hell do you think it goes?" Lew asked.

"Toward the killer," Daniel said as he drew his Sig Sauer .45 caliber pistol. Lew drew his own weapon as well.

"Look here," Art said as he examined the back of the door.

"There's a normal latch and lever. The killer could easily have opened the door from this side and left it cracked open as he made his way into the Consistory. Then he would just have to slide it shut and latch it," Art said.

Daniel looked back at Lew and gave a nod of his head in the direction of the tunnel.

"This way."

"Should I call for back-up?" Lew asked.

"I doubt the killer is waiting at the end of this cavern. Let's keep this to ourselves for now," Art said.

Daniel took point, his forty-five caliber pistol extended straight ahead, as the men crept down the cave-like hallway hugging the wall.

A few minutes later the men reached the end of the tunnel, encountering a similar door.

"How far have we come?" Art asked.

"Three hundred eighty-seven paces," Daniel said without hesitation.

Art smiled.

"Do we go through?" Lew asked.

"Do we have a choice?" Daniel responded as he gripped the door lever with his free hand. Lew nodded he was ready.

***

Daniel moved the latch an inch at a time keeping his .45 pointed at the opening. The door opened smoothly as they slid it open far enough to squeeze through. Daniel could see lights in the next room. He felt a slight chill as his nose took in the musty air. He gave a hand signal to follow him as he weaved his way through several stacked desks, cabinets, and chairs. He surmised they were in a storage room.

Daniel held up a closed fist to signal the others to stop as he approached the lighted room. As he came through the opening, his peripheral vision caught a flash of color and movement as he leveled his large bore gun at a man's head.

"Sweet Jesus, don't shoot."

The young man's eyes were wide as a full moon as he threw his hands up into the air. Detective Lew sprang out right behind Daniel, and immediately recognized the man's City of Denver work uniform.

"Easy kid, we're cops," he said pulling out his badge.

Daniel holstered his weapon as the young man peered closer to see the detective's credentials.

"You gave me a frickin' heart attack," the kid said.

"Sorry about that, kid," Daniel said.

"What the heck are you guys doing here?" the young man said as Art came into the lighted hallway.

"Where is *here*, exactly?" Art asked.

"You don't know where you are?" The young man said.

"Look..." Lew raised his eyebrows at the man.

"Jeff."

"Okay, look...Jeff, it's a little hard to explain right now. We just need to know what this place is," Lew said waving his arms around in a sweeping motion.

"You're in the basement of the State Capitol building," Jeff said with a confused look.

"The State Capitol?" Art asked.

"Yep." Jeff said.

"Have you seen anyone strange down here? People that shouldn't be here?" Lew asked.

"Just you three."

"Look at these, Art," Daniel said pointing to the narrow gauge railroad tracks embedded in the floor.

"Where do these tracks lead to Jeff?" Art asked.

Jeff turned and looked down the long cavernous hallway before looking back at the men.

"The boiler plant."

The three men followed the tracks down the catacomb hallway until they reached the enormous boiler plant. Detective Lew flagged down a guard and jogged over to talk to him. Daniel scanned the room, looking for the exit.

"Let's try those doors over there," Daniel said pointing.

Daniel and Art shouldered open the heavy door just as the boiler plant manager shouted, "Not that door!"

Art and Daniel stumbled out onto the loading dock under the gaze of a half dozen Denver Police officers.

"Who the *fuck* are you numbnuts?" barked an angry plain clothes detective.

At their feet was a woman's lifeless body surrounded by a pool of blood.

"Whoops," Daniel said. "Sorry."

An annoyed crime scene photographer gave Daniel a disapproving look as she crouched beside the dead woman. Detective Lew followed them through the door a few seconds later.

"It's all right...they're with me." Lew said.

"What the hell is going on, Tom?" the detective shouted upon seeing his colleague.

"Shit, let me try to smooth this over," Lew told Art as he side-stepped the body and made his way under the crime scene tape.

"Let's just back track, shall we," Art said.

Daniel and Art retreated into the boiler plant and closed the door leaving it cracked about an inch.

"That can't be a coincidence," Daniel said.

"I agree. Let's see what Tom has to say when he gets back."

It was another five minutes later before Detective Lew rejoined them.

"You're not going to believe this." Lew said.

"About an hour ago some waitress saw the victim laying there and came over to give her some money; then she saw all the blood."

"Do they know how long she's been dead?" Art asked.

"Coroner says at least twelve hours." Lew said.

"*Twelve hours?* There must have been a hundred people that saw her this morning." Daniel said motioning to the parking garage.

"You know how it is in the city. I've seen people step over dead bodies blocking the sidewalk." Lew said.

"I don't get that," Daniel said.

"A lot of folks won't look at the homeless—embarrassed, scared, whatever it is—they don't want to deal with it. From a distance it looked like she was just sleeping. Add to the fact they might be running late for work… I'm not too surprised." Art explained.

"It's a damned shame." Lew said.

"Did you mention the tunnel to them?" Art asked.

"No, no…I kept that gem to myself for now. I told them we were doing a canvass in the Capitol of the night crew that may have been coming and going and we came through the door by mistake."

"Good. Until we know more we need to keep a lid on it. We don't even know if this is related to our scene." Art said.

"Do you know how she was killed?" Daniel asked.

Lew looked at Art for a long second before looking back at Daniel. "Her throat was cut."

8

Daniel walked the three blocks back to the Consistory on the street level with Art and Tom. Daniel marveled at the cobalt blue sky as he soaked in the warm sun. It was a stark contrast to the two murders connected by a secret tunnel system below.

Coming into the lobby, they passed Ranger and the older Mason snoring on the plush couch.

"What do you say we take a fresh look at the crime scene?" Art said as they descended to the library. Judge Paul Whittier was at the bottom of the stairs.

"Where on Earth did you three come from?"

"It's a long story, Paul, but when we're done here, you and I need to discuss something we found." Art said.

The seasoned judge raised an eyebrow but Daniel noticed Art never broke stride on his way to the library.

While Daniel took another look around the room, Art and Tom spent time reviewing the crime scene photos.

"I think it's safe to say this scene was staged." Art said.

"That means murder," Daniel said.

Art nodded in confirmation as Tom continued studying the crime scene photos on his laptop.

"If it's murder, what do you think the motive would have been?" Tom asked.

"Paul said Seaton's been under a lot of stress," Daniel said.

"Yes…Seaton's mysterious research project." Art said. "Did you examine the books on the desk, Tom?"

"Briefly. There's a Masonic almanac, some books on nineteenth century masonry in Colorado and the west, and some letters and personal journals of some Masons I've never heard of."

"Journals?" Art said, as if remembering an important fact.

"What is it?" Daniel asked.

"If memory serves, Seaton always kept a personal journal of his notes during research projects."

"Could that be one of the journals here on the table?" Daniel asked scooping them up.

51

Art took each leather bound book and perused the contents.

"None of these are in Seaton's handwriting." Art concluded.

"So where is *his* journal?" Daniel asked.

"Maybe he left it at home?" Lew said.

"Tom, can you contact his wife and see if she knows anything about the journal? Also, has anyone checked Seaton's car?"

"His wife is down at the station being interviewed, but I'll text the detective in charge. The coroner has the keys. I'll call the Coroner's office and have them bring his car keys back here."

"Thanks, Tom."

Daniel waited until Tom had left the room before speaking again.

"So I've been doing a little thinking, Uncle Art."

"I thought I saw your wheels turning," Art said smiling.

"Do you think it's a coincidence that an assassin tried to kill you on the same day you get a postcard from Seaton?"

"You know I don't believe in coincidences," Art said as he thumbed through one of the leather bound journals.

"And don't you think it's interesting how the tunnel took us directly under the State Capitol?"

Art looked up from the journal and frowned.

"Daniel, we've been through this. There is absolutely no evidence linking Senator, excuse me, *Governor* Barclay to the assassinations. There could be a hundred people with the means and motive to kill a sitting Governor. Hell, Tim Hoines wasn't exactly shy in going after the Russian mob in Denver. *They* had a real motive for killing him."

"Why kill all those kids, though?"

"You said it yourself...practice." Art said.

"So how would Seaton's research piss off the Russian mob?" Daniel asked.

"How would it threaten the Governor?" Art retorted.

Daniel exhaled deeply. He pursed his lips as he turned away from Art and ran his finger down a row of books.

There were several minutes of deafening silence before either man spoke. It was Daniel that broke the silence.

"Regardless of who hired these guys, Seaton obviously stumbled into something key."

"I agree." Art said.

"And I'll bet that key piece of evidence has something to do with his journal," Daniel said.

"Assuming there is a journal," Art said.

Daniel folded his arms and stood slumped against the bookshelf.

"Okay, let's look at this from another angle. Why would this Gerovit team target you and Seaton at the same time?"

Art thought in silence for a moment before answering.

"Technically they didn't," Art said.

Daniel shot him a puzzled look.

"According to the police, Seaton was killed between midnight and one a.m."

"What's your point?" Daniel said.

"If this was a coordinated attack, why not try to kill me in my home last night? Why wait until daylight with witnesses around?"

Daniel nodded, his eyebrows drawing closer together.

"For that matter, why not stage your death as a suicide like Seaton's?" Daniel said.

Art was silent for a moment and then raised his finger as his eyes lit up.

"Simple. Seaton's death was planned, mine was an afterthought."

"Okay...*why* was it an afterthought?" Daniel said.

"A better question. What made the killer drop everything and drive four hours up to the Facility to take a shot at me?" Art said.

"You think the man I caught is the same one who staged this crime scene?" Daniel asked.

"What do you think?" Art said.

"I think its two different people. The one who came after you is an amateur. The guy that staged *this* scene is an expert in killing. If this crime was planned, as you say, then this guy was chosen for the job. The kid I caught was good, but clearly no expert." Daniel said.

"So you think he was the "B" team?" Art asked.

"He may not even be a part of their team. Just some pinch hitter called in to tie off a loose end."

"So, why not use the professional?" Art said.

"There could be a lot of reasons; time, other priorities. Hell, when we'd take down a high valued target, we often left the search and interrogation of local villagers to the conventional forces."

"Get in and get out." Art said.

"Exactly."

"If this kid you caught is not part of their team, then maybe his allegiance is subject to change."

"What do you have in mind?" Daniel asked.

"Maybe I can give him some incentives to playing ball with the Sheriff." Art said.

"By incentives, you mean money." Daniel said giving his uncle a disapproving look.

"Oh, don't give me that look. I'm sure you paid off a few 'tribal elders' back in the day to get the information you needed on a bigger fish."

Daniel conceded the remark with a sly smile.

***

Art pulled his cell phone from his shirt pocket and dialed Sheriff Charlie Bishop in Routt County, Colorado. The phone rang four times before Charlie picked up.

"Funny you should be calling." Sheriff Bishop said.

Art had known Charlie Bishop for nearly twenty years. He was a simple man of few words and Art had to fight to get a simple good morning.

"Charlie…something wrong?" Art said.

"Oh, ya know…typical Monday. What's the story on the guy you caught this morning?"

"I was hoping you could enlighten me. Has he made any statements?"

"He asked for a glass of water." Bishop said.

"Anything else?" Art said with growing impatience.

"Not a word," Bishop said.

Art waited for more but none was forthcoming.

"Jesus, Charlie. Have you *even* tried to talk to him?"

"Wouldn't do much good, I'm afraid.

"A couple of Feds came by about an hour ago and picked him up." Bishop said.

"You just turned him over?" Art asked.

Bloodlines

"Well, not me. The Coroner released him."

9

The words hit Art in the stomach like a sledgehammer.

"Coroner." Art said.

"Yep."

"Charlie, so help me God, I am running out of patience. What the hell is going on up there?"

Charlie huffed into the phone before answering. "Your boy took some kind of poison. At least, that's what one of your chemistry folks said it looked like when they took a sample."

Art wondered which member of his staff hadn't bothered to call him with this critical news.

"How in the hell did he get access to poison? Didn't your deputies search him?"

"You know how it is, Art. My guys are looking for guns and knives, not little white pills."

Art dropped his head into his left hand and rubbed his brow. Daniel stepped closer.

"The Feds just showed up out of the blue and took the body?" Art said.

"Actually, they showed up first. We told the suspect he was being transferred into their custody and that's when he asked for the glass of water." Bishop said.

Art was silent as he pondered the news.

"Shit Art, they had official paperwork. Said he was a person of interest in some big federal murder case."

"What agency were they from?" Art said.

"Hell, I don't know; Feds. They all look the same to me. I didn't actually see the paperwork, the Coroner did."

"Look Charlie...I apologize. I know you didn't want any of this to happen. It's been a hell of day."

"So I gather."

"Can you talk to the Coroner and see if they happened to keep a copy of the paperwork?"

"He's up in the hills right now on a natural death but I'll corral him when he gets back in."

"I'd appreciate that, Charlie. You have my number." Art said before hanging up.

"That didn't sound good," Daniel said.

Art briefed Daniel on the events back in Routt County.

"You think they could have been Feds?" Daniel asked.

"No way. You and I have seen the federal government in action. It would take them two days and ten meetings to get a custody transfer order signed and delivered, especially on a high profile case." Art said.

"These guys are good." Daniel said.

"How could they have known he was in custody?"

"Obviously, they were monitoring local law enforcement radio traffic and heard their boy got caught."

"Monitoring the police bands?" Art said.

"Standard practice in an extraction. It's what *I* would have done," Daniel said.

"Well, this leaves us in a bit of a pickle now, doesn't it?" Art said.

"At least we're still breathing," Daniel said.

Art chuckled at his nephew's ability to always find a bright side.

"All right, nothing we can do about that business right now. Let's go back to what we were talking about before." Art said.

"Planning."

"Exactly. If my death was unplanned then the killer expected to get what he was after here in the Consistory." Art said.

"But he didn't…so he came after you." Daniel finished the thought.

"Which leaves the obvious question, why me?" Art said.

"Obviously they thought you knew something. They wanted you dead." Daniel said.

"Not that I knew something…that I might *discover* something." Art reasoned. "If they thought I knew something, they would have planned my death to coincide with Seaton's. It wouldn't have been an afterthought."

"So what were you supposed to discover?" Daniel asked.

They stood in silence for several minutes before Daniel spoke up. "Let me see that postcard again."

He read the inscription aloud.

Tom Adair

"Looking forward to our 14th Degree
I am sorry to burden you with extra work
Remember to relieve yourself and give the ancient
adoration after lustration"

"I know I should know this, but remind me again about the Fourteenth Degree." Daniel said.

Art gave him a disappointing look.

"The Perfect Elu degree unifies the earthly and spiritual qualities of man. We strive to be free of prejudice, intolerance, envy, and all that make us slaves. Please tell me you have not forgotten the charge." Art said.

***

Daniel closed his eyes for a moment.

"Virtus junix mors non separabit," Daniel said.

"Whom virtue unites, death cannot separate," Art translated.

"Seaton knew you weren't going to the fourteenth degree this year. His message must have some other meaning." Daniel said.

"Seaton is a scholar on Masonic codes, but this message doesn't appear to be coded."

"Do you know much about codes?" Daniel asked.

"A little, but I'm hardly an expert." Art confessed.

"The first half of the message seems to set up the context. It's as if he's setting the stage for you."

"So the second half is what he's telling us to do." Art said tapping the postcard.

"It's a place to start. Does that last sentence make any sense to you?"

Art studied the message again. "I'm drawing a blank."

Daniel let out a sigh in frustration, "I gotta take a leak." He crossed the library and pushed through the bathroom door.

***

Art followed Daniel a few seconds later but stayed outside the bathroom door. He heard Daniel washing his hands and opened the door to see Daniel staring back at him in the mirror.

"You're staring, Art."

"What? Oh, sorry. I was just thinking of Seaton's message. He said to relieve myself." He took a step into the bathroom.

58

"And you think he meant to go to the bathroom?"

"Maybe. After that he mentions the lustration. Lustration in the Fourteenth degree involves washing the hands. It's like a purification ritual." Art explained.

"Followed by the sign of adoration," Daniel said as he raised his arms above his head.

"Don't forget, you have to tilt your head back." Art said. As both men imitated the movement, Art noticed the small wood trimmed panels in the lower ceiling above the sinks. He touched the edge of the panel with his fingertips and pushed.

Daniel smiled as the small panel popped open like a false ceiling tile. He slid a Shurfire P2X flashlight from his pocket and illuminated the dark compartment. Nothing. Art moved to the right and checked the panel above the second sink. As Art popped the panel up and slid it to the side, Daniel activated the flashlight.

That's when Art saw it—the edge of a dark brown leather spine.

"Eureka," Art said as he snatched the journal from its perch. Grabbing the front cover by the corner, Art opened the journal. Unlike the aged journals Seaton had been studying at the library desk, this one was brand new. Instead of old world style calligraphy on aged yellow paper, this journal had block letters on bright white lined notepaper. The writing seemed to be coded.

"Can you make it out?" Daniel asked as he looked at the journal over Art's shoulder.

"The section headings are in English but the rest of this looks like gibberish," Art said.

"Maybe we should start at the beginning, what does the first section header say?" Daniel asked.

Art flipped the pages back to the first entry and read the words aloud. "Alexandria, Virginia."

***

Sarah pulled into her driveway a few minutes after six and found Daniel leaning against his 1967 big black Camaro which had been backed in. Daniel called it 'combat parking'. She knew he kept the car at Art's town home a few miles away for when he came into town. Two large gift-wrapped packages were on the hood.

Sarah hadn't seen Daniel in two months and the mere sight of him sent a spark through her body. She wasted no time exiting the truck and embracing him. She was convinced there was no safer place on Earth than in his arms.

"It's really good to see you," she said.

"It's been too long."

"Are those for me?" She took a step backward and glanced over at the packages.

"Yep, that and more," he said.

Sarah gave Daniel a quizzical look. He smiled and pinched his fingers in his mouth whistling loudly. Sarah turned towards her side yard as she heard a clanking sound and was surprised to see a beautiful Belgian Malinois bounding towards her.

"This is Ranger. Ranger, this is Sarah."

"He's beautiful," Sarah said, as she got down on one knee and ran her fingers through his thick, brown coat. "Is he yours?"

"I just got him a few weeks ago. I wanted to keep it a surprise."

"Did you get him from the pound?"

"Actually, his trainer was a good friend of mine."

"Was?"

"We're still at war," he reminded her.

"So...he served with you?"

Daniel nodded.

"Same unit?"

"Same one; same as Ranger here. In fact, you are looking at the most decorated canine in the United States Army. He's even received the Dickin Medal."

"What's that?" she asked.

"It's a British medal for gallantry."

"British? How did he get a British medal?"

"That's classified," he said smiling. "Maybe you can get him to tell you about it sometime. It's quite a story."

"So he's like a furry Rambo, huh?"

"Rambo ain't got nothing on Ranger here," Daniel said patting Ranger's head.

"Well, it's a pleasure to meet you, Ranger," Sarah said extending her hand.

Ranger promptly raised a paw into her outstretched hand.

Bloodlines

Turning away from Ranger, she asked, "Can I open my presents?"

"Those we might want to open inside," Daniel said as he slid his arm around her and pointed her towards the house.

She walked to the front door and punched the deactivation code into her alarm panel as her two guests squeezed by behind her.

Rounding the corner and coming into the living room, Sarah froze in mid-step. Perched atop her mantle was a very large, framed watercolor of a cobalt blue horse with red eyes. The horse was blowing fire from its nostrils. Ranger froze too and let out a low growl at the painting.

"I guess your mom's been by, huh?" Daniel said.

Sarah's mother, Nancy, was an award-winning interior designer committed to reshaping her only daughter into her vision of a modern lady.

Sarah lived in the home of her deceased grandfather and she kept it looking much like he had. Her maternal grandfather had been an avid outdoorsman. He taught her self-reliance and the skills of a tracker while her friends were dressing dolls. The hand-crafted furniture and taxidermy made her house look like a Cabela's showroom.

Her mother's taste ran more in a Contemporary style. Sarah's childhood home was minimalist to say the least. Sleek-lined furniture with white undertones was contrasted with bright accents and explosive-colored artwork. To Sarah, it felt more like living in a museum; cold and devoid of emotion just like her mother.

Sarah looked back at Daniel and rolled her eyes. Her mother was constantly leaving 'little improvements' as she called them. Sarah would keep them around for a week or two until her mother either came by to replace them, or give them to a more gracious client. In many ways, Sarah was running from the home of her upbringing just as Nancy was. The irony, however, escaped her mother.

Daniel had placed the presents on an old wooden dining room table her grandfather had crafted as a young man in the 1930s. One box was long and narrow. The other was about the size of a basketball but square. Both were wrapped in butcher paper—most likely from the Facility labs—and sealed with red

61

evidence tape. Each box was adorned with a large bow made from yellow crime scene tape.

Cute. Only Daniel would do this for her. "I love the wrapping job," Sarah said.

"Nothing but the best for my girl."

Sarah winked at him. She liked the way his words sounded. "Can I ask what the occasion is?"

"Do I need an occasion to give you a gift?"

"I suppose not, which one should I open first?"

"Dealer's choice."

Sarah ran her fingers along the long, narrow box. "Flowers?"

Daniel smiled. "Better."

"Better, huh? How can I pass that up?"

Sarah dug into the paper and tore the package open. Her eyes lit up as they followed the length of the 18 inch blued barrel. She grabbed the black synthetic pistol grip and hoisted her gift out of its Styrofoam packaging.

"Whoa!" Sarah said.

"It's a Remington 870 tactical shotgun with adjustable stock, 600 lumens tac-light, and Trijicon Reflex sight. I even added a mercury recoil suppressor."

"What…no laser?"

Daniel laughed. "Forget the laser. A tac-light is all you need."

"Thank you! I love it." Sarah checked to make sure the chamber was empty before she shouldered the weapon. "It's much lighter than I expected."

Daniel watched as she swung the shotgun around engaging invisible targets.

"This is too much, Daniel. You can't afford this," she said.

"Don't worry about what it costs. I don't have any expenses thanks to Art."

"You're going to spoil me."

"You love it," he said, not able to hide his smile.

Sarah had to admit she did, and for a second it made her uneasy. She brushed aside the fleeting though, and tore into the second package.

Inside the box she found five boxes of twelve gauge shotgun shells, and a trendy-looking bullet resistant button-down shirt made from the famed Columbian designer Miguel Caballero. Sarah held up the shirt and gave it a once over.

"That'll stop a forty-four magnum at point blank range," Daniel said.

Sarah gave him a quizzical look then turned her gaze back to the shirt. The gears started turning in her head as she glanced at Ranger, then back at the items lining her dining room table.

"Daniel...what's going on?"

"What do you mean?"

"I mean *all this*," Sarah said waving her arm across the table. "Ranger, the shotgun, the tactical gear...don't get me wrong, I love the stuff, but you're not telling me something. We agreed you wouldn't keep secrets from me."

Daniel's expression turned from joy to dread in an instant. It was as if an invisible hand had erased any trace of happiness from his face.

"Something has happened," he said. Then he explained to her the events of the day.

"Oh my God...and you think it's the same assassin that killed the Governor?"

"No doubt."

"And you think they'll come after me?"

"No, I don't. If they thought you were a threat, they would have made a move on you like they did Art. Hell, they apparently didn't consider me a threat."

Big mistake, Sarah thought.

He put his arm around her. "It just makes me feel better that you have a little more protection, that's all."

"The department gives me a bullet proof vest, you know."

"Yeah, but this is more fashionable," Daniel said holding up the shirt. He had a point.

Sarah hugged him and planted a kiss on his lips. She felt her stomach drop as the kiss deepened and lasted several more seconds before her cell phone chirped.

Sarah looked at the caller ID and with horror read her mother's name. *How does she do that?*

"Hi, mother."

"Sarah dear, your father and I were just thinking it would be wonderful if you joined us for dinner tonight."

"Oh, that's really sweet, Mom, but Daniel is in town and has to leave tomorrow. I was going to do something with him," Sarah said.

"Daniel…he's the mechanic?"

The word mechanic was laced with disapproval. Nancy had tried unsuccessfully to pick a suitor for her only daughter. Although handsome, wealthy, and successful, none shared her interests and fewer still approved of them. First and foremost on that list was her occupation followed by a close second of her possession of firearms. 'It just isn't ladylike to own a gun,' her mother often observed.

Although they had been dating for a year, her mother never fully acknowledged Sarah's love for Daniel.

"Bring him along dear; we never get to see him. I'm sure your father would like the chance to visit."

Sarah smelled a trap, but she also knew that the best way for Daniel to win over her parents was by spending more time with them. Daniel had a gift of bringing people together he said he learned while serving as a Green Beret.

She cupped the phone muting the speaker and asked Daniel if he wanted to go. After a nod of the head, Sarah accepted and hung up the phone.

"I hope this doesn't ruin any plans you had for a romantic dinner," she said.

"No, not at all. I like your folks."

Sarah raised her eyebrow and snorted, but accepted the comment as face value.

"Let me just grab a couple of things for Ranger before I forget," he said.

Daniel returned with a large duffel bag and handed Sarah a stainless steel dog bowl which she in turn filled with water.

"Here's his bag of essentials. I'll go grab his food."

As Daniel ran back outside, Sarah unzipped the bag and began removing the contents. The first few items were the standard fare for dogs. A leash, some throw toys, and a food bowl. Underneath, however, lay an assortment of items rivaling the gifts she had just received. Sarah removed a K9 Storm ballistic vest with an olive drab American flag patch, a laminated sheet of command words, muzzle, and what looked like a pair of high tech swimming goggles. She was holding the goggles up by the strap when Daniel came back in the room.

"They're called doggles," Daniel said.

"They look weird. He actually wears these?"

"Usually just when we skydive, but sometimes when we're out walking the grounds at night."

"Oh, so he sky dives too," she said looking at Ranger. Sarah squinted as she examined the odd lenses and attachment on the brim. Daniel could see her studying the goggles intently.

"Night vision and infra-red capable," he said.

"Is the Army going to miss these?" she asked.

Daniel answered with a shrug of his shoulders.

"And this?" Sarah touched a small plastic orb on top of the vest.

"It's a strobe light. It's meant to disorient anyone the dog is charging. It's activated by a voice chip inside; actually, a bark activated chip," he added.

"Just the *essentials*, huh?"

"Well, it's easier to keep all his gear together. You never know," he said dismissively.

"I see," she said smiling, placing the goggles back in the bag.

"He does like to wear the vest at night though. I think it makes him feel needed, so if you could keep it on him at night that would be great."

"Speaking of clothing," Sarah said as she gave Daniel a once over. He was handsome enough in his polo shirt and khaki pants, but for some unexplained reason she wanted to dress him up a bit for dinner.

"Do you mind putting on a dress shirt and tie?"

"That's why I keep one here, isn't it?"

"Do you keep one somewhere else?" Sarah asked.

"Actually…no."

***

Reaper felt the phone vibrate in his pocket and glanced at the number on the caller ID. He recognized it right away.

"Did you find it?" Barclay snapped.

"No. It's not in the residence or in the library," Reaper said.

"Well, it has to be somewhere. I saw the damned thing myself!"

"My team is looking into all known associates, his financial records, and his phone records. If he has another hiding place, we'll find it."

"That's not good enough," Barclay said.

"You have a better suggestion?"

"Look, I *need* answers. Do you have any idea how much money I have invested in this little scheme of ours? Millions. My campaign is just getting off the ground and a scandal like this is the type of thing that can bring us all down. Your people need to do more!"

"We have invested quite a bit ourselves, remember?" Reaper said. "My team is working around the clock. We'll find the journal."

Barclay wasn't as optimistic. "What about this Von Hollen character; could he have the journal?"

"If he had it he would have given it to the police and my man would have alerted us. Trust me…he doesn't have it."

"What if he's conducting his own investigation? Did you ever think about that?" Barclay snapped.

"And why would he do that?"

"It might have something to do with your man trying to kill him."

"Unlikely," Reaper said.

"Has your team connected this researcher with Washington D.C.?" Barclay asked.

"Not that I am aware of, why?"

"I did a little checking on my own. Art Von Hollen filed a flight plan to D.C. tomorrow morning." Barclay said.

Reaper was silent for a moment as he contemplated this new intelligence. His analytical mind raced through the known facts until he remembered the postcard. He cursed himself for not demanding a transcript of the message.

"The old man must have sent the journal to someone in D.C. You need to get ahead of them and tail the Von Hollens' to their meet point," Barclay said.

"Von Hollens'…plural? His nephew is with him?" Reaper asked.

"Don't tell me you're afraid of some washed out soldier," Barclay said.

Reaper didn't care for the flippant attitude his employer had adopted. "Need I remind you that in all likelihood it was this 'washed-out' soldier that took out Marat?"

"We don't know what happened to Marat. All we know is he got caught. You're damned lucky he only got interrogated by Sheriff Taylor and the Mayberry squad," Barclay said. "We can't afford any more mistakes like that."

Reaper suppressed a flash of anger and took a deep breath. He had warned the Governor about sending an inexperienced operative into the field alone and it had nearly blown the mission.

"I guess I'm going to D.C." Reaper said.

"I have a jet waiting to take you in two hours. Follow them to their meet and grab the journal. Whatever you do…don't stop until you get that damned journal. No more failures."

10

It was a few minutes after seven when Sarah's pickup thundered down her parent's driveway at the end of a windy road in Cherry Hills Farm. Daniel smirked at the large statue of Poseidon hoisting his trident above the large fountain.

"She just had to pick Poseidon with his trident, didn't she?" Daniel said.

"I'm sure it's nothing personal," Sarah joked as she elbowed him in the arm. She knew the trident was the symbol of his military rival—the Navy SEAL.

Sarah removed the Glock 17 nine millimeter pistol from her Crossbreed holster and slid it under the seat. Since joining the Sheriff's office, Sarah carried a gun everywhere except court and her mother's house. She knew it was pointless to ask Daniel to do the same. He was always armed. He probably had it tucked somewhere her mother would never feel in a casual embrace. Sarah never even saw his weapons unless she was undressing him.

Daniel came around to the driver's door, and they walked up to the front door together, holding hands. They stood patiently outside the five hundred pound doors as Sarah rang the buzzer.

"Don't you think it's weird to ring the doorbell to your own house?" Daniel asked.

"It's not my house anymore. I'm a guest just like you," she said.

The huge wooden doors glided open as Nancy greeted them with a smile on her face from one diamond earring to the other.

"Oh, look at you two! Aren't you just the picture of the perfect couple?"

Sarah gave a half-hearted smile and hugged her mother. Daniel offered a firm but demure handshake.

"Come in, come in. Your father is waiting in the study. I know he's dying to see Daniel," she said.

Theodore Richards stood near the far window with one arm propped against a glass bookshelf. His other hand held a small tumbler glass filled half way with a caramel-colored liquor.

Bloodlines

"Saaaarah! Come over here and give your dad a hug."

Unlike her mother, Sarah's father never discouraged his daughter from following her dreams, especially in matters of the heart. He lifted her off her feet in a bear hug followed by a peck on the cheek. He offered a firm handshake to Daniel.

"Daniel, how's the weather up in Steamboat?"

"Fine, Mr. Richards. It's good to see you again."

"Oh, call me Ted, please. We don't rest on formalities here. Can I pour you a drink?"

"I'd love one. What's you poison?"

"Stranahan's; it's distilled right here in Denver," he said with a tinge of pride. He poured a glass for Daniel as Nancy offered Sarah a Chardonnay.

"Do you have any beer?" Sarah asked.

Nancy waived her hand back in forth in front of her face. Sarah had learned years ago it was a subconscious attempt by her mother to 'erase' any spoken words that were unpleasant to her.

"*Try* the Chardonnay. It's Californian," Nancy said.

Sarah took a sip and winced.

"Uhm, that's...*interesting*," she said suppressing a cough.

"Oh Sarah, *really*...you look like you just swallowed cough medicine." Sarah was thinking the exact same thing. She didn't have the same taste for wine that her mother did.

"What can I say, Mother; I guess there's still too much Tom in the Tomboy."

Ted retrieved a Negro Modelo beer from the small fridge and popped the cap for Sarah.

"Here you go, sweetie," he said as he shot a disapproving look towards Nancy.

"Sarah honey, I'm just dying to know what you think of the new Bristolé?"

"Come again?" Sarah asked.

"I think she means the painting," Daniel whispered.

"Oh yeah, the painting. It's real...*colorful?*"

"You hate it," Nancy said with petulance.

"It's just doesn't seem to go with the rest of my stuff, Mom."

"What do you mean? It's very 'western'. It's a horse for heaven's sake!"

69

"A *blue* horse! There's fire and smoke coming out of its nostrils. Not quite a Remington, is it?" Sarah shot back; her voice slightly elevated.

"I'll have you know that Jean Claire Bristolé is one of the finest new artists in the Santa Fe Arts District. Even the Governor has one."

Sarah glanced over to Daniel but he was looking for safety at the bottom of his whiskey.

"Now ladies," Ted interrupted. "Am I going to have to send you two to your rooms without dessert?"

Sarah smiled and took a deep breath before eyeing her mother.

"I'm sorry, Mom. I haven't really had a chance to look at it in the light. Can I hold onto it for a little longer?"

Nancy's eyes beamed with excitement as she clapped her hands together. It was a dance they had perfected over the years that always ended the same. In a week or two, Nancy would replace the art with something even more hideous.

"You'll love it, I promise. The piece really grows on you."

Sarah offered a flat smile and looked at Daniel as if to say *please shoot me if that ever happens*. He returned an almost imperceptible grin.

"Sarah dear, will you give me a hand in the kitchen?" Nancy said. Sarah took her arm and followed her out the door and down the hall.

***

"Nancy is cooking dinner?" Daniel asked. He realized how incredulous he sounded as the words slipped past his lips.

Ted winked. "No, but she's dynamite at take out."

"Ah, so that's where Sarah picked up her skills?"

"Not too good in the kitchen, eh?" Ted asked.

"Let's just say she likes to use the smoke detector as a timer," Daniel said.

"I'm afraid we didn't prepare her too well in that arena, not that we didn't try. Sarah likes to march to the beat of her own drum, if you know what I mean." Ted said.

"That's what I love about her."

Ted seemed to ponder that statement for a moment as he took another look out the darkened window. He turned and pointed to a pair of leather recliners in front of a large white marble fireplace. Daniel sank into the deep upholstery and nearly spilled his drink. He didn't expect the leather to be so soft.

"So how is your job treating you, Daniel?"

"I can't complain."

"Still doing the hunting guide thing up at Art's place?"

"Among other things; I do construction and mechanical repairs, too."

"Ah," Ted said letting the words hang in the air like thick cigar smoke.

"You know, Daniel, if you ever wanted to try something a little more...*challenging*... I could get you an entry level position at my investment firm."

Daniel suppressed a smirk as he looked down into his whiskey.

"I didn't mean that to sound so condescending. I just want you to know I can provide options for you."

The word 'challenging' was still hanging in his mind.

He wanted to tell Ted that he was once one of the more elite soldiers in the world. That he had fought the enemies of freedom on every battlefield, on every continent, for less pay than a librarian. He wanted to tell him about the four languages he spoke, or the education he had acquired that would have shamed any Ph.D. Instead, Daniel just swirled his glass and took the high road.

"I appreciate the offer Ted, I really do. It's just that my Uncle Art really likes having me around. It may not be glamorous work, but it needs doing," he said.

"Of course, of course, I completely understand. Just know that I'm here for you if you change your mind."

Daniel nodded. "Thanks."

"The most important thing to me is my Sarah. As long as she's happy, I'm happy," Ted said.

"On that we can agree, Sir."

"You know, I've never seen Sarah quite so smitten as she is with you."

Daniel waved him off as he took a sip from his drink.

"No, I mean it. She thinks the world of you, son."

"The feeling is mutual, I assure you." Daniel said.

"You two have been dating for, what is it now, a year?"

"Pretty close."

"Any plans for the future?" Ted asked with a hint of caution. Daniel nearly choked on his drink.

"Are you asking me my intentions?"

"Oh, no." He said with a dismissive wave. "I was just curious how things were going, that's all. Our Sarah isn't getting any younger, you know."

The comment was something Sarah had warned him about months ago. Sooner or later, the 'wedding card' would get dealt.

"As you say; she likes to march to her own drumbeat. But, I promise you, the moment that changes I'll be back here with my hat in my hand."

Ted offered a wide, toothy smile, apparently satisfied with the answer.

***

Sarah was helping her mother set the table when she heard three soft knocks on the back door.

"Who could that be?" Sarah asked.

"It's the delivery boy," Nancy said.

Nancy threw open the door and began instructing the Asian teenager how to arrange the food on the various platters. As he exited the back door, Nancy handed him a hundred dollar bill.

"You just tipped him a hundred bucks." It was more like an accusation than a question.

"What? Oh, well good help is hard to find. Jung-Yoon is studying for his Masters in Biochemistry."

Sarah sensed for a moment that her mother might try to suggest him as a suitor but Sarah interrupted her train of thought.

"And you're paying his tuition all by yourself? That's sweet, Mom."

"If you must know, I ask him to do the occasional errand."

"What kind of errands?"

"Sometimes he stops by the liquor store and picks something up for dinner. Sometimes I ask him to get the dry cleaning…"

"The dry cleaning, Mother? Really? If you need help…" Sarah interrupted her.

"Good lord Sarah, you make it sound so sleazy. He's very dependable and I pay him well. It's not as if he's an indentured servant."

Nancy was right of course. Most people were lucky to have any job, and this kid could have done a lot worse.

***

Dinner was engaging to say the least. Sarah winced as her mother quizzed Daniel on everything from marriage and grandchildren to career choices. He gave as good as he got. It reminded Sarah of a story Daniel had told her about a parley he once had with an Afghan militia commander. In the end, she decided it was a draw.

By ten o'clock she was ready to have Daniel all to herself. She gave Daniel the signal they had pre-arranged and backed her chair from the table.

"It was a lovely dinner, Mrs. Richards. Thank you so much for inviting me," he said.

"Oh, do you have to go?"

"I'm afraid so. Art and I are scheduled to depart at eight o'clock tomorrow morning."

"I've got to get up early for work, too," Sarah added.

"Where are you two boys jetting off to?" Ted asked.

"Washington, D.C."

"Is this business or pleasure?" Nancy asked. "You must find time to visit the National Gallery of Art. One of their board members is a sorority sister of mine. I'd be happy to arrange a private tour."

"Thanks Mrs. Richards, but I'm afraid we won't have much time for sight-seeing. Art has an important project he's working on."

"Well, you just call Sarah if you change your mind."

"Wilco…I mean, I will," Daniel said. "Thank you."

Once in the truck Sarah holstered her Glock, locked the doors, and turned the key. The ride home started off with a comfortable silence. Sarah asked about caring for Ranger yet twenty minutes later she was peppering him with questions about the assassin and his trip to D.C.

"I don't understand. Why would they resurface again, a year later?" Sarah said.

"I think it's safe to say they feel threatened," Daniel said.

"Threatened by what? We never found anything to link them to the killings. Hell, we have no idea who *they* are!"

Daniel didn't respond. He sat quietly looking at the passing scenery as Sarah drove the distance back to her home.

"What are you thinking?" she asked.

"Sorry, I'm not being a very good conversationalist am I? I'm just trying to figure out a game plan."

"We could try calling the FBI."

"Last time they got involved, I went to jail remember?"

"Technically, you were already in jail," she said hoping to crack a smile. It worked.

"Technically," he said.

After the sniper had killed a witness, Daniel nearly caught him after a harrowing chase. But, the police caught Daniel instead and fingered him for the murders. He was still in jail when the Governor was killed and Sarah knew how much it bothered him to have failed in capturing the killer. She squeezed his knee and smiled.

Sarah maneuvered her truck into the driveway and took note of how dark the yard was. They sat in the car for a few seconds as Sarah turned off the radio, unfastened her seatbelt, and unlocked the door.

"You forgot to turn on your lights again," Daniel said. She could sense the concern in his voice. He had installed a number of flood lights after a serial killer had stalked her almost a year earlier.

"I know, my bad. Maybe you should come up and make sure I get in all right?"

"I thought you'd never ask," he said.

Sarah led him up the stairs by the hand. She opened the front door and deactivated the alarm before closing the door. When she flicked on the light, her heart skipped a beat as Ranger sat a few feet away staring at them through his tinted doggles.

"Sweet Jesus!" Sarah whispered.

"Come," Daniel said snapping his fingers. Ranger bounded over wagging his tail. He sat obediently to Daniel's right.

"I thought he was supposed to be a guard dog?" Sarah joked.

Bloodlines

"He knows you and I belong here. Trust me; you'll know when a stranger comes in. Oh, that reminds me. Tell your mother not to drop by when you're not here. You need to be present when he meets new people."

Sarah thought an encounter with Ranger might be just the thing to keep her mother away but pushed the thought from her mind. She didn't want to give her a stroke.

"Can I get you a beer?" Sarah asked.

"I guess that depends."

"On…"

"On whether I'm staying here tonight or driving home," Daniel said.

"You said your flight isn't until eight."

"I did."

"And your bags are packed?" Sarah asked drawing a finger over his chest.

"Yup. I'm ready to go," he said.

Sarah stepped around him and stood behind him. She pressed her lips to his ear. "So there's nothing you need to do before you go?"

"I did have one thing in mind," he said.

"Does that 'thing' involve me?"

Daniel just smiled as he drew her close. His grip was firm and commanding. Sarah felt goose bumps erupting on her skin. He didn't just take hold of her body. He took hold of her soul.

"That was the plan," he said.

"Good, because I have a few plans of my own Mr. Von Hollen."

Sarah grabbed his tie and began leading him back to the bedroom.

"I guess these ties aren't so silly after all," he said.

"I'm just getting started with it," she said with a devilish smile. Sarah took Daniel by the shirt and spun him into the room before kicking the door shut.

11

That same evening; Eastern Arapahoe County, Colorado.
Wes Hammond, Governor Barclay's chief of security, leaned into his employer's ear and whispered, "Last question."

Governor Barclay pointed to a lanky tenth grader in the front row of the town hall meeting hoping to get a softball question. He regarded town hall events as a necessary evil to maintain his affable public persona.

"Why do you want to run for the Presidency when you're already rich?" the young woman asked.

Little bitch.

"What a wonderful question, young lady." Barclay said before folding his hands and making a show of reflecting on the question.

"The Presidency is a calling, I consider it my duty to serve the people and lead our nation forward. As my campaign slogan indicates, I'm 'all in' and it has nothing to do with money. In fact," he said raising a finger, "I pledge here and now that I will donate a portion of my annual salary to a worthy charity."

The small crowd erupted into applause as Barclay flashed his practiced smile to the farmers and ranchers before him. Truth be told, he hated them. Barclay regarded them as simple-minded fools, necessary to a degree, but unwelcome in his grand design. His chief of security touched him on the elbow and held out a hand to the door as Barclay waved to the crowd.

It was Hammond's job, among other things, to keep Barclay on schedule. Hammond was the first private security chief to ever serve the Governor's office. Up until Barclay's administration, security and protection had been handled by troopers of the Colorado State Patrol. But Barclay was a man with many secrets, and police officers had the annoying habit of reporting crimes when they witnessed them. It was a risk he just couldn't afford, especially now.

The move was another in a long line of public affair victories for Barclay and his political team. As designed, the local press heaped praise upon him as a fiscal watchdog. One reporter went so far as to inflate baseless claims of 'threats' to the Governor's family to justify the replacement of sworn officers with private contractors. Barclay was happy to pay the costs from his vast family fortune. It was a small price to pay in a world where secrets and scandals could ruin a man.

Hammond held open the rear driver's door to the black SUV while he surveyed the parking lot. Once inside, the Governor virtually disappeared behind the tinted windows.

Barclay overheard his security chief announce into the security team's radio network that they were en route back to the Governor's Mansion in downtown Denver.

"Wes, I'd like to take a little detour tonight. Have someone meet us at the spot."

Hammond acknowledged the order with a nod in the rearview mirror and placed a call on his cell phone. Thirty minutes later, they met one of Hammond's men in a deserted parking lot and switched vehicles. Hammond got behind the wheel of an old Chevrolet Suburban after handing his colleague the Governor's cell phone. Barclay sat in the front passenger seat and pulled a ball cap down over his head.

The ruse was something Hammond developed while protecting other affluent men with secrets. While en route to their destination, the other security agent would drive a planned route that would ensure the Governor's SUV, with custom license plates, would trigger numerous automated toll booths and at least two red light cameras. The driver would place calls with the Governor's personal cell phone to other security agents waiting at the Mansion as well as general phone extensions at certain government offices and his private attorney. Should an accusation ever be made, Barclay had ample evidence proving he was miles away at the time.

It was just after eight-thirty in the evening when the beige SUV turned down the secluded gravel road twenty miles east of the bustling downtown districts. There wasn't a street light within five miles and the only neighbors were a den of coyotes. Thousands of acres of corn and prairie grass surrounded the early twentieth century farm house. By all appearances, it was a working farm during the day. The thirty-five year old proprietor leased out her acreage for a pittance of its value. Her only stipulation was that the work must stop before sundown. Most of the workers were illegal, and had neither the time nor inclination to make inquiries of the secretive land owner.

***

Barclay had completed a thorough background check of the property owner before joining her elite list of clientele. He picked up additional information about her life as the two spent time together. Elizabeth Trevet had been a normal teenager from a normal home in central Ohio until her second year in college in southern California. Drowning in debt and disillusioned at employment forecasts, she succumbed to the sweet song of a man who convinced her that the troubles she faced were worth the cost of her flesh. Within eight weeks she had paid off her college loans, and by the time she graduated she had a business degree, a wad of cash, and a plan.

She spent the next eight years building an impressive client list of Hollywood celebrities, business men, athletes, and politicians in southern California before an influx of eastern European crime syndicates forced her to relocate. If there was one lesson from college that she valued, it was that successful businesses always adapted to the environment. Elizabeth studied her options like a blue chip stock broker before settling on the Mile High city. Denver was an opportunity waiting to be exploited.

The region boasted several championship sports franchises, a growing gambling infrastructure, and several fortune 500 companies. The establishment of an international airport ensured a steady stream of customers from around the globe. Some came for billion dollar business deals, some for the numerous conventions, and others just for her.

A series of shell corporations insulated Elizabeth from the escort service she ran in Denver for her 'common' clients, but the farmhouse was designed for her VIP clientele. It was a perfect location in a world where personal privacy was eroding with surveillance cameras, facial recognition software, and RFID readers. Celebrities and politicians were especially sensitive to being seen in public, or even so-called 'private' parties. It only took one drunken fool with a cell phone camera to tweet an image of infidelity to millions of followers in seconds. Anonymity had become the pinnacle service in her industry.

Bloodlines

Those who could provide it reaped the rewards of the world's oldest profession.

She ran a clean house; no drugs, no gangs, and no hassles. Her customers paid ten thousand dollars a night for an experience. A night of pleasure and passion guaranteed to erase their insecurities and shore up their egos. Her only employee was a former mob enforcer. His duties were to keep the farm safe and stay out of sight.

Elizabeth told Barclay she knew that one day her luck would run out. Crime was best viewed as a sprint, not a marathon she mentioned. Since her arrival in the Centennial state, Elizabeth had secretly been building her investments in legitimate corporations. She bought a home just outside of Aspen and in five short years she estimated she could retire from her current profession and live out the rest of days as an upstanding member of the community. She would live a life of opulence earned from so many years on her back.

***

A metal gate blocked the road about a quarter mile from the farmhouse. Hammond reached out and punched the private access code into the keypad. Each VIP was issued a unique access code. In addition to opening the gate, the code would alert the small staff that the customer had arrived. There was only one other car parked outside the farmhouse, an old beige Ford pick-up truck that was used to ferry special customers arriving on international flights. Elizabeth once told Barclay the last thing Elizabeth needed was limousines or expensive sedans that looked out of place here.

A single red porch light glowed under the starry sky. It was the signal that entry was permitted. Governor Barclay pulled the brim of his hat a little lower and trotted up onto the wrap around porch with Hammond a few feet behind. Once in the formal sitting room, Hammond took a seat in a red velvet chair and snatched a magazine from the end table while Barclay made his way up the narrow staircase. He stopped outside the third door on his right and rapped on the door.

Elizabeth stood five feet eight inches high in her three inch heels. Naked, her breast-length blonde hair accented her opal blue eyes and skirted the tassels dangling from her nipples. Her bronzed skin didn't reveal a single tan line and was unblemished by the tattoos or piercing found on most prostitutes. In other attire, Elizabeth could easily pass for an A-list supermodel or European nobility.

"Nice to see you again, Aaron," she said running her hand along the length of his arm.

"I don't have a lot of time," he said brushing past her. He stood at the foot of the bed and yanked at his tie.

Elizabeth came in behind him and began rubbing his shoulders.

"Soooo tense. How can you do your job with so much stress," she said rubbing at the knots.

"Let's just do this, all right."

Not being one to mince words, Elizabeth spun him around and unbuttoned his dress shirt. She tossed it onto a small chair before pushing him onto the bed and straddling his chest. She rubbed her moist loins gently across his navel as he laid his head back and closed his eyes. He never showed any indication that he heard the digital recording devices being engaged.

***

Wes Hammond sat patiently in the formal sitting room reading a magazine while his boss conducted other business upstairs. Hammond had been to the farmhouse at least three dozen times since joining the Governor's security staff. It was one of the few times he felt comfortable letting his guard down.

As he thumbed through the pages of his magazine he caught a flash of light in the corner of his eye. The flash came from outside and Hammond immediately set down the magazine and sat straighter in his chair. A second later the reading light next to his chair went out and Hammond reflexively padded the pistol on his hip.

A door opened down the darkened hallway and Elizabeth's burley enforcer stomped down the hall towards Hammond. For a split second, Hammond caught the reflection of what looked like a bank of television monitors on the window opposite the room before the door was closed, to within a sliver of the door frame.

"Sorry about the lights, but its protocol whenever we get a possible intrusion," the enforcer said.

Hammond nodded in understanding and joined the man at the window looking out over the vast property. In the distance they watched as a blade of light sliced through the darkness with a slight bounce. It appeared to be out near the main gate but neither man could be certain.

"It's probably some local kids spotlighting for deer. Stay here while I go out there and check it out."

"I'm going to get my principle," Hammond retorted.

The enforcer latched onto his elbow like his hand was a bear trap.

"This has happened before, it's probably nothing. Up to you, but I seriously doubt your boss will be happy if you interrupt his festivities over a false alarm."

Hammond paused for a moment and considered the ramifications of being wrong. The fact of the matter was that the farmhouse had a lot more at risk and if their security wasn't freaking out, he shouldn't either.

"All right, I'll try to watch you from here," Hammond said.

"Here, take this radio. If something looks hinkey, I'll call you up."

"Good enough," Hammond said.

The enforcer threw open the creaky screen door and tromped out into the darkness without an ounce of hesitation. He looked to be in his late fifties and reminded Hammond of his grandfather. The man had short cropped silver hair, the build of a linebacker, and the swagger of a grizzly bear.

As Hammond watched the man disappear down the road, he thought briefly of his boss. Prudence dictated that he at least verify his status and his thoughts ran back to the reflection in the window. Taking a final peek out the front door, Hammond crept down the hallway until he saw the unmistakable sliver of light emanating from behind the cracked door. Placing his ear against the door, he listened for any sign of another occupant.

Hearing none, he gave a soft rap on the door.

Nothing.

Using the tips of his fingers, he pushed it open one centimeter at a time until the whole room was visible. What he saw caused his heart to skip a beat.

No less than ten monitors flashed images from both inside and outside the house. He saw the enforcer crouched by an outbuilding on the monitor in the lower left corner. He seemed to be fine. The only other activity he could see was located on the center monitor, which was also the largest.

There on the screen sat his boss sitting on a bed using exaggerated hand movements and talking to a beautiful naked blond. He was still wearing dress pants, socks and shoes. Hammond inched closer to the screen. Barclay looked to be in a heated discussion. Hammond glanced down and saw a pair of padded headphones with a cord leading to the monitor.

He glanced behind him and then to the monitor showing the enforcer before putting the right headphone pad up to his ear.

"I tell you, this has never happened to me before." It was the Governor's voice.

"It's all right, baby. What can I do to help you?" a woman's voice said.

"Nothing! I just can't concentrate until I get that damned journal back!"

"Talk to me baby, what journal?"

The Governor shook his head in frustration as he dropped his arms to his side.

"I swear to god if I never hear the name Seaton Adiago again, it will be too soon!"

"What are you talking about, sweetie?" She grabbed his shoulders and straddled his lap. The Governor was silent.

"Forget about him, concentrate on me." She flung her hair around and brushed it against his face before arching her back and thrusting her ample breasts within an inch of his mouth. The trick worked and soon Barclay was back to the business at hand.

Hammond stood for a brief moment mesmerized by the activity on the main screen when he caught a glimpse of movement on the lower monitor. The enforcer was returning to the house. Hammond placed the headphones back on the desktop and scurried out the door and into the hallway. There was no way of getting back to the sitting room without getting caught, so he turned right and headed for the kitchen.

The full moon allowed for some illumination through the large picture window over the sink. He had the second cabinet door half way open when the enforcer walked in behind him.

"I thought I told you to stay put," he said.

Hammond turned around and feigned surprise.

"I was just getting a glass of water."

The enforcer glanced at the open cabinet next to the sink and then back to Hammond.

"Second one on the left," he said with a nod of his head.

Hammond grabbed a glass and began filling it from the tap.

"Everything all right out there?"

"Like I said...kids."

Hammond nodded as he took a slow drink. He couldn't tell if the enforcer was eyeing him suspiciously, or if he always had that expression.

The enforcer gave him one last look from head to toe. "You got your water. Now get back up front. This area is off limits to guests."

Hammond nodded and brushed past the enforcer on his way back to the sitting room. With every step he could feel the man's eyes burning through his back.

12

August 6th; Littleton, Colorado.

Daniel sprang up the stairs and into the Gulfstream cabin five minutes before eight. Art was sitting at a four seat table near the aft of the aircraft. Art noted the time with an exaggerated arm movement.

"I was beginning to wonder if you'd make it," Art said.

"I'm never late for a deployment, Uncle Art."

Art smiled as he eyed his nephew.

"You've got quite the spring in your step this morning. I take it your date went well?"

"Really well," Daniel said.

Art waited for more but none was forthcoming. "By really well you mean…"

Daniel was visibly taken back by the question. "Jesus Art, this ain't a locker room."

"What? No, I don't mean…you know…" Art's eyes darted back and forth searching for the right words. "I just mean, I've been worried about you two. These long distance relationships can be hard. It's difficult for a romance to evolve when each date feels like you're starting from scratch."

"Oh, well I think things are going good. I'm not sure she's ready to kick things up a notch. I'm not sure I am, either."

Art chuckled as he leaned back in his chair.

"Daniel, you are the single worst liar I know. That includes the criminals, mind you."

"That obvious, huh?"

"Completely transparent. Let me ask you this, what are you afraid of?"

Daniel folded his hands and rested his chin on crossed thumbs. "I'm not afraid of anything."

Art inhaled deeply, interlaced his fingers behind his head, and arched his eyebrows.

"You know what I think? I think you're afraid of not measuring up to the person you *think* she deserves. I think you're afraid you don't make a difference anymore. I watch you around the facility, you know. I see you on the range and with the students. You try so hard to be mediocre, to not stand out. What did you call that before?"

"A gray man."

"Yes...a gray man. Daniel, the fact of the matter is you can't help but stand out. I know it's been difficult transitioning from your former life into the civilian world. I get it. But I want to ask you something very important. Do you know why you were so successful as a soldier?"

Daniel shrugged his shoulders.

"You were successful because you don't know how to fail. That former life of yours...that mission...it's over, son. You served your country proud, you served your family proud, and you have nothing to regret. This...this life...your life...this is the new mission. The objective is to grow old and die happy with a wonderful woman at your side. And you, my boy, are off to a good start," he said jabbing a finger into the table. "I have every confidence you will excel at whatever it is you choose to do."

Daniel pinched his lower lip between his thumb and forefinger before he spoke.

"I'm not scared of failure, Uncle Art, and I don't have any regrets about my service. Not one."

"But," Art said.

"I've done things, things that aren't easy to understand sitting stateside while eating an apple pie, and watching a ball game on TV."

"You're worried she *won't* understand? Have you forgotten what she's been through?"

"I haven't forgotten. I'll never forget, but certain knowledge can erode trust. It can legitimize uncertainty...change the way you view the world...view the ones you love."

"This knowledge hasn't changed the way I think of you," Art said.

"I guess," Daniel said.

"Look Daniel, neither of us can know for sure what Sarah will think, but I do know this; she is a woman of great character. And women of great character deserve men of great character, and that she has in you. Men of honor don't require a uniform."

Art let that last point sit in the air a moment before opening the journal and laying it out on the desk.

"I made a call to a friend last night who just happens to live outside Washington, D.C., and he's agreed to take a look at the text. He's perfect for this code stuff," Art said.

"Who is he?"

"Name is Herb Degroat. He retired from the NSA a few years back and works at the George Washington Masonic Memorial Library."

"Jesus, the Masonic library? Do you think he knows Seaton? What did you tell him?"

"I thought it best not to say anything for now. I don't know if he knew Seaton, but it's not the type of news I want to toss out over the phone."

"How do you know him?" Daniel asked.

"Herb was a guest speaker a few years back at the Facility. He gave a well-attended lecture on the history of cryptic writing using invisible inks. It was quite something."

"Well, it's a place to start I guess. Maybe we can at least figure out what was so interesting about Alexandria."

Art spent the four hour flight going over each page of the journal looking for any clue that may help explain Seaton's murder.

Aside from the section headings, none of the text made any sense. The same could be said of the drawings. Seaton was not a gifted artist but it was clear he thought certain images were important enough to. One image looked like a heart with leaves on the inside. Another was a small oval with an apple, or some other fruit in the center. An image on a later page looked like a corkscrew with small notches cut into it. None of it made any sense to him.

Daniel dutifully took digital photographs of each page while Art made notes on a separate notepad.

"Art, we're starting our decent into Manassas so buckle up." The pilot's voice announced over the intercom. Art pushed the blue button on the control panel.

"I thought we were landing in D.C.?" Art said.

"I thought so too, but since 9/11 D.C. is a restricted flight operations zone. It takes a couple of weeks to get the proper clearances. Manassas Regional is the best I can do."

"Okay, no problem Dave. Did you check to see if they have rental cars by chance?"

Bloodlines

"Way ahead of you, boss. I got a luxury sedan with GPS waiting for you at the terminal building."

"Thanks Dave, you're a life saver."

The landing at Manassas regional airport was smooth and uneventful. Daniel collected his two large black nylon gear bags while Art tucked the small leather journal into his shoulder bag. Dave helped load their other baggage into the trunk of the rental car before taxiing the plane to one of the service hangers.

Art took the front passenger seat and punched the address of their hotel into the GPS even though Daniel assured him he had already plotted their route.

Traffic was light during the lunch hour until they reached Interstate 95. The local traffic report announced a roll-over accident near Newington backing up traffic all the way to Woodbridge.

Art used the time to call Herb and arrange a meeting time in his office at the George Washington Masonic Center Library. Two hours later, after checking into the hotel and downing a bag of fast food, they pulled into the parking lot northwest of the memorial.

Daniel picked a spot near the top corner of the downward sloping lot on Shuter's Hill and backed in.

Herb was waiting for them at the bottom of the enormous stairway leading up to the Parthenon-like entrance. He greeted both men with the customary handshake and greeting.

"I trust you didn't have any trouble finding us?" Herb said.

Daniel looked up at the nine story tower and said, "It's kind of hard to miss."

"Is this your first time here?"

"First time for me," Daniel said.

"Well then, I think a tour is in order," Herb said.

Art rested a hand on Herb's shoulder. "If it's all the same to you, Herb, I'd prefer to get started on this translation."

"Suit yourself, we're not going anywhere."

Herb entered his meager office and gestured to the chairs surrounding a small circular table.

"All right, let's see this code that brought you half-way across the country in such a hurry."

Art pulled the journal from his shoulder bag and slid it across the table.

Tom Adair

"Art tells me you used to be with NSA?" Daniel said.

Herb settled his half-moon bifocals on the edge of his thin nose as he opened the journal and scanned the first page.

"Thirty two years," Herb said.

"What got you into that line of work?"

My father was a Navajo code talker in the Pacific Theater; forty-three to forty-five," Herb said peeking over the wire rimmed glasses.

"I grew up hearing the stories and I fell in love with the idea."

"You know, Daniel's Great Uncle was a code talker," Art said.

"He was?" Daniel said, surprise in his voice.

"You didn't know that? Your maternal grandmother's youngest brother I believe." Art said.

"Grandma was Comanche, not Navajo." Daniel said.

"Oh, there were Comanche code talkers. Part of the Army's 4th Infantry Division. About a dozen participated in the invasion of Normandy," Herb said.

"I've never heard any of this," Daniel said.

After a moment of silence Art continued, "Your dad mentioned it once while he was courting your mother. Honestly, I forgot about it until just now."

"What was his name? There weren't too many of those guys, and I'm kind of a buff on that particular topic. Maybe I've got some biographical information I can pass along."

"I can't remember, but I'm sure we can figure it out." Art said.

"Well...one mystery at a time I guess," Herb said as he turned the page and ran his finger across several coded words.

He studied the pages for several minutes with an occasional grunt or nod of the head. Several times Art watched as he flipped back and forth between several pages and jotted notes on a small pad of paper bearing a watermark of the Masonic square and compasses. Finally, he settled on the page containing the rendering of the heart emblem with leaves, spun the journal around to face them, and jabbed it several times with his finger.

"Now this is interesting," Herb said.

"You recognize it?"

"It looks like the Military Badge of Merit."

"Who's military...ours?" Art asked.

"Yes," Herb said. "They were reportedly first issued in seventeen eighty-two by General Washington himself to three non-coms for unusual gallantry or extraordinary fidelity to the cause of freedom."

"Non-commissioned soldiers," Daniel clarified for Art.

"Yes, that's right, and given personally by General Washington himself," Herb said.

"You said *reportedly* first issued in seventeen eighty-two?" Art said.

"That's right," Herb said.

Art stared at the old researcher but Herb quickly looked down and away. It was a classic sign of avoidance Art had witnessed many times from suspects.

"Herb...why do I get the feeling you're holding something back?" Art said.

Herb pulled his bifocals from his nose and laid them across the pages of the open journal.

"Why are you here, Art?"

"I need to understand this code."

"And why is understanding this particular code so important to you?" Herb said rapping his fingers on the open pages.

Art wasn't ready to reveal things that might place Herb in the same danger that befell Seaton. He leaned forward in his chair and chose his next words carefully.

"Because I swore an obligation to an old friend; now tell me...brother to brother...do you recognize this code?"

"I should hope so...I designed it."

13

Reaper waited nearly forty-five minutes in a small parking lot north of Reagan National Airport off the George Washington Memorial Parkway.

Parked in the shadow of a large shade tree, he scanned the tail numbers of over a dozen corporate jets. None matched the number he had memorized.

It was not until he called one of his team members at the ops center to run a trace on Art Von Hollen's credit cards that he was informed of the rental car. Using that information, it was a simple task for his team to hack into the On Star navigation system and provide a location for the vehicle he was now watching. He had wasted valuable time though.

Nestled in a shady spot along Ridge Lane, Reaper ate a fast food lunch as he peered through his compact binoculars every few minutes. In truth, he didn't like American fast food, but it provided a good cover story should a wandering police officer stumble upon his stake-out. He was just another guy having lunch.

He had not seen his targets enter but was certain they were inside the opulent building. Reaper didn't care for the look of the building, or the people inside. His grandfather had taught him everything he needed to know about the secret society which propagated political opinions dangerous to the security of the Soviet state. Better they infect America with their poison called *freedom*.

He set down his binoculars and checked the time on his Sturmanskie watch after hearing his phone ring. He glanced at the caller ID and saw Barclay's number. He answered without a word.

"Do you have it?" Barclay asked. Reaper could hear the tension in the man's voice as it cracked.

"No," he said.

"What do you mean 'no'? You told me you were going to snatch it as soon as they landed," the governor barked.

"You told me they were landing in Washington, D.C.; not Manassas, Virginia. Regardless, I will have it soon enough."

"Manassas…where the hell are you?"

"They're inside a Masonic memorial. I have eyes on their vehicle."

"I don't pay you to watch vehicles. Why aren't you in there getting that journal?" Barclay demanded.

"This isn't a shopping mall crowded with people. I can't just walk into a building like that unnoticed."

"So what's your plan?" The Governor's voice reached a crescendo of anger and impatience.

"I will have it shortly; either from their vehicle during dinner, or from their hotel tonight."

"Just try not to leave a bloodbath in your wake and call me the moment you get that journal. I've got a meeting to get to."

Reaper closed the phone and shook his head. Barclay was coming unhinged. Men like that had an enormous capacity for poor judgment. He dialed another number into his phone and waited three rings for the party to answer.

***

Art leaned back in his chair and let out a deep sigh. "*You* designed it?"

Herb nodded and folded his hands over the pages of his scripted work.

"Of course…Seaton attended your lecture at the Facility. I completely forgot," Art said.

"Seaton called me a few weeks ago for some help in designing it."

"Did he say what he wanted it for?" Art asked.

"No," Herb said. "And I didn't ask."

"Did he say what he was researching?" Art pressed.

"Why aren't you asking Seaton these questions."

"I can't, Herb," Art said. "I…"

"Arthur, I'm sorry you wasted a trip but I gave an oath of secrecy to Seaton. I cannot speak to you further on this. I suggest you contact him if you want more information."

"There's no easy way to say this, Herb. Seaton was found murdered yesterday morning at his desk."

"Murdered?" Herb gasped.

91

Tom Adair

"I'm afraid so," Art said as he relayed some of the information they had discovered at the crime scene.

Herb slumped in his chair, and set his bifocals down on the table. "And you think he was killed because of what's in this journal?"

"That's our working theory, yes," Art said.

"*Jesus*, Art," Herb said leaving his mouth agape.

"Can you translate the code for us?" Daniel said. "It could help lead us to the killer."

Glancing at Daniel then back at Art, Herb said, "It's based on a book code. You see, the letters in the journal are what we call cipher text. You need a key to unravel the true meaning of the message. I designed this code to be used with a book as the source of that key."

"What book?" Art asked.

"That's just it. In theory you could use almost any book. I left that up to Seaton."

"So it would have to be a book Seaton had access to on a regular basis, and seeing as how he was a librarian that could be any book in the library. This will be like looking for a needle in a stack of needles," Daniel said.

"Is there any way to narrow down the possibilities of which type of book the code would origin from based on what you see here?" Art asked.

"I'm afraid not."

"But you said almost any book could be used," Daniel said.

"Yes…ideally it would be large volume, but not like a dictionary. More of a story or treatise," Herb said.

"*Treatise*…how long of a treatise?" Art asked flipping through his note pad.

"Oh, I dunno…seven…eight hundred pages to be on the safe side," Herb said.

"What are you thinking, Art?" Daniel asked.

"Do you remember the books on Seaton's desk in the library?"

Art thought back to the crime scene and mentally filed through the images in his memory before his eyes lit up. Scanning the bookshelves behind Herb, he saw the familiar symbol of the two-headed eagle. Art rose, walked to the case,

92

and pulled the heavy volume out with a finger. The heavy book landed like a brick on the table in front of the retired NSA agent.

"Morals and Dogma," Herb said.

"This was on Seaton's desk. I remember seeing it there." Art stepped back around the desk.

"How long would it take you to decode the journal entries using this volume, Herb?" Art asked.

Herb tapped the nineteenth century book as he scanned the pages of the journal. "Assuming this is the source of the key…two, maybe three days."

"That's the earliest?" Art said. Art leaned back in his chair, stared at the ceiling as he scratched his head, then exhaled deeply.

Herb shrugged his shoulders. "I didn't design it to be easy to crack, Art."

"You said Seaton only contacted you a few weeks ago about the code, correct?" Daniel said.

Herb nodded in assent.

"What are you thinking?" Art said.

"If Seaton only started using the code a few weeks ago then his original work could be uncoded. Maybe it's still in his office," Daniel said.

"If Seaton went to the trouble to design a code, my guess is that he destroyed the earlier notes," Art said.

"Seaton didn't share a lot of information with me about his research. Mostly, he wanted to talk about a code. He had done some preliminary research that was troubling him and he decided to encrypt his findings," Herb said. "But there was one thing he did ask about."

"What's that?" Art asked, leaning forward in his chair.

"He asked about a woman named Prudence Corbin. Her husband William was an infantryman in the Continental Army and member of a traveling lodge Washington attended. Apparently, William died in battle but his wife stayed on under Washington to cook and sew for his officers. I dug into her story and found a colleague that had a letter she had written in seventeen-eighty regarding an encounter with General Washington."

"What did the letter say?" Daniel said.

"I don't know. I gave the contact information to Seaton. A few days later he called back to ask about the Badge of Merit and who it was awarded to. I read him the official names and dates. He sounded very excited. He even had me double check the information which, of course I did."

"Did he say why he was so interested in that particular award?" Art asked.

"No, and when I pressed him for more information he swore me to secrecy." Herb said.

Art rested his chin upon folded hands as he tried to figure out his next move.

"Where is this letter?" Daniel said.

"It's at a small private museum in Middletown, Pennsylvania."

"Could you arrange a viewing of this letter with your friend?" Art asked.

"That shouldn't be a problem. Let me dig out the address for you. I'll also make copies of the journal pages; be right back."

"Art, what the *hell* did your friend get himself into?" Daniel asked.

"Better question…what are *we* getting ourselves into? Seaton must have uncovered a snake pit."

Daniel shook his head as he thumbed the cover of *Morals & Dogma*. "What does a letter written by some woman in 1780 have to do with a team of professional killers and the assassination of Governor Hoines?"

"I have no idea, Daniel, but it appears our next clue awaits us in Middletown."

Daniel glanced down at his watch. "There's no way we're going to get there before they close for the day."

"No, probably not. Based on the number of journal entries, I don't think Middletown will be our last stop. It's going to take Herb a few days to decode the entries and I need some time to wrap my head around this. Let's get some dinner and hash this out. We can fly out in the morning."

"Sounds like a plan."

***

Bloodlines

Reaper checked the building again with his binoculars and not seeing the Von Hollens, he decided to call his inside man at the Governor's office. The phone rang twice before it a familiar voice answered. "Hammond here."

"Something has your boss rattled, what is it?" said the voice on the other end of the line.

"I don't know for sure. He's been on edge since last night."

Reaper shifted the phone to his other ear. "What happened last night?"

Hammond hesitated for a moment while he chose his words carefully.

"He was at the farmhouse. I saw something there that concerned me, but I'm not sure how to handle it."

"What farmhouse? What are you talking about?" Reaper asked.

"You know, the blonde...the...brothel. I thought you knew about this," Hammond said.

"Tell me what you saw from the beginning."

Reaper was stunned as he listened to Barclay's chief of security recount the events of the night.

As the story unfolded he remembered a report a few weeks earlier from his team. Every week Barclay would drive long circuitous routes through the city for hours and place calls to various offices. The Gerovit analysts were unable to make sense of the vehicle routes and surmised Barclay was doing private business dealings in his car.

Reaper clenched his teeth as he realized how easily he had been fooled. Then he caught something Hammond said.

"What did you just say?"

"Barclay, he started talking about some journal he needed."

"And you say this was on a video surveillance system in the house?"

"Yeah, the whole place is wired."

"And you didn't think it necessary to call me?" Reaper said.

"In case you forgot, I don't have your number. The rules are you call me."

Reaper now questioned the wisdom of that decision but pushed the issue out of his mind. "Did he say anything else?"

"Just the guy's name. It was a strange name, ah, Adidas or something..."

"Adiago."

"Yeah, that was it," Hammond said snapping his fingers.

"What did the woman say?"

"Ah, nothing. She told him to forget about it and got him back to business if you know what I mean."

Forget about it? Hardly.... If his name had been Joe Blow maybe, but Seaton Adiago? *This was not good.* His mind raced through various solutions to the problem at hand.

"I need you to go back out to that farmhouse and take care of this," Reaper said.

"Their security is pretty tight. I'm not sure how we're going to bluff our way in and take the tapes without being discovered."

"I'm not telling you to bluff your way in. I'm telling you to take them out. Grab all the tapes and intel you can, then burn the place to the ground."

Hammond was silent. He couldn't believe what he was hearing.

"Look...you pay me for surveillance, not wet work."

"Consider this a promotion then."

Hammond glanced down the hallway, then turned to face the wall. In a hushed tone, he said, "This isn't what I signed on for. Why can't *you* handle this?"

"Because I'm *here* and you're *there*. Besides, we're too exposed in Colorado."

"I...I don't know," Hammond said.

"I know about your previous work in Chicago, Wesley. This should be a walk in the park," Reaper lied.

"That was a long time ago."

"Regardless, either you take care of this problem or you *become* the problem. Do you understand me?"

Hammond clenched his fist and punched at the wall stopping a half inch short of touching it. He took several deep breaths and regained his composure.

"Wesley?"

"I understand."

"I want it wrapped up tonight."

"Tonight? Look, I'm going to need..."

"Tonight!" Reaper hissed before ending the call.

Reaper glanced around the neighborhood and made a mental checklist for his team members to follow up on. Catching sight of movement near the memorial entrance, he lifted his compact binoculars. He recognized the men immediately.

Subconsciously he fingered the bullet scar on his left hip and recalled the events in a Denver hotel almost a year earlier. It was the last time he had laid eyes on the younger man coming down the stairs and he regretted not killing him that night. He dropped his gaze and saw what he was looking for. There in his right hand was a leather bound book.

That has to be the journal. Reaper watched as the older man took the book and tucked it into a shoulder bag before climbing into the passenger side of the vehicle.

The younger man popped the hood and spent several minutes in the engine compartment before Reaper's phone vibrated. It was his surveillance analyst.

"*Da,*" Reaper said in his native Russian.

"The On Star GPS just went off line. I think it has been disconnected."

Reaper watched as the man threw a small component onto the pavement, stepped on it, and closed the hood. Within seconds, he started the engine and began to pull away.

Reaper silently cursed his bad fortune as he pulled out after the vehicle and raced to catch up.

14

Art buckled his seat belt and braced an arm against the door as Daniel sped out of the parking lot.

"Doesn't handle much like your Camaro does it?" Art said.

Daniel smirked as he checked his mirrors and maneuvered out onto King Street. "Sorry, I just want to make sure we aren't being followed."

"Is that what you were doing under the hood?"

"The vehicle's GPS can be activated even if the unit is turned off. It's better to just yank out the transponder."

"I suppose I'll be paying for that," Art said.

"Cheaper than a funeral."

"You really think someone is watching us?"

"Yesterday they tried to kill you, Uncle Art. I'd say it's a certainty."

"Well, what do you say we put some distance between us and them," Art said as he punched his pilot's number into his cell phone. Dave answered on the second ring.

"Dave, I need you to get the plane fueled and a flight plan filed to Middletown, Pennsylvania. I also need you to book us some hotel rooms near the airport."

"I'm already refueled. I'll head over now to the tower and file the plan. I'll ask some of the pilots around here for a recommendation on hotels. When do you want to depart?"

"We're going to grab some dinner before heading back. Let's plan on departing no later than ten tonight," Art said.

"I'll be waiting." Dave said.

"Thanks." Art clicked the phone shut.

Daniel made a number of turns and U-turns watching for a tail but never spotted one. He turned north onto Pitt street and headed into Old Town Alexandria.

"Do you actually know where you're going?" Art asked.

"Just making sure we don't have a tail."

"You learn that in the Army, too?"

"Among other things…it's a bit easier to spot a tail in the Hindu Kush." Daniel said with a smirk.

Daniel found a parking spot on Pitt street under the large sweeping branches of an ash tree. The block was a mix of new and historic brick buildings and red brick sidewalks.

"I had Tilly research wild game restaurants in the area and she said Boone's Bar & Grille has the best reviews." Daniel said.

"I would think you'd go for seafood in Virginia," Art said.

"I guess you've spoiled me with elk."

***

Reaper followed a parallel route one block over and circled the area twice after locating their vehicle. He found a parking spot one block north of Pitt Street, grabbed a drink from a cafe, and positioned himself on a set of stairs giving himself an unobstructed view of the Von Hollen car. Five minutes later his phone vibrated; it was his intelligence analyst, Pavel.

"They filed a flight plan to Middletown, Pennsylvania," Pavel said.

"When do they leave?" Reaper asked.

"Twenty-two hundred hours."

"Tonight?"

"*Da.*"

"Middletown, how far is that by car?"

"Four hours from your position."

Reaper checked the time and cursed under his breath. By his calculations, the targets would be on the ground at least an hour ahead of him. With the vehicle GPS disabled, he'd have no way to track them.

"Do we have assets in place to meet them?"

"Not yet."

Reaper's mind raced through several options but none provided him the tactical advantage he was looking for. Tailing the vehicle was his only option, and it wasn't a good one at that. Tailing the car through a busy downtown district was one thing, but following it on an open highway was something entirely different. He wouldn't have the option of parallel routes, or buildings to dart behind if traffic was light.

And, he reminded himself, he wasn't tailing an amateur. He had to adjust the odds in his favor.

"Do a search of Masonic lodges or museums in Middletown, and get back to me in thirty minutes." Reaper ordered. He ended the call and dialed Barclay's number.

"We have a problem," Reaper said.

"Do you have the journal yet?"

"Not yet."

"May I ask just *what in the hell you are waiting for?*" Barclay's voice rose.

"This isn't some 'has been' I'm dealing with here. He's a former tier one operator."

"And just what the *hell* are you?" Barclay said.

Reaper wanted to reach through the phone and tear out his throat. He'd handled politicians before; and sometimes killed them. He wondered if that day would soon come with Barclay.

Ignoring Barclay's question, he said, "They are preparing to fly out of state in a few hours. I need you to stop that flight."

"How do you propose I do that?" Barclay said.

"Reach out to your sources in Homeland Security and have them ground the flight."

"By saying what?"

"Tell them it's a safety inspection. Tell them there's a terror threat. Whatever it takes, but stop that flight. If they have to stay in town tonight I can hit them at their hotel."

"Fine, but I want this finished tonight. Do you understand me?" Barclay said.

"Understood." Reaper shut the phone and shoved it into his pocket. Taking one last look down the street, he made his way over to the target vehicle.

***

The street was dark by the time Art and Daniel left the restaurant. Art held out his hand as they crossed Pitt Street to the car.

"Why don't you let me drive a bit?" he said.

"Why not?" Daniel said, as he fished the keys from his pocket and tossed them to Art.

They were ten feet behind the car when Daniel spotted a major problem. He scanned the street as casually as he dared and checked the reflection in the window of the car behind theirs. Nothing. He shifted to Art's left and clenched Art's arm above the elbow like a vice.

"Let's get some coffee, Art," he said directing Art away from the car and back across the street.

"What is it, Daniel?"

"We're burned. Act naturally and follow my lead," he whispered.

Daniel led Art into the coffee shop and scanned the patrons without detecting a threat. He spotted the exit sign above the hallway leading to the bathrooms.

"This way," he said.

Art waited until they exited the rear of the building before speaking.

"Daniel, what is going on?"

Daniel didn't slow their pace as he turned right and ducked along a narrow, brick path between two buildings.

"The tail light."

"What about the tail light?"

"It had a hole punch in it."

"Daniel, I don't understand what you're saying. Will you stop for a second?"

Daniel stopped and looked behind them for the killer he knew would be coming.

"We don't have much time, Art. Right now they're watching the front of that coffee shop but in five minutes when we don't come out they'll be going in. We need to get moving."

"Wait...how do you know someone is following us?"

"The tail light had a small hole punched in the lens. It's an old low-tech trick for tailing a vehicle at night. The red-colored lens will have a bright white spot in it. You can see it clearly from quite a ways back."

"And you're sure the damage is new?"

"I specifically checked the tail lights when we picked up the car. Call it an old habit. Now we have to keep moving."

"Where are we going?"

"We need to find another ride. If we can get to a large hotel, we can slip on a shuttle to the airport."

"I have money for a cab," Art said.

"Too risky...cabbies call in their fares. They might be monitoring the channel," Daniel said.

Daniel kept a brisk walking pace as they rounded the corner onto St. Asaph street.

Art felt his phone vibrate and pulled it from its holster. He read the name of his pilot on the caller ID readout.

"Now is not the best time, Dave," Art said as he scanned the street and tried to keep pace with Daniel.

"We got a problem, Art." Dave said.

"Just one?"

"Homeland Security called the tower and grounded the plane. They said it had something to do with an anonymous call about a terrorist cell, if you can believe that. I told them who we were, but they said procedure was to have an FBI agent come out and interview us. He's supposedly on the way now. What do you want me to do?"

Art stopped dead in his tracks as he tried to digest the information. Daniel immediately stopped and faced Art. He watched Daniel as he scanned the street.

"Be cooperative, Dave, but buy us some time. Make them get a warrant to search the plane."

"Art, what the *hell* is going on?"

"I wish I knew. Suffice it to say, we won't be coming back there. When they clear you to leave, head back to Steamboat Springs and tell Tilly I'll contact her soon."

"Roger that, Art."

Art hung up and filled Daniel in on the problems with the plane as they continued to walk.

"Shit, this ratchets things up to a whole new level," Daniel said.

"I can't see how the FBI will buy the terrorist cell thing given who we are. We can still rent a car at the airport and drive to Middletown," Art said.

"And what do you think will happen when they search the rental car back there and find my gear bags stuffed with two assault rifles and tactical gear? Once Gerovit figures out we're not coming back to it, they'll drop a dime to the bureau and connect the car to the plane. We have to assume that shortly we'll be on every terror watch list for mass transit."

Art's eyes grew wide as he realized the implications.

"We're in new territory now Art, are you up for this?"

Art bit his lower lip as he remembered the sniper that tried to kill him and the images of his friend killed at his desk.

"Yes," he said with a stern nod. He took a half step then paused. "What about Herb? Do we need to warn him?"

Daniel thought about that for a moment.

"I don't think so. These guys don't want to draw attention to the real reason of our expedition. My guess is they just want to pin us down while they make a play for the journal."

The news made sense and was a relief to Art. The last thing he wanted was another friend to die.

"So what now?" Art asked.

15

The challenge for Hammond was leaving the Governor's security detail without alarming him. His opportunity came when he remembered the fundraising dinner planned for that evening. The rich and elite would be dropping twenty thousand dollars a plate for a few minutes of face time with the future President of the United States. The timing couldn't be better.

Barclay would be miles away from the farmhouse surrounded by some of the richest, most well respected elites of the state in one of the most secured residences along the Front Range. Barclay would be so busy pressing palms and kissing cheeks, he'd never notice Hammond's absence.

Once Barclay was into his third glass of wine, Hammond left instructions with his second in command and slipped out the side entrance next to the kitchen. If all went according to plan he'd be back before they served dessert.

Jogging down the walkway, he met the dark SUV waiting for him in the alleyway. Within ten minutes they were speeding east on Interstate 70 towards the farmhouse.

Hammond had his driver kill the lights and slow their pace to a crawl as they traveled the last quarter mile on the dirt road. Once at the security gate Hammond entered the Governor's code and the large iron gate swung open with a moan. Hammond was sure they could get to the security room before the lone bodyguard grew suspicious. After all, Barclay was the most coveted client of the brothel.

The driver parked next to an outbuilding and the two men racked a shell into their shotguns and slipped on their ski masks before exiting the vehicle.

"Keep your gun hidden until you reach the objective," Hammond reminded his cohort.

They entered the farmhouse with military precision. The driver turned left down the hallway towards the surveillance room as Hammond bounded up the stairway. At the top of the stairs, Hammond heard the distinctive ka-boom of a twelve gauge shotgun on the main floor followed by three shots from what sounded like a pistol. The driver had engaged the bodyguard and Hammond had to act fast. The door to the bedroom was just beginning to open as he booted it with all his strength.

Elizabeth screamed as Hammond thrust the barrel of his shotgun into the face of the man on the floor. Even through the blood streaming from his nose, Hammond recognized the first round draft pick and ordered him to leave.

"If you want to live, get your ass outta here and don't say a damned word. You call the cops and we'll come for you."

The man clasped his hand over his nose and stammered from the room before tumbling down the stairs. Hammond struck Elizabeth on the side of the head with the butt of his shotgun as he heard the roar of the sports car outside. The blow was just enough to get her attention but not enough to cause serious injury.

"Shut up! Where's the fucking surveillance tapes?"

"I...I have money...I can get you money!" she wailed.

"I don't want your money, I want information. Are all the tapes in the room downstairs?"

Tears streamed into her open mouth that she huffed close to hyperventilation. She nodded while avoiding his gaze.

"No backups?"

Elizabeth shook her head violently from side to side.

"Bullshit!" He said slapping her cheek with an open hand. The blow caused a new wave of uncontrollable sobbing.

"Where do you keep the backups?"

"They're...they're on the computer."

Hammond racked another shell into the shotgun and thrust the muzzle onto her bare chest.

"You better not be lying to me!" he snarled.

"I'm not lying!" she screamed.

"Get up. Let's go see," he said as he grabbed her by the arm and yanked her from the bed. Hammond slammed her face first against the bedroom wall and pressed his body against her naked back. The smell of expensive French perfume was intoxicating. He snaked his lips through her tangled hair until they were resting on her right earlobe.

"All I want are the backups, Elizabeth. You cooperate and you'll be okay. You screw with me in any way and I'll make sure you die the most painful death you can imagine. You got that?"

Whimpering, she managed a slight quiver of her head in affirmation.

"Good girl," he said as he ordered her to place her hands behind her back and slid a pair of flex cuffs over her wrists. He cinched them tight.

Hammond led her down the stairs with one hand clenching her tangled blonde hair.

"Coming down, Johnny," he called out to his driver. There was no response. Hammond's adrenalin surged when he reached the bottom of the stairs, turned the corner, and saw the body of his driver lying supine on the floor just outside the surveillance room door.

"Oh my God," Elizabeth muttered.

Hammond immediately lowered his profile using his captive as a human shield.

"Johnny!" he hissed. The man's body lay motionless with a large pool of blood forming around his neck and head. Inching towards the open door, Hammond rested the shotgun over Elizabeth's shoulder. He pushed her head into the room.

"Tell me what you see!"

"He's down...he's bleeding."

Hammond shifted his position slightly and took in the room one small visible sliver at a time until he saw the enforcer on the floor. He was laying on his right side, his back to the door, and breathing in shallow, labored breaths. Hammond noticed a large pool of blood on the floor around the man's neck. He challenged the man with several stern commands but he just laid there unresponsive.

Hammond spun his captive and slammed her face first into the wall just inside the door way.

"Don't move a fucking inch!"

He leveled his shotgun at the man's head as he inched closer. Hammond could feel time stop as every movement and sensation seemed amplified. *The most dangerous animal is the wounded one,* he reminded himself. Once he was within a foot of the dying man's body, he rocked his buttocks with his foot.

That's when it happened. The man rolled onto his back and Hammond glimpsed the black 9mm handgun as the muzzle swung towards his head. Uninjured, the enforcer might have been fast enough but with all the blood loss, he was moving at half his normal speed.

Hammond dove to the floor a split second before the bullet spat from the gun and sailed over his left shoulder. Landing in a heap, he thrust the shotgun muzzle against the man's left temple and jerked the trigger. Splinters of bone, blood, and brain matter showered the console and monitors a few feet away as Elizabeth let out a wild scream and ran from the room.

By some miracle, the woman made it out onto the driveway before her feet rose above her as Hammond yanked her hair sharply back. The wind was knocked out of her as she smacked the gravel with a thud. She tried desperately to gain footing as Hammond dragged her by her hair back up the stairs and into the foyer. Once inside, he released his grip and her head dropped to the wooden floor like a bowling ball.

"Enough of this horseshit!" he spat. "Get up and show me where the video is stored."

She curled into a fetal position and received a swift kick to her kidneys. "Get up!"

He nearly dislocated her shoulder as he pulled her arm and brought her to her knees. Placing one foot on the floor, it took all his strength as he pushed her back towards the bedroom.

"Where!" he demanded.

She nodded at the computer tower standing sentinel next to the bank of monitors. Hammond pushed her to the floor on top of her blood-soaked enforcer and without her hands free to break her fall, she face-planted into the remnants of his skull cavity.

Hammond yanked the cables from the tower and set it by the door. Crouching next to her, he grabbed a fist full of hair and curled her head to face him.

"Where is the back-up drive?"

Elizabeth gagged on the mineralized chunks of brain matter as she tried to clear her throat.

"There…on the shelf…the dictionary."

As Hammond yanked the thick book off the shelf, a palm-sized computer drive tumbled from the hollowed out compartment of the pages. Across the top was a label for the current month. He was sure she had other drives for other months stashed away somewhere, but he had what he'd been sent to retrieve. He tucked the drive into his coat pocket and turned back to his captive.

"Please…you have what you want…I won't talk..." she said as her lips quivered. Elizabeth was still shaking her head when he leveled the muzzle at her beautiful face and pulled the trigger.

16

Sarah sat transfixed by the poorly acted cop drama rerun playing out on her television. She'd seen the episode before and didn't like it then either. However, she lacked the enthusiasm to extricate herself from the couch to go to bed.

She couldn't sleep anyway. Sarah never slept well when she was on call. She knew the minute she'd enter a deep peaceful sleep her phone would ring and jolt her out of bed.

She glanced over at Ranger who was laying on the floor facing her, motionless, and staring. He was a good dog but his staring was kind of creepy. It was as if he were awaiting a command to pounce. Every muscle in his body looked ready to spring into action. Like Daniel, he was now a warrior without a war. *At least he wasn't wearing those dog goggles.* She reminded herself to bring it up the next time she spoke to Daniel.

After reviewing her options of another forty-five minutes of bad television and dog staring, she powered off the T.V. and decided to head to bed. She made it halfway down the hall before her cell chirped. *Of course.* The caller ID said Lopez.

"Hey Manny, what's up?"

"Did I wake you?"

"Would you hang up if I said yes?"

"Funny, Sarah. We got a homicide…multiple homicides actually."

Sarah felt a small surge of adrenalin as she made her way to the kitchen counter to grab a pen.

"What do you got?"

"Two bodies out east of Bennett in a small farmhouse. Looks like the killer tried to torch the place but I'm told the fire wasn't extensive. I've got Andy en route as well," he said.

Andy Vaughn was her closest friend and mentor in the crime lab and one of the best bloodstain pattern analysts she'd ever met. She liked to think of him as the older brother she never had. Homicides were best worked in teams, and she couldn't have hoped for a better partner. Sarah jotted down the time of the call, address, and a few directions.

"I may have to call you back when I get closer to guide me in," she said.

"Just look for the flashing lights. It looks like Tesla's laboratory," Manny said.

"Look at you…throwing out the lab geek references, nicely done."

"I'm not just another pretty face, Sarah."

Manny was right.

An hour and a half later she turned down the dirt road towards the artificial Aurora Borealis. She passed over a cattle guard and the remnants of an iron gate that probably once blocked the driveway was now littered with emergency vehicles. The deputy outside the gate tipped his hat upon recognizing her. Her heart skipped a beat as she noticed the dozens of first responder tire tracks blanketing the road. She found an open spot next to Andy's SUV and grabbed her camera.

Sarah stepped over several fire hoses as she made her way up onto the porch. She checked in with the deputy standing guard and found Andy just inside the foyer.

"Hey Sarah, I'm surprised I beat you out here?"

"Why is that?"

"You've been so wound up for a homicide lately; I figured you'd race out here at a hundred miles per hour!"

"I'm *sure*," she said punching him in the arm. "I don't *want* people to die, but how else am I supposed to learn?"

"What are you talking about? I bought you the complete first season of CSI on DVD for Christmas," he joked.

"Yeah, thanks for that," Sarah said.

"How long have you been here?" she asked.

He glanced at his watch, "About twenty minutes."

"So what do we have?" As she asked the question, she glanced around at the damage. The floors were wet, but the black mark trailing down the hall was unmistakable.

"Well, we got a pour pattern along the floor here from some kind of accelerant; probably gasoline," he said pointing along the trail. "It goes from the room back there where the bodies are to the front door."

"So why didn't the house go up in flames?" she asked.

Andy pointed up to the small spigot on the ceiling.

"Sprinkler system. It activates when the sensor detects heat from a flame."

"An old farm house with a fire suppression system?" Sarah said. "Seems kind of odd."

"Yeah, well…this ain't your ordinary farm house. Follow me down here," Andy said as he motioned down the hallway. Out of habit, Sarah traveled along the wall so as not to disturb shoe impressions; though the water would have certainly destroyed them.

Sarah's eyes were drawn to the two charred bodies stacked on top of each other like cord wood. Andy crouched next to the bodies and pointed with his pen. They smelled like burned pork and Sarah made a mental note to avoid bacon for the next few days.

"One male and one female; the female's on top. Obviously we won't move the bodies until the coroner gets here, but it looks like she caught a shotgun blast point blank to the face. The guy underneath looks to have taken one to the face, too."

"Sweet Jesus," Sarah muttered.

"Yeah. Based on the spatter on those monitors there I'm guessing the guy was on the floor when he was shot."

Sarah hadn't even noticed the bank of monitors against the wall when she walked in. She looked around the room at the soot covered electronic equipment, headphones, and dangling cables.

"What the heck was this room used for?"

"Surveillance. I'm not surprised you didn't see the cameras; they're pretty small." Andy said pointing up towards the corner of the ceiling.

"Drugs?" Sarah asked.

"Not sure yet. I've only looked around the main floor. Manny and Vegas are upstairs."

"Are these the owners?"

"That's the assumption right now."

"Do we have an ID?" she asked.

"Manny is looking into it."

Sarah studied the bodies and looked up at the soot covered blood spatter on the monitors.

"So were they both shot on the floor?"

Andy rubbed his chin with the back of his latex covered hand before answering.

"This is where it gets interesting. You see that spatter pattern up there on the wall near the door?"

Sarah stood and examined the bloodstain from a few inches away. "It looks like there's brain matter mixed in there."

"Right, so to me it looks more consistent with the woman's injury. Also, her hands are bound with flexible handcuffs, but the man's aren't."

"So was he killed first?"

"Maybe, but there's more," Andy stood and walked out into the hallway. He bent down and took a knee. "If you get down here, you can see a skeleton pattern of blood pooling on the floor."

Sarah remembered that blood dried from the edges in and as time passed the outer ring of a blood pool would dry while the center stayed liquid.

"Whose blood…did he get hit out here first?"

"I haven't seen another wound but we have to move her first to be sure. What I have found are three nine millimeter casings back in the room there. I also found two twelve gauge shotgun shells." He said pointing back through the doorway. Andy turned back to the diluted blood pool on the floor. "Now this pool looks pretty large to me and I don't see any drag marks from here back into the room."

Sarah turned on her Surefire flashlight and held it at a low angle to the floor over the blood pool.

"What are these lines here?"

Andy smiled. "You're getting much better at this, Sarah. All right, to me these look like folds of fabric," he said.

"Like clothing?"

"Some could be, but others are pretty large so I'm guessing maybe a tarp or even a comforter maybe. You see," he said pointing down the hallway towards the foyer, "there are no drag marks or blood drops along the floor or outside. That tells me a body may have been wrapped up and carried out."

Sarah nodded as she tried to imagine the activities.

"What do you want me to do?" Sarah asked.

"You're the primary. You give the orders on this one," Andy said.

Sarah frowned as she contemplated the situation.

Bloodlines

"Don't worry…I'm not going to let you do anything crazy, but you need to learn to take lead on a major case. This is no different than any other crime scene if you take away the bodies…the arson…the ballistics…"

"Okay, okay, I get it." Sarah said letting loose a smile.

"You seem to have a good start down here. I'll head upstairs and we can regroup in a half hour."

"Sounds good."

Sarah found several blood droplets and swipes along the wall and railing leading upstairs and photographed them as she moved towards the voices. "Manny?" she called out.

"Back here, Sarah."

Macabre traces of blood along the upstairs floor and walls guided her back to the bedroom. She poked her head past the doorway and took in a disturbing sight.

Detective Sal Vargas had an array of sex toys and devices sprawled out across the white silk bed sheets.

"Richards, good! You need to get a photo of this stuff." He was holding what looked to be a padded harness.

"Aw c'mon, Vegas! Tell me you guys took pictures of the room before you started dragging all the crap out?"

He held up a point and shoot digital camera and waved it back and forth. "Jeeze Richards, is it your time of the month or what?"

Sarah mentally ran through the steps necessary to kick him in the groin and felt much better.

"That's right, Vegas. Piss me off anymore and I'll swab your desk and throw it in a rape kit," she said with a devilish grin.

The comment was enough to shut him up for now as he moved away from the bed so she could take pictures.

Manny chuckled, "That'll teach you, Sal. You want us out of the room while you take pictures, Sarah?"

"Nah, you have overall pics. If I need you to move I'll let you know."

"Did you see the blood on the floor?" Vargas said in a conciliatory tone.

"I followed the trail up the stairs. Looks like the first blow started in this room, huh?" Sarah crouched down to photograph the small blood stains grouped on the floor halfway to the bed.

"There's a live twelve gauge shell on the floor by the foot of the bed there," Manny said pointing.

"An unfired shell?" she asked.

"Nothing grabs your attention like racking a pump shotgun," Vargas said.

Sarah thought back to her conversation with Andy about the woman.

"Andy said her hands were bound. So maybe he racked a round to intimidate her."

"There's also a boot print on the door," Manny said pointing.

Damn, Sarah cursed herself for walking right past that clue but pushed the self criticism from her mind. *I would have found it eventually.*

Sarah held her flashlight at a low angle to the boot print and examined the door and frame.

"The door jamb isn't damaged so the door must have been partly open," she said.

"Did you bring the static cling machine?" Vargas asked.

"It's called an electro-static dust print lifter, and yes, it's in my truck."

Twenty minutes later, Sarah had taken nearly a hundred photographs of the room and its contents. She set the electro-static dust print lifter, or ESDL, device on the floor next to the door and affixed a thin sheet of metal-coated film over the boot print. She then affixed an index card sized metal plate a few inches away from the film and bridged the gap with the hand-held device. When she activated the unit, the film was drawn against the door. After powering down the device, she pulled the film from the door and checked to make sure she got a good boot print with her flashlight before sealing it in a protective folder.

"Hey Sarah, you ready to compare notes?" It was Andy.

"Sure. Well...it looks to me like it may have started up here and ended downstairs," she said. "I got a right boot print off the door here and a little bit of blood in the room. It looks like the blood trail goes from here downstairs."

"Yeah, I saw those coming up." Andy said.

"There is also a live shotgun shell so maybe the killer racked a round to force the victim's compliance?" she offered.

"Holy moley!" Andy said as he saw the sex toys arranged on the bed. "Do you think she was a pro, or just kinky?"

"Ya know, Andy…the more I do this job the harder that question becomes," she said.

"I hear ya; being a CSI is kind of like being an archaeologist sent to work in Hell. Anyway, I'm thinking she's a pro."

"Why do you say that?" Sarah asked.

"It's that video room. If she was just some kinky housewife I could see her having a camera in her bedroom…*maybe*. But a whole house of cameras, even outside? No, that seems like a pro to me. Another thing, there's cords for a computer but no computer drive. I also found a hollowed out book that looks big enough to hold one of those palm sized back up drives," he said.

"Maybe it held something else like cash or jewelry," Sarah said.

"Maybe, but why keep it in there? Plus, she has a pretty good rock on her right hand that wasn't taken. Oh, I looked at the sprinkler connections to the water line and they're those new colored flex hoses which means they had to have been installed in the last few years."

Sarah took in the information as she tried to make sense of the pieces of evidence.

"Are you thinking blackmail?"

"It's a place to start. The only thing I see missing for sure is the computer which presumably held the surveillance footage."

"Maybe they were here for something else and just took the footage to cover their tracks," Sarah reasoned.

Andy nodded. "At this point, your guess is as good as mine."

"Well, once we figure out who our victims are, we should know more," Sarah said.

She looked over her notes and tapped her finger on the page.

"Hey Manny, how did this call come in?"

"Anonymous 911 call. Sounded like a kid to me. Dispatch said the call came from a house two miles away so I sent Detective Riley over there to do some follow up. He should be back pretty soon," Manny said checking his watch.

"Cool, okay Andy what else do we need to do?" Sarah asked.

"How about I wait for the coroner while you search the out buildings?"

"Sounds good. Let me know when they're ready to move the bodies."

Sarah was just entering the second outbuilding when she saw the Coroner's van pull up in the driveway. So far her search had been a bust. Everything around the house looked like a typical farm. The one Ford pickup was filthy and looked like a clan of raccoons lived in it. She saw another set of headlights coming down the drive and recognized Detective Riley's car when he pulled along side the coroner's van. Sarah trotted over and met Manny as they reached the car together.

Detective Bret Riley hadn't been in the investigations division long, but he was becoming a good investigator. He and Manny had gotten off to a rocky start during the infamous sniper killings the previous year, but the two had made amends.

"Tell me you got something," Manny said as Riley exited the car.

"How about a witness," Riley said.

"No shit; a witness to the killings? Where are they?" Manny said looking into Riley's empty car.

"Well, sort of a witness I guess," Riley said.

"What do you mean *sort of* a witness? What did they see?"

"The caller is a fourteen-year old kid. Apparently, the female resident likes to walk around naked and isn't a big fan of closing her blinds. I guess she figures no one is around. Anyway junior accidentally discovered this neighborly peep show a few months ago and has been sneaking onto the property a couple times a week ever since."

"He saw the murders?" Sarah asked.

"Unfortunately no, he was walking through the field on the south side coming up to the house when he heard the gunshots. It freaked him out a bit so he kept his distance. He snuck a little closer after everything got quiet, and did see a man dragging something large to a dark SUV in the driveway. The vehicle then hauled ass up the road with its lights off."

"So, basically he didn't see shit," Manny said.

"Yep, typical teenager." Riley said.

"Could the suspect have been dragging a body?" Sarah asked.

"Kid said it was as big as the suspect, but it didn't have any form. He called it a…" Riley flipped the page of his notebook, "…big blob."

"You think the killer took a body from the scene?" Manny said.

"Andy sure thinks so. There's a blood pool in the hallway downstairs that doesn't link to any other trail in the house."

"Another victim?" Riley asked.

"Or maybe another suspect," Manny said.

"We'll know for sure when we get the DNA back," Sarah said.

"All right, well…let's table that for the time being. Where are we at, Sarah?" Manny asked as he opened his notebook.

"I'm just about done out here. Everything looks like what you'd expect to find at a farm house. I've been searching the out buildings but nothing but old tractors, fencing, and junk. The place could use a new coat of paint, too," she said jabbing him in the side. Manny didn't look amused and Sarah took a more serious tone. "I'll keep looking though."

Sarah and Manny turned to go back to the main house.

"Wait…" Riley said.

Sarah and Manny turned in unison to see Riley staring at the roof. She looked in the direction of his stare.

"What?" Sarah said.

"That antenna there…what is that all about?"

Sarah strained her eyes in the darkness for a second before pulling out her flashlight and shining it towards the peak of the roof.

"What…that thing?" she said wiggling the light back and forth over it.

"That's an antenna? It looks like a small hat box," Manny said.

"No…that's an antenna," Riley said. "My brother-in-law has something similar on his house."

"What is it used for?" Sarah asked.

"It transmits and receives data I guess," Riley said shrugging his shoulders. "You're the lab geek, don't you know?"

Sarah shot him a withering glare. "I'm not a geek," she corrected him.

"Maybe the couple had satellite internet service. We are in the boonies out here," Manny said.

Sarah's mind was racing as she processed the information from the crime scene. Then it hit her.

"I don't think so...that antenna is on the north side of the house," Sarah said.

"So what?" Riley said.

"She's right," Manny said. "Satellites are in the southern sky. If they wanted a satellite signal it would be pointed the other direction."

"Andy said it looked as if the killer might have took the computer hard drive and surveillance footage...he also found evidence of a possible back-up drive," she said.

"Yeah...what are you getting at?" Manny said.

"Well, a small drive only holds so much data right? I mean, even a terabyte only stores like a thousand hours of video."

"I'm not following," Riley said.

"Look, she's got cameras all over the place. That's a ton of data to store; more than some little portable drive could handle."

"You think there's another computer somewhere?" Manny said.

"It's a hunch," Sarah said biting her lower lip.

"It makes sense," Manny said. "If I had blackmail worth killing for I'd want another back up copy in case the original was stolen or confiscated by the police."

"The question is where," Sarah said.

"Sarah, how far would an antenna like that transmit?"

"What am I...Bill *fucking* Gates? I don't know."

Manny chuckled. "Okay, she'd probably want it close enough to get to but maybe not inside the house," Manny said.

"I checked the house and outbuildings. I didn't find a computer," Sarah said.

"The antenna." Riley said pointing up towards it.

"What about it?" Sarah said.

"If it's not pointing at a satellite it would have to be pointing towards the other computer wouldn't it?"

Of course! Sarah thought. None of the outbuildings were on the north side of the farm house. She must have missed it.

"Fan out and search the area." Manny said.

Bloodlines

The three spread out and began sweeping the property to the north of the farmhouse. Sarah spotted the derelict structure first.

"Over here!" She shouted as she flooded the small shack with her flashlight. It looked like an old outhouse with a caved in roof. Sarah squatted next to the weathered wooden door as Manny and Riley rushed to her side. She heard some kind of small fan running.

"Whatcha' got, kid?" Manny said.

"Do you hear that?"

Manny and Riley stood frozen as they strained to hear anything in the dead silence of the prairie. Sarah heard the unmistakable sound of a mechanical hum.

"Open this thing up," Manny said as he reached for the door. He unhooked the small latch and swung the door open slowly.

A small weatherproof box sat upon a concrete pad. There on top of the box sat a boxy antenna pointed back towards the farmhouse.

"Well what do we have here?" Sarah said.

17

Daniel looked up and down the street as he formulated a new strategy, covertly palmed the butt of his Sig Sauer 1911 in his waistband, and checked his watch. Six minutes. If they hadn't entered the coffee shop by now, they would be any second. They had to keep moving. The question was which way to go? Piece by piece the plan took shape in his mind until a broad smile crossed his face.

Art looked winded after finally climbing aboard a Dashbus on King Street and settling into a seat with Daniel near the back. Daniel checked his watch and made some mental calculations. Unlike Art, he hadn't broken a sweat.

"Do you mind telling me where we are going?" Art asked between labored breaths.

"I spotted an Amtrak station near the Masonic center earlier today," Daniel said.

"I thought you said they'd be looking for us at any terminal?"

"I'm counting on it."

"Daniel, you've lost me again," Art said shaking his head.

"We have to assume he knows we're headed to Middletown but he doesn't know *how* we're getting there. Right now I'll bet he's hacking into the GPS locators on our phones to pinpoint our location. Our only hope is we get to that station before they track our location and get eyes on us."

"So, how is hopping on an Amtrak train going to stop them from finding us?"

"I didn't say we were getting on the train, Uncle Art."

***

Reaper waited five minutes before growing suspicious and passing by the front of the coffee shop. He stole a glance through the large window but didn't see his targets. He waited another few minutes down the block as he leaned against a building and pretended to read a free real estate guide he found in a rack next to a business. He was confident his targets didn't know his face, but he also knew that Daniel Von Hollen would instantly recognize him if he saw him. A warrior could always spot another in a crowd. It was their gift.

Reaper waited for a couple to enter the coffee shop and followed in close behind using their bodies for concealment. He scanned the patron's faces in seconds but didn't see the Von Hollens. He watched the bathroom door for a moment before admitting to himself that they weren't in the coffee shop, and must be on the run.

He dashed out the back door and scanned the area but there was no sign of them. Reaper punched in the number to Pavel who answered on the first ring.

"*Da*."

"I've lost them Pavel. Have you been able to hack their phones?" Reaper said cursing himself for not giving the order days ago.

"It took some time to cross reference incoming and outgoing records from the facility but they're coming on line any minute now."

Reaper made his way back to his observation spot to watch their vehicle. He waited fifteen minutes before Pavel called him back.

"Do you have them?"

"*Da*. They are at the Amtrak station approximately one kilometer west of your location. I am sending the coordinates to your phone."

Reaper watched his screen for the download to be received.

"I've got it. Have you determined where they are going?"

"I have hacked into the passenger manifest but they have not purchased a ticket."

Not yet, Reaper thought. "Keep checking. When is the train departing?"

"You'd better hurry, there is a train departing the station in five minutes!" Pavel said.

Chort! Reaper cursed under his breath as he dashed across the street and was nearly hit by a cab as he threw open the door to his car. The engine roared to life as he smashed the accelerator pedal and raced to the station.

Reaper used his offensive driving skills to maneuver through the slow-moving evening traffic. He had to make several turns to avoid red lights but he made it to the station without a moment to spare. He punched Pavel's number into his phone as he raced down the grassy slope to the train.

"Have you found them?"

"They are on the train but there are no tickets in their names." Pavel said.

Reaper cursed as the train began to move. He had seconds to act and without hesitation he sprinted across the platform and jumped onto the stairway of the closest car.

***

Art and Daniel watched from the shadows as the train departed the station.

"That was pretty dangerous crawling under the train like that, Daniel."

"It seemed safer than the alternative. Thanks for distracting the platform officer for me, Art."

"Do you think it will work?"

"I wedged them in there pretty tight. Best case scenario is that they'll waste an hour discretely searching this train for us. Worst case scenario is that they'll have to split their team and some will continue canvassing the city for us. Let's just keep a lookout for any tails and be ready to move."

Daniel led Art down Callahan and across Duke Street to a large black iron fence. He moved through a small field along the east fence line of the parking lot as he searched for activity. The parking lot was nearly empty, and after several minutes of observation he was convinced the coast was clear. He pointed to a row of aging vehicles bearing the seal of the United States Post Office.

"Dare I ask?" Art said.

"We need a ride," Daniel said.

"Your plan is to steal a postal truck?"

"It's perfect if you think about it. There's only a skeleton crew in here and no one gives a second look to a postal truck. It's the last thing these guys will be looking for."

"Daniel, I'm not comfortable with this. You're talking about stealing a federal vehicle. This is exactly what I have spent a lifetime chasing criminals for. Why don't we just use our cash to buy a car?"

Bloodlines

Daniel lowered his head and exhaled deeply before speaking. "Look Art, I get it okay? The fact of the matter is that we don't have time. We have to keep moving, or we'll get caught. Our only advantage is that the killers don't know our location. The longer we stick around this city, the more likely they'll find us."

Art put a hand to his brow and shook his head.

"Maybe we should just go to the police, Daniel."

"And tell them what? You know they won't take this seriously. They have no jurisdiction over a murder in Colorado. They'll just tell us to call Denver, or worse, hold us for questioning on terrorism charges."

Art bowed his head and said, "Of course you're right. It's just that stealing a car is not something I'm all that comfortable with."

"It's not like we're taking some civilian's ride. No one is going to miss it, Art. They have a dozen of these things sitting around. We can even dump it near a police station so they find it quickly, but it's your call."

Art weighed their options. Committing a crime was a line he said he would never cross, but considering what was at stake... He bit his lip and silently nodded his head.

"I suppose you know how to hot wire one of those?" he asked.

"In point of fact...yes, but I don't think we'll need to. They keep the keys in the ignition."

"Seriously?" Art said.

"Trust me, I did the same thing during my selection process training op," Daniel said.

"Really."

"It's like I said...no one ever steals a postal truck."

18

August 7th; Middletown, Pennsylvania

Art was jolted from his uncomfortable sleep as the truck bounced into a deep pothole. He rubbed his eyes and stretched out his arms. "Where are we?"

"We're here," Daniel said.

Art glanced at his watch and squinted at the sun breaking over the horizon. He noted the rows of Colonial style homes on either side of the street and wondered if any were from General Washington's time.

"Do you know where this museum is?" Art asked.

"It's close, but, we need to ditch our ride first."

"What do you have in mind?"

"I know you're worried about this thing so I came up with a plan while you were napping. Once we ditch it, we're going to need to grab a few supplies and get some breakfast. How much cash do you have?"

Art checked his money belt. "About three thousand," he said nonchalantly. "Herb said she gets to work at about eight so we have a little time to kill," Art said.

Daniel checked his watch as he drove up onto the walkway leading to the public library and stopped in front of the main doors. "You see? By nine the cops will have this thing towed and on its way to the impound lot.

"I'm just glad we didn't get caught," Art said as he took a handkerchief from his pocket and wiped down the interior.

After inhaling a large breakfast at a local café, they stopped at a convenience store and bought three pre-paid cell phones from the clerk. Daniel handed one to Art and tucked the other two into his pocket.

They waited outside the small Colonial style home until an attractive middle-aged woman with short brunette hair and a pair of rosy cheeks came out. She was wearing a blue full length period dress from the eighteenth century, white bonnet, and black laced boots.

Bloodlines

Art stepped from the side of the building as she strolled up the walkway.

"Are you Janice?"

"That I am...you must be Arthur," she said extending her delicate hand.

"I am, and this is my nephew, Daniel," he said. Daniel extended his hand and greeted her with a slight bow of the head. She looked them over from head to foot.

"I must say the girls are going to enjoy seeing two strapping gentlemen grace our presence today. We don't get too many male visitors," she said winking at Art. The wink had the desired effect, and Art blushed.

She led them in passed the ornately decorated parlor and up the stairs to the library. Art noted a plaque on the wall that read *Daughters of the American Revolution*. He sat at a large oak library table with Janice as Daniel took a position by the window overlooking the street.

"Herb tells me you're interested in the Prudence Corbin letter?" Janice asked.

"That's right, do you know much about it?"

"Honestly, I had never even seen it until a few weeks ago when a man from Denver called me to inquire about it."

"Seaton...his name was Seaton," Art said.

"Is it true he was murdered?" she asked in a hushed voice.

"We're still investigating, but the letter may help shed some light on what he was researching. Can you tell me about it?"

Janice walked over to her desk and retrieved a file folder from the top drawer. She opened it and laid the letter on the desk. It was encased in a plastic sheet protector.

"Our records indicate it was donated over sixty years ago by a family member who lived here in Middletown. Prudence was the wife of a revolutionary soldier named William Corbin, an infantryman. After his death she stayed on with General Washington's staff as a seamstress and cook.

The letter is to her sister Elizabeth in New York and dated September twenty seventh, seventeen-eighty. Mostly she talks about her general welfare and activities which are common of letters of that day, but there is one notation of historical curiosity."

"What did she say?" Art asked.

125

Janice turned the letter around so Art could read it and slid it closer to him.

"Prudence makes a brief statement about General Washington cutting away a piece of purple cloth from his jacket and asking her to shape it into a heart with the word 'merit' stitched in it," she said pointing to that portion of the letter.

Art put on his reading glasses and examined the letter more closely. He pulled Seaton's journal from his hand bag and opened it to the page bearing the picture Seaton had drawn of the badge.

"She goes on to say Washington then handed her a thumb sized medallion with an apple and the word 'fidelity' printed on it and told her to attach it to the top of the heart shaped patch."

"Sound familiar?" Art said looking towards Daniel.

Daniel nodded and turned back to the window. Art took a moment and read the two page letter again.

"Prudence mentions an Ensign John Henry DeFrance from Lancaster County, Pennsylvania. Does that mean anything to you?" Art asked, looking at Janice.

"Apparently he is the man the patch was made for but I'm not sure why. I'm afraid we only research women of the American Revolution. I can refer you to my counterpart at the Sons of the American Revolution if you'd like," she said.

"Thank you Janice, but I think I'll ask Herb to look into that." Art said.

"Do you have any other letters from Prudence?" Daniel asked, without looking away from the street below.

"No, just the one. I'm afraid we don't have much correspondence from women during that period of the war; especially from women living among the troops."

Art leaned back in his chair and pinched the bridge of his nose. They had traveled all night and were no closer to understanding the mystery than when they had left the Denver Consistory.

"May I ask what Seaton wanted to know about the letter?" Art asked.

"As best I can remember he just asked me to read it to him. He seemed most interested in Ensign DeFrance. Like you, he asked me if we had any other records on him."

"So he wasn't interested in Prudence?" Daniel asked.

"I can't be sure, but he didn't ask me anything else about her. He didn't even ask if she had written any other letters. Most of our calls are from genealogists and they want to know everything about the letter writer and their family connections. Your friend didn't ask a single question about her husband or her family."

"Would it be possible to get a copy of this letter, Janice?" Art asked.

Janice leaned into Art as if she were afraid of being overheard. "It's all so mysterious. Do you really think this letter has something to do with that murder?"

Art was beginning to wonder himself. Was this letter a clue, or simply a wild goose chase? Remembering the events of the last forty-eight hours, he convinced himself that it had to be important. There was something in this letter that had prompted a team of assassins to kill his friend and try to kill him. Now that same team was chasing them across the country.

No, this is a clue worth killing for, he thought as the letter shook in his hand.

Janice reached out and tugged gently on the letter until Art released his grasp.

"I'm sorry I can't be of more help to you," Janice said.

Art regained his composure and managed a slight smile. "You have been a big help, Janice."

"Well…I'll go make that copy," she said as she glided from the room.

***

Reaper tapped the steering wheel with his thumbs as he turned down another dull suburban street in Middletown. He had wasted over an hour chasing ghosts on the Amtrak train before returning to Alexandria.

Pavel had listened online to police radio traffic in Alexandria but had nothing to report during his search. Now Reaper was following an icy cold trail in pursuit of his targets. He drove the streets looking at every home, business, and vehicle in vain. He wasn't even sure his quarry hadn't already gotten what they came for and moved on. The lack of intelligence was maddening.

Middletown was a small community of less than ten thousand people, but it might as well have been a million. As he drove past a small car dealership his phone rang. It was Pavel.

"Do you have them?"

"Perhaps. I just heard something interesting on the police radio in Middletown. A stolen postal truck has been found on the front steps on the public library. I am sending the coordinates to your phone."

"Why should I care about a postal truck, Pavel?"

Reaper was frustrated that his analyst was grasping at straws.

"It was stolen sometime last night from Alexandria."

Reaper sat up straight and pulled the car to the curb. *A postal truck... How clever*, he thought. This Daniel Von Hollen was turning out to be a tough target.

"Is their plane still locked down?" Reaper asked.

"Hold on, I'll check."

Reaper heard Pavel typing on a keyboard and speaking into another phone.

"No, the FBI searched it and released it this morning. The pilot filed a flight plan to Colorado and is en route."

"Are you sure?"

Reaper heard Pavel typing again. "According to the transponder, it is over Ohio," he said.

"Does Gregor still have eyes on the vehicle?"

"He checked in a few minutes ago. The vehicle is unmoved and no one has approached it." Pavel said.

Reaper considered a number of options and adjusted his plan.

"Have Gregor plant some jihadist materials in the car and then tip off the FBI. By midday they won't be able to get a ticket on a roller coaster. Tap the phones of the girlfriend, offices, and homes. I want all the security protocols in place."

"Da, I have flags on their bank accounts and credit cards. I have also checked flight manifests from Harrisburg airport; nothing yet."

"Reaper thought for a moment. "No...they will be searching for another vehicle. Stay on the police radio and place taps on the phones of their friends and families."

"*Da.*"

Five minutes later Reaper parked on the street a block from the library and practiced his best East Coast accent as he approached. A single police officer was filling out paperwork as the tow truck driver pulled the chains off his flat bed. Reaper tapped on the officer's window.

"Mornin', I'm Bobby Singleton from the postal workers union. I see you found our missing truck?"

The officer looked up and nodded with a 'no shit' expression.

"Hey do you mind if I jot down a few numbers from the truck? I need to get the mileage and ID# off the dash to our field rep so he can get the paperwork moving," Reaper said rocking back and forth on his heels.

"Be my guest," the officer said with a dismissive wave.

Reaper strolled over to the truck trying to soak in as much detail as possible.

The tell-tale streaks of black fingerprint powder covered the white metal dashboard. He looked for a rectangular patch of removed powder signifying a fingerprint was lifted with tape but found none. The same was true of the rearview mirror. The streak marks confirmed the vehicle had been wiped down and after a brief look he waved to the officer and made a b-line for his car.

After closing the door, his calloused hands choked the steering wheel as he thought of his targets. He was not accustomed to dealing with such skilled men. He was accustomed to having a target, a time table, and encyclopedia of intelligence to pour over. It was as frustrating as standing at the North Pole and being ordered to search south.

The brief surge of anger faded as quickly as it had risen. He turned the key in the ignition and gave the postal truck one final contemptuous glance as he rolled past without any more of a clue as to where to go next.

19

Art entered the Laundromat and picked a seat near the back of the room as Daniel fed quarters into several machines and started them before joining him.

"Remind me again why we're here?" Art asked.

"I can't spot a tail, but in case we're being watched, they'll likely use a laser mic on the windows to record our conversation. The laser senses the vibrations in the glass from our speech and translates it into words." Daniel explained.

"So the machines mask the noise," Art said.

"Exactly."

Art thought the action was unnecessary, but he couldn't shake the feeling that Daniel's tactics had kept them alive so far. Art pulled one of the pre-paid cell phones from his pocket and dialed Herb.

"Herb? It's Art."

"Art, I didn't recognize the number."

"Yeah, well…my phone died and I have to use one of those pre-paid ones."

"It sounds like you're in a factory," Herb said.

"That? Oh, that's nothing. Have you been able to decipher any of the text so far?"

"I stayed late last night and made some progress. It turns out Seaton introduced a second cipher. I don't think he understood my instructions completely but I'm pretty sure I figured out how to untangle it all. I sure wish I had my old computers at NSA though."

"Tell me you found something interesting," Art said.

"Keep in mind I've only gotten a dozen or so pages decoded and a lot of the notations seem to be trivial data. He mentions the letter from Prudence Corbin and a description of a Badge of Merit issued to someone with the initials 'JHD'."

"John Henry DeFrance," Art said.

"So you've seen the letter?"

"Yes, this morning. I had Janice make a copy for us."

"When was it dated?"

Bloodlines

"Um, hold on," Art said fishing the letter out of his bag. "September twenty seventh, seventeen-eighty," Art said.

"Now, you see...that's the strange part. I've triple checked our records and called in a favor from a friend at the Smithsonian. The Badge of Merit was only awarded three times and none were given to this guy you mentioned—John Henry DeFrance."

"I see," Art said reading through the letter again.

"There's something else you should know."

"What?"

"There's another drawing on one of the pages I haven't decoded yet. It's an oval with an apple in the center."

"Yes, I seem to recall that image," Art said, pulling the journal from the bag, and flipping a few pages forward.

"Yes, I see it here. Does it mean something to you?"

"You mentioned the date September twenty-seventh, seventeen-eighty."

"Yes."

"I did some research. In September 1780, George Washington issued medallions to three soldiers in the New York State Militia. It is believed to be the first honors ever bestowed by the United States military. They were called the Fidelity Medallion and featured an apple on them. An inscription on the medallion read *Amor Patriae Vincit.*"

"The love of country conquers," Art translated. "What were these fidelity medallions awarded for?"

"The capture of one Major John Andre."

Art's eyes narrowed as he racked his brain for the familiar sounding name.

"The British officer conspiring with Major General Benedict Arnold for the capture of West Point," Herb said.

Art sat silent for several seconds as he processed the information.

"Art, are you still there?"

"Yes, Herb. I don't suppose Mr. DeFrance was one of the three soldiers?" Art said.

"No. I can't find any mention of him in the documents I've reviewed."

Art stroked his goatee as he tried to make sense of the revelation.

"All right, thanks Herb. Can you keep working on decoding the journal?"

"Are you kidding? This is the most intriguing project I've had since I left the NSA."

Art laughed. "Okay, I'll call you later."

"What if I find something important? Can I call you at this number?"

Art glanced at his nephew and knew the answer without ever asking the question. "No, I'll call you."

"Suit yourself. Hey, Art?"

"Yeah, Herb?"

"Stay out of trouble, all right?"

"You know me," Art said.

"My point exactly," Herb said.

Art huffed before ending the call.

Art spent the next few minutes briefing Daniel on the conversation while Daniel scanned the street outside.

"This town is getting too cozy for me. We'll need to find another place to hold up," Daniel said.

"No more stolen cars," Art said.

Daniel turned towards Art and winked.

"What the hell have we gotten ourselves into?" Art stared down at the journal, exhaled deeply, and shook his head.

"I've got a better question," Daniel said.

Art looked up with a glimmer of curiosity.

"Who the hell is John Henry DeFrance?"

20

Sarah and Andy spent most of the morning filling out chain of custody receipts from the crime scene. Neither one had slept. Sarah noted Andy was on his third energy drink but she avoided them. She had already drained one pot of coffee which took the edge off her fatigued muscles, but did little for her temperament. Add to that the fact she had called Daniel twice but spoke only to his voicemail. She was worried about him.

No… Daniel can take care of himself. She placed the last barcode label on the evidence bag.

Sarah heard the exam room door open and turned to see detectives Lopez and Vargas stroll into the room.

"Hey guys," Andy said.

"Ah, the glamorous work of a CSI," Vargas said as he surveyed the mound of bags and paperwork.

"Yeah, well I'll take paperwork over talking to perverts any day," Andy said.

"Present company excluded," Sarah added with a wink at Vargas.

"Funny," he said.

"Are there any new leads in the case?" Sarah asked.

"*Shit*, we don't even have an ID on our victims yet. I pulled some records on the property and vehicles and they're all registered in some blind trust. The DA is working on a warrant but that could take all day." Manny said.

"Patrol hasn't ever responded out there on a call?" Andy asked.

"I spoke to the east district deputies and none of them ever went out there. The local farmers never met their neighbors, either." Manny said.

"I can head over to the coroner's office and take their fingerprints for I-AFIS entry." Sarah said.

"That's the nation-wide fingerprint database?" Vargas asked.

"Yep. It takes a little longer but we might as well get it out of the way. We'll have to do it eventually," she said.

"Where's the computer at? You know the one from the outhouse?" Manny asked.

Andy pointed to a large bag on a four wheeled cart. "Right there…where are you going to send it?"

"Probably the Front Range Computer Forensics Lab," Manny said.

"Should be ready to check out in an hour or so," Andy said.

"How long will it take them to analyze the data?" Vargas asked.

"Given the circumstances, I think we can have them expedite the process. Those guys are buried in back log and court orders. I wouldn't expect anything sooner than the end of the week or next, at the earliest." Andy said.

"We really need this analysis done a-sap. If I call in a favor, can you two run it over there?"

Sarah exchanged glances with Andy and shrugged her shoulders. "I guess so. Right now this case is top priority."

"Good, I'll make some calls so be ready to go soon," Manny said.

"If we can get some pictures of these guys, maybe we can wrap this thing up with a bow," Sarah said after the detectives left the room.

"We're never that lucky," Andy said.

"Keep your fingers crossed," Sarah said with a demonstration.

"I'm more interested in what else might be on that computer," Andy said.

"You still think she was a pro?"

"Absolutely, and if we can find a client list or pictures of her, we might be another step closer to figuring out who killed her and why. There is something valuable on that computer Sarah, and I want to know what that is," Andy said.

"Something worth dying for," Sarah said.

"No…" Andy corrected her, "something worth killing for."

21

Middletown, Pennsylvania.

Daniel had considered several factors in selecting the diner. The proximity to the highway, residential traffic, layout of the dining room, and most importantly, the recommendation from the clerk at the hardware store.

"Remind me again why we're here?" Art said.

"We need alternate transportation," Daniel said.

"We've been sitting here for over an hour. Aren't we drawing attention to ourselves?"

"Good thought, order some desert." Daniel said waving to the waitress in thick-soled shoes.

"I assume you have a plan?" Art said.

"We're heading to Annapolis."

"What's in Annapolis?"

"I have an old friend there. Trust me, these guys won't expect us to double back."

"And just how are we getting there?" Art said.

Daniel unfolded a sheet of paper from his pocket and slid it across the table.

"A boat?"

"It's perfect. Fifteen foot fiberglass hull with a 75 horsepower motor recently overhauled. They're only asking a thousand, and the owner is right on the water," Daniel said.

"Judging from the picture, I'd say that price is inflated."

"She ain't pretty I'll grant you that, but we can take her all the way down the Susquehanna River to Annapolis."

"Are we going to see one of your Army buddies?"

"Marine, actually. I don't want to risk contacting the guys in my old unit. It'll be the first place they'll look to acquire us." Daniel said.

"So what do we do when we reach Annapolis?"

"Then…we evaluate our situation. We won't get there until tonight and by then Herb should have more of the journal decoded."

"How are we getting to this boat owner, do you even know where this is?"

Daniel held up a finger as he caught a glimpse of what he had been waiting for.

"I need a hundred bucks, Art," Daniel said as he snatched the flyer from the table.

Art unzipped his money belt and held out the bill. Daniel plucked it from his hand and said, "Get ready to go."

Art watched as Daniel met the man driving a residential plumbing van and pointed at the flyer. Within seconds, Daniel waved for Art to join him.

Art pinned a twenty dollar bill under his water glass and muttered to himself, "I sure hope to hell that kid knows what he's doing."

Art listened as Daniel wove a fanciful story to their driver about reconnecting with his long lost dad on a cross country bus trip. Now they wanted to buy a boat and go fishing like they did in the old days. The driver didn't seem to care a bit about the story, but it helped pass the time of the thirty minute drive.

Once at the boat, Daniel was all business. He didn't offer any stories or personal information. He just paid the man for the boat and even convinced the seller to throw in an extra five gallon can of gas and nautical map of the river. Ten minutes later, they were cutting south through the water on their way to the coast.

Art let the wind blow through his graying, dark hair as he gazed upon his nephew with pride. His placid composure was in stark contrast to his rugged features chiseled from years of combat. His father would have been proud.

"Daniel?"

"Yeah?"

"I'm very impressed with how you've handled all this."

"Come again?"

"I mean, I'm glad you know what you're doing. If it weren't for you, I'd have been shot the other morning and Seaton's death would probably be just another tragic suicide."

"Not to mention we'd miss out on this wonderful vacation together, right?" he said smiling, as he inched the throttle forward and glanced to port.

"Well…I think I'll check on the investigation back in Denver," Art said. He fished the pre-paid cell phone out of his pocket and dialed the number for Paul Whittier at the Consistory.

"Paul? This is Art."

"Art, where have you been? I've been calling you all morning," he said.

"Has something happened?"

"I wanted to ask *you* that. We've been sitting on pins and needles here. The brothers are very upset about Seaton's death and they want answers."

"What have you told them?"

"Only that you were working on the case with the Denver police, but sooner or later we have to give them some answers," Paul said.

"What have you heard from Detective Lew?" Art asked.

"He's checking local parolees and canvassing the neighborhood. So far, nothing. He did pass along something interesting, however."

"What's that?"

"Someone ransacked Seaton's home on the day of the murder."

"Good God, was Barbara home?"

"No, no, she was at the police department being interviewed. Thomas sent his crime scene folks over there and they did get some fingerprints. Nothing has turned up in AFIS as of yet," Paul said.

"I doubt this man left fingerprints. They're probably from guests or family that isn't in the database." Art said.

"What have you found out?" Paul asked.

"My friend is making progress on breaking Seaton's journal code but we've run into a little snag," Art said.

"What kind of snag?"

Art spent several minutes recounting the events of the last twenty-four hours. All except their current destination. Art thought it better to keep that tidbit secret.

"This makes no sense, Art. What would some old letter from the American Revolution have to do with Seaton's murder?"

"Honestly Paul, I'm at a loss, but my gut tells me we'll know more when we find out who this John Henry DeFrance character is. Maybe he has some connection to Colorado," Art said.

"Did you say DeFrance?"

"Yes... Why? Does that name ring a bell?"

The line was silent for several seconds and Art checked the phone to see if the connection had been lost.

"Paul?"

"I seem to recall a Judge from my District named DeFrance... Alison DeFrance, I believe."

"Is she retired?"

"What? Oh heavens... *He's* long dead, I'm afraid. He served in the late eighteen hundreds, if memory serves. Long after the Revolution. I can't imagine it's anything but a coincidence."

"Maybe..." Art said pondering the revelation.

"You want me to follow up on it?" Paul asked.

Art considered the question for several seconds. The chance that this judge was related in any way to their current mystery was unlikely, but Art also knew that the leads in Denver were all but gone. There was no harm in looking into Judge Alison DeFrance. Moreover it gave Paul and the others something to keep them busy while Herb translated the next clue... *If there were a next clue.*

"It wouldn't hurt to cover our bases, but let's keep this between us all right?"

"I can make some general inquiries through my staff. I'll say I'm working on a historical project and include several other judges from that era. They love that PR puff stuff," he added.

"Great, just try not to raise any eyebrows," Art said.

"I was a prosecutor for fifteen years, Art. I think I know how to conduct a discrete investigation."

"That you do."

"I'll check back with you in a few days," Art said.

"All right, but you be careful out there. We're counting on you, Art."

It was a fact Art didn't need to be reminded of.

"I'm in good hands," Art said looking at Daniel.

"Well then, good luck." Paul said.

"You, too."

Art closed the phone, looked out over the passing landscape, and let out a deep breath. It was one of those odd moments in an investigation when things seemed to be accelerating and stalling at the same time. He hoped their efforts wouldn't lead them to another dead end.

"Phone please," Daniel said reaching out his hand.

"Do you want me to dial her number?" Art asked.

Daniel responded by snapping his fingers twice. It was probably for the best. Art didn't think he could remember Sarah's number off the top of his head. He relied too much on speed dial. It was amazing he had remembered Paul's and Herb's numbers.

Art leaned over and in one smooth motion Daniel snatched up the phone and tossed it over the side of the boat.

Art shook his head, "That's littering, you know."

***

Reaper sipped his coffee as another over the road truck driver departed the truck stop without his quarry. His stake out was based on an educated guess, not a hunch. His targets would never risk booking a flight or renting a car. Conventional tactics dictated that they travel by the most inconspicuous and convenient means possible; hitching a ride with an over the road truck driver by his estimation.

Daniel Von Hollen, however, was proving to be anything but conventional. Knowing he was at a dead end, Reaper rolled down his window, spat, and punched Pavel's number into his cell phone.

"Give me an update."

"Still nothing on the police radio, and no new activity on their cell phones. I hacked into the CALEA software for their telephone providers and set up taps for the girlfriend, secretary, office, and the Denver police detective."

CALEA was the acronym for the Communications for Law Enforcement Act. It was also the common name of the software used by cell phone providers to allow law enforcement to 'tap' or listen to suspect conversations without their knowledge. Unlike law enforcement, the Gerovit didn't take the time to get a court order.

"Good work."

"I also set up a pen registry so we can see the exact moment anyone calls those numbers. I'm making a linked chart now based on their past call history to see if I have missed anyone of importance," Pavel said, a hint of embarrassment in his voice.

"Do we know who they went to see in Middletown?" Reaper asked.

"*Nyet.*"

Reaper's hands tightened around the steering wheel as a wave of intense frustration swept over him.

Without another word he hung up the phone and dialed a new number.

Governor Barclay answered in labored breaths.

"Tell me you have it."

"I've lost them."

"What?! Shit, hold on," Barclay said as Reaper heard him cup his hand over the phone and order someone out of the room.

"What do you mean you've lost them?"

"A minor set back. They have nowhere to run. I will have their location soon enough."

"Where are you?"

"Pennsylvania."

"And what are you doing to get that journal?"

Reaper was getting annoyed at his employer's tone but he didn't let it show.

"There are some things you are better off not knowing. A man in your position must be insulated from such things, yes?"

"I don't have to remind you what happens if that journal gets out into the press, do I?"

"No, Governor, you do not."

"Then see to it you get it back before we both regret it. I won't be going down on this ship alone, my friend."

The comment took Reaper off guard for a moment. He was not used to being threatened and certainly didn't regard his employer as a friend.

"It will be done. In the meantime, I suggest you keep a low profile and..."

"Are you insane? I've announced my campaign. I can't keep a low profile, you idiot. Now you listen to me...you find that journal and you find it fast. I'm not letting some lab rat and his army brat nephew get in the way of becoming the next President of the United States," Barclay snapped.

Reaper licked his teeth as he watched an overweight prostitute climb into a red eighteen wheeler across the parking lot. His employer's petulance gnawed at his gut. The appeal of having intimate ties with the next President was losing its luster more and more, but for now Reaper had to play it out. There was too much at stake if their association were made public now.

"Trust me Aaron, this is what I do. I will find that journal…and then I will kill them both."

"See to it that you do, and don't bother calling again until the deed is done."

Reaper tossed the phone aside in disgust as the line went dead.

22

Sarah and Andy arrived at the Front Range Computer Forensics Lab a few minutes past one in the afternoon and found a parking spot by the door.

"Hey, rock star parking," Andy said.

"Does that make me your groupie?" Sarah joked.

Their jovial mood was somewhat tempered by the stressed out looking man standing just inside the doorway. His body trembled with impatience as he shifted his considerable weight back and forth. Marv Dangle reminded Sarah of a short chubby Marlboro man complete with a greased blonde handlebar moustache.

Sarah had met him a few times before but always remarked how sweat seemed to pour from his brow, even in winter. She didn't know a thing about his personal life and she counted that as a blessing. As far as computer forensics went the man was a genius. One of his software developments was even used by the Secret Service but he would never say which one.

"Okay, it's showtime!" Andy said as he grabbed the computer tower and followed Sarah to the door.

Marv didn't open the door for them. Annoyed, Sarah pushed the door open, trapping him against the wall.

"Hey Marv, thanks for getting us in on such short notice," Andy said as he balanced the evidence bag and extended his hand.

Marv ignored Andy's hand. Instead, he snatched a crusty white handkerchief from his pocket and blew his nose.

"I'm very busy," he said as he motioned for the pair to go inside to the lobby. After checking in at the main desk and getting visitor badges, Marv led them through a maze of cubicles filled with electronic racks, monitors, and energy drinks.

Marv's cubicle resembled the home of a hoarder. Dozens of books and hundreds of papers were piled on the desktop and floor like pick-up sticks. There was no discernable order or orientation to the mess that Sarah could see. His trash can was overflowing with empty Dr. Pepper cans and Sarah spotted partially eaten doughnut poking out from behind his monitor. The carpenter ants feeding on it made her cringe.

Marv grabbed the computer tower from Andy and cleared a space next to his monitor on the desktop.

"You guys must have some serious juice. I was working on a court ordered discovery project due by the end of the week. I guess now it will be continued," Marv said as he adjusted his thick-framed glasses.

"It's that double homicide from out east," Sarah explained.

Marv offered an expression of complete indifference.

"You know, the one that's been all over the news," she said.

"I don't watch the news. I don't watch television," Marv said.

Sarah glanced around his cubicle and the comment suddenly made sense.

"I have to make a mirror image of the hard drive before we poke around in there. What are we looking for?"

Andy pulled out a copy of the search warrant and handed it to Marv. "Surveillance footage from last night showing the murders and any other documents that might tell us who the victims are."

Marv looked over his shoulder at the warrant, "You don't know who your victims are?"

"It's a long story," Sarah said.

Over the next several minutes Marv mumbled to himself and one time even let out a boisterous laugh as his fingers danced across the keyboard. While the hard drive hummed like a small lawnmower, Marv opened a mini-refrigerator, cracked open a fresh Dr. Pepper, and took a long drink. Sarah was about to ask a question when Marv's phone rang.

"Marv," he said. "Um...now is not a good time." Marv glanced back at Sarah and scooted his chair to the corner of his cubicle. Sarah could barely make out his hushed voice as he carried on the conversation.

"I...no... I can't..."

There was a long pause as Marv listened intently to the voice on the other end of the line.

"You wouldn't... Okay, okay, I'll call you back later," he said and then hung up the phone.

"Girlfriend Marv?" Sarah prodded.

Marv looked up at her like a teenager caught masturbating by his mother.

"No…it…was…Detective Vargas."

"Sounded pretty serious," Andy said.

Marv's eyes darted back and forth. "Um, he just needs help with his computer," Marv said.

"Porn scrubbing, eh?" Sarah said as she jabbed Andy in the arm and snorted like a pig.

Marv offered the first timid smile Sarah had ever seen from the man before turning back to his monitor and punching new commands into the keyboard.

"Here we go," Marv said as new file folders opened up on the screen. "We're in."

"There, that one," Andy said pointing to the video file dated the previous day.

Marv double clicked on the icon and started playing video from the various cameras throughout the house. The images danced from camera to camera in a dizzying collage.

"Is there any way you can isolate the various cameras and stream them individually by location?" Sarah asked.

Marv fixed a look of disapproval on her, "Of course I can."

He punched new commands into the software and fifteen minutes later the video was ready.

"Which camera angle do you want?" Marv asked.

"Let's see the bedroom," Andy said.

Marv double clicked on the icon and began playing through the video. The first few minutes were benign but then a woman came in and began undressing. Sarah heard Marv swallow deeply and watched him shift uneasily in his chair.

"Is there audio?" Sarah asked.

Marv clicked an icon and turned the speaker volume up a few notches. They watched for several seconds as Elizabeth primped and preened her appearance.

"You can skip though this stuff, Marv," Sarah said.

He exhaled deeply as he clicked the mouse on the scroll bar and slid it to the right. The images flashed until just before the end of the video.

"Hold it right there, Marv!" Andy said pointing towards the screen. "Back it up a few frames so we can see the John."

"Do you recognize that guy?" Sarah asked.

Bloodlines

Marv shook his head as Sarah immediately recognized the young football star that had been this year's first round draft pick.

"Is that who I think it is?" she asked.

"Looks like it to me," Andy confirmed. "Okay Marv, keep going."

The three watched in silence as the events of the homicide played out in front of them like a movie. Marv deftly switched from camera angle to camera angle like a prime time television producer as he tracked the two suspects waging a small war against the occupants.

"You were right, Andy…there were two suspects," Sarah said.

"Blood doesn't lie, kid. Look…right there…looks like one of the suspects takes a round there. See him collapse on the floor?"

"Whoa!" Sarah exclaimed as she watched the final shootout between the suspect and a man. "That was intense," she said.

"Can you zoom in so we can see the license plate on the vehicle, Marv?"

"It's too dark and far away. It's not like television you know."

"Print me a still of that anyway. Maybe we can see that vehicle on the toll road cameras," Andy said.

"Andy…we need to go back further. My gut tells me these guys came looking for something that happened on another day," Sarah said.

Andy nodded, "Marv, can you open up the previous day's footage?"

Marv mumbled under his breath as he repeated the process to stream the video from the new file folder.

"There," Andy said pointing to the icon, "Open the bedroom footage."

Sarah and Andy watched intently as the middle-aged wiry man came into the room and fumbled with his clothing.

"Turn up the volume, Marv," Sarah said as she strained to hear his voice.

There was something very familiar about the man's voice but she just couldn't put her finger on it. Sarah's eyes widened as she heard the name Seaton Adiago.

"Wait...play that last part back and turn it up," Sarah ordered.

Marv replayed the section as Andy leaned in towards the monitor.

"Does that name mean something to you, Sarah?" Andy asked.

Sarah caught herself before she revealed what Daniel had told her in confidence. She trusted Andy, but the mention of Seaton's name just linked these murders to the one in Denver. Sarah wanted to consult with Art before bringing Andy in the loop.

"No, I guess it's just such a strange name," she lied. "Keep going Marv."

The trio watched for several more minutes as the woman and the stranger re-started their lover's dance. Then, in a moment of pure ecstasy the man turned and tilted his head giving all three a perfect view of his face. Sarah said the only thing that came to mind as they stared at the most powerful man in Colorado politics.

"Holy fuck sticks."

23

"Ummmm…I think this just went way past our pay grade," Andy said as he stood transfixed by the image of Governor Barclay on the screen.

"Who's that?" Marv asked.

"You're kidding me, right?" Sarah asked before regaining her composure.

"Ah, it just looks like someone we know Marv," Andy said.

Marv shrugged and punched a few keystrokes as Andy and Sarah exchanged a look of amazement.

"I think we'd better call Manny on this," Andy said as he placed his phone to his ear and walked outside of the cubicle.

Sarah made one-sided attempts at small talk with Marv until Andy returned. He handed Sarah his cell phone, "Here, Manny wants a word,"

"You two sure know how to ignite a shit storm," Manny said.

"How is this my fault? I didn't pay for some seedy hooker," Sarah said.

"Sorry, I'm getting hammered here. Bottom line is we're getting pulled from the investigation. I've been told in no uncertain terms to slam the lid shut on this and transfer my files to someone better suited for special investigations."

"Who's going to be handling it?" Sarah asked.

"Special Investigations, but technically Lieutenant Manilow will be lead."

"Manilow? Well…it's as good as solved then. Remind me again how many homicides he's investigated during his illustrious career at Internal Affairs?"

"You're preaching to the choir, but it's out of our hands now. This is the 'Ape' case of the year."

Sarah knew an 'APE' case was an acronym for acute political emergency though she had never worked on one.

"You can expect to get pulled in for debriefing when you get back. If it's anything like mine, they'll practically threaten you with charges of obstruction if you leak any information about the case—*even* within the department," he continued.

"Greeeeeat, the threat of criminal prosecution is always a morale builder," she said. At that moment Sarah thought of Barclay's comment about Seaton Adiago and his journal. If she told Art of the revelation and it ever got back to Manilow it might ruin her career. *That is a bridge crossing for another time.* She swept the thought away.

"So what about the analysis of the video and computer files?" Sarah asked.

"Stop everything and bring it all back for Manilow. He'll be waiting for you in the crime lab."

More good news.

Sarah broke the news to Marv who seemed somewhat relieved. Sarah was sure he thought any dent in his backlog was a small victory.

"I can't release the mirror image I've placed on our server, it's against policy," Marv said.

"I'm sure they'll be calling your supervisor about that," Andy said as he bagged the computer tower and affixed fresh evidence tape. "Thanks for your help, Marv."

The first few minutes of the car ride back to the crime lab passed in agonizing silence, but Sarah finally had to speak her mind.

"How is Manilow supposed to conduct an investigation without the Investigations Division?"

"I know, it's pretty messed up, but can you blame them really? I mean, it's the Governor for Pete's sake."

"That doesn't give him a pass on murder, Andy," Sarah said and instantly regretted it.

"Murder? Bad judgment maybe, but not murder. The guy's in the wrong place at the wrong time. His presence shouldn't cloud the investigation. Plus, he's running for President. Can you imagine being the sheriff that derailed the star of your own political party?"

Sarah was thankful she hadn't mentioned Seaton's name in her off-hand rant.

"No, I know. I guess I'm just feeling sorry for his poor wife. I mean, it sure doesn't fit their public profile."

"I know you didn't vote for the guy, but you may not know the whole story. Maybe his wife is a bitch. Maybe she won't touch him with a ten foot pole, you never know."

"You're right, I shouldn't judge when I don't know the whole story," she lied. She may not know about his marriage but she knew he was involved in Seaton's murder one way or another.

"This thing could blow up on the national news. I mean, can you imagine how many other rich and famous people might be in that surveillance footage? We watched ten minutes and saw two of the most recognizable people in the state."

Marv didn't recognize them.

"Maybe Manilow is on the tape. Maybe that's why he took over the investigation," Sarah joked.

"Even prostitutes have standards, Sarah," Andy said as they exchanged high fives.

Lieutenant Manilow and Sergeant Marshall were waiting for them, arms crossed, in the parking lot when they arrived. As promised both were given stern warnings about divulging any information about the case, even to other members of the crime lab.

"How are we supposed to handle future lab requests on the case?" Andy asked.

"There won't be any," Manilow said. "Any future forensic analyses will be conducted by the CBI."

"But the CBI works for the Governor," Sarah protested.

The comment drew a withering gaze from Manilow as he dressed her down.

"The Governor is not the *subject* of this investigation Ms. Richards…he is a victim." Manilow spat. "You had better remember that if you value your career."

"We're all on the same page here, sir. I'll make sure all of our crime scene reports, notes, and photos are sent up immediately," Andy said.

***

Hammond quietly entered the meeting room. He tip-toed around the head of the table as the governor's campaign manager laid out her five point plan to secure the women's vote. Upon reaching Governor Barclay, Hammond placed a hand on his shoulder and whispered into his ear.

"Something has come up...may I have a word?"

Aaron Barclay gave a dismissive wave and replied "Five minutes," before returning his attention to his campaign manager. Hammond silently crossed the room and took a seat on a plush leather couch.

Fifteen minutes later, once the meeting broke and the self-assuring handshakes were exchanged, Barclay joined his security chief. Hammond waited until the last staffer closed the door behind them before speaking.

"I just got a call from a friend in law enforcement. There has been a terrible tragedy at the farmhouse."

Barclay looked genuinely surprised at the comment.

"What sort of tragedy?"

"Sometime last night Elizabeth and her bodyguard were murdered."

"Murdered? Do...do the police have any suspects?"

Hammond had been relieved to find out that they did not but didn't let it show.

"No, but there's a bigger issue at play."

"What's bigger than murder?"

"First, let me assure you that I have taken steps to protect you."

"Protect me? Protect me from what?"

"Were you aware she had the house wired for surveillance?"

Hammond watched the color drain from Barclay's face followed by his eyes glazing over with a deer in the headlights stare. "Sir, I've taken care of things. The information is compartmentalized and I have every confidence we can keep this under wraps. We have some very loyal allies at the helm. Of course, you may want to consider a few appointments for key people to the Department of Public Safety, or the Bureau of Prisons."

Barclay finally turned to Hammond. His fearful expression was replaced with one of pure anger.

"Look, no one is blackmailing us... I thought it would give us some added leverage." Hammond said.

Bloodlines

"You listen to me, Wes, and you listen good. That surveillance footage will cease to exist...do you understand me?" He said stabbing a finger into the armrest of the couch.

"Sir...it's in evidence... I mean, the cat is out of the bag."

"Fuck the cat!" Barclay hissed. "I am not going to watch my political career get derailed by some two bit piece of ass. You find a way. You find a way to make that evidence disappear, you hear me? I don't care if you have to break into that evidence room yourself. I pay you a hell of a lot of money to protect me... Well...it's time to earn your pay."

Hammond shrunk in his seat at the dressing down. He had an idea of how Barclay dealt with those that betrayed him. He also knew the Governor had powerful men that wouldn't hesitate to kill him if they felt he was a liability.

Resigned to his new task, Hammond met Barclay's icy stare and slowly nodded.

24

Annapolis, Maryland
Daniel pulled into the small seaside wharf and tied off the mooring rope to a tarnished cleat. He smiled at the sight of his old friend sitting in a wheel chair up at the parking level.
"Art, I'd like you to meet my friend, Chris. Chris…this is my Uncle Art."
"It's a pleasure meeting you, Art," Chris said as he extended his hand. Art noticed he had only three fingers. Chris's upper body was muscular in stark contrast to his lower thighs. His high and tight haircut was the tell-tale badge of a Marine.
"Any friend of Daniel's…" Art said. "You're a Marine?"
"Retired, of course," Chris said.
"Oo-rah," Daniel said.
"Semper-fi," Chris replied as Daniel leaned over and hugged his old friend.
Chris drove his mechanized wheelchair into a custom van and offered Art the front passenger seat while Daniel took a seat in the back.
"So you boys met in the service?" Art asked.
"Yeah, what…nineteen ninety-nine, right Danny?"
"Uh-huh."
"Ol' Danny boy swooped in and saved my ass after I stirred up a hornet's nest in one of the Earth's armpits."
"Chris here was a scout/sniper."
"And you were a PJ at that time," Art said.
"Yep."
"Enough said." Art replied.
Twenty minutes later Chris pulled into the driveway of a modest ranch style home and slid the gear into park.
"Tammy and the girls are visiting the folks all week so we have the place all to ourselves," he said.
"I can't tell you how much we appreciate your hospitality, Chris," Art said.
"Think nothing of it. *Mi casa su casa* as they say. Art, you can take the girls room upstairs. Danny, you get the couch."

"Just like old times, huh?" Daniel said.

"Yeah, except now I got a wife so no puking in the tub and for God's sake lift the lid."

Daniel's lips formed a wide smile. He forgot how much he had missed the banter from his old friend.

"Can I get you boys something to eat? Danny...how about a beer?"

"I'm going to lay down for a few hours, I'm beat." Art said. "Maybe after dinner we can run out and grab a fresh pair of clothes?"

"Sounds good, Art. I'm going to give Sarah a call and check in," he said glancing at his watch. "She's probably worried I haven't called her."

Chris frowned. "You Army boys are so pussy-whipped."

After Art left the room Chris wheeled over to the couch and patted Daniel's knee.

"It's good to see you, brother."

"You too, I promise we won't trash the place," Daniel said.

Chris swatted dismissively through the air. "Shit, I'm not worried. So tell me about this Sarah girl, is it serious?"

Daniel smiled. "Sometimes."

"What the hell does *that* mean?"

"You know man, it's hard. She's in Denver... I'm up in Steamboat, but when we're together...it's like..."

"Yeah?" Chris said sitting up and leaning forward.

"Yeah. She could be the one."

"Wow, I never thought I'd hear that from you. So what's she like...you got a picture?"

Daniel fished a picture of her from his wallet and handed it to Chris.

"Holy shit, dude...she's a ten per center. How in the hell did you manage that?"

"I ask myself that every day."

"Well...tell me about her."

"She's smart...she's...tough, hell, she's damned near perfect for me. She's a hunter, too."

"Wow, hot *and* a hunter. Sounds like you hit the lottery, dude. So what does she do?"

"She's a CSI like Art, and a good one. I mean, she's like a pit bull, you know? She won't give up. Sometimes that's a bad thing, I guess."

"How is that a bad thing?" Chris asked.

"I worry about her. Sometimes she runs off all half-cocked. She's like a new recruit all full of piss and vinegar on their way to war."

"Ready, shoot, aim huh?"

"I guess, but I can understand why she does it. She had this thing happen to her in college and it changed her."

"Was she…" Chris let the words hang in the air.

"No, but her roommate was, and she blames herself for not being there to stop it. Ever since then, she's been on the hunt for monsters and if she finds one…look out. I mean when she gets on a scent she'll peg the red line. Last year she chased a guy down a mountain in a blizzard with nothing but her Glock. He nearly killed her."

"Ballsy. She sounds like one tough lady," Chris said.

"She is, but she's inexperienced."

"Doesn't sound like it."

"You know what I mean. You and me have dealt with the worst of the worst. Uncle Sam didn't send us out looking for some junkie who held up a liquor store."

"Well, you know her better than me but it sounds like she's one hell of a gal, and that, my friend, it just what you need. Take it from me, there comes a day when you can't jump out of helicopters anymore and you need a strong home front," he said rubbing his stump.

Daniel smirked and said, "I'll bet you could still fast rope with the best of them."

"Well sure, it's the landings that give me trouble," he said laughing.

Daniel glanced down at this watch. "Speaking of Sarah, I'd better give her a ring."

"Use the bathroom if you want some privacy. In a house full of girls it's the only place I can have a sane thought."

Daniel closed the door to the bathroom and punched Sarah's number into the pre-paid cell phone.

"Richards."

"Hey babe, it's me."

"Daniel...I didn't recognize the number. Are you okay?"

"Yeah. We had a little trouble with our phones and had to ditch them."

"That sounds ominous. What kind of trouble?"

"Nothing we couldn't handle. How are you doing?"

"Hold on a minute," she said. Daniel could hear her open and close a door.

"Daniel, something happened today that you have to hear."

"What's going on...is everything okay?"

"No, not by a long shot," Sarah said. "I'm in the fingerprint lab but if someone comes in I'll have to change the subject." She spent the next few minutes describing the double homicide at the farmhouse and their brief analysis of the computer.

"You're kidding me?" Daniel whispered as he sat on the edge of the tub. "And Barclay actually mentioned Seaton and a journal?"

"It was clear as day. We knew right away we had stepped in a pile of...well, you know...and when Andy called back to the office we got the door slammed on us hard. Manilow has everything. Daniel, they even threatened us with prosecution if we talk about the case to *anyone*."

"Jesus."

"I know, right? Who does that?"

"Did you say anything about the murder at the Consistory?"

"No, I didn't dare, but I'm telling you."

"I'm glad you did. This takes things to a whole new level though."

"Maybe I could leak something anonymously to the media or something?" Sarah said.

"No, don't do that. You don't know who you can trust and Barclay surely has moles in the press."

"I can't sit on my hands knowing he may have committed a murder, Daniel."

"You can do anything you want on your last day of work, Sarah."

"Real funny."

"I'm not asking you to sit on your hands, just take it down a notch until I can talk it out with Art. He'll know what to do."

"Maybe Art could talk to the sheriff...you know explain it to him privately?" Sarah suggested.

"The sheriff will know someone talked and he won't need to guess who spilled the beans," Daniel said. "Look, you did the right thing telling me. We're on it and making some progress. Let Art and I draw fire on this one, okay?"

"I don't like the sound of that, Daniel."

"It's just an expression babe, don't worry about us."

"Where are you?"

"With a friend."

"You don't want to tell me," she said in a deflated tone.

"I don't want you to have to lie if you're asked."

"Can you at least tell me when you're coming back?"

"We're going where the information takes us. I wish I knew more. The journal is encoded and it's taking time to decode it."

"Oh, I wish I was with you. I feel useless out here and getting sidelined is really pissing me off."

"You need to throttle it back, Sarah. We're in the tall grass now and there's no way to tell where the lions are."

There was a long silence.

"Sarah…you still with me?"

"Yes, it just pisses me off," she said releasing a deep sigh.

"We'll figure out what to do. Let me talk it over with Art and I'll call you back tomorrow okay?"

"Okay… Stay safe, all right? You'll call me tomorrow?"

"I'll call you tomorrow."

"Love you."

"Love you too babe, be safe and sit tight."

Daniel set the phone down next to the sink and splashed some water on his face. He considered waking Art to formulate a plan but decided against it. Daniel knew the value of a good night's sleep and right now…they needed every advantage they could get.

***

Sarah ended the call with a deep sense of despair.

What if this case gets buried for political expediency? What if the killer gets away with it? Then she had a thought that sent chills through her spine. *What if the killings are related?*

Sarah found herself picking at her nails and flexed her hands in frustration. She flipped open her phone and called her best friend Jenny Fletcher at the Westminster Police Department.

156

"Jenny? It's Sarah."

"Hey trouble, what's up?"

"Can you come over tonight? I really need to talk to you about something?"

"What is it...Daniel?"

"No...well, sort of...not really."

"What is it, Sarah?"

"I don't want to talk about it over the phone."

"Oh my God, are you prego?"

"Jenny!" Sarah said.

"Okay, just checking...*jeez*. I'm working mids tonight. Can it wait until tomorrow?" she asked.

Sarah rolled her tongue under her lower lip in frustration.

"Yeah, sure, tomorrow will work."

"You sure? 'Cause I could come over tonight, but I won't get there until like one," Jenny said.

"No, tomorrow is fine. It can wait until then." Sarah said.

"Okay...it's a date. I'll bring the beer and you can serve the ice cream."

"Great."

"Give me a preview though...it is juicy?" Jenny asked.

"Jenny...yeah, it's juicy."

"Good, my gossip tank is running low."

"I'll call you when I get off work. Should be around five," Sarah said.

"Okay, see you then."

Sarah hung up the phone with a trace of regret. She promised Daniel she wouldn't tell anyone but Jenny could be trusted. Jenny was the toughest cop she knew next to Manny. She was also the first female officer ever to qualify for the Westminster SWAT team. If nothing else, they could go to the range for some hundred and twenty-four grain therapy.

25

Reaper's satellite phone rang only once before he saw Pavel's name and pressed the call button.

"We have a problem," Pavel said before describing the conversation between Daniel, Sarah, and her friend. Reaper digested the information in silence.

"Did you get a fix on his location?"

"*Nyet*, but the call pinged a tower in Annapolis. I have placed the number on the grid and with a few more calls we should have his position," Pavel said.

Annapolis? Reaper thought. "Hammond assured me all the loose ends were tied off. I see now that is not the case," Reaper said through gritting teeth.

"Maybe we can use this to our advantage," Pavel said.

"How?"

"He values the girl. If we take her, it may force him to come out into the open."

The thought had already crossed Reaper's mind. He was walking a tight rope but was convinced they could keep a lid on the journal. Right now, the Von Hollens were chasing shadows from the lies of a crazy, old man. They had no hard evidence. The kidnapping of a CSI would bring too much attention. His prey was in the dark, on the run, and close to capture. It was only a matter of time.

"The girl is not the problem," he said.

"And what if she tells her friend, or someone else?"

"We'll send her a message she can't ignore."

***

Hammond's phone buzzed in his pocket. He put a finger in his free ear and bowed his head as he strained to hear Reaper over the voices in the room. He listened in silence as his head rose an inch and his eyes scanned the crowd for eavesdroppers. Pinching the phone between his cheek and shoulder, he pulled a business card from his shirt pocket and scribbled an address onto the back side.

Bloodlines

"I understand," he said after several seconds. "I have someone in mind."

Hammond ended the call and waved another security officer over to his post. Once in pace, he ducked around a corner and scrolled through his phone list until the name 'Dustin' came up. He was a man of many talents but moderate in intelligence. Most important, he got results without asking too many questions or sharing secrets. Hammond pressed the send button and waited for an answer.

"I didn't expect to ever hear from you again, now that you have your new gig," the man said.

"I have a job that calls for your...specialties."

"What kind of job?"

"I need you to send a message to a young woman."

"A young woman, huh? Is she hot?"

"It's not that kind of message. We just need to scare some sense into her."

"What's your message?"

"I like what you did to that reluctant land owner on the highway deal. I think something similar should get our message across," Hammond said.

"Anything else?"

Hammond explained a brief note he wanted left behind and stressed that Dustin wear gloves when writing it.

"The price has gone up, you know?"

Hammond frowned. "How much?"

"Twenty percent. Half now, half upon completion in the normal account."

"Agreed, but we want the message sent tonight."

"That won't be a problem." Dustin said.

Hammond checked his watch and ran through their planned schedule for the rest of the day.

"Call me when it's done," he said.

The line went dead and Hammond dialed the number to a source at the Arapahoe County Sheriff's Office.

***

The drive home was a complete blank for Sarah. The radio was tuned to a local talk radio program but she had no idea what they were discussing. Her thoughts were of a farmhouse and a prostitute whose murder may never be solved.

Hoisting the heavy duty bag over her shoulder, Sarah labored up the front steps and slid her key into the lock. She turned it slowly to the right until the latch clicked. She depressed the thumb lever and gave the door a bump with her hip before gasping in alarm.

"Sweet Jesus!" she blurted.

Just inside the door Ranger sat at attention, his tail sweeping the wooden floor. Sarah hadn't become accustomed to her new roommate yet.

In truth, he was weird. It was the staring. He would sit and stare at her all day, and the only thing Sarah could think about were the corpses she had seen at crime scenes that were fed upon by their pets.

Dropping her bag, she trotted to the kitchen and got a jerky treat for him.

The next few hours were passed in a trance. Sarah hadn't felt this tired in weeks. Sitting on the couch she channel-surfed in rhythmic pulses, barely allowing each new program to materialize before switching to the next. Ranger was curled up on the couch next to her when his head abruptly popped up.

Jumping from the couch, he ran to the back sliding glass door and looked back at Sarah through his wagging tail.

Sarah exhaled deeply. "All right."

On her way to the door, she remembered Daniel's suggestion and grabbed Ranger's tactical vest off the kitchen table. He stood ramrod straight as she fastened the vest over his body and let out a little whimper of impatience.

He shot through the open door, banging his vest against the frame, as he darted out onto the deck. He raised his nose and sampled the air as Sarah closed the door behind him. She shuffled back to the couch, laid down, and without planning to…fell asleep.

***

Sarah slowly opened her as she heard the scratching at the sliding glass door. She blinked several times in rapid succession as she took in her surroundings. She had no idea what time it was.

Bloodlines

Ranger let out a sharp bark and Sarah pulled herself from the depths of the couch to let him in. As she approached the door, she noticed his tail was rigid and pointing straight up. *That was odd.*

Ranger burst past Sarah as she opened the door and nearly knocked her off her feet. His nails clicked across the floor as he sniffed around the couch.

"Sorry buddy, no scraps."

She brushed past him and plopped back onto the couch. She flipped through the news stations hopeful to catch a glimpse of the farmhouse killings. Seeing none, she tapped the screen to her iPad and scanned the news sites with similar results. She hadn't really expected to see a breaking story but it was worth the look.

Ranger circled around the ottoman and lay on the floor facing her like the Sphinx. His beady eyes met hers as he looked up from the floor.

"Dude…you're creeping me out," she said as he dropped his gaze. She made a mental note to bring the subject up with Daniel when he called tomorrow.

Sarah tapped her slippers on the floor, then leaned back to prop her feet on the ottoman.

A wave of fear suddenly flushed through her body as the hairs on the back of her neck stood at attention. As a hunter, her grandfather had taught her to listen to her senses when they sent a signal. Goosebumps erupted on her arms and she reached for a blanket draped over the back of the couch.

She turned back, seeing movement. Ranger's head snapped up and he let out a low steady growl. Rising slowly to his feet, she watched as Ranger dropped his head, his growl growing in intensity.

"Ranger…what the hell?"

Ranger started a slow stalk towards her bearing his teeth.

"Ranger, down," Sarah yelled. She shifted upward in her seat and glanced at her Glock on the kitchen counter. For a brief moment she considered standing up and making a dash but thought better of it. Predators responded to the flight of their prey by giving chase.

"Ranger! What has gotten into you? DOWN!"

161

Ranger let out a series of vicious barks, streams of spit flinging from his dagger-like teeth as he arched his body preparing to pounce.

Sarah rolled up a magazine in a makeshift baton a half second before he launched ninety pounds of flesh tearing ferocity at the couch.

26

Sarah closed her eyes, drew her knees into her body, and screamed as she felt Ranger's body slam into the couch. She swung her makeshift baton wildly but never made contact with Ranger's body.

It took her a full second to realize Ranger had not attacked her after all. She opened one eye at the sound of hollow wumps to see Ranger violently thrashing a thick rope against the wooden floor.

Her mind was slow to recognize the object, but when she did, she sprang towards the kitchen. She swiped her Glock from the counter and pointed it at the snake. Her new shotgun would have been better.

"Ranger...LEAVE IT!"

Ranger ignored her as he continued to thrash the snake in all directions. Seconds later, the head separated from the body as it whipped through the air and landed in a heap by the door. The headless body was writhing back and forth as it spewed blood from the severed end.

Ranger spat out the head and launched a new assault on the body tearing it open and clawing at it with his paws. Sarah continued yelling until he finally stepped back and gave one last insulting bark.

Sarah opened the door and kicked the limp carcass over the threshold. Ranger tried to follow but Sarah swung the door closed. She fell back against the door and slid down until she was sitting on the floor. Ranger stood on all fours, panting heavily, and wagging his tail back and forth. She could swear he was smiling.

She laid the Glock on the floor and held out her arms to her furry savior. She turned her face away as he slobbered her with kisses. She clasped his face with both hands and held it firmly in front of her.

"I will never doubt your loyalty again, Ranger."

He let out an annoyed whimper as he broke free of her hands and sat on his haunches.

Sarah took several deep breaths before opening the door and examining the body. Ranger had thoroughly shredded the skin. *So much for a hatband.*

Her eyes narrowed as they settled on the tail. Duct tape? *Of course; no way had a snake like this got into her house by accident.*

She immediately scanned the yard and street for threats. Nothing. Her mind immediately kicked into work mode and she bent down to examine the duct tape. She considered how she would process it for fingerprints and hoped the thrashing hadn't obliterated them. She turned to get her crime scene camera when she saw the small white envelope tucked under her front mat.

She knelt down on one knee and reached for it as a year old memory flashed through her mind. The last time she found a note on her door step she was being hunted by a sadistic killer of women.

Sarah gasped as she spun around in the direction of the park and the bench that man had once occupied. Her eyes darted between dark shadows until her pulse slowed and she regained a measure of composure.

He's long gone.

Fighting an urge to grab the note, she ran inside for her camera. The last thing she wanted was to leave her own fingerprints on the possible evidence. She took two dozen photographs of the family room, Ranger, and the front porch. She made certain she had good images of the snake body and duct tape wrappings before dropping it into a large paper bag.

Satisfied with her photos, Sarah shouldered the camera, and plucked the note from under the mat. Even using gloved hands, she was careful to handle the envelope by the edges.

She flipped open the loose flap and drew out the card inside. She turned it over and read the brief message handwritten in blue ink.

Back off this case!

Sarah flipped it over again and looked for more information but the card was blank. She flexed the envelope open and looked for something else inside…nothing.

"Back off this case," she murmured. *What case?*

Confused, Sarah tucked the note back into the envelope and slipped back into the house. Sarah dialed the number for dispatch as Ranger sat by her side, sweeping the floor with his tail. Eight minutes and forty two seconds later a deputy called out over her portable radio that he was on scene.

After placing Ranger in her bedroom, she met the deputy on the porch and gave him a quick tour.

"I guess you pissed someone off," he said.

"Apparently," she replied.

"Do you want me to get a detective out here?" he asked.

Sarah was just about to answer when her cell chirped. Manny's name was displayed on the caller ID.

"Too late," she said. "Hey, Manny."

"Did I hear over the radio that someone threw a rattlesnake in your house?"

"I'm not sure how but yeah...a rattlesnake."

Her eye caught the brass plate of the mail slot in the front door and she made a mental note to fingerprint it.

"*Jesus*, Sarah," Manny said.

"Tell me about it."

"Dispatch said there was a note telling you to back off some case?"

"Yeah."

"What case?"

"It didn't say. Kind of inconsiderate, isn't it?"

Manny chuckled under his breath. "You mean to tell me you have more than one case?" he said. "Do you have any murders or high profile cases coming up in trial?"

"The only high profile murder I've had is the one we were just ordered to drop," she said cupping her hand over the phone.

"Do you think that's what the note is referring to?"

"I don't see how. I mean, how much more backed off can I get? I've been threatened with arrest if I even talk about it. Manilow scares me a hell of a lot more than a snake," Sarah admitted.

"I hear you." Manny said.

There was an uncomfortable moment of silence before Manny spoke his next words.

"Maybe you should take a few days off, Sarah."

"I don't need any time off."

"I didn't say you *needed* it. Take it anyway, at least until we can get our arms around this."

The idea hadn't occurred to her but the more she rolled it around in her head, the more sense it made.

"Maybe you're right."

"You know I'm right," he said.

"You could head up to your cabin and do some pre-season scouting," he said.

"Maybe, I'll have to check with the office first. They may not give me any time off."

"*What?* Believe me…you'll get some time off, and if you don't, I'll make the call for you."

"Don't do that, Manny, I don't need any special treatment."

"It's not special; I'd do it for anyone."

She knew in her heart it was true.

The deputy remained on scene for another thirty minutes writing his report and gathering the evidence. Sarah helped him fingerprint the mailbox slot in the door and lift a partial finger print.

She watched the tail lights of the deputy's car turn the corner, then Sarah rechecked the locks on her windows and doors before surveying the park one last time.

Sarah turned out the lights and grabbed her Remington tactical shotgun. Racking a shell into the chamber, she sat in a leather recliner facing the door with her battle-tested dog curled at her feet. The second hand on her grandfather clock punctuated the silence, click…click…click, as she surveyed her surroundings under the soft glow washing in from the streetlights. Minutes later, Ranger's gentle snore signaled permission for her to drift off into a deep sleep.

27

August 8th: Annapolis, Maryland

Art awoke to a pair of almond eyes staring at him. A sand-colored Siamese cat sat on his chest. "Well, hello there."

Startled, the feline launched from the bed as he outstretched his arms and rubbed his eyes. The red numbers on the alarm clock read zero-six-hundred.

Art dressed in his only set of wrinkled clothes and made his way downstairs. Chris and Daniel were already sipping coffee at the table.

"Hey Art, can I pour you a cup?" Chris asked.

"Please," was all Art could manage.

"How did you sleep?" Daniel asked.

"Heavy. I don't remember a thing."

"Well, it's been a pretty exciting couple of days. Your body isn't used to the scramble," Daniel said.

Art smoothed his hair out with one hand before saying, "Is that a polite way of saying I'm old."

"Not old, just…"

"Just what?" Art asked.

"You know…"

"Old," Chris said as he placed the coffee before Art with a smile.

Art chuckled as he raised his eyebrows and nodded in affirmation. "I guess you're right, but I'm not dead."

"Chris and I were just discussing a few things," Daniel said changing the topic.

"Such as?"

Daniel spent the next few minutes repeating the information Sarah had shared with him the night before. Art sat emotionless as he stirred another sugar cube into his coffee.

"So…what do you think?" Daniel finally asked.

Art pursed his lips as he looked from Chris to Daniel. "I think its great news."

Daniel shot a look of surprise to Chris, "Funny…I was thinking pretty much the opposite."

Art smiled. "I'll admit it presents a few challenges."

"Said the Spartans at Thermopylae," Chris said.

"I'd wager they had better odds," Daniel said.

"This is good news for us, my boy," Art said raising his mug in salute.

"How do you figure? We're talking about a man who might be President next year. You know what he's capable of," Daniel said, stealing a glance at Chris.

"I do, but now at least we know. The toughest part of an investigation is determining the 'who'. Now we just need the evidence."

"Oh...is that all?" Daniel said.

"I'm not saying we aren't in danger. We know who our enemy is, and that's a good thing isn't it?"

Daniel shrugged his shoulders. "It takes a lot more to defeat an enemy than just knowing his name."

"Why don't you just go to the press?" Chris said.

"No, they'll bury the story. Besides, we don't have any evidence." Art said with a wave of his hand.

"What about the surveillance video?" Daniel asked.

"If we tell Sheriff Westin we know about the tape he'll know it was Sarah that told us. You know what that means."

"You'll offer her a job?"

Art let out a deep belly laugh, "Nothing would make me happier Daniel, but not under those circumstances. If she gets fired or prosecuted it would mean the end of her career."

"Can we go around Westin...maybe through Manny?"

"Same problem I'm afraid; we'll just have to pretend it doesn't exist for now," Art said.

"What if Barclay finds out about it?"

Art hadn't considered the possibility until just then. "Good point." He ran his thumb back and forth over the rim of his mug as he contemplated the threat.

"I may have an answer to that. I'll make a call once the sun comes up in Denver."

"Let's hope it's not too late already," Daniel said.

"What else is on our agenda today?" Art asked.

"My vote is to sit tight and rest up. No one knows where we are and until Herb deciphers more of the journal we have nowhere to go. I could use the time to do some op planning and set some things in place for contingencies."

"In other words we're hiding?" Art said.

"We're regrouping," Daniel corrected him.

"I see." Art said rolling his eyes.

"Chris's gonna make us breakfast, we can head into town and get some clothes, shower, whatever."

"And then what?" Art asked.

"Then we wait."

***

The windows of the glossy, black limousine reflected off the cloudless, blue sky as it pulled in front of the Governor's Mansion and came to a stop. Watching the arrival from the second story window, Hammond turned to get the Governor and saw the First Lady standing in the doorway. Barclay's wife, Gloria was twirling a plastic stir stick in her third gin and tonic of the day. At fifty six, she had the looks of a woman half her age. She came from old plantation money in South Carolina and met the Governor while the two attended Yale Law School. She stretched her arm across the door as Hammond tried to pass.

He stopped abruptly in his tracks and looked into her pale blue eyes.

"Mrs. Barclay...can I help you with something?"

Her eyes dropped across his broad chest followed by the gentle caress of her finger.

"Actually, that is something I've wanted to discuss with you Wesley," she said in her trademark southern drawl.

Hammond sighed as he gently swept her hand out of his path. It was the third such advance in recent weeks and sooner or later the Governor was bound to find out.

"Off to find my husband a new whore then?"

The comment struck Hammond like a hammer blow. He turned to look at her over his shoulder.

"Oh darling...of course I knew of little Elizabeth. Such a lovely young woman, smart too, I hear. I hope she rots in hell," Gloria said as she downed the gin. She circled Hammond dragging her finger across his shoulders and chest until she was facing him.

"Aaron and I have a very…*special* relationship. I let him have his whores so he'll leave me alone. But, I am a woman with needs and you are a man. Since we're both here…under the same roof, I think we should get to know each other better." she said as she poked his chest.

"Mrs. Barclay…"

"Oh Wesley, don't be such a boy scout. I'm not looking for a husband. I have every intention of occupying the White House with that wretch. But, that is a business arrangement and what I'm talking about is purely personal."

Just as the corner of his lips began to curl, Hammond heard his boss call out behind him in the hallway.

"*Gloria*, if you're finished harassing my head of security, we need to get going."

Hammond felt his stomach implode as Gloria swatted a dismissive hand towards her husband.

Barclay made his way down the elegant staircase and past the pillars in the grand hallway as Hammond caught up to him.

"Sir, let me assure you…"

Barclay cut him off, "Gloria is a beautiful woman. She's also a manipulative bitch that usually gets what she wants." He stopped at the threshold of the door and faced Hammond. "But, she's *my* manipulative bitch. Do we understand each other?"

"Absolutely, sir."

Hammond led Barclay outside and held open the rear door to their SUV. The first few minutes of the ride were passed in an uncomfortable silence. Hammond watched as Barclay poured a scotch and raised the driver's partition as the driver turned north onto Interstate twenty-five. Barclay took a sip and turned to look out the window as he spoke. "I trust everything went well last night?"

"We delivered the message but we can't gauge the effect until he calls her."

"And the other matter?"

"I've made arrangements to get access to the evidence room tonight."

"How did you ever get them to let you in?"

"Simple…I lied. I told them we wanted to tour the facility and review the security protocols for a possible joint storage venture with the department of corrections. I implied if the proposal went through it would mean a lot of money for the agency, and we would share personnel costs."

"That's it?"

"They ate it up. On the tour I'll excuse myself for a phone call, find the case evidence box, and place the device to wipe the hard drive."

"And when they find out the drive has been wiped?" Barclay asked.

"By then it won't matter. Nothing connects you to the device. They'll be too worried about covering their own asses to point the finger of blame at anyone."

28

Sarah watched the rain drizzle and dance across her window as she waited for Jenny to arrive. Like most Colorado storms it had arrived without notice and would be gone within the hour. Ranger hadn't left her side all day except briefly to go outside.

Against her wishes, Sergeant Marshall had given her the rest of the week off and now she struggled with what to do with her unexpected vacation time. She spent an hour scrubbing the snake blood from her floors and had Ranger checked by a local veterinarian for signs of injuries. Thankfully he was all right. Sarah was comfortable with the idea of protecting herself, but it was nice to know she had backup.

It was six-thirty and Jenny was predictably late in arriving. When Sarah's cell rang she expected to see her friend's name on the caller ID. Instead, she saw the four-ten area code.

"Hello?"

"Hey babe, it's me."

"Daniel! Thank God you called."

"Is everything all right?"

"Where are you? You sound like you're at a football game."

"We're in a food court at the mall," he said. "What's going on?"

Sarah told him about the previous night's events; how Ranger saved her from the snake and the ominous note.

"Of course, it would have been nice if they mentioned which case they wanted me to back off of," Sarah said with a trace of sarcasm.

"Are you safe? Maybe you shouldn't stay there tonight," he said.

"I'm not letting them scare me out of my house. Plus, I have my new boyfriend to keep me safe," she said stroking her hand through Ranger's coat as he lay beside her.

"Boyfriend? *What?* Oh, you mean Ranger. I just think you might be safer at your folk's house, or maybe Art's apartment."

"I'd rather face another snake attack than a night of talking etiquette and my biological clock with my mother thank you."

"You don't really mean that."

"Mmm...maybe just a little," she said laughing.

"All I'm saying is that it wouldn't hurt to have some people around you for a few days," Daniel said.

"Jenny should be here any minute."

"Is she staying the night?"

"Why, does that turn you on?"

Daniel was silent and realizing she may have made him uncomfortable, Sarah didn't give him an opportunity to answer.

"Sorry, trying to inject a little humor," she said.

"It's just a mental picture I didn't expect," Daniel said.

Sarah suddenly felt the urge to change the subject.

"How is the investigation going?"

"Slow. We should be getting an update soon, but honestly, I have no idea what's around the corner."

"Welcome to the world of criminal investigations," Sarah said. "Are you safe at least?"

"Safe was never my area of operations, but yeah, we're safe."

"Good."

"Listen, I don't think you should say anything to Jenny," Daniel said.

"She's my friend, I trust her Daniel."

"It's not about trust; it's about keeping a lid on this thing until we get the evidence we need. Every person that knows something is a potential leak and leaks...wait," he said and was silent for a moment. "Are you sure you didn't tell anyone about the surveillance video?"

"Yes, I'm sure. Why?"

"You didn't even allude to it with someone, someone like Jenny?"

"No, I mean, I told her I had something important to talk to her about."

"You were going to tell her...even after we agreed to keep it quiet, weren't you Sarah?"

"I have to talk to *somebody* about this Daniel. I'm all alone out here and I can't call *you.*"

"Listen, I know it's hard to keep secrets but think of the consequences. You could get fired or prosecuted. Think of your career and all the criminals you won't be in a position to catch down the road?"

"And what about the criminal I know about?"

"Look, the video isn't going anywhere. Sooner or later they have to examine it and someone will connect the dots. Seaton has a very unique name," Daniel said.

He was right, of course. Once the video was examined it would be impossible for anyone to ignore the information about Seaton. Plus, she reminded herself, the defense attorneys would get a copy in discovery and surely they would blow the whistle.

"I guess you're right," she said.

"You know I am," Daniel said.

"Oh hey, that reminds me. Can you do me a favor?" Daniel said.

"Sure, anything."

"Can you get my go bag from Art's place and keep it at your house?"

"I guess so. Do you need something particular?"

"No, Art just reminded me that some workers will be in there and...you know..."

"You don't want people going through your stuff."

"Yeah. Also, there is a black day pack above it. Can you get that too?"

"Any rocket launchers or mortar tubes you need me to pick up while I'm there?"

"Funny. No, that'll do. Just keep them close for a few days."

Sarah heard the unmistakable sounds of a car engine in her driveway. "Okay, listen Jenny just pulled in. Will you call me tomorrow?"

"You know it, but can you make sure you get those bags tonight? The workers are coming first thing in the morning."

"Sure, Jenny and I can make it a field trip."

"About Jenny?"

"All right...I won't say anything."

"Good. I know it's tough, just hold out a little longer okay?"

"Okay, I love you. Gotta run."

"You too, and stay safe."

Sarah rushed to the door to meet Jenny, and hold Ranger back from 'staring' at her.

29

Daniel was relieved to see no signs of a tail or surveillance as Chris drove the trio past his house twice before entering the garage. Daniel flicked on the light to the kitchen and held out one of the new pre-paid cell phones from the mall.

"Here Art, can you call Manny before Paul and Herb? I'd like to get some security at Sarah's place as soon as possible."

"Sure, Daniel. I understand." Art took the phone and set it on the table. "I'm going to brew some coffee...you boys want any?"

They both nodded and Daniel leaned over to Chris.

"Do you still operate a ham radio?"

Chris offered a quizzical look as he nodded and asked, "Yeah, why?"

"I need to make a private call."

"I thought that's what the pre-paid cells were for?"

"They work great for civilians, but the guy I need to call will certainly have his phone line monitored. I don't know his cell. It's been a few years since we last spoke."

"Military?"

"Signal squadron, third battalion, tenth special forces group."

"I should have known he was a Colorado boy. Do you have his radio call sign?"

Daniel wrote it on a slip of paper from memory and checked his watch.

"If he keeps to his routine, he'll be monitoring for a few more hours."

"Something you two worked up while deployed?"

"He's kind of a life line for a few guys on the team and other elements in special forces. Just in case we got compromised overseas and needed to dial nine-one-one," he said smiling.

"Never hurts to have a back-up plan for the back-up plan?"

"Isn't that how I came to save your ass?" Daniel said as he patted his friend on the shoulder.

After turning on the coffee machine, Chris led Daniel up to the attic. Closing the door he fired up his radio, tuned to the correct frequency, and called out into the darkness of space. On the third try, he got a response.

"Do we know each other?" came a voice on the other end.

Daniel snatched the transmitter from Chris's hand and depressed the call button.

"BJ, this is Blackbird."

"*Blackbird?* Good to hear your voice. I heard you lost your backstage pass."

"Yanked by security, but I'm still crashing concerts. Listen, I need a favor and I need it quick."

"Name it."

"I have a snow white that needs a moat built and the drawbridge raised."

"Heavy or light?"

"Light. CI only. Make it a blue light special if you can," Daniel said.

"Where's the castle?"

"Standby..." Daniel held the transmitter to the table and tapped out Sarah's address in Morse Code with a pen.

"Copy that. How will I know snow white?"

Chris couldn't help but interrupt, "Look for the smoking hot redhead."

Daniel chuckled and said, "Got that?"

"Copy, Wilco first thing after reveille."

"I owe you one," Daniel said.

"You owe me a case of beer and a sit-rep on your life. I miss hearing from you, Blackbird."

"Same here. Talk soon."

Daniel handed the transmitter back to Chris and let out a sigh of relief.

"I followed most of that, but what the hell is a CI?" Chris asked.

"Oh, civilian intrusion. Basically it's a less-lethal intrusion alarm. I can't have him setting claymores in her backyard, now can I?"

"If only..." Chris said holding out his fist which Daniel bumped.

"Let's go check on Art." Daniel said.

Jenny rubbed Ranger's ears after a warm reception at the door.

"Oh, he's so sweet Sarah."

Sweet? Sarah thought, hardly. "Yeah...he's great."

"So what's this big secret you have to get off your chest?" Jenny said cutting to the chase. Jenny was nothing if not direct. She was the same way with men.

"Do you mind if we take a quick trip to Art's place? We can talk along the way."

"Whatever floats your boat, but let's grab something to eat first. I'm starving." Jenny said.

"Great, just let me grab a few things." Sarah said as she ran back to her room. She could hear Jenny walking around the living room.

"You two sure make a cute couple," she called out.

"Thanks, it isn't easy with him so far away but we're managing."

"You know Sarah, most of the cops with a military background have a lot of tattoos. Daniel doesn't seem to have any."

Sarah came back into the room and spied Jenny holding a photo of a bare-chested Daniel she kept on the hutch.

"He was just a mechanic. He never really got into all the soldiering stuff," Sarah lied.

"Right...mechanic," Jenny said.

"Actually, he does have one tattoo," Sarah said.

"Really...where?" Jenny said.

"On his butt cheek," Sarah said giggling.

"His butt cheek! What is it?"

"It's nothing, really."

"Oh no, you can't leave me hanging...cough up the details," Jenny said.

"He has..." Sarah hesitated before continuing, "A little pair of green feet."

Jenny was unable to contain her laughter. "Green feet...what the *hell?* I figured it was a dagger, or missile, or screaming eagle, you know, something cool."

"I'll admit I was surprised, too. But, I've gotten used to them." She gave Jenny a wink as her lips curled into a smile.

"So tell me about the first time you saw it." Jenny poked Sarah's shoulder with her finger.

"Oh no, I've said too much already."

"I'm going to find out eventually," Jenny said.

Not if I can help it, Sarah thought, remembering her vow to keep Daniel's past a secret from her friends and family.

"Over my dead body."

"Don't tempt me!" Jenny said playfully punching her in the arm.

Sarah checked her Glock, slid it into her Crossbreed holster on her waist, and fluffed her shirt to conceal it.

"C'mon, we can chat in the truck," Sarah said as she called for Ranger to follow.

They spent an hour catching up on recent events in their lives over fast food. Mostly they talked about Jenny and recent crimes she had responded to. Sarah didn't want to talk about recent events in a public place. After dinner, they climbed back into Sarah's big Ford truck and offered Ranger a few French fries.

Firing the big diesel engine to life, Sarah pulled out onto the dark street and eased the accelerator forward on their way to Art's town home a few miles away.

"Okay, you got me alone now Sarah, what's up?"

Sarah had thought long and hard about what she was going to tell Jenny. Jenny was masterful at spotting a lie and Sarah was terrible at telling them, but she had the perfect mix of truth and fiction.

"I'm worried about Daniel," she said.

"What about him?"

"I guess I'm worried about the relationship…being long distance and all. It really puts a strain on things and I'm worried he might find someone else up there."

Jenny studied her friend for a full three seconds before answering, "Bullshit."

"What?"

"You heard me."

"Well, thanks for the support."

"You're lying to me, Sarah."

"I *am* worried about him," Sarah said.

"Of course you are, but not because you think he'll leave you. Even I can come up with something better than that."

"Jenny!"

"Oh don't bother," Jenny said swiping at the air. "I know you better than you know yourself. I can always tell when you're lying to me."

Sarah pursed her lips and cursed under her breath. "How?"

"It's *obvious*. First, guys fall all over you. Shit, even officers at my department talk about you!"

"Really?" Sarah asked.

"Plus, I've seen you two together. More importantly, I've watched *him*. You remember a couple months back when we all went bar hopping in LoDo? Girls were giving him the slut eye all night long and he never looked at one of them. Even when you were in the bathroom." she said poking her arm. "He's totally into you girl. You add to that Ranger, the new shotgun, our little jaunt to get his go bag. C'mon Sarah even a blind man could see the clues. Daniel is in love with you."

"You saw the shotgun?"

"Kinda hard to miss. Now…spill it."

Sarah hated how easy others could read her. It was one reason she knew she could never work undercover. She convinced herself she could tell Jenny a *little bit* of the truth. She knew Daniel was in love with her, he would understand.

She spent the rest of the ride giving Jenny the Cliff Note version of the events from the murder at the Consistory to the rattlesnake Ranger had killed the previous night. She left out only the part about Governor Barclay.

"*Holy fucking shit*…what is it with you?"

"Me?" Sarah asked. "Why is any of this my fault?"

"I thought your luck hit rock bottom last year with that serial killer, but now…"

"I know…it's like a curse or something."

"I never get cases like this," Jenny said.

"Look, you can't tell *anyone*. I promised Daniel I wouldn't say anything okay?"

"Awwww, I think it's cute the way he underestimates you."

"Jenny! That's not nice."

"I'm just sayin'…you can handle yourself."

Sarah's eyes narrowed as they pulled up to the town house and put the truck in park. She glanced over at Jenny.

"What is it?" Jenny said, seeing her concern.

"That light there. I've never known it to be on a timer."

"Maybe Art forgot to turn it off."

"Art? Not likely."

"Let's check it out," Jenny said.

Sarah unbuckled her seat belt, slipped from the truck, and made her way to the front door. Jenny followed as Ranger sped past both of them and made it to the door first. Sarah inserted the key and turned it slowly until she heard a click. With Jenny on one side of the doorway and her on the other, Sarah swung the door open and froze as she carefully peeked inside.

Ranger let out a low growl as the three took in the ransacked room. Jenny drew her Sig Sauer pistol a half second before Sarah drew her Glock.

"Go," Sarah said to Ranger as he darted through the room and down the darkened hallway.

"Maybe we should call the cops," Sarah whispered.

Jenny held up her thumb and pinky finger to her ear like a phone, "I'm here."

Before Sarah could respond, Jenny was through the door sweeping left while Sarah moved right. Jenny took the lead and lit the hallway with six hundred lumens from her tactical light. Room by room, they searched the house until they got to the back door and saw Ranger looking out the open sliding glass door. The vertical blinds were swaying back and forth from the breeze.

Jenny switched on the porch light and surveyed the small fenced yard before closing and locking the door, and drawing the blinds.

"I'd say we just missed them. Do you smell the aftershave?" Jenny said.

Sarah sniffed the air and caught the faint odor.

"Good nose," Sarah said.

"Yeah, well…it's a popular brand with the losers in my life."

Sarah peeked out the window. "Do you think we scared them off?"

"Hard to miss the sound of your tank pulling into the drive," Jenny said.

"We're lucky they didn't want a fight," Sarah said.

"I'd say *they're* the lucky ones," Jenny said as she holstered her pistol. "You sure know how to show a girl a good time."

Sarah didn't answer. Gun in hand, she surveyed the damage.

"This wasn't a burglary."

"Art needs to get a new maid then," Jenny said.

"Look around, nothing of value was taken. They were searching for something," Sarah said.

Jenny followed as Sarah made her way upstairs and entered one of the bedrooms.

"Since when does Art have a grandkid?" Jenny said as she looked around the nursery. The room contained a crib, rocking chair, and changing station with noticeable child safety locks holding the doors closed. One wall was adorned with a six foot graphic of Noah's Arc while the ceiling was plastered with glow in the dark star decals.

"He doesn't, this is Daniel's idea of concealment."

"Come again?"

Sarah walked over to the changing station and rolled it away from the wall. Removing the back panel, she pulled his go bag and black day pack from the shelves inside.

"Crooks never search a baby's room," Sarah said.

"I never thought of that. Maybe I should put a nursery in my place," Jenny said.

"Yeah, I thought about it too until I realized my mother's reaction."

"Good point," Jenny said.

30

Art hung up the phone and laid the pen from his aching hand upon three pages of scribbled notes as Daniel's eyes begged for an update.

"So...what do we know?"

Art rubbed his eyes before picking up the first page.

"I'm more confused than ever," Art said.

"What did Herb say?" Daniel asked.

"Seaton is pretty clever. He used a rotating cipher that correlated to the day of the week he was making the entry; seven in all. It's why Herb had such a hard time deciphering it."

"He has it figured out now?" Daniel said.

"It looks that way. He's about two-thirds through the journal and he's found something interesting. Seaton has been on this case for months. He's tracked down obscure letters and documents from Masonic libraries and museums all along the eastern seaboard. One thing of note is that King George issued an arrest warrant for Charles DeFrance in November of seventeen eighty."

"An arrest warrant for what?" Daniel asked.

"Treason, which is odd because the same could be said of all soldiers in the Colonial Army."

"King George singled out an ensign in a state militia?" Daniel asked.

"That's right. Unfortunately, there isn't any indication so far in the journal of why he was singled out."

"What else?"

"There are a lot of scattered references to names and places but no real detail of why they are included. Herb isn't sure how each one is connected, but he's working on cross referencing the information with other sources. But one name stood out among the others. There is a reference to a Hawkins Boone DeFrance in the late eighteen hundreds."

"A descendant of Charles perhaps?"

"He must be. His name comes up in a letter from a wealthy sea merchant who played a big role in financing the Confederacy during the Civil War but according to Herb he is also known to have aided the underground railroad to free the slaves."

"That seems contradictory," Daniel said.

"Wouldn't be the first time a man said one thing in public and did another in private," Art said.

"Do we know what the letter said?"

"The letter was to the merchant's brother, a Mason in the north, but Seaton didn't transcribe it in the journal. The only notations mention some kind of 'grand plan' for cessation, and Daniel, are you sitting down? The notation includes the name Augustus Barclay."

"*Fuck me...*" Daniel said as he leaned back and interlaced his fingers behind his head.

Art arched his eyebrows and nodded slightly. "Herb obviously keyed in on Barclay and did a little background check. Amazingly, he has almost no historical footprint despite being one of the wealthiest men in Virginia. His circle of friends indicates he was on the side of the Confederacy but Herb has found very little of value on him. In any event, Seaton regarded his name with importance because it is circled and underlined numerous times in the journal. Herb said it was the only name in the journal highlighted like that so it may have been a pivotal discovery."

"None of this makes sense," Daniel said.

"It made sense to Seaton. We need to figure out what he saw in all of this."

"Whatever it was, he paid for it with his life. Which reminds me, have you called Sheriff Westin about placing a guard at Sarah's?"

"That was going to be my next call." Art said.

"If possible, see if one of these guys can do it," Daniel said handing Art a folded piece of paper containing six names.

"Former military?"

"Rangers mostly," Daniel said.

"You really expect them to try again?" Art asked.

"Considering what you just told me?"

"You're right," Art said. "I should have done this sooner. Come to think of it...I need some guys to cover Tilly too." He punched the sheriff's number into his phone with lightning speed.

Hammond and his associate did their best to look interested as they were led inside the property evidence warehouse by the exhausted female technician. It took thirty minutes to reach the homicide section of the warehouse. All along the way, the technician rattled off facts in the drone voice of someone who had given the same tour a thousand times before.

Hammond spotted a familiar set of clothes in a large glass cabinet against the wall.

"What is that?" Hammond asked the heavy-eyed technician.

"Those are drying cabinets. They allow us to dry evidence before final packaging. Those clothes are from a double homicide out in the east part of the county," she said.

Hammond made an exaggerated expression of surprise as he fished his phone from his pocket and held it up.

"Oh, this is the Governor calling. Can you give me some privacy please?" Hammond said to the young technician.

She hesitated for a moment. Her eyes dropped to the floor and she pursed her lips. Hammond could see that she was not going to leave him alone without a little encouragement. He pretended to answer the call.

"Yes Governor, can you hold on for one second please? I need to clear the room," he announced before cupping his hand over the mouthpiece.

"Young lady, do you really want me to tell the Governor to wait any longer?"

He could see the wheels turning in her mind.

"I *promise* not to open any of the evidence," he added with extreme sarcasm.

That last comment seemed to strike a chord with her as she slowly nodded her head and looked at Hammond's associate.

"Perhaps you could show me where you store the drugs and other contraband we will be sending you?" the associate said extending an arm.

"I'll catch up in a few minutes," Hammond said as the young technician turned and lead the other man out of the room.

Hammond placed the phone in his pocket and checked his watch. He would need at least four minutes to complete the scrubbing of the hard drive. He jogged over to the drying cabinet and read the label on the evidence tag indicating the case number and storage shelf location for the case evidence.

Scanning the shelves, it took less than thirty seconds to find the evidence he was looking for. He found the computer hard drive packaged in a large paper bag. With one last look over his shoulder, Hammond pulled the scrubbing device from his jacket. The palm-sized device was glossy black with no markings. It had a single button on the side as well as one red and one green LED light on the face.

He pressed the button and held it down as he slapped it against the computer tower through the paper bag. A faint whirling sound hummed from the small device and Hammond felt a slight vibration in his hand. He held it firmly against the side of the computer tower until the red light changed to green.

He froze as an unfamiliar voice shattered the silence of the cavernous room.

31

"Is someone in here?" a female voice called.

Hammond stashed the scrubber in his jacket and peeked through the evidence bags to the doorway across the room. There stood another young woman in the same property evidence uniform.

He snatched his phone from his pocket as she began walking towards the evidence shelves and launched into a one-sided conversation with his phone.

"Excuse me, what are you doing back here?" the woman asked as she came face to face with him. Hammond held out a finger to the woman as he pretended to strain and listen to the fake caller.

"Sir, you are not supposed to be here." the woman said.

"Let me call you back, Governor," he said as he ended the fake call and set a withering gaze upon the twenty-something woman standing before him.

"Just what in the hell do you think you are doing? I had to cut off a call with the Governor of all people. I thought I had explained to your colleague I needed privacy for that call!" he barked.

"Who are you?" she said as a look of confusion washed over her face.

"Who am I? Are you completely inept? I am here on official orders from the Governor's Office. Didn't anyone tell you about our inspection?" Hammond said.

"I...um... No, sir," she said biting her lower lip and avoiding his gaze.

Hammond let out a deep sigh and placed a gentle hand on her shoulder.

"Listen..." he raised his eyebrows.

"Karen," she said.

"Okay, Karen. Look, I understand that maybe you weren't privy to all the details of our inspection. I suppose there is no need for me to tell the Sheriff about this. I'd hate to see you punished for an honest mistake."

She looked up at him with puppy dog eyes that began to well up with tears.

"Th…thank you," she muttered.

"It will be our little secret," he said.

Hammond couldn't contain his devilish smile as he watched her nod and stare at the floor in total submission.

"Why don't you take me to find the others, and we'll forget this ever happened."

***

Art slammed the phone down on the kitchen table.

"That went well, huh?" Daniel said as he sat across the table.

Art rubbed his eyes and massaged the bridge of his nose with two fingers.

"Manny already requested a guard at Sarah's house but the Sheriff says there's no money in the budget."

"That's bullshit," Daniel said. "Doesn't he remember what happened last time some psycho targeted her?"

"Oh, I'm sure he doesn't need reminding. This is pure office politics. I could hear Bart Manilow in the background feeding him talking points."

"He's had it in for her since she started working there," Daniel said.

"He has it in for any woman who challenges him."

"So what are we going to do about it?"

Art had already asked himself the same question. Once it was clear that sheriff Westin wouldn't help, he made up his mind.

"Do you know any former Rangers with the Littleton police department, Daniel?"

"You don't want to use the sheriff's guys?"

"No. If Westin finds out one of his deputies went off the reservation, he'll go ballistic."

"I'll make the call," Daniel said as he fished a phone from his pocket.

"Good, I'll call Paul. Herb mentioned a DeFrance in the eighteen hundreds. Maybe Paul has found something."

Art checked his watch and dialed Paul's home phone. After exchanging brief pleasantries with Paul's wife, she got Paul on the phone.

"Art, I was beginning to wonder if I'd hear from you today."

"It's been quite a day."

"You're telling me. I think I may have something of interest for you on Judge DeFrance."

"Really? What do you have?"

"My staff combed through the newspaper archives for any mention of his name. In an article dated May eighteenth, eighteen seventy-six Judge Alison DeFrance was hailed for donating a substantial amount of money to the Masonic widows and orphans' fund. Apparently, the donation was in response to the disappearance of his chief aide, Martin Handler. The newspaper article suggested the aide was probably killed by renegade Indians in retribution for the Sand Creek massacre."

"Interesting." Art said.

"There's more… I had my staff search the court archives surrounding that date and found a notation in the record wherein Judge DeFrance allocated monies for his aide to travel to Brigg's Ranch on a matter described as being 'of great importance' to the court. The aide was never heard from again. Now, believe it or not, I got in touch with the great-great granddaughter of Judge DeFrance. She lives in Leadville.

"She was familiar with the story of the missing aide. According to her grandfather, Judge DeFrance sent his aide to meet a cousin who was coming out from Williamsburg, Kentucky. Her grandfather said Alison was very distraught over the disappearance and never seemed the same afterward."

"Did the cousin ever meet the aide?"

"The cousin was never heard from again either," Paul said.

"Any idea why the cousin came out to Colorado?"

"No, but she did mention something about exchanging a key."

"A key to what?"

"She didn't know but her Alison once told her it was spiral shaped. She remembered it was something she'd never heard of before…a spiral shaped key," Paul said.

Bloodlines

Art's mind flashed back to the image drawn in Seaton's journal and the corkscrew shaped image bearing a snake's head.

"I think you may have something, Paul. Do you have any idea where Brigg's Ranch is?"

"Not a clue."

"Okay," Art thought for a moment. "I'm going to send you some help tomorrow." Art said.

"Who?"

"Do you remember Sarah Richards?"

32

August 9th; Denver, Colorado

This was only the second time Hammond had been called
here for a meeting. The Governor conducted state business from
his official office in the mansion, but he was prohibited from
conducting campaign business from behind that desk. Unofficial
business was done from the luxury of his private office. It was a
space that only the most wealthy and well-connected allies had
seen.

Hammond was sure this would be a dressing down about
the first lady. He stood before the red velvet lined mahogany
case waiting for Governor Barclay to end his phone call. Two
dozen antique and modern handguns hung from the cabinet wall
bathed in the warm sunlight. Hammond had never seen the
Governor fire a weapon and wondered if the display was meant
to placate certain donors.

Ever since the episode with the First Lady, Hammond
detected a hint of animosity from his boss. There had been no
specific exchange of words, but his gut told him he was treading
in dark territory. Perhaps the Governor suspected an affair was
already underway.

The thought was ridiculous given his constant presence with
the Governor, but jealousy was not rational.

Hammond heard Barclay end the call and turned to see him
crossing the room towards him.

"Have a seat, Wes," Barclay said pointing towards a high
back red leather chair. "Would you like a drink?"

Hammond looked uncomfortably towards the crystal
decanter sitting on the table next to him. He knew that the amber
alcohol inside cost more than his months' salary.

"No, thank you, Governor."

"You're declining my hospitality?" Barclay said with
unwavering eyes. For a moment Hammond wondered if it was
poisoned but he pushed the thought away. He dutifully poured
two fingers into a tumbler and took a sip.

Barclay waited for him to rest the glass upon the table before turning to the guns in the cabinet.

"A wonderful collection, don't you think?"

Hammond could see Barclay staring at him in the reflection of the glass.

"Yes sir, very impressive."

"Guns have been a source of power and control for centuries, Wes. My great grandfather carried this one during the Indian wars."

"Is that right?" Hammond asked.

Barclay opened the cabinet door and fingered a Lugar pistol emblazoned with gold highlights and a black swastika on a red background. He snatched it from the wall and held it up in profile for Hammond to see it closer.

"This German Lugar was presented to my father by a two-star general following the war. To me, it symbolizes the failed ideology of a madman."

Hammond nodded slowly, choosing to keep quiet.

"You see Wes, leading a world superpower is every man's dream. The control, the power, it's...intoxicating." Barclay said it in a professorial tone.

"But, attaining such power takes sacrifice. Past generations relied almost exclusively on the power of guns." Barclay placed the Lugar back on its peg. "But guns are merely a tool. Real power comes from the control of information. Information can change governments; it can change the will of the people. Any cretin can shoot a gun, but only those who control the information will rule the next millennium."

Hammond felt a bead of sweat race down his forehead as he tried to understand the meaning behind the lecture.

"Everything went well last night?"

"Yes sir, you have nothing to worry about."

Barclay paused and stared at Hammond for several seconds. They were the longest and most uncomfortable seconds Hammond had ever endured with his employer. He broke eye contact to take another sip.

"We've seen our share of bumps in the road in this campaign, haven't we?" he said, placing a hand on Hammond's shoulder.

"Yes, sir."

Tom Adair

"I'm not oblivious to the bullet we've dodged Wes, or my role in the events. Elizabeth was a...*distraction*, and I appreciate your efforts to put that embarrassment behind us."

"Like you said, I'm paid to protect you Sir."

"Yes, you are, and paid handsomely."

"Yes, sir."

"Wes, I was destined to lead our nation into a new era. It is my birthright. But, there will be those who will resist these changes. I need assurances from you that you're as committed to our success as I am."

Hammond wasn't sure how much more he could do to demonstrate his loyalty. In the last few days he had killed two people, threatened a cop, and destroyed evidence in a murder case.

"Sir, you have my complete loyalty."

"Good...I'm glad to hear that." Barclay said as he lifted the decanter and poured himself a glass. He held it up to Hammond and the two clinked tumblers in a toast before adding, "Because, you and I are in this together..."

***

Sarah struggled to open her eyes as she shifted her head on the pillow. The room was still barely lit by the pre-dawn sky and for a moment she didn't know where she was.

Then she heard it; a faint buzzing sound.

In an instant Sarah's mind flashed to images of the rattlesnake and she sprang up in bed to swipe her Glock from the nightstand. Her eyes darted back and forth across the room, straining to see the source of the buzzing sound.

Then she saw Ranger.

Laying on his left side, Ranger lifted his head for a moment, glanced at her, and dropped it back on the floor.

Shouldn't you be barking? The buzzing stopped and she focused her gun on the bedroom doorway.

Slowly, she peeked over the side of the bed as if she'd find a sea of snakes writhing on the floor. Her shoes were there on the floor next to the bed, but she felt a genuine fear of reaching for them. Her senses were supercharged which made the silence even more disturbing.

Then the buzzing returned.

192

Bloodlines

Sarah edged to the end of the bed. Taking a breath, she leapt as far as she could and spun back towards the bed when she landed. Ranger didn't move a muscle. Sarah looked at the darkness under the bed and flashed back to her childhood. *What are you— six years old?*

Her head snapped left as she listened for the buzzing again. She leaned against the open door and looked back at Ranger. He wasn't coming. *What was wrong with him?*

Walking on her toes, she crept through the doorway towards the buzzing noise. It took a few seconds before her eyes settled on Daniel's go bag next to the couch.

It was at that moment she recognized the sound of the ring tone. Daniel had once told her it was the sound of a mini-gun firing.

Sarah set her Glock on the armrest and unzipped the side pocket. She held up the phone and hit the send button.

"Daniel?" she asked.

He answered on the first ring. "Hey, you got the bag."

Yeah, I just about shot it, but I got it.

"Wait a second," Sarah shook her head. "Why are you calling me on this phone?"

"I couldn't say anything before, but I think your cell is bugged."

"Bugged? Are you serious?"

"Yeah. I'm sorry, Sarah. This is a safe phone."

Sarah felt a sudden shudder at the invasion of her privacy.

"How could they get a warrant to tap my phone?"

"I don't think it's the cops doing the tapping?"

Jesus.

"So, I can't use it at all?" she asked.

"No, don't change a thing. Just be careful what information you're sharing over your phone. If these guys realize you know about the bug, we lose our advantage."

"How is *this* an advantage? They're listening in on my private calls, Daniel."

"I know, just try to ignore it for a while."

"Why can't I just use this one?"

"This one is just for us, okay? I don't know who else they might have tapped."

193

Sarah bit her lip but went along. What else could she do? "I assume you have some kind of plan?"

"I'm working on it, but there are a couple things I need to talk to you about."

Sarah sat down on the floor and crossed her legs. "Fire at will," she said.

"First, a friend of mine will be stopping by this morning to install some intrusion devices. Introduce him to Ranger and give him full access to the place."

"Who is this friend?"

"Someone I trust with my life, and yours. His name is BJ," he added.

"When is he coming?"

"A few hours at most."

"Okay, what else?"

"How would you feel about getting back into the investigation?"

"Are you kidding? Of course I want to, but Manilow won't let me anywhere near this case. Plus, I've been given the rest of the week off because of the snake incident."

"That's good timing for us. We were thinking of an unofficial investigation."

Relieved for the first time in days, Sarah's eyes lit up with excitement. "I'm in, what do you want me to do?"

33

Five minutes before eleven Sarah pulled into the parking lot of the Jefferson County judicial complex. nicknamed the Taj Mahal, it was the picture of government excessiveness. The marble floors, walls, and golden elevators seemed out of place in the rural setting of the foothills west of Denver.

Sarah drew her Glock and slipped it into the glove compartment. As a civilian, she'd never make it past the magnetometer—even with her badge. At least she wouldn't have to remove her belt and shoes.

After passing through the designated law enforcement security line, she took the elevator to the fourth floor and found Judge Whittier's clerk pecking away at a computer keyboard.

"Hi, I'm Sarah Richards; Judge Whittier is expecting me."

"Ah yes, come on back," the woman said buzzing Sarah through the security door. The clerk led her down a drab hallway that was in direct contrast with the opulent interiors of the public side of the door.

The clerk rapped three times, paused, then knocked again. Sarah could hear the judge call out from behind the door and the two entered.

"This is Sarah Richards, Your Honor," the clerk said.

Judge Whitter rose from his desk and crossed the room with outstretched hands and a broad smile.

"Sarah, it is a pleasure to meet you young lady; Art speaks very highly of you."

"Thank you, Your Honor," she said gripping his bear-sized hands. His hands were calloused, not at all what she had expected from a judge.

"Please, call me Paul," he said. He nodded to his clerk who pulled the door shut as she left his office.

Sarah glanced at the taxidermy adorning his walls and settled her eyes on a very large bull elk.

"That's a beautiful elk."

"Thank you. It's not as nice as the one in your house, though is it?"

Sarah shot him a puzzled look.

"I must confess to a tiny lie. We have met before, but back then I held you in my arms." Paul said.

"You knew my grandfather."

"Very well, actually."

"I'm sorry, my mother never mentioned you growing up."

"I didn't know your mother. As I said, I met you only once. Your grandfather and I mostly knew each other from lodge."

"I see."

"He was a remarkable man, your grandfather," Paul said.

"That he was, Your Honor."

"Paul," he corrected her.

"I'm sorry; habit."

Sarah watched as Paul returned to his chair and offered one to Sarah as he sat down.

"So are you up to speed on our little project?" he asked.

"A little. Daniel said that a judge here in the eighteen hundreds sent his aide out east to meet a cousin and exchange some kind of key. But he also mentioned that neither man was ever heard from again."

"Basically, yes."

"That's sad. Daniel mentioned that the meeting was at someplace called Brigg's Ranch. Do we know where that is?"

"I think Art was hoping you might know. At that time, much of eastern Colorado was in Arapahoe County."

"Originally, Arapahoe was part of the Kansas territory and the sheriff's office actually pre-dates statehood. I asked some east district deputies who work in that area and none of them have ever heard of it," Sarah said.

"So it must be a historical place."

"I'm sure one of the families out there would recognize the name, but I don't know where to start." Sarah said holding up her hands.

"I'll place a call to the assessor's office and see what we can find out. That brings up another problem however," Paul said.

"How do we find a one hundred and fifty year old crime scene?"

"Exactly; that's where you come in."

"Me? I'm no expert in that. Art's people at the Facility would have the gear and know-how, not me."

"I've already spoken to Tilly and they have a team ready to respond."

"So where do I fit in?"

Paul unrolled a large scale map of Arapahoe County across his desk and placed several large law books on the edges to hold it down.

"Since I understand you have some time on your hands, Art was hoping you could talk to some of the ranchers out east and see if you can pinpoint a search area." Paul said.

"Sure, I can do that. But ranches back then were hundreds, if not thousands, of acres. It will be like looking for a pebble in a riverbed," she said.

"I'll keep my staff combing the archives. Maybe they can come up with something to get you in the ballpark."

Sarah placed both hands on the edges of the map and leaned over it—like a perp would on the back of a squad car. "We're going to need a miracle," she said.

"Lucky for us," Paul said, "Art Von Hollen is in the business of miracles."

34

August 9th; Washington, D.C.

After losing his targets in Pennsylvania, Reaper decided to return to the Gerovit ops center. He'd rather be in Annapolis but without a target address he might as well be in Omaha. He thought it better to review the intel first hand and access some of his personal computer files.

Reaper finished a small cup of Turkish coffee in the Gerovit operations room as he reviewed intelligence reports for the operation. Compared to his normal operations, these reports were anorexic. It was obvious that Daniel Von Hollen was an expert at escape and evasion. The reports also made clear that he had a network of resources that were not a part of his normal digital footprint.

Most of the men targeted by the Gerovit team were creatures of habit; easy picking. A few with military training or professional security details made tracking a little more challenging. Look far enough back into a target's past however, and the weak link was usually exposed.

This was not the case with Daniel Von Hollen. Prior to the last eighteen months, his past was a work of fiction dreamed up by one of the most cunning organizations in the world; the United States Army. Nothing the Gerovit found could be relied upon as fact.

Reaper's resource in the Denver Russian mafia was forced to flee the Von Hollen town home when a large pickup truck pulled into the driveway the night before. So far, the information pulled from a few documents revealed nothing that would lead them to their quarry.

The phone intercept between Daniel and Sarah raised few alarms among Reaper's analysts. No one bought the line about the construction workers, and the consensus among Reaper's team was that Daniel wanted her to get his 'go bag' for him for additional technical gear and weapons following the failed attack on her. It had a ring of truth, but Reaper couldn't shake the feeling he was being played.

"Where is the Richards woman?" Reaper asked the analyst sitting a few feet away.

He pulled up her cell phone location on one of the three computer screens before him.

"She is at the courthouse," he said.

Court, what a waste of time. The Soviets knew how to deal with criminals and it wasn't filing legal motions for months on end.

"What about the secretary?"

The analyst punched in her tracking code.

"Still in her office."

"Phone calls?" Reaper asked.

"Nothing from the targets. Mostly calls from students, faculty, and a few requests for forensic services," he said.

"Anything from..."

"Sir, I have something you need to hear," another analyst said interrupting him.

Reaper spun his chair in the opposite direction and slid across the floor to the workstation.

"What is it?" he asked.

"I have been monitoring Governor Barclay's phones and those of his security detail. A few minutes ago the Governor made a call on a clandestine phone to our banker friend in Zurich."

"What do you mean 'clandestine phone?'"

"Barclay purchased and activated phones in the names of his children months ago. We installed software on them to alert us when they are activated. Until today, he had used only one to call the prostitute. He hasn't used that phone since her death. This phone was activated today," he said pointing towards the number on the computer screen.

"What did he want?"

"He asked about opening a new contract and allocated two hundred and fifty thousand dollars. He did not say who the contract was for, he just asked about the possibility of finding someone reliable to do the hit."

"Curious," Reaper said as he read over the transcript.

"Sir, I thought we had an exclusive contract for such jobs," the analyst said.

"Apparently," Reaper said, "we have some competition."

"Do you think he is unhappy with our search for the Von Hollens?"

"Undoubtedly, but no one outside of government has our resources."

"Perhaps he merely wants additional eyes in the field," the analyst said.

Reaper considered that for a moment but it didn't add up. The idea of adding more searchers looked good on paper but in reality was more complicated. Uncoordinated teams often covered the same ground and followed the same leads. This was a counterproductive measure and increased the chances the target would detect them.

No, this was something else.

"Keep an eye on it and report to me the minute he names a target, or picks a contractor," Reaper said.

***

As Daniel discussed with Art their plan, Chris packed food for them. Daniel began stowing clothes and their meager personal items into two back packs. Daniel knew Art was relieved to have along a change of clothes.

Finished in the kitchen, Chris set a small stack of printouts on the coffee table near Daniel.

"I found a couple reliable-looking used cars on line. They're all within thirty minutes of here. I can lend you the cash and some travel money for a little while as long as I get it back soon," he said.

"You'll get it back with interest," Art said as he reached to pick up the papers.

"Are you sure you want to go all the way to Kentucky?" Chris asked. "It's over ten hours away by car."

"It's the only lead we have at this point," Art said.

"You're more than welcome to stay for another day or two. Maybe your friend will come up with a better lead by then," Chris said.

"We've stayed too long, Chris." Daniel said.

"Tammy and the girls are gonna be real upset they missed you."

"They're part of the reason we're leaving." Daniel said. "You know the longer we stay, the more we put you and your family at risk. These guys are good, and it only takes one slip in op-sec to bring them to your door."

"Shit, I'm not worried about some mercenary," Chris said.

"I am. These guys aren't your typical mercs."

"In that case, you boys should take along a little insurance." Chris said.

Daniel stopped packing and looked up to see his friend wheeling his chair across the room to a wall mounted gun safe. Chris spun the combination lock back and forth until Daniel heard a click.

"The PX is open for business," Chris said as he turned the handle and swung the heavy steel door open. He grabbed a black rifle from just inside the stack and handed it to Daniel.

"That's the original Springfield SOCOM chambered in seven point six-two," Chris said.

Daniel shouldered the rifle and swung the carbine around the room to check the feel.

"I topped it with a four power scope."

"Well, it ain't a SCAR but it'll do," Daniel said.

"Extra mags are on the shelf in front of you. What else do you need?"

Daniel scanned the shelves for a moment and then said, "How about that Glock thirty-seven for Art and a couple boxes of ammo."

Daniel was just about to shut the door when his eye caught something else.

"I'm taking these radios, too," he said grabbing a pair of civilian walkie talkies.

"Those aren't secure, dude. I just use them for hunting with my girls."

"Just in case." Daniel said as he tucked them into his pack. "Thanks, Chris. I owe you."

An hour later Daniel watched as Art literally kicked the tires on the used car they had found. He could tell from Art's expression that he wasn't impressed.

"It just has to get us there, Art."

Art looked up at him with gloom.

"She ain't pretty, I'll give you that, but trust me...she's perfect." Daniel said, eyeing the hatchback.

Art dropped his shoulders and pulled the folded cash from his pocket. Daniel noticed he hadn't even tried to negotiate as he stripped ten one-hundred dollar bills from the stack and handed them to the elderly man in coveralls.

"Gentlemen, it's been a real pleasure," the old man said as he pocketed the money and handed over the key.

Daniel took the driver's seat and drove it off the front lawn. The car handled poorly but was inconspicuous which is exactly what they needed. Chris helped them load their gear into the hatchback before turning to Art and extending his hand. Art clasped it with both hands.

"Chris, I can't tell you how much I appreciate your hospitality. When this thing is finished, I'm flying you and your family out to Colorado for a very special vacation."

Chris looked taken back by the offer as a smile overcame his face. "Not necessary. I still show a debt on the balance sheet with Daniel here."

"You don't owe me anything, you never did." Daniel said.

"You watch your six, cowboy," Chris said.

Daniel looked Chris straight in the eye and gave him a firm handshake, placing his free hand on his friend's shoulder. "Oo-rah."

***

The past two hours driving had been spent mostly in silence. Daniel's gut churned like it used to when he left the safety of a military base for dangers unknown. Once again they were exposed and a mix of excitement and anxiety battled inside him. Daniel turned south on interstate eighty-one as Art fumbled with the broken window crank handle on his door.

"They don't make 'em like this anymore, do they Art?"

Art shot him a look of contempt as he gave up, tossed the handle onto the floor mat, and adjusted the air vent in front of him.

"I'm surprised they ever made them like this at all?" Art spat.

"Aw, c'mon. What's not to love?"

"Love is fickle," Art said checking his watch. "We have eight hours of driving ahead of us. Do you think she's up to it?" Art said tapping the dashboard.

Bloodlines

Daniel smirked as he inched the fan power up a notch.

"So what's the plan once we get to Williamsburg?" Daniel asked.

Art swallowed hard, "I'm still working on that. Hopefully Herb will have something new for us by then."

"Do we still have family in the region?"

"I'm sure some of my cousins are nearby, but I haven't stayed in touch like Tilly has with her kin."

"When were you there last?" Daniel asked.

"High school," Art said.

"Mom told me once that something made you and Tilly leave; the rest of the family soon after. You want to talk about it?"

"That was almost forty years ago…it's in the past," Art said as he turned away and looked out the window.

"I only mention it because, you know, we're heading back there."

Art cast a contemplative gaze upon his nephew.

"It's nothing," he said.

Daniel wasn't so sure but he didn't pursue it.

"Keep it under the speed limit," Art said. "We can't afford to get popped on radar."

Daniel glanced at the speedometer needle as it bounced on the fifty-five miles per hour mark. "I don't think that'll be a problem."

Art looked over and huffed, "Then let's hope we don't have to outrun anyone."

"Oh, how I love a challenge."

35

"How's the vacation going?" Manny answered, seeing Sarah's name on his caller ID.

"Oh, you know, about what you'd expect."

"You got into another shooting?"

"Very funny," Sarah said. "You have anything going on today?"

"Nothing much?"

"Great. Can we meet? I need your help."

"That sounds ominous," Manny said.

"Sarah...you there?" He said after not hearing a reply.

"I'm here. Can we meet?"

"Sure. How about your place around six."

"See you then," Sarah said abruptly ending the call. She hated being rude but the less she said over the phone, the better.

Several hours had passed when Sarah noticed Ranger's head come up from the floor at the imperceptible sound of Manny's car pulling into the driveway. She leaned back on the couch and peeked through the blinds. Two detectives made their way up the stairs.

For once, she was relieved to see Sal Vargas. He was just the sort she needed for this off-the-books assignment.

Sarah opened the door just as Manny raised his hand to knock.

"C'mon in, gents," she said as she swung the door wide. "Can I get you guys something to drink?"

"Beer for me, if you got it," Manny said. "We're off duty."

Vegas stopped mid-way through the door as Ranger let out a low growl. Sarah saw his hand slowly move to the holstered gun on his hip.

"Oh, I wouldn't do that," Manny said as he gently grabbed his partner's arm.

"Ranger! Leave it!" Sarah barked back.

Ranger complied by sitting, although his haunches looked like coiled springs as he kept his gaze fixed on Vargas.

"What's with Cujo?" Vargas asked relaxing his arm.

"A fine judge of character if you ask me," Manny said chuckling.

Sarah rubbed Ranger's head before embracing Vargas in a hug. "See? Hugs for friends," Sarah said looking back at the dog. His tail began sweeping the floor.

"Do I get a hand job if he bites me?" Vargas asked.

Sarah's eyes narrowed as she turned back to face Vargas, placing her thumb and her middle finger together.

"I snap my fingers and you won't ever have to worry about that again."

Vargas held up his hands, "Okay, okay, take it easy. It's only a joke."

"Much like your manhood," Manny said as Sarah walked past and exchanged high fives.

"Sure, sure, pick on ol' Vegas but I get more action than both of you," he said as he walked past Ranger in a wide arch.

Sarah grabbed two beers from the fridge, twisted off the caps, and set them on the table. She pulled out a chair and sat, motioning the two detectives to do the same.

She spent the next fifteen minutes going over the events of the past few days and the clues uncovered by Art and Daniel. It was risky, but she told them everything. They already knew about the Governor and Seaton anyway.

"So that's why we were pulled off the investigation," Manny said as if unraveling a puzzle.

Vegas swirled the amber liquid in his bottle before speaking, "I never trusted Barclay."

"I'd only vote for him at gunpoint…even then I'd take the caliber into consideration," Manny added.

"Have either of you heard of the Brigg's Ranch?"

Manny looked at Vargas who was taking a final swig from his bottle.

"I've never heard of it, but I haven't worked out there since I was a young deputy. You heard of it, Vegas?"

"It's not ringing a bell. I assume you asked the east deputies?"

"Yeah, none of them were familiar with it, either. I thought about going to the Assessor's office and looking at land records but that might send up a flare to Manilow. I can't get caught," Sarah said.

"*We* can't get caught," Vargas added.

Manny leaned back in his chair as he scratched at the label on his beer bottle with his thumbnail.

"Do you realize how difficult it's going to be to find this place? We're talking two-hundred square miles," Manny said.

"At least," Vargas added.

Sarah shrugged her shoulders with indifference. "What choice do we have?"

"Pretend we never heard any of this," Vargas said, staring down the neck of his empty bottle.

Sarah shot him an incredulous look.

Vegas huffed and shook his head. "Okay, whatever...I'm in."

Manny got up from the table and walked over to the large window over-looking the park. He parted the blinds with his forefinger and tapped his foot on the hardwood floor. Sarah watched him stand in silence until she couldn't bear it anymore. "Manny?"

He took a deep breath, turned, and narrowed his eyes as he looked at Vargas and finally at Sarah.

"Make no mistake. We cross this line...we better go all the way. If we find the bodies, we might...might keep our jobs. But if we fail," he paused looking back and forth between the two, "we could lose a helluva lot more than just our careers."

"I'm not afraid of Barclay," Sarah said defiantly.

"That's because you're young. This guy has power and connections we can't even imagine," Manny said.

"You're forgetting about the surveillance tape. That's our ace card. If he comes after us we can go public. Hell, he names Denver's murder victim. That sounds like leverage to me," she said.

"Assuming we can ever get access to the video. What if Manilow locks it away," Manny countered.

"But at trial..." Sarah began before Manny cut her off.

"What trial? You think Manilow is going to rush this thing to trial just to save our asses? The killers had masks and the one witness we do have can afford better lawyers than the President." Sarah rubbed her face with both hands as she realized the truth of the matter.

"So, where do we start?" Vargas said as he broke the silence.

"Strasburg is the oldest community in the eastern part of the county. I say we start there," Sarah said.

"Anywhere in particular?" Vargas asked.

"How about that diner on Main Street. That's been there fifty years I bet. If anyone knows this Brigg's Ranch, chances are they will. Every rancher in the county eats there regularly," Vargas said.

"It's a place to start," Manny agreed.

"When do you want to go?" Sarah asked.

"Vegas and I can't do this on office time. Lucky for you tomorrow is Saturday. I say we hit it early." Manny said.

Vargas cleared his throat and pleaded with puppy dog eyes to his partner.

"Okay, mid-morning then."

36

It was five minutes past ten p.m. Sarah had spent most of the last two hours transfixed on Daniel's small cell phone resting on the kitchen table. Over the past thirty minutes she pleaded, even bargained, with it to ring.

When it finally did, it took two rings for Sarah to snap out of her trance-like pose and snatch it from the table.

"Daniel?"

"It's me. How are you doing?"

"Better now, where are you?"

"We're in a roadside motel. Art's asleep and I'm just checking the perimeter."

"Are you going to tell me where this roadside motel is?"

There was a two second pause before he answered, "We're safe."

Sarah decided she didn't much care about their exact location as long as they were all right.

"I met a few of your friends today," Sarah said. "BJ, the mysterious installation guy and an off-duty cop from Littleton named Colin."

"Good, he's there?"

"Yep. He came up to the door a few hours ago and introduced himself. I recognized him from a crime scene class I taught a few months back. You want to tell me why he's parked outside my house?"

"After the other night we thought you could use a little backup."

"I don't need any backup. I have Ranger."

"How is Ranger?"

"He stopped staring at me, so that's a big plus. Earlier tonight I thought he was going to take Vegas out after he put his hand on his gun."

"Not a good move."

"I think Vegas got the message," Sarah said.

"So how did you get Colin to waste a perfectly good Friday night?"

"Art is paying him."

"Daniel?! I don't need Art paying for a private security guard for me!"

"Four actually; we have them going in shifts."

"I don't need protection," Sarah protested.

Daniel seemed to ignore the comment as he pressed on with a question.

"Did BJ go over the security system?"

"No, I had to head to the courthouse before he was finished."

"He's planted a series of pressure plates and laser trip wires around your yard. Avenues of approach that you or the neighbors wouldn't use. If one of the sensors gets tripped, then the silent alarm will engage."

"If it's *si-lent*, how am I supposed to know it's tripped?" Sarah said.

"Take the phone and walk out into the backyard."

Daniel walked her along a path from memory until she reached a section of her fence next to a large elm tree.

"Now, look at the street light forty yards to the south."

"Okay?"

"Do you see the blue light?"

"Yeah, I've never noticed that before," Sarah said absently.

"I know, BJ put it there."

Duh, Sarah thought.

"You should be able to see it from every south and west facing window in your place."

"Wouldn't it have been smarter to connect it to a light in my living room or something?" Sarah asked.

"Think of it as an early warning signal. I wanted something you could see whether you were coming or going. Besides, you have a whole house alarm system that should activate if someone gets inside."

Sarah didn't like being perceived as a damsel in distress. She knew in her heart that Daniel didn't think of her that way, but others like BJ and Colin might. Like always, she would have to prove the stereotype wrong.

"Are you two any closer to getting the evidence you need?" Sarah asked, changing the subject.

"I don't know. Our lead is pretty flimsy. I just keep telling myself if we keep pushing forward, maybe we'll get a break. I don't think Seaton made notes with the intent of someone else figuring them out. His journal is more like a series of post-it notes in shorthand. Personally, I think we need a miracle."

Sarah thought back to what Judge Whittier had said about Art and miracles and prayed he was correct.

"How did the meeting with the judge go?"

"Not encouraging. His staff found a place called Brigg's Ranch that may have some bodies buried on it. Manny and Vegas are meeting me tomorrow in Strasburg to see if we can locate it, but so far no one in the sheriff's office has ever heard of the place."

"It's my experience that the village elders are the best source of intel."

"This isn't Afghanistan, Daniel."

"Small towns are all the same. I don't care if it's Afghanistan or Colorado. It may take a little effort to gain their trust but once you get it…those elders will unlock every mystery."

"Well, we're meeting at an old diner. Maybe someone there has heard of the ranch."

"Sounds like a plan."

"That's the least of our worries though," Sarah said.

"Why do you say that?"

"Assuming we even find the ranch, we could be talking about hundreds of acres. I doubt the graves have headstones. *Hell*, the victims may not even have been buried. It could take months to find the graves. You guys can't stay on the run that long."

"We're not on the run. We're following leads."

"You know what I mean. You guys have to pop up on radar sooner or later, and what happens then?"

"Sounds to me like you're the one worrying now."

"I *do* worry about you, *and* Art."

"I can handle myself."

"You're not Superman, Daniel. We've both seen what these guys do to their enemies."

"I hear you. Look…Sarah, I've had the best training a man can have and I've been in tougher situations than this. They don't know where we are and that's a huge advantage."

"Just promise me you'll be careful."

"My old command sergeant major preferred we proceed with surprise, speed, and violence of action. Careful ain't in the manual."

Sarah sighed as she realized Daniel didn't want anyone thinking of him as vulnerable. The difference was that he and Art were alone. They didn't have a battle hardened dog, off-duty cop, or alarm system. They were in uncharted territory with an enemy that could be lurking around the next corner. She pushed the thought from her mind as she tried to focus on her own circumstance.

"Before I forget, I need to call you on your cell," Daniel said.

"But they'll hear us," Sarah said.

"That's the point. I want them to think everything is normal. Just make small talk and make sure you don't mention our leads."

"Got it."

***

Reaper sat up and adjusted the volume on his console as the computer alerted an incoming call to Sarah's cell. He maneuvered the cursor over the Record icon and tapped the mouse button. He had been manning this station for hours with only minor breaks to use the bathroom and refill his coffee. A day old tray of smoked herring and rock hard bread were his only nourishment.

He listened to the voices hoping to detect some minor clue revealing their location. An errant word, an identifiable sound in the background…anything. She talked about her plans to go fishing over the weekend. *Was that code for a search?* Her profile indicated she was an avid hunter and angler so it was probably just what it sounded like. The male didn't say anything revealing. He just asked questions and gave one word answers.

There was something about the conversation that bothered Reaper. He couldn't put his finger on it at first. It was subtle, but they didn't sound like they usually did. Actually, *she* didn't sound like the voice he had heard before.

Then it hit him. She didn't sound worried. She didn't ask where he was or when he was coming back. It was almost as if…

Reaper slammed his fist onto the console knocking his cup over and spilling coffee onto the floor. His chief analyst Pavel froze as did the other analysts in the room. Several seconds passed before Reaper regained his composure and turned to face the others.

"What's wrong?" Pavel asked.

Reaper shook his head in disbelief as he spoke, "They know we're listening."

37

August 10th; Williamsburg, Kentucky.
Art woke early to a darkened room, outstretched his arms, and sat up to find Daniel staring out the window.

"Did you get any sleep?" Art said noting the perfectly made bed next to his.

"I slept a little in the chair," Daniel said without looking back. Art guessed he was scanning the parking lot.

"You're no good to us if you're tired," Art said.

Daniel broke his outward gaze and turned his head half way to Art giving a blunt reply, "I'm fine."

Art held up his hands in mock surrender. It was wrong to bring it up with a professional of Daniel's caliber.

"How do you want to approach this today?" Daniel asked.

Art ran his fingers through his hair and rubbed his head as he shook off the funk of sleep.

"I'd prefer to check property records at the courthouse, but its Saturday. I've ruled out the police department, too. We don't want to send up any smoke signals to our pursuers. We may be able to access newspaper archives at the public library. With any luck, this DeFrance character has been written up somewhere."

"They won't be open for hours," Daniel said.

"Then we can take our time getting ready."

"What about trying to reach out to one of the cousins?"

"I'd prefer to keep our presence a secret."

"Might be kind of hard in a small town," Daniel said.

"It's a chance we'll have to take. It's been a long time since I was here. I doubt very much anyone would recognize me now," Art said rubbing his graying goatee.

***

An hour and a half later the two felt refreshed after a shower, shave, and donning fresh clothes. Art took his turn behind the wheel and made their way over to Main Street. Art parked a few doors down from Angie's diner.

He spotted a large banner hanging over the street announcing the Harvest Days Parade and craft show scheduled for later that morning. The thought of the parade conjured up wonderful childhood memories. He remembered it being one of the most talked about events of the year. Small town festivals often shut down local businesses and he hoped their trip to the library wouldn't be sidetracked by marching bands and a pie eating contest.

Settling into a quiet booth at the back of the room, the two ordered coffee as they looked over the menu. An older man wearing a white apron and hat sauntered out from behind the lunch counter with a stainless steel pot and topped off their mismatched cups.

"What's good here?" Art asked the older man.

"Everything but Angie," he snorted.

"Your wife?" Daniel asked.

"Forty-eight years," the man replied.

"That's incredible," Daniel said.

The man leaned over to Daniel as if he were about to reveal top secret information.

"Her father caught us in the back of his Oldsmobile one night. He told me I could marry her, or go to jail." he said letting the words hang in the air before breaking into a broad smile. "I can't help but think if I took option two I'd be a free man by now."

A gray-haired woman half his height stopped at the table and slapped his arm with a menu.

"You leave these boys alone."

"Angie I presume?" Art said.

"In the flesh, but don't get any ideas. I'm a happily married woman," she said lightly jabbing her husband's arm with a fork.

"I warned you," the old man said as he turned and disappeared back behind the counter.

"You boys look tired and skinny. I'm making you biscuits and gravy," she said as she plucked the menus from their hands and started for the kitchen.

"Sounds...*good?*" Daniel said as he shook his head and snickered.

"Makes you wonder why the family ever moved away, huh?" Art replied.

Bloodlines

They ate their breakfast in silence as the diner filled to near capacity. Daniel kicked Art's foot under the table.

Art looked up from his plate, "What?"

"Don't look now but there's a middle aged woman with way too much makeup and large hoop earrings staring at you three tables over on your left.

Art turned slightly but felt Daniel kick him again.

"I told you not to…oh, now you've done it. She's coming over," he said. Daniel inched his chair away from the table and set his silverware down.

"Arthur…is that you? Well, as I live and breathe," she said patting her heart.

Art looked up and tried to place the familiar voice.

"It's me…Patty Anne," she said with a broad smile.

"Patty Anne, of course," Art said as he dabbed the corners of his mouth with his napkin.

Patty Anne slid a chair out and plopped down with her heavy handbag in her lap. Art pursed his lips and cast a curious look to his nephew.

"This is my nephew, Daniel."

Patty Anne did a double take as she looked the younger man over from head to toe.

"You're Max's boy?"

"Yes ma'am."

"I see the apple didn't fall far from the tree," she said with a devilish wink.

"So, how have you been Patty Anne? How's your father?"

"Art…what are you doing here?" she said, leaning in with a conspiratorial whisper.

"Having breakfast."

"No, I mean *here*…in Williamsburg. You shouldn't be here."

"Maybe I've been away long enough," Art said.

"There ain't no statute of limitations on *murder,*" she whispered before looking over her shoulder for eavesdroppers. Daniel shifted in his seat as the words ricochet around his head. Art looked around the room as well then leaned into her and whispered, "It was self defense."

"Call it what you want, but you still should've stayed away. Do you know who the sheriff is?"

215

"Someone I know?"

"Its Frank junior, you fool. If he catches you in town, well…you better not stick around to find out."

"I don't plan on being here long, Mitts."

"Oh, dear. No one has called me that since high school," she said batting her eyes and playfully swatting her hand at him.

"I heard about Joan. You two were quite the couple. Al and me would have made it to the funeral but we didn't have the money."

"No need to apologize," Art said.

"So how is Tilly?"

The question was laced with more than mere curiosity.

"Tilly's fine."

"Is she still working for you out in Wyoming?"

"Colorado," he corrected her, "and yes, she's still working for me."

"Funny how she never did marry. Some of us figured you two might get hitched after Joan…" she caught herself as she realized how terrible it sounded.

Art smiled and said, "We're just friends."

"Of course, of course. I'm friends with her on Facebook you know. We don't talk much though."

"Well, I'll tell her you said hello," Art said.

Patty Anne leaned in close to Art and rested her hand on his forearm.

"I'm serious, you need to get out of town."

"The past is the past."

"Not for Frank junior. You don't know him, Arthur. He's just angry, I mean all the time. If he finds you in town, Lord…well, I don't want to think about it."

Art stripped thirty dollars from his money clip and pinned them to the table with his coffee mug.

"Perhaps you're right. I trust you won't mention you saw us to anyone for a few days?" Art said.

"Oh, you're secret is safe with me," she said drawing her pinched fingers across her lips.

"Thanks, it was great seeing you Mitts."

Patty Anne placed her business card in his hand and winked at Daniel, "Give me a call and we can catch up."

Bloodlines

Art reviewed the realtor card and slid it in his shirt pocket, "I'll do that."

Daniel scanned the street as they exited the diner. He grabbed Art's arm and turned him sharply away from the path to their car. A second later a police cruiser passed from behind and turned a few blocks down onto a side street. Daniel lead them south for a block and then turned down an alley. He stopped between two dumpsters and faced his uncle.

"Now might be a good time to fill me in."

"Daniel…"

"Murder? What the hell was she talking about Art?"

"It's nothing."

"Murder isn't *nothing,* Uncle Art."

"It wasn't murder. If it was, I would have been arrested a long time ago," he said looking up and down the alley. Daniel's gaze didn't waver.

"We all have secrets Daniel, I don't have to remind *you* of that."

"*My* secrets have to do with national security."

Art took a deep breath as he stared at his shoes. This was the last thing he wanted to talk about. It was an event that changed his life, and that of his friends. In many ways, it was the reason he got into law enforcement and forensics, in particular.

He leaned back against the wall and met his nephew's gaze. If anyone would understand his actions, it would be Daniel.

"It was the end of our senior year in high school. Our baseball team won our division and we had a bonfire party out at the gravel pit. It was your typical high school party; booze, loud music, fast cars, that sort of thing. It seemed like the whole school was there.

"After a while some of us decided to head into the woods. A friend of mine had pilfered a bottle of gin from his folks and we were going to mix it with fruit punch. We called it Jungle Juice," Art said as an after thought.

"Aunt Joan was with you?" Daniel asked.

"Tilly too, and a few others. Anyway it was late…maybe one in the morning when all of the sudden this deputy sheriff pulls up to the edge of the trees and shines his spotlight on us. He had the overhead lights on and squelched the siren."

"This was that guy, Frank?"

"Yep, Deputy Frank Hatch. Senior, apparently."

"What did you do?"

"We scattered. All except Tilly. She's always been a goodie two-shoes. Straight A's in school and a senior princess in Jobs Daughter's. She wasn't going to run from the law."

"So she got arrested?"

Art chewed on his lip as a glassy film coated his dark eyes.

"Deputy Frank, that's what we called him, was a mean drunk with a badge. Everyone knew it. On really bad nights, he'd drive across the tracks to find some poor black kid to beat. Sometimes they got worse than a beating."

"Did he ever beat up women?" Daniel asked as he anticipated the direction of the story.

"There were rumors," Art said before continuing. "At first it looked like he was just scolding her. He made a big show of dumping out the bottle of gin. He tossed the bottle a few feet into the air and smashed it with his nightstick like a Major League ball player. We thought that was the end of it; that he would give her a tongue lashing and drive away."

"But he didn't drive away, did he?"

"No...he didn't," Art said as he met Daniel's eyes.

"What happened next?" Daniel asked in a soft voice.

"It all happened so fast. I remember him brushing his hand against her cheek and pushing back a lock of her long blonde hair. She swatted his hand away. He said something to her I couldn't hear and she slapped his cheek.

"That's when he lost it. He grabbed her by the shoulders and threw her against the hood of his car. I wanted to call out, but I was too scared."

"Then what?"

"I thought he was going to cuff her and take her to the station. But, he didn't. He pushed her face down onto the hood of his patrol car and started hiking up her dress and ripping down her panties. She was screaming for help and struggling. He was just too big for her."

"*Jesus*...what did you do?"

"Joan wanted to run...go for help. We were hiding there in the trees together. I can't explain it, but I felt a rage build in me that I had never felt before. I was like an animal. I remember digging my fingers into the bark of that tree I was hiding behind.

Bloodlines

It felt like several minutes had passed but looking back it was probably just a few seconds before I took off at a run towards them. I vaguely remember Joan calling out 'No'.

"Deputy Frank must have been too distracted because he never heard me coming. I grabbed the nightstick he dropped to the ground when he attacked her, and I just started hitting him. The first one was to his back but then I concentrated on the back of his head."

Art paused and closed his eyes. "I remember him sliding off of her and going to his knees. I just kept hitting him…three…maybe four times. I can't remember. All I remember is that he didn't get back up."

Daniel placed a gentle hand on Art's shoulder, "You did what you had to do to save your friend."

"He was a *cop,* Daniel."

"He was a *criminal,*" Daniel corrected him.

"Still, I could have run for help. I could have shouted at him, pulled him off of her. Maybe he would have stopped if he knew witnesses were around."

"What about the next time? What about the next teenage girl that found herself alone with Deputy Frank? Bottom line is that you stopped an evil man from committing an evil act. I'm guessing you're standing here today because the law agreed."

Art wiped a tear from the corner of his eye and cleared his throat. "We didn't know what to do. Joan came out of the woods and we did our best to calm Tilly down. She was shaking like crazy and just catatonic. I remember her makeup being smeared and soaked with tears. Her lip was swollen and there was a trickle of blood coming out of the corner of her mouth. She could barely stand. We ran back to the bonfire and I drove Joan's car back to my folk's house. Dad was a doctor and we couldn't think of anywhere else to go. He looked her over and then called the other parents.

"We all met down at the sheriff's office. It was late and we beat the sheriff there. Joan and I waited in the hall outside his office, but we could hear our parents yelling at the sheriff."

"Was the sheriff a reasonable man?"

"I don't know. He didn't have the reputation of Deputy Frank, but he put up with him. He had to know something like this would happen sooner or later."

"How did the town respond?"

Art nodded his head as if he had forgotten to mention that part.

"Officially, it was like it never happened. I've never seen anything like it. Even the local papers ignored the story. They just posted an obituary, but there was never any mention of the attack, Tilly, me...nothing. I think secretly people in town were...*relieved.* Not a very Christian response, but I think a lot of parents slept better knowing their kids wouldn't go through what Tilly did. Our folks were well-liked and I don't think anyone questioned what happened that night."

"Things couldn't have been the same for you though," Daniel said.

"Not by a long shot. Our parents didn't want us to be the subject of gossip and rumor so my dad sent us to Lexington. He put us up in an apartment and paid for us to go to the community college. A few months later he moved his practice up there, too. Your dad was already off to boot camp so that wasn't an issue."

"What about Tilly's parents?"

"Her dad had died in the mine a few years earlier and her mom was kind of...*detached.* It's probably the reason the three of us were so close. I suppose we became Tilly's family after that night, in a sense. We've rarely spent a day apart since."

"I had no idea, not even a hint," Daniel admitted as if acknowledging a failure.

"It's not the kind of thing you advertise. I'm not proud of what I did, Daniel. I still wonder if I could have saved Tilly without killing that man, but I can't undo the past. I have to live with that decision for the rest of my life."

"I think, because of that decision, Tilly *can live* the rest of her life."

Art didn't respond. Instead he looked up and down the alley.

"We'd better get going, Daniel."

Daniel held out his hand and stopped Art in his tracks.

"One more thing, Art. I take it Frank junior, the current sheriff, is the son of Deputy Frank?"

Art nodded.

"Sons have a funny way of avenging their fathers, no matter how scummy they were. To be on the safe side, let's do everything we can to get what we came for without running into him."

"Agreed."

38

Sarah pulled into the dusty diner parking lot to find Manny and Vargas waiting for her. Manny's personal Toyota Camry was the only foreign car in the dirt parking lot. Actually, it was the only passenger car at all. The parking lot looked more like a used car lot specializing in pickup trucks and SUVs. There was even a John Deere tractor parked along one side of the diner.

Manny sprang from his car but Vargas pulled himself up like a man twice his age.

"Long night?" Sarah asked.

"I feel like one of those rodeo clowns that got trampled by a bull," Vargas said.

"And, what was her name?" Sarah said in a mocking tone.

"Funny. I need a cup of coffee," Vargas said as he brushed past her, hand on his lower back.

Manny smiled and put his arm over Sarah's shoulder as they walked to the door. "You could have ridden out here with us you know."

"I know. The thought of being trapped for two hours with Vegas was a deal breaker," she said smiling. "Truthfully, I just needed some quiet time," she added.

The diner was about two-thirds full and the locals eyed them all the way to a small table in the corner. The waitress brought coffee without being asked. She dropped three menus on the red checker tablecloth and cast a suspicious eye at each of the strangers.

"I'll give you folks a few minutes to look these over," she said before leaving.

Sarah sat quietly looking around the room while Vargas nursed his coffee. She felt strangely over-dressed in jeans and a button-up shirt. Boots, dirty coveralls, and a worn Carhartt jacket, seemed to be the dress code of the day. The ranchers dressed like her grandfather. She figured they didn't have much besides a strong work ethic, dirty fingernails, and a faith in God.

The old barn wood walls of the small diner were adorned with black and white photos of good days gone by in the small ranching community. Hay harvests, parades, and the marker at Comanche Crossing.

When the waitress returned, Sarah ordered the *huevos rancheros* with green chile. Manny got down to business.

"Say there…Joy," he said glancing at her name tag. "We're looking for a place called Brigg's ranch. Ever heard of it?"

Joy put a hand on her hip as she looked to the ceiling, "Ahhhh…can't say that I have. Who's asking?"

Sarah couldn't help but notice that the entire dining room instantly fell silent.

Manny pressed his lips together as if he was afraid to answer. "Just curious?"

"Just curious, huh?" Joy said with the authority of a school teacher catching a student with a hidden note. "You wouldn't be land developers from California, would ya?"

Vargas spit his coffee back into his cup as he held back a laugh. Manny cracked a smile, too.

"No. Definitely not land developers," he said.

Joy tucked her pen back above her ear and made it clear she wasn't going to budge until he answered.

"Well then, why are you askin' about it?" Joy said.

Manny looked around at the other patrons and leaned a little closer to Joy.

"We're from the sheriff's office," Manny said cracking open his identification to show his badge.

Joy snatched the ID from his hands and scrutinized it like a traffic cop.

"This here badge says *Detective*. What kind of crime would bring you all the way out here?" Joy asked looking over the rims of her half-glasses.

"It's nothing like that. We're just looking for some information from the land owner."

"Information, huh?" Joy said again, tossing the badge back on the table. "Well, I need some information from you first. What'll you have for breakfast?"

Manny and Vargas had barely finished giving their order when the waitress abruptly turned and walked away.

"What about the…" Manny began before she cut him off.

"Never heard of it," she said with a wave of her hand.

"She sure does live up to her name," Sarah said.

Vargas stared at her ass as she sauntered back to the kitchen before Sarah hit him in the arm.

"She's old school, all right. I'll bet the manager makes her wear two hairnets," Vargas said popping his eyebrows up and down.

"Ewwww…that's gross, even for you Vegas," Sarah said.

"I'm just sayin.'" Vargas said.

"I suppose she resembles the woman you took home last night," Sarah said.

Manny shook his head subtly as if to warn her.

"Sit back kid, you're gonna love this," Vargas said.

Sarah suddenly regretted ever bringing it up.

"I'm good," she said holding up her hand.

Vargas ignored her comment and plowed ahead.

"So I'm chatting up this stunning blonde at the bar. I'm buying her drinks and she tells me she's *vajazzled*."

"Va-what?" Sarah asked.

"You know, like bedazzled but down there," he said pointing towards his crotch. "Piercings," he added.

Sarah's face scrunched as she held back her gag reflex. She turned to see an older man at the next table shake violently as he held in his laughter.

"Anyway," Vargas said lowering his voice, "I dropped fifty bucks in booze on her only to find out she's a dinosaur."

"Come again?" Sarah said.

"You now, a lick-a-lotapus."

Sarah looked at Manny for clarification but he just stared at his coffee.

"Do I have to spell everything out to you, Richards?" Vargas said. "I thought you had all those college degrees."

Sarah ran the name through her head again until it clicked.

"Not that there's anything wrong with that. I just wish she would have been up front about it." Vargas explained.

"So then, how did you hurt your back?" Sarah asked.

"There were a couple B team players in there so I just worked my magic."

"What magic?"

"Women respond to me, Richards. I have a swimmer's body," he said sucking in his gut.

"Where…in your freezer?" Sarah chided.

Bloodlines

Sarah jumped as she heard silverware crashing into a plate on the table next to them. The old man was bouncing in his chair again holding in his laughter.

The three investigators worked through their meals and tried to ignore the eyes of the diner that were settled upon them. They each dropped cash on the table after reviewing the bill and receiving a facetious, "Y'all come back real soon" from Joy.

"So what now?" Sarah asked.

"Now we do what all good cops do when they've run out of leads." Manny said.

"We're going to the golf course?" Vargas asked.

"We're knocking on doors," Manny corrected him.

As they exited the diner, they found the old man in overalls leaning up against Sarah's Ford chewing on an unlit pipe.

"I have to say…I had a great time listening to your conversation. You three argue like my kids used to."

"Glad we could entertain you," Vargas said.

"You were in the military, weren't you?" Sarah said surprising them all.

"What makes you say that?" the old man asked, cocking his head.

"Sniper…Recon maybe?" Sarah prodded.

The old man pulled the pipe from his mouth, his brow now furrowed.

"Right on both but, how…"

"It was the way you laughed. You held it in like you were going to burst. It reminded me of a friend I know who spent some time behind enemy lines."

The old man lit his pipe, smiled, and winked at Sarah. "You say you're looking for the old Brigg's place?"

"You know where it is?" Manny asked.

"I know where it was. The Brigg's have been gone for quite some time. A man bought the place back in the eighties. He leases out most of the land for cattle, but he still lives in the barn."

"The barn?" Sarah asked.

"The roof on the house collapsed in the blizzard of oh-three. He's a bit of a hermit; kind of a strange fellow. He doesn't come into town much. I suggest you stay in your truck little lady and let these two boys knock on the door," he said.

"Can you tell us how to get there?" Manny asked.

"Take this road about five miles 'til you see the old church. One of the walls is caved in. Turn east and go until the road ends. You'll see the barn about two hundred yards up a two-track past the gate."

"Thanks for your help." Sarah said shaking his hand.

Twenty minutes later Sarah pulled up alongside Manny's car just outside the gate. She grabbed her binoculars off the dash and focused on the structure in the distance. The barn made of faded bare wood tilted slightly to one side. It looked to Sarah as if a mild wind could bring it all down. She spotted some goats and chickens milling around the grass, but no people. A pair of mules was taking shelter under an old lean-to.

Manny rolled down his window and yelled over to Sarah.

"Why don't you stay here while we check it out."

"I can handle myself," she said.

"I know you can, but some of these guys can be real constitutionalists. Plus, he may not respond well to a bunch of vehicles thundering down the driveway," Manny said.

"Whatever," Sarah said waving him off as she peered through her binoculars.

Manny rolled down the two track road at five miles an hour. He parked at a slight angle out front, got out of his vehicle, and rapped loudly on the closed doors. Sarah caught some movement along the side of the barn and froze as a man with a long gray beard holding a shotgun made his way towards her friends. Sarah slammed on the horn as she fished her cell from her pocket and scrambled to pull up Manny's number. The man was ten yards from the corner when she slammed her thumb onto the transmit button.

"Sarah…?" Manny asked.

"Shooter eleven o'clock!"

She watched as her friends drew their weapons and took cover behind the car. She could see them screaming at the man but couldn't hear the words. She let out a deep sigh as the old man leaned his shotgun against the barn and put his hands in the air. Sarah threw her truck in gear and thundered towards the barn.

By the time Sarah skidded to a stop and jumped from her truck, Manny and Vargas were holstering their weapons. Vargas broke open the man's side by side shotgun and removed the shells before resting on it like it was a cane.

The old man looked like a nineteenth Century trapper. His tangled gray beard qualified him for a spot in the band, ZZ Top. He was pudgy in dirty coveralls and stood over six feet. His ponytail looked like he salvaged it from the north end of a south moving horse. He flashed a row of tobacco-stained teeth as he laid eyes upon her and spit a large brown glob onto the ground.

"Is this the Brigg's Ranch?" Manny asked.

"Who's asking?"

Manny dug his badge out of his pocket.

"Sheriff's office."

The grizzly man leaned right and looked past Manny.

"That don't look like a sheriff's car."

"We're detectives," Vargas said.

"I don't answer to nobody but the sheriff himself. You boys ever heard of posse comitatus?" he said defiantly.

"Naw," Vargas said, "Can you spell it for us?"

Manny held out a hand to his partner, "Vegas…just…hold on a sec."

"Sir, we're just looking for the Brigg's ranch. One of the guys in town told us this was the place."

"What do want to know fur?"

"Well, this is going to sound a little strange, but there was supposedly a couple of men that were murdered near here in the late eighteen hundreds."

The man's eyes narrowed and he leaned over to spit another glob of brown juice onto the ground.

"Since when do the cops investigate crimes that old? Don't you have enough rapists and killers out there to keep you busy? The television is full of 'em."

Sarah watched as Manny took a step closer to the man as if he were about to confide a great secret with him.

"Listen…" Manny said.

"The name's Bob."

"Great. Listen Bob, I'm going to level with you. I don't want to be out here on a Saturday looking for a century old crime scene. The fact of the matter is…it's politics," he said. "If you could just let us look around a bit, it would mean a lot to me. The sheriff has been riding my ass to get this thing done and I could really use a break."

Bob eyed him like a used vacuum salesman and spat a glob inches from Manny's shoe.

"You want to look around, you get yourself a warrant. While you're at it, you can bring the *real* sheriff out here. Until then you can get the hell off my property," he said with a dismissive wave of the hand.

He held out his hand to Vargas and waited until the detective gave him back the shotgun.

"I'll leave the shells by the gate," Vargas said.

"Sir?" Manny said.

The man huffed at Manny and stopped mid-step to soak in a long, head to toe look at Sarah whereupon he shook his head and exhaled.

"Sir?" Manny tried again.

"Don't come back without a warrant," the man said as he walked to the large double doors and went inside.

The three investigators gathered around Sarah's Ford.

"Well, that went over like a cum pancake," Vargas said.

"Gross," Sarah said.

"That's gross? What about Grizzly Adams back there eying you up?"

"Look, we need to figure out what to do. We're running out of time," Manny said.

"Did you notice how he didn't deny the murders?" Sarah asked.

"Yeah, but what good does it do us if we can't get a look around?"

"Maybe we *should* get a warrant?" Vargas said.

"Based on what? We try to get a warrant and the judge will laugh us out of his chambers. We're talking about the *eighteen hundreds*. Not to mention what will happen to us when the sheriff finds out about it."

Sarah had been quietly running through their limited options but she couldn't shake the eerie feeling of Bob undressing her with his eyes.

Then she remembered the warning from the man at the diner about her not getting too close.

"Wait, I think I have an idea."

Bloodlines

Sarah went to the back of her truck and opened the topper door. She reached in and uncased her hand-crafted Kadel longbow. She attached the spool line to the laminated riser of exotic cocobolo and osage wood. Their contrasting light and dark colors complimented each other perfectly, making the bow look like a piece of fine furniture or art, rather than a weapon. She bent the sleek bow back and looped the string over the top nock. She grabbed the string and drew the bow, squeezing her shoulder blades together as she sighted down the arrow before letting down the forty pound draw.

"You're not gonna shoot the guy, are you?"

"Not exactly."

Sarah leaned the bow against her truck and took off her long sleeve shirt exposing the skimpier tank top beneath.

"How do I look?" she said letting out her long chestnut hair and tossing it back.

Manny placed a firm hand on her bare shoulder.

"What the hell are you doing, Sarah?"

"I'm playing the only card left in the deck."

"Which is?"

"Me."

"No way."

"You saw the way he was looking at me. It's probably been a long time since he's talked with a woman. I'm going to use that to our advantage."

"First of all, that's the stupidest thing I've ever heard. The guy is a loon and he has a shotgun. No way you're walking up there with a bow in hand looking like Sheena queen of the jungle."

"It might work," Vargas said.

"You're not helping," Manny snapped as he pointed a finger at his partner.

Sarah turned without another word and made her way to the large wooden doors of the barn. She was sure the old man was watching her through the slats in the weathered boards so she added a little swagger to each step.

"Sarah!" Manny hissed.

"Just hold on, give her a chance." She heard Vargas say behind her.

Sarah reached the door and rapped loudly with the back of her free hand. She took a step back as she heard the latch being removed.

The large door cracked open and a musty stench smacked her in the face.

39

The old man poked his head out and stared right at her chest. As uncomfortable as it was, her decision to go without a bra under the thin tank top was paying off today.

"Hi there, I'm Sarah."

The man chewed on his tobacco, eyes still fixed upon her chest.

"I know you told us to leave, but this was going to be my only day off this week and I had planned to go bowfishing until this thing came up."

For the first time, his eyes drifted away and he seemed surprised to notice she was holding a longbow.

"You hunt?"

"Since I was nine," she said. "My grandfather taught me."

"Uh-huh," he said chewing more on his tobacco.

"I see you got a nice big irrigation canal running alongside the property."

The man's gaze was now crawling all over her body as he chewed, and Sarah did her best to suppress her gag reflex.

"You got any carp in that canal?" she asked.

"Yeah, big as those goats there," he said pointing to the yard.

"You like carp?"

"Yeah."

"Great, I'll make you a deal. You let me shoot a few carp out of that canal and salvage my day off and you can eat what I shoot."

The old man stroked his beard as he considered the proposition and leveled his blueish-gray eyes on her.

"You'll eat dinner with me?"

Sarah's stomach churned like a bucket of worms at the thought but offered the most non-committal nod she could muster. The old man smiled and slammed the door shut.

Sarah walked back to the truck feeling the old man's eyes glued to her ass.

She rounded the tailgate with a triumphant nod.

"We're in."

"Seriously?" Manny asked.

"Well technically, I'm in. He's letting me bowfish along the canal. It looks like it runs for miles and it'll give me a chance to check out the property.

"And what if you don't see anything?" Manny asked.

"Then I'll prod him for more information over dinner."

"Whoa…dinner? You can't be serious."

"That was the deal. I catch the carp and he cooks them for us."

"Us? No way I'm eating carp. I'd rather chew on an alley cat." Vargas said.

"He might have one in the freezer," Sarah joked.

"Oh, great; dinner at Wolfman Puck's then?" Vargas said.

"I'm glad you find this so amusing," Manny said.

Sarah frowned and gave Manny a disappointing stare. "Look…does the guy creep me out? Hell yes. That's why I'm depending on you two to watch my back in there. Let's not forget why we're out here though. We can't allow Barclay to get away with murder. Can you imagine how dangerous he'll be if he gets in the White House?"

"What if Bob decides to eat us?" Vargas said.

"I'll give him something else to focus on."

"That's what I'm afraid of," Manny said.

"Speaking of that, you may want to turn the high beams off," Vargas said motioning to her chest.

Sarah brushed him off with a scowl, grabbed her bow, and headed up the berm to the edge of the canal.

***

Daniel found a parking spot near the library that kept the car secluded from view of the main road. Before getting out, Art called Tilly to check in. She answered on the first ring.

"Things a bit slow today?" he joked.

"I'd ask you the same thing but I already know the answer don't I?" she said.

"Come again?"

"Imagine my surprise to hear from our old high school friend Patty Anne this morning," Tilly said in an accusatory tone.

That was fast, he thought.

Bloodlines

"So I take it you're in Williamsburg?"

Art held his breath. He hadn't expected Tilly to divulge their location over the phone but, the damage was done.

"Yeah, just a rest stop I'm afraid. We have a long drive ahead of us."

Tilly sounded as if she hadn't heard the last statement.

"Arthur...have you completely lost your mind?" she whispered.

"I suppose that's debatable."

"Not from where I'm sitting. Patty Anne tells me that there's a new sheriff in town. Are you planning on dropping in...maybe trading patches?" She was laying the sarcasm on thick.

Art switched the phone to his other ear. "Look, I know this isn't ideal but, we'll be outta here in fifteen minutes. In a couple of hours we'll be in another state."

Art could hear her breathe a sigh of relief.

"Well, see to it that you don't dilly-dally around."

"Wouldn't think of it."

"No, I know you wouldn't think of it, but you'd do it."

Art sighed in frustration.

"Tilly, I just wanted to call and make sure the men I hired have arrived."

"First thing this morning. They sure are a serious looking bunch"

"Good," Art said. "Listen, I've got to go. I'll call you tomorrow when we're at our next stop alright?"

"Do be careful, will you Art?"

"Always."

Art ended the call and held his face in his hands.

"What is it Art?" Daniel asked, placing a hand on his shoulder. Art looked over and sighed.

"I'm afraid we don't have much time."

40

Washington D.C.

Reaper's fatigue ebbed as he listened to the call streaming at the adjacent work station. He hadn't put much hope in getting any useful intelligence from the target's work phone, especially after the Richard's phone tap seemed compromised.

But, this call seemed to be a massive stroke of luck. He snapped his fingers at another analyst at the mention of Williamsburg and motioned for them to find the location of the city. Once the call was finished, he cued up the recording and listened to it again. He wasn't about to miss a vital clue. As he made a notation another analyst interrupted him.

"A computer search has revealed a Williamsburg, Kentucky with a Frank Hatch Jr. serving as county sheriff."

Reaper's lips spread into an evil grin as he eyed his chief intelligence analyst Pavel.

"We've got them."

***

Daniel's senses were firing on all cylinders as he led the way to the front of the public library. The parking lot was filled to capacity due to the Harvest Festival gathering on the street, and they blended in with the crowd.

The interior of the library was bright, filled with fall colors from decorations and displays. One whole wall was covered in pre-school art depicting the pilgrims and Indians sharing a Thanksgiving feast.

Art tugged at Daniel's sleeve as he walked over the information counter. He addressed the older of the two women sitting behind it.

"Hello there young lady, I was wondering if you could help me."

"This *is* the help desk," she said, not looking up from a printout she was reading.

"Yes, well, I'd like to search your local newspaper archives. I'm looking for any mention of a man named Hawkins Boone or, perhaps, Hawkins Boone DeFrance?" Art said.

"Year?"

"Ah, I'm not exactly sure."

The older woman looked up from her book and fixed a disappointed gaze upon him. "Then I'm not *exactly* sure I can help you."

"I'm not looking for a specific article, just any reference to him at all."

The older woman pried the glasses from her narrow beak-like nose and let them dangle from her neck by a gold colored chain.

"Follow me," she said as she rose and came around the counter. Daniel noticed the attractive younger assistant batting her large brown eyes at him. She couldn't be more than twenty he thought.

The older woman led them through a maze of book cases until they reached a bank of four microfilm terminals.

"Wait here while I get the first batch," she said.

Art exchanged a worried look with Daniel as he thumbed the scroll wheel on the antiquated machine.

"That thing looks older than me," Daniel said.

"I'm sure it is. This might not be the best idea I've had," he admitted.

A moment later the woman returned and dropped a small box of dated film rolls on the counter.

"This is the last ten years. When you're finished with that, let me know, and I'll get the next batch."

She turned without so much as a smile and headed back to her desk.

"Thanks for all the *help*," Art said putting an emphasis on the last word.

"This could take a while," Daniel said.

"Let's start with major holidays. Newspapers often run puff pieces around that time. Maybe we'll get lucky and they featured him in a biographical story."

"Maybe check this time of year, too. This Harvest Festival seems to be a big deal."

"Good idea."

Art loaded the first roll and began scanning the headlines. It took fifteen minutes to get to the end and he quickly loaded another.

"I never realized how much I depend on search engines," Daniel said.

"Yes, well...there's a reason these things are mostly found in museums. As good as they were, their time has come and gone."

"Maybe I can find a computer with an internet connection. I'm feeling a bit useless at the moment," Daniel said.

"It can't hurt. I'll keep plodding through these," Art said.

Daniel followed the path back towards the help desk when, passing by a large wall of windows, he spotted a problem.

A sheriff's car was parked behind their car. Daniel stood next to a small potted tree and plucked a magazine from a table next to a wingback chair. Looking over the pages of the open magazine, he watched the deputy behind the wheel talking into his hand held radio. Then a second sheriff's car pulled up.

Shit, he murmured.

Then a third car pulled up and a serious looking man wearing black sunglasses got out and started pointing at the other two deputies. Daniel knew what a commanding officer looked like, and decided it was time to move.

He set down the magazine and turned to get Art when he ran into the younger help desk clerk standing behind him.

"Hi," she said as she grabbed his arm to steady herself.

"Oh, I'm sorry. I didn't see you."

"Yeah, I could tell. Are they here for you?" she said nodding her head towards the window.

She didn't miss a thing.

"It's kind of a long story," he said.

"You don't have to explain. Everyone hates the sheriff," she said smiling and batting her eyes at him again.

"Maybe you could point me towards the back door?"

She looked right and left and pointed towards the east end of the building.

"That way leads to the city park."

"Thanks, I owe you."

She reached out and grabbed his arm as he took a step.

"Wait! I have something for you," she said holding out a folded piece of paper.

Daniel opened the note and read the name Hawkins Boone DeFrance followed by an address and phone number.

"Mrs. Jackson doesn't trust the internet. I figured I'd save you boys a few days of searching," she said rocking back and forth on her heels.

"How did you…"

"He was registered to vote," she said.

"And this is his phone number?"

"No…it's mine," she said gushing in embarrassment.

"Right," he said offering her a boyish smile. "Thank you…"

"Corey," she said.

"Right…Corey. Well, I have your number," he said holding up the note. "I gotta run."

Daniel left her standing by the small tree and hustled through the aisles back to Art.

"Back so soon?" Art said as Daniel placed a hand on his shoulder.

"Sheriff's here, we gotta go."

"Are you serious?"

"C'mon, Art. We don't have much time," Daniel said looking back.

"What about our search?"

"I have a lead," Daniel said holding up the paper. "But we won't be able to follow it up if we don't get out of here."

Daniel led the way as he snaked between the bookshelves. He poked one eye beyond the bookshelf and down the wide hallway towards the entrance. Sheriff Hatch and two deputies were coming through the doors at breakneck speed. At least their guns weren't drawn.

If they crossed the hallway now, the sheriff would spot them for sure. Daniel was just about to turn and search for an alternate route when he saw Corey run out from behind the group of lawmen and wave them down. The three men stopped and turned to face her. Daniel wasn't about to wait for another opportunity.

"Let's go," Daniel said as he grabbed Art by the shirt sleeve and dragged him across the hallway. He was almost positive he could see Corey give him a wink as he darted across the open hallway. The two picked up speed as they maneuvered past patrons until they came to the rear exit. Daniel closed the distance but Art called out to him, "Daniel, the door!"

"No choice!"

The fire alarm belched an ear-splitting siren as Daniel slammed into the push bar and shouldered the door.

Daniel didn't break stride as he raced across the parking lot and into the tree lined park. He stopped behind a large bush and waited for Art to catch up.

"We're not going to outrun them for long," Art said looking back at the library.

As if on cue, the three lawmen came running out the emergency exit, paused for a second to look around, and then ran full steam towards the park.

"I hate being right," Art said as they darted along the far side of the tree line.

"This way!" Daniel said as he spotted an opening.

They spilled out into a gathering crowd of marching band students, boy scouts, and local politicians. Daniel slowed his pace as they entered the depths of the crowd and headed for the far side of the street.

Once in the shadow of a large fire truck, Daniel peeked through the gap behind the cab to see the lawmen on the opposite side of the street looking in all directions. One went left, one right, and the sheriff began pushing through the crowd.

Daniel turned and ushered Art through the doors of a bar called Ted's. The dark smoky interior was just what Daniel was hoping for. He would have preferred a few more patrons but he didn't plan on staying.

As they made their way towards the back of the room the bar tender called out, "The bathrooms are for customers only."

"Two buds," Daniel yelled back holding up two fingers.

He passed through the swinging saloon doors separating the main room from the back hallway, breezed past the bathroom doors, and out the back door and into the alley. Thankfully there was no alarm.

They made their way north down the alley and emerged on the next block. Daniel looked across the street at a small gas station and saw an opportunity.

"How much money do you have left?"

Bloodlines

"We're down to five hundred," Art said.

"That'll do, wait here." he said holding out his hand.

Daniel dashed across the street to the teenager filling the tank of a thirty year old Honda dirt bike. The bike was spackled with dried mud and the headlamp casing was caved in. After flashing the money and exchanging a few words, Daniel kick-started the bike and roared back across the street to Art.

"You can't be serious?" Art said.

"Here, put this helmet on," Daniel said as he inched forward to let Art get on the back.

"This is a really bad idea," Art yelled over the coughing muffler.

Daniel rocked the throttle as he yelled back over his shoulder. "Trust me."

41

Annoyed, Manny removed the vibrating phone from his short pocket. "Keep an eye on her Vegas," he said nodding towards Sarah. He looked at the caller ID and saw sheriff Westin's name.

Shit.

"Yes sir," he answered.

"Manny, I'm sitting here with Lieutenant Manilow and we've got a bit of a shit storm brewing."

Shit, shit, shit. "Sir, before you say anything, I can explain."

"Explain what?"

"What?"

"Lopez, have you been drinking?"

"No…sir."

"Then shut up for five minutes and listen to what I have to tell you."

Sheriff Westin spent several minutes telling Manny how Hammond lied his way into the property evidence room. He told Manny about the wiped hard drive and, though he couldn't yet prove it, his suspicions that the governor had ordered it.

"This guy has crossed a red line Manny."

"Yes sir," Manny said, feeling a bit uncomfortable with the direction of the conversation.

"We're going to get to the bottom of this thing first thing Monday morning. I want you to go over all your notes from the double homicide and figure out a game plan on how to move forward without the tape. You'll be quarterbacking the case from here on out."

"What about the governor sir?"

"You let me worry about that," he said as a goat standing in front of Manny's car let out a loud 'bahhhh'.

"Where the hell are you?" Westin asked.

"Ah…petting zoo sir. Yeah, my kid wanted to go so…"

"Get it done," Westin said cutting him off.

"Yes sir."

Manny hung up the phone and rested his head on the roof of the car.

"Good news?" Vargas asked.

"Clock's ticking now. We've got until tomorrow to find those bodies."

***

As Sarah suspected, the canal had not been fished for years. There were only deer tracks along the burm, and the waters were loaded with carp. She took her time walking the elevated edge as she looked for anything that could have been a landmark used as a meeting place a hundred years ago.

An endless field of grass waved under a slight breeze as she navigated along the canal under a canopy of century old cottonwood trees. They might be the only witnesses left of the murders…if they even happened. Sarah looked around for fifteen minutes before realizing that she had no idea what she was looking for. She didn't know what a century old grave would look like. Sarah decided the best approach was to gain the confidence of the old man. Maybe he knew something useful and didn't even know it.

Sarah skewered three large carp and used an old piece of barbed wire she found sticking out of the ground as a string to carry them back to the barn. She offered a wink to her surprised colleagues waiting by Manny's car and rapped loudly on the door.

The old man must have been watching her because the door opened immediately, and for once the old man stared at something other than her chest.

"I'm back," Sarah said.

The old man stepped aside and motioned for her to follow him. Manny and Vargas followed closely behind.

"Put them over there," the old man said pointing to a food caked laminate countertop next to a sink full of dirty dishes. The makeshift kitchen looked like something from a third world village.

The old man took a seat at a four top card table in the center of the room illuminated by a mechanics lamp dangling at the end of a long extension cord. He slammed a dusty bottle of scotch on the table followed by three mismatched metal coffee mugs.

241

Sarah kicked up dust as she crossed the dirt floor back to the table. She couldn't help but notice she wasn't offered a mug.

"You catch 'em, you clean and filet 'em," the old man said dismissively.

Sarah turned on a heel without saying a word and walked back to the kitchen area to work on the fish. She could feel his eyes plastered on her ass as she walked back to the kitchen but tried to brush the thought away.

"She's a cop?" the old man asked.

"Criminalist," Manny said.

Even from the kitchen area, Sarah could hear their conversation clearly. But she continued to work on the fish in silence. She glanced back at the table to see the old man pull out a pouch of tobacco, load a fresh wad into his mouth, and wink at her.

"Married?"

"Who her? No." Vargas said.

"What'll you take for her?" he said, chewing on the tobacco.

Sarah fought the urge to turn around. She'd let her colleagues handle it. "Come again?" Manny asked.

"She's not spoken for...what'll you take for her?"

"What did you have in mind?" Vargas asked.

"Vegas, please," Manny said holding up a hand.

"Can't hurt to hear his offer," Vargas said without cracking a smile. Vargas turned to the old man. "Are you thinking cash money or do you got something to trade?"

Sarah tightened her grip on the filet knife and imagined Vargas' face on the carp before her.

The old man didn't seem to be joking when he said, "I've got three good goats and that shotgun."

"That's it? Maybe you should take another look at her, *Bob*. That's a prime grade 'A' specimen there with a lot of child bearing years ahead of her. You're going to have to up the ante and throw in a mule or two if you want us to take you seriously."

Sarah spun around towards Vargas so he could see the knife in her hand. Vargas simply winked as if to say 'trust me.'

"Okay, enough Vegas. She isn't ours to trade for, Bob."

The old man looked irritated but not deterred. "Maybe I should talk to her father then?"

Bloodlines

"I'll be sure to pass along your offer and let him know where you live," Manny said.

The old man nodded as if the deal had only hit a minor roadblock and downed his scotch.

Sarah could see Manny was growing impatient with the old man's salivating as he stared at her across the room. She was getting creeped out herself. *Goats? Really?*

"So about those murders, what can you tell us?"

"What murders?"

"You know which murders. Stories like that may fade from the papers but not the people. I'll bet you were told all about the rumors when you bought this place from the Briggs. Isn't that right?"

For the first time a hint of guilt escaped past the hermit's hard eyes. Manny was trained to detect such micro-expressions and seized upon the moment.

"What do you care if we find some old crime scene? We're going to find the graves eventually, Bob. You really want to fight us each and every step of the way because we aren't leaving until we find them. You gotta ask yourself if you're willing to take on that fight. You got no skin in this game…yet." Manny said with a hint of a threat.

It must have worked because the old man shifted in his chair and poured another shot.

Manny never needed to coordinate his interrogation strategy with Vegas. On this issue they were always perfectly aligned. Given his proclivity for debauchery, Vegas typically played the good cop. He tried to identify and appeal with the subjects' darker desires. Sarah knew it was a skill that Manny found hard to stomach.

Vargas reached out a hand and gently tapped the man's forearm.

"Your cooperation might go a long way with Sarah's father," he said.

The old man's eyes widened. "You think?"

"Oh…yeah, you'd be helping her career. Trust me, I know her dad. Any man that helps his daughter out has a foot in the door."

The man spit a glob of tobacco onto the dirt floor as he stole another glance at Sarah.

"Would she be here for the digging?"

Manny let out an imperceptible sigh as he knew the hook had set.

"You bet, she could be here for days," Vargas said.

The old man nodded several times as he wiped a stream of saliva from his tangled beard.

"Well...the story I heard was that two rustlers were killed and buried after they got caught trying to grab a mare by the loafing shed, but I never dug around or anything."

"When was this?" Manny asked.

"Eighteen hundreds sometime, I never did ask further."

"Can you show us this loafing shed?"

"I can show you were it was, it ain't standing there no more."

Sarah watched as Manny excused himself from the table and came over to her.

"Believe it or not we got an area to look at," he whispered.

Sarah didn't hide her surprise. "Seriously, how'd you get him to talk?"

"Vegas got it out of him." Manny said.

"Really...I guess I owe him one."

He winced. "Let's wait and see if this pans out before we start giving high-fives. How fast do you think Art's team can get down here?" Manny asked.

"I'll call Judge Whittier but, I suspect they could be here tonight."

"The sooner the better, I want to get into this before the old man changes his mind."

42

The mountains outside Williamsburg

It took a few minutes to skirt the parade crowds and get out of town. It was a stroke of luck that the kid with the dirt bike had a general idea of where the DeFrance man lived. Daniel snaked through the tree-lined roads until he reached the two lane highway and turned east. With each passing mile, the evidence of modern civilization faded. Streets of modern residential homes turned to the occasional small boxy home and corral, then scattered double wide trailers. Lawns sprouted rusty appliances and broken down cars with barking dogs chasing their bike with increased frequency.

He couldn't help but notice the pure beauty of the hill country though. Daniel finally spotted what he was searching for and pulled across the opposite lane. He brought the dirt bike to a stop in front of a dilapidated shack of a store with a small 'post office' sign hanging in the window. He slid the kickstand out and steadied the bike as Art got off.

"Watch the bike Art," he said as he checked the highway and headed into the shop. Daniel was all smiles when he came out a few minutes later.

"Got it."

"How far?"

"Maybe ten miles," Daniel said as he slammed the kick start and throttled the engine to a roar.

They wound their way over the snaking roads to the back hollars not concerned with modern conveniences. Daniel slowed the bike to a crawl as they came to the gate of the property. It was marked with a sign that read *Trespassers will be shot...survivors will be shot again.*

"What do you think?" Art said as he read the warning.

"No turning back now. Just keep your eyes open," Daniel said.

Daniel pulled to a stop fifteen feet from the broad front porch and took note of the King Shepard dog looking out a large window at the front of the house. He thought it strange that the dog didn't bark. Daniel slid the kick stand out and leaned the bike as he and Art dismounted into the mud. He subconsciously brushed the butt of the 1911 handgun tucked on his hip.

The rustic old cabin was dark and ringed by towering oak and walnut trees. Daniel scanned for any signs of activity around the detached garage and shed, but saw nothing. A car was hidden in the garage under a large oil stained tarp. Daniel pulled back the tarp to reveal the front hood and ornament.

Art let out a long whistle, "Looks like a forty-nine Oldsmobile V-eight."

Daniel dropped the tarp and walked towards the front porch. The air was still; quiet.

Too quiet.

Daniel was just about to ascend the stairs when the hairs on his neck stood on end. Soldiers like him had developed a sixth sense in the field. It was what had kept him alive.

He held up a closed fist to Art and froze. Daniel took a deep breath before speaking.

"Sir, we're no threat to you."

Silence.

"Mr. DeFrance, we've come a long way. We just want to talk." Daniel said, not moving an inch.

"Start by tossing that pistol," a voice came from somewhere way too close for Daniel's comfort.

He turned slightly to his left and saw a shadowed figure partially obscured by a large tree. The man leveled a Browning automatic rifle in his direction.

Against his better judgment Daniel lifted the pistol with two fingers and tossed it toward the man. The man slowly approached until he was close enough to bend down and pluck the pistol from the ground.

Daniel admired the man's field craft. It had been a long time since someone had gotten the drop on him.

He judged the man to be in his late sixties although he had the physique of a twenty year old. He stood about five foot eight with buzz cut silver hair. His hawkish features were accentuated by his clean shaven face.

The man got to within ten feet and kept the heavy rifle leveled at Daniel's chest.

Daniel caught a glimmer on the man's ring finger and instantly recognized the triangle shaped engraving.

"Virtus Junxit Mors Non Separabit…whom virtue unites, death can not separate," he said.

Daniel watched a wave of calm roll over the old man's face.

"You say you boys are traveling men?"

"Yes sir," Daniel said.

"Where from?"

"Colorado," Art said. "We've come to talk to you about John Henry DeFrance."

Hawkins Boone slowly lowered the rifle and took a more relaxed stance.

"Who sent you?"

Daniel thought of the only person that really mattered at the time.

"Alison."

43

Sarah stood on the spot where the old loafing shed once stood. Tilly insisted on coming to help when Sarah called her before frying up the fish.

Tilly and the Facility team arrived faster than she expected on Art's private plane, and were now unloading their gear. She wasn't sure what they would find, if anything.

So far Sarah had avoided making small talk with Bob, but she could still feel his eyes upon her. She wished he'd go back in his barn and leave them alone to work.

Sarah could see Sandi Thorpe, Art's bloodhound handler at the Facility, let her dog Mitch out on a twenty foot lead while another team member, Ben Locke, who she had met briefly, unpacked a ground penetrating radar unit.

Mitch was one hundred and twenty pounds of nose, lips, and saliva that could pull a truck off its wheels. His reputation was the stuff of legend with the local agencies as the four-year-old dog had caught more criminals than most cops with twenty years on the job.

"Where do you want us, Sarah?" Sandi asked.

"Start in this area and work out in a spiral if you can," she said motioning around with her hand.

"Search it up..." Sandi said as Mitch snorted at the ground.

Sarah watched as the dog moved from one clump of grass to the next, zigzagging back and forth until he suddenly stopped and sat on his haunches.

"Whoa, I've never seen that happen before." Sandi said.

"What?" Sarah asked.

"Mitch has never signaled a hit that fast. Has anyone taken a leak out here?"

"Not that I'm aware of, although I wouldn't put it past the landowner," Sarah said glancing over her shoulder at the old man fifty yards behind her.

"Flag it." Sandi said. "Ben can run radar over it while Mitch and I keep going."

Bloodlines

Sarah planted a PVC pin flag where Mitch had indicated and watched as the dog pulled his handler outside the glare of the artificial light and into the darkness. "Vegas, stick with her and do what she says," Sarah yelled as she held out the small bundle of extra pin flags.

"My kind of gal," he said as he hurried to keep up.

Sarah trotted over to Ben to see him attaching the final cable to the box antenna of the radar unit.

"I've got a spot to check," Sarah announced.

Ben looked up and pushed his glasses back on the bridge of his nose.

"This isn't the way I normally do things. We should really set up a grid, take soil samples, and do some test runs before we just start running wild. I'd also like to take readings with the magnetometer and clear out any metallic trash that might be here."

Tilly walked over to join them.

"We're on the clock, Ben." Tilly said. "Art is depending on us to get this done as soon as humanly possible."

"Well, you can have it done fast or you can have it done right," Ben said.

Tilly gave Ben a firm look that Sarah thought could only be described as one a mother gives an obstinate child. It took only a second for Ben to back down.

"All right, all right, let's do this thing," he said.

Sarah dragged the antenna back and forth in ten foot swaths as Ben monitored the color screen. On her third pass, he stopped her.

"We might have something. Go back to the beginning, move over a foot, and run along that line again."

Sarah did as she was told. As she passed by the pin flag Ben called out, "We've got a sizable anomaly there."

"Is it a grave?"

"An anomaly…big enough to be a grave though." Ben said.

Sarah went over to the monitor as Ben played the image back. She watched as the horizontal lines representing the layers of soil suddenly jumped in a garbled mess before returning to their normal parallel arrangement.

"Let's get digging." Tilly said.

Sarah took some photos while Tilly motioned for four grad students to set up their excavation grip and begin clearing the topsoil. Sarah knew that most forensic digs took days, sometimes weeks, but that was a luxury they didn't have.

Besides, she reminded herself, it really didn't matter in the long run. If these were the bodies, the killer was long dead. Sarah watched as the grad students expertly shaved the grass like a barber and began attacking the soil with trowels. She crossed her fingers and said a silent prayer for success.

***

As Reaper was loading his gear bag, Pavel ran into the operations team room.

"I'm glad I caught you," Pavel said.

Reaper kept packing after making eye contact with his chief analyst.

"What is it, Pavel?"

"We just intercepted some phone calls from the secretary's office. She's assembling a team of scientists to search for a grave site."

"Is that out of the ordinary?"

"No, and we wouldn't have thought anything about it, but she specifically mentioned Arapahoe county murders and…she was talking to Sarah Richards."

Reaper stopped packing as the name hit him.

"What do you think they are up to?" Pavel asked.

"I don't know… Hammond has taken care of the prostitute case. Have you heard any traffic from the targets?"

"Nothing."

Reaper's eyes narrowed. "It could be a coincidence. Has the Richards woman said anything about a new case she's working?"

"No, her phone traffic is down considerably from the week prior. I believe she may be using another phone."

The 'go bag.' He remembered the previous phone call from Daniel to Sarah.

"What do you want me to do?"

Reaper scowled as his mind raced for a new plan.

"I can't be in two places at once and we don't have another team to send to Colorado."

"I can go," Pavel said.

"*Nyet*, you're needed here my friend. I need someone I trust implicitly monitoring communications."

"Who then?"

"I have an idea who I can get to help."

Reaper turned back to his gear bag and drew out the satellite phone. He punched the Governor's private number and waited for him to answer.

"Yes?" Barclay answered on the first ring.

"It's me." Reaper said.

"Do you have it? I told you I don't want to hear from you until you have it in your hands."

"No, but we have tracked it down to a small town in Kentucky. My team and I are departing in minutes, but we have another problem."

"What is it now, you idiot?"

"Art Von Hollen has assembled a team to include the Arapahoe County Sheriff's Office. As we speak, they are searching for old grave sites in the county."

"So what?"

Reaper wished for a moment he was meeting personally with Barclay so he could hit the man across the face.

"We have reason to believe that they are searching for historical graves."

"So send a team to intercept them."

"*My* team is going to Kentucky. Besides, we can't assault a bunch of cops at a crime scene. This will require something special."

"Maybe you and your team just aren't up to the task at hand. Why not just wait and see if they find anything. If they do, we handle it like we did the computer."

"We got lucky with the computer. Besides, I don't think we can risk tapping into that well twice," he said.

"What could they possibly find?" Barclay said.

"Bodies. Do you want to wait for the evening news to see?"

"*Jesus*, I'm at a party here," Barclay complained.

Reaper shook his head as he gave the phone a look of contempt, directed at Barclay.

"Focus Governor, your party will have to wait."

251

Barclay was silent. Reaper wasn't sure if he was still on the phone.

"Did you say they were looking for historical graves?" Barclay asked.

"Yes, why?"

"I just remembered something that may be useful."

"What?"

"You let me worry about that. Do you have a location for me?"

"Yes." Reaper gave him the specific coordinates.

"You get your team and get that journal. No mistakes."

Reaper looked at the phone as Barclay abruptly ended the call.

"What is it?" Pavel asked.

Reaper tossed the phone back in the bag and folded his arms as he replayed the conversation in his mind.

"Something isn't right. Keep monitoring the lines. I want to know what Barclay's up to."

***

It had been a very long night, but they had made significant progress. After so many setbacks, Sarah felt her luck was finally taking a turn in the right direction.

They hit the first body after a foot of digging. The second came about an hour later and was partially covered by the first. Technically, they should have called the coroner's office but Sarah wanted to get a better look at the bodies before involving them.

She was shocked to see a trio of dark SUVs thunder down the two track road to the barn and pull up into the drive.

"We may have a problem," Sarah said to Manny as she motioned towards the barn.

"Did you call the coroner?" Manny asked.

"I didn't; did you?"

Manny and Sarah casually strolled towards the group with Tilly trailing a few feet behind. They met a serious looking heavy chested woman stomping across the field from the lead SUV.

"Who is in charge here?" she thundered.

Manny raised his hand. "I am."

252

"Under Colorado law, I am hereby taking control of this dig," she announced handing Manny a tri-folded photocopy of a state statute.

"And, who are you?" Manny asked.

"Dr. Teresa Russell. I'm the state archaeologist, and as you can see, any buried body of antiquity falls under *my* jurisdiction. My office will be handling the processing and collection of all the remains and associated artifacts. Are you the land owner?"

"I'm Detective Lopez, Arapahoe County Sheriff's Office; this is my criminalist Sarah Richards."

"How did you know we were here?" Sarah asked.

Dr. Russell shot Sarah a disapproving look and addressed Manny instead.

"How we find ourselves here is irrelevant to the law. You are hereby commanded to stop your processing."

"We don't even know these bodies are old. They could be recent deaths," Sarah countered.

"So…this is an official investigation then?" Dr. Russell said looking around.

"Well…" Manny said searching for the right words before he was cut off.

Sarah recognized Melvin Stokes, a veteran investigator of the coroner's office, come over from the second SUV. He joined the conversation and extend a hand.

"Detective Lopez," he bellowed, "What the hell is going on?"

"We were just about to call your office, Melvin." Manny said.

"Is that so?" Melvin said.

"Yeah, why don't you come take a look," Manny said.

The group followed Manny, all except Tilly. Sarah noticed her punching a number into her cell phone.

Sarah watched as Dr. Russell came unglued when she saw the degree to which the graves had been excavated. The next several minutes were spent arguing each person's position until it was finally agreed upon that the coroner's office would supervise the dig and if the bodies were determined to be of antiquity then the site would be turned over to the state archaeologist's team. After the shouting had died down, Dr.

Russell pecked away at her cell phone and replayed her hysteria to the party on the other line.

Just then, Manny reached out and grabbed Sarah's arm as he saw the approaching SUV coming down the road.

"*Shit*...the sheriff is here," Sarah said.

"Let me handle this. You stay here and keep an eye on Dr. Russell. I don't trust her." Manny said, and walked away.

Sarah watched in dread as Lieutenant Manilow exited the vehicle with the sheriff. Manny waved the old man Bob over to their little gathering and was soon joined by Melvin Stokes. Sarah couldn't decide if she was relieved to see that the archaeologist hadn't been called over.

The men talked for several minutes before Dr. Russell noticed the impromptu meeting. She darted across the field with Sarah close behind.

Dr. Russell unleashed a torrent of complaints to the sheriff. She cited a litany of legal statues and court rulings giving her authority over all sites of antiquity and suggested his staff should understand the law if they were to enforce it. She even implied Native American tribes might lodge a protest to the handling of their ancestors.

When Sheriff Westin didn't budge, the woman laid into Melvin Stokes.

"Under Colorado statute, you have the authority to arrest the sheriff. I demand you do so forthwith!" Dr. Russell screeched.

Melvin squirmed.

Sarah saw Melvin squirm as he searched for the right words.

Sheriff Westin's toothy smile oozed confidence as he addressed the state archaeologist.

"Dr. Russell; I'm going to save Mr. Stokes from trying to find a politically correct response to your ridiculous demand."

"Read the law, Sheriff Westin, the coroner or their representative has the authority to arrest the sheriff," she said waving her photocopy of the statue in the air.

"True enough," he agreed. "Tell me though; how exactly do you see Mr. Stokes here handcuffing me?" he said resting his hand on the butt of his sidearm.

"More importantly, whose jail do you think he's going to book me into? You can't possibly think that my deputies will throw me in a cell, do you?"

Dr. Russell's defiant expression suddenly looked deflated. "Moreover, do you think any of the other sheriffs, my *friends*, will allow Mr. Stokes to throw me into one of their cells?"

"I expect that everyone will follow the law," she said.

"I think today, right here, you might do well to consider me and my armed deputies to be the law," the sheriff said.

Sarah struggled to contain her smirk as she watched the archaeologist's eyes bulge from their sockets. She had apparently never been talked to that way.

"On that note, Dr. Russell, until we know for certain that these bodies are historic in nature, my crime lab will be handling the dig. You are free to observe but any attempt to interfere with our duties will be met with arrest," Westin said.

Sarah noted he didn't bother hiding his smirk.

Dr. Russell scowled and began punching a number into her cell phone as she turned her back on the group.

"Ms. Richards?" Westin said.

"Yes, sir?"

"Consider your vacation over. Supervise this dig and coordinate the findings with Detectives Lopez and Vargas."

"Yes, sir," she said not hiding her smile.

Sarah returned to the graves and tried to understand what had just happened. History suggested that she would have been placed on leave, or worse, with Manilow on scene. The man didn't hide his disdain for her.

There's something else going on.

She decided not to look a gift horse in the mouth. For now she would thank her lucky stars she wasn't terminated on the spot.

44

DeFrance Cabin; Kentucky

Inside the cabin, Art marveled at the appearance of the place. It looked like a staged photo for some magazine. The King Shepherd curled into a ball on the floor next to the coffee table. Nothing was out of place. There were no dishes in the sink, no junk mail on the table.

Art noted with interest that even the labels on the food cans were all aligned and facing out. It was clear to Art that the man was extremely organized. Hawkins Boone motioned for each man to take a seat on the couch in the main room. "Thank you Mr. DeFrance," Art said.

"Call me Boone."

Boone propped his rifle against the fireplace on the far wall and lit the kindling. He walked over to the couch, pulled the pistol from his waistband, and handed and handed it back to Daniel, butt first. Daniel quickly tucked it back in his holster. Boone turned around a chair from the table and sat facing his guests.

"Alison, huh?" Hawkins said.

Art looked over at Daniel. They hadn't actually discussed what they would say in this moment.

Art decided honesty was the only way to go. Normally he would hesitate to share too much of their story but Boone was a fellow Mason, and Art suspected the DeFrance family knew more about this mystery than the Von Hollens. He spent nearly an hour recounting the events from the murder at the consistory to their arrival on his property. Boone sat quietly absorbing the information. Art then revealed the attempt on his life and the assassination of Governor Hoines the year before and how he thought it might be related.

"He was a friend of yours," Boone said.

"Yes. He was a good man," Art added.

"And you two think all these events are related?"

"Absolutely," Daniel said.

Bloodlines

Daniel had stayed quiet for most of the conversation, Art noted. This was the first time he had spoken in an hour.

Hawkins Boone turned to Daniel and looked him over from head to toe.

"What's your story then?"

"Sir?"

"No offense to your uncle here, but it seems to me that you're the reason you've both stayed alive to this point."

"He is," Art said.

"Military?"

"Yes, sir."

"Branch?"

"Army, by way of Pararescue."

Boone nodded as if he had just unraveled a deep mystery.

"Did you serve sir?" Daniel asked.

"I was not allowed that honor."

"You could have fooled me," Daniel said.

Art was still hung up on Hawkins' answer when he asked, "What do you mean you weren't *allowed* that honor?"

"I had another obligation," he said.

"Meaning?"

Art followed the man's gaze to the wooden mantle above the stone fireplace. Perched on the stone was a flintlock rifle, several leather bound books, and a silver box about the size of a large dictionary. The box was covered in ornate scrolling and seemed very out of place compared to the other simple items in the cabin.

"I've waited my entire life for you two to show up."

"Sir?" Daniel asked.

"It didn't work out too well for my great grandpa the last time this meeting was supposed to happen on the plains of Colorado."

Art and Daniel exchanged puzzled looks which Boone picked up on.

"Where's the key?"

"We don't have it," Art said.

Boons' eyes narrowed as he calmly stood and walked to the fireplace. With the speed of a man half his age he snatched the rifle, spun around, and leveled the barrel directly at Daniel's head.

"Son, you just made the biggest mistake of your young life." His index finger hugged the trigger as the icy words flowed from his lips.

45

Piece by piece, Sarah and the excavation team removed tiny bits of soil from around the bodies until they sat upon a crude dirt pedestal. Using bamboo and horsehair, it had taken hours to brush and scrape away the packed soil. The team even used tiny surgical scissors to cut away roots woven through the bodies.

One of the grad students shouted in excitement as she brushed away a clump of dirt from the cranium of one of the bodies.

"I've got a bullet hole," the student said.

"Are you sure?" Sarah asked.

"See for yourself."

Sarah crouched next to the student and snapped a picture with the team camera. She then had the student hold a small 'L' shaped scale and snapped another. She pulled her cell from its cradle and called Manny over from the group of on-lookers to see the bullet hole.

Manny squatted and examined the small round hole in the man's forehead. Sarah noticed Dr. Russell carefully inspected the clothing that had been dislodged from the bodies during excavation. The woman snapped on a pair of latex gloves and gently rubbed the fabric and fingered the buttons.

"Look, see here? Look at the construction of these buttons. Look at the stitching. These clothes are from the nineteenth century." Sarah watched as she drew a pair of Teflon tipped forceps from her jacket pocket and dipped them into the lapel pocket.

"Hey, careful!" Sarah shouted.

Dr. Russell withdrew a small leather bi-fold wallet. Ignoring Sarah, she opened it and partially withdrew a colorful currency bill with the number fifty emblazoned on it.

"Is that money?" Manny asked.

"Yes. More precisely, it's a fifty dollar bill from the Confederacy."

"The Confederacy?" Sarah asked.

"I think that more than proves these graves are of historical significance. I shudder to think how much damage you've already done, but this is now *my* dig." Dr. Russell said with a dismissive wave of her hand.

"May I see that bill?" Sarah said.

Dr. Russell laid the bill upon a paper evidence bag. The printing was on one side only and Sarah took several photographs of the faded bill. She noted the picture of the man on the bill was circled in dark ink.

"Who is that on the bill?"

"I'm not sure. Is that important?" Dr. Russell said.

"Somebody circled his picture," Sarah dryly noted.

Dr. Russell seemed to ignore the comment as she cradled the bill and stomped over to the sheriff.

"Sheriff Westin? Take a look at this please," Dr. Russell said as she showed him the bill.

"This bill is dated 1864. Based on its presence and the style and construction of the clothing materials on the skeletons, it is quite obvious that these artifacts are well over the fifty year statutory requirement. This is not a crime. This is a site of antiquity and I demand you turn it over to me.

"If you refuse, I will have no other choice than to call Governor Barclay and tell him you are violating the law." Dr. Russell placed a hand on her hip as she fixed her gaze upon the sheriff.

Sarah knew Sheriff Westin didn't like being threatened, especially by some holier-than-thou bureaucrat.

"Did Governor Barclay send you out here to stop this dig?" Westin prodded.

"Governor Barclay fully supports the preservation of historical artifacts. These treasures belong to all of the people, Sheriff. They belong in a museum, not a police evidence locker."

"Sheriff Westin," Sarah interrupted. "May I bring you up to speed on some of our confidential findings?" she continued with a nod in a direction away from Dr. Russell. "Allow me a moment to consult with my staff, Dr. Russell. I'm sure we can come to an understanding."

Dr. Russell looked like a Cheshire cat, Sarah noted, as he took Sarah by the arm and led her several yards away. Lieutenant Manilow followed.

"Sheriff, there's more to these bodies than some historical dig. When was the last time you heard of the state archaeologist coming to a remote crime scene?"

"I share your skepticism Sarah, but if I'm going to defy the Governor I'm going to need some ammunition."

"Like what?" she asked.

"Manny told me about the video from the farmhouse. Can you swear to me that Barclay was on it?" the Sheriff asked Sarah.

"Absolutely."

"And he mentioned the name of the murder victim in Denver?" the sheriff prodded.

"Yes sir, it was clear as day. Watch the video yourself and you'll see."

"Be that as it may, what relevance does *this* crime scene have on the case?" Westin said.

"Frankly sir, we don't know yet. But, Art Von Hollen thinks it's very important. I think once we get the evidence back to the lab we'll have a better idea."

"How do you suggest we do that? The evidence seems to be on her side. By every account, these graves are over a hundred years old."

"There's no statute of limitation on murder, sir," Sarah said.

"True, but the murderer died long ago. It's not like we're going to present this case to the DA."

Sarah chewed on the inescapable fact for a few moments before Manilow spoke up.

"Sir, if I may. The Arapahoe County Sheriff's Office pre-dates statehood. Our office began in eighteen fifty-five as part of the Kansas Territory."

"What's your point, Bart?"

"Sir, if there is no statute of limitations and we've had continual jurisdiction over this plot of land since the bodies were buried, then legally, it's our case. An inability to present a case in court is no grounds to forfeit our investigative authority. It's no different than a murder-suicide."

Westin cracked a smile as he considered the comment.

"That's pretty thin legalese, Bart."

"Nonetheless, if we think this is a murder then we should investigate it as such."

"Sir, I am in total agreement," Sarah said.

She exchanged a brief look of surprise with her nemesis as Sheriff Westin considered the option.

"All right, let's do this. Sarah, tell Manny to get that woman off our crime scene and send Detective Vargas over here, will you?"

"Consider it done," she said as she ran back to Manny.

46

"Wait!" Art shouted loudly.

Daniel didn't move a muscle as the muzzle settled on his head. It wasn't the first time he had found himself in this situation.

Boone kept the rifle pointed at Daniel but drifted his eyes towards Art.

"You don't want to do that." Art said.

"I'm pretty sure I do."

Art shouted the words that Masons only utter when in great peril. The message seemed to work as Boone rested his finger alongside the trigger guard.

"You say that you're here because of Alison?"

"Yes," Art said.

"Then explain to me how it is you don't have the key?"

"The spiral key," Art said remembering the image in the journal.

"Of course."

Art explained how he had seen the image in Seaton's journal.

"Then how the hell did you expect to open the box?" Boone said nodding towards the silver box on the mantle.

"The key is for the box," Art said trying to make sense of the revelation.

"Isn't that obvious?"

"What's in the box?" Daniel asked.

Boone looked at Daniel. "No, son. You don't get to know that without the key."

"Did Alison have the key?"

"Of course he did. The key and the box were never kept together." Boone said.

"I see," Art said.

"You know what I see?" Boone said in an irritated voice. "I see two men who claim to be here for the box, but know nothing about what's inside. They don't even know there is a key or where it is. How do I know you boys aren't treasure hunters looking for the find of the century?"

"I can assure you we're not treasure hunters," Art said holding out his hand in a calming manner.

"Assure me with something more than words," Boone said with an icy tone.

Daniel had spent a lifetime reading people; Art too, for that matter. He recognized a bluff when he heard it and this was not one of those times. Taking an extreme chance, he made the man an offer.

"Mr. DeFrance, I understand your distrust. A week ago I would have thought this whole story was crazy, but give me a chance to prove to you we're here to help."

"Talk fast."

Daniel slowly opened his jacket and pulled his cell phone from the inner pocket with two fingers. Boone responded by taking a half step and anchoring the rifle butt harder into his shoulder.

"Easy…" Boone said. "What's that?"

"Just a cell phone."

Boone eyed the device showing a mix of curiosity and suspicion. "I've heard of them."

"Right now, I have a friend searching for evidence from Alison's clerk; the one that was supposed to meet your great grandfather in Colorado. Let me prove to you we're sincere."

Hawkins Boone nodded in agreement as he brought the rifle to a combat ready position.

Daniel dialed the number and activated the speakerphone before placing it on the coffee table in front of him. It took several rings before a female voice answered.

"Daniel?"

"It's me, Sarah. Art is here, too."

"This isn't the greatest time, but you're not going to believe this… We found the graves."

"Seriously?" Daniel asked.

"Yep, we've had a hiccup with the state archaeologist but believe it or not Sheriff Westin told her to stuff it and we're taking charge."

"That's great, Sarah," Art said. "Are you sure you have the right graves?"

"We're pretty sure. We even found Confederate money on one of the bodies."

"Describe it," Boone interrupted.

"Who is that?" Sarah asked.

"Describe the money. What do you see?" Boone continued.

"It's okay, Sarah; he's a friend. Describe the money," Art said.

"It's a fifty dollar bill with a man's face in the center. It's not Grant, some other guy and his face is circled. The artwork is pretty cool actually…"

"You said the face of the man was circled?" Boone interrupted her.

"Yeah, circled in ink," she said.

Boone looked as if a great weight had been lifted from his shoulders. He lowered the rifle and set the butt on the ground.

"Sarah, have you found a spiral shaped key?" Art said.

"Not yet, we still have to get the bodies out of the ground. We're taking everything to the lab tonight and I can do a more thorough search there. What does this key look like?"

"Silver. Spiral shaped with a snake's head at one end," Art said recalling the image from the journal.

"I'll look for it. Should I call you on this number?"

"Yeah babe, thanks." Daniel said. "Listen, we've got to go all right?"

"Hey, if it's there, I'll find it," she assured him.

"I have no doubt," Art said before Daniel ended the call.

Boone slumped back into his chair and let out a deep sigh. For a man so fit, he looked completely exhausted. He stole a look at each man as he cupped his hands over his chin.

"You boys like a good story?"

47

Williamsburg, Kentucky

Reaper had requested four battle-hardened veterans from the Gerovit ranks. He wasn't about to take any chances with so much on the line.

He briefed the men and personally flew the group's private jet to Kentucky. The men offloaded into the last two SUVs at the rental office. The men had done their research and worked out their plan on the plane ride and were driving at high speed to the local sheriff's office.

Reaper had dealt with small town sheriffs before. In his experience they kept themselves preoccupied with local matters and rarely, if ever, dealt with federal authorities. In the south, the 'Federals' were something akin to a barn cat. Necessary but unloved.

After a brief discussion with the dispatcher, Sheriff Hatch burst through the lobby doors and approached the five men wearing dark suits.

"I'm Sheriff Hatch."

"Special Agent Phil Nance," Reaper said producing a fabricated badge and ID. He breathed a sigh of relief as the sheriff invited him back to his office.

"Can I get you some coffee?" Hatch said.

"No Sheriff, thank you," Reaper said in perfectly accented English.

"How can I help the FBI today?"

"I think you and I are looking for the same man."

"Who's that?"

"Arthur Von Hollen,"

Sheriff Hatch adjusted himself in the chair.

"What are you looking at him for?"

"Terrorism."

Sheriff Hatch raised an eyebrow at the unexpected claim.

"Terrorism? Hmm." Hatch said. "What did he do?"

"I'm afraid I can't go into that, but I assure you that we need to stop him now. We have credible evidence he's planning an imminent attack."

"I'm looking at him for the murder of a police officer," Hatch said.

"I think you and I can agree then that the sooner we get Von Hollen into custody the safer everyone will be."

"We chased him this morning from the public library but he eluded my officers."

"Yes, well, he's traveling with an extremely dangerous man. This man was dishonorably discharged from the Special Forces and now works as a mercenary."

"I see," Hatch said.

"You need to tell your officers to consider them armed and dangerous."

"Already done. My guys won't take any chances with a cop killer."

"Good."

"To be honest Agent Nance, I could really use your help finding these guys. Can you turn on a satellite or something?"

Reaper contained a chuckle as he stood and buttoned his suit coat.

"In my experience, Sheriff Hatch, the best way to track a man is to start at the trailhead."

***

Fifteen minutes later the two dark SUVs followed the Sheriff's car into the library parking lot and stopped in the handicap spots near the entrance. The parking lot was half-full. The library was showing a midnight silent movie as part of the harvest festival. Three of Reaper's men instinctively fanned out in a perimeter but kept their sub-machine guns under their coats. The other man followed Reaper and the Sheriff through the double doors to the information desk.

"I need some help, Florence," Sheriff Hatch said to the older woman behind the information desk.

"Picture books are in the children's section," she said without looking up from her romance novel.

Sheriff Hatch shifted uneasily and avoided eye contact with the FBI agent.

"This here is Agent Nance with the FBI."

The older woman looked up from her novel and caught Reaper's hard stare.

"Agent Nance is looking for the men that stopped by the counter yesterday."

She regarded the man for a moment then looked back at the sheriff. "How would I know where they are?"

"Perhaps you could tell me what they were looking for?" Reaper said.

"They were looking for a man that lives around here. I don't remember the name."

"Did you direct them to any particular book or reference?" Reaper asked.

"I put them at the microfiche projector with about ten years of newspaper archives."

Reaper nodded to his assistant to search for the machines and he ducked between two bookshelves and out of sight.

"Ma'am, these men are wanted in the murder of a policeman and may be planning a terrorist attack so any assistance you can provide will be saving American lives," Reaper said.

"My God…they killed a policeman? Corey did you hear that?" the woman said to the younger assistant.

It was then that Reaper noticed something odd about the younger woman. It was almost imperceptible, but Reaper caught it. She never looked up from her magazine.

It occurred to him that any person in a dull job would be riveted by the arrival of the FBI. This was probably the first time FBI agents had ever come to this tiny town and she was more interested in her magazine than a manhunt for two cop killers?

Reaper rounded the Sheriff and leaned on the counter next to the attractive young woman.

"Excuse me…"

She looked up from her magazine and pointed towards her name badge.

"Yes of course… Corey. Well Corey, did you speak to the men when they came here?"

"Nope," she said popping the letter "p".

It was all the confirmation he needed.

Bloodlines

"Corey, I've spent my whole life catching liars. Some say I have a gift for it, I don't know," he said with a charming smile. "You know how I can tell when someone is lying to me?"

Corey rolled her tongue under her upper lip and stared at her magazine.

"They won't make eye contact when they lie…just like you're doing now," he said.

"Corey, if you know something you'd better tell us," Hatch said adjusting his duty belt.

"You realize that it's a federal crime to assist a fugitive. And these aren't just any criminals, these are cop killers. You could do twenty years in a federal prison." Reaper said.

The young woman looked up, her eyes wet.

"Just tell us where they went," Reaper said in a calm but determined voice.

48

Boone poured each man a glass of water before settling into his chair. Daniel was surprised to discover that Boone didn't have a trace of alcohol in the rustic cabin. Their host took a sip from his glass and seemed to gather his thoughts before speaking.

"That silver lock box was given to John Henry by General Washington himself," he noted with pride.

"May I?" Art asked.

Boone nodded and Art approached the mantle with some trepidation. If true, this was an item of immeasurable historic value. Just outside of arm's length, Art felt the weathered foot-wide floor board giving way. The board moaned in protest as he shifted his weight and stepped back.

"I forgot to mention that," Boone said. "I'm afraid it's a long way down to the mine."

"The mine?"

"Beneath us is an old coal mine test tunnel. Never really panned out, but it's there nonetheless. The access ladder is under the floor panel over there," he said pointing towards the kitchen. "Maybe later I can take you down there if you're interested."

Art smiled and stepped over the loose board and came face to face with the ornate box. The craftsmanship was unlike anything he had ever seen. The ornate scroll patterns surrounded an oval shaped inset on the face that contained a large oak tree with expanding roots. Next to the tree was a punch mark with the letters PR.

"PR?" Art asked.

Boone smirked before taking another sip from his glass.

"The box was made by a personal friend to General Washington; a master silversmith."

"Paul Revere," Art said.

"Mm-hmm," Boone hummed.

Art lifted the box as if it were unexploded ordinance and inspected it with care. He noted a strange C-shaped opening on the locking mechanism.

Bloodlines

"This is where the key fits?"

Boone nodded. "No key...no access."

"Have you ever tried picking the lock?" Daniel asked.

Boone leveled a gaze upon him. "The lock is booby-trapped. If you open it without the key a chemical explosive will destroy the contents.

"What kind of explosive?" Daniel asked as Art set the box back upon the mantle and backed away.

"How should I know? Whatever they had back then. I've never opened it," Boone said.

"So you have no idea what's inside?" Art asked.

The older man shook his head.

"What I know of it comes from my daddy, and his daddy before him," he said. "During the war for Independence, there was a great act of treason."

"You're referring to Benedict Arnold?" Art said.

"That was only part of it. There was something else, something more sinister. A plot that threatened to dismantle everything that Washington was fighting for."

"What was it?" Art asked

"I was never told." Boone said.

"How did Alison get involved?"

"Well now...that's where I can shed some light."

Boone rose and walked to a handcrafted hutch. He opened the top drawer and opened a faded yellow envelope. Walking back to his seat, he sat down. He opened a folded letter and reviewed the contents for a moment.

"John Henry always made sure that the key and the box were never together unless the nation was threatened by the same families."

"Families?" Daniel said.

Boone paused as a puzzled expression shaped his face.

"Of course. There are families that work to reshape this nation and those like mine that strive to maintain Washington's dream."

"So Alison discovered a threat to the Republic?"

"No. Alison had the key. We heard about the threat from someone else who knew of our family pact with General Washington. This was back in April of 1865." He said holding up the letter.

271

"What was the threat?" Art asked.

"Lee had been defeated and the Confederacy was doomed to collapse. A group of prominent families had gathered in Virginia to discuss the future of their movement."

"Was one of the families named Barclay?" Art asked.

Boone nodded. "He was there. As was Nathan Forrest, Jefferson Davis, and some other folks you probably never heard of. The letter even mentioned a friend of Barclay's son; a young fiery actor who had recently played a role in The Marble Heart and was apparently quite handsome according to the woman who wrote this letter. The actor was also the angriest of the group, but the older men dismissed him and he ran from the house in a rage."

"Who wrote the letter?" Art asked.

"Grand-daddy said she was one of the servants of the house. She was a brilliant young black student known to our family only as Sally. She volunteered to spy on the Barclays for us. She endured a lot of hardship and died much too early for the cause. Interestingly, the Barclays and some other families never concealed their words in front of the slaves. I suppose they thought of them as ignorant or worse. They couldn't have been more wrong.

"Anyway, a few of the southern families wanted to regroup and begin a new assault on the North. Barclay and others seemed to realize the war was lost. So they devised a plan to retreat and regroup."

"How?" Daniel asked.

"In the west."

"The west?" Art asked.

"Yep. You see, Barclay and Forrest devised an unconventional plan to fight the carpetbaggers. Forrest favored a guerilla war but Barclay wanted to rebuild their forces out west for an eventual two front war against the north. The southern Confederates would lay low and drag out Reconstruction until the federal troops were gone and then move to retake the north once they rebuilt their forces."

"So your family contacted Alison and requested the key," Art said.

"The Barclays were high on our watch list. When we heard of this plot, there was a family meeting. It was decided it constituted an emergency. They thought it was too risky to move the box without knowing the contents so we sent for the key. Alison couldn't travel so we arranged to have a cousin meet him on the plains east of Denver. Alison picked the spot.

"Jefferson Davis was the man circled on the Confederate bill your friend found. It was a signal agreed upon for the meeting since the aide had never met my great grandfather."

"So what happened?"

"No one knows. Alison suspected that someone in his office may have betrayed him and sent agents to meet or follow them."

"The Barclays knew?"

"It's possible. They watched us, too. They just didn't regard our family as much of a threat. There were always rumors of the silver box, but I think the Barclays dismissed it as legend after the older generations died off. Their descendants probably didn't know anything about the contents either."

"So what do you plan to do if Sarah finds the key?" Art asked.

"Based on what you've told me, we don't have much choice. We have to open it."

"Then what?" Daniel asked.

"One bridge crossing at a time, son."

"I think maybe..." Art's words were cut short by a low growl from the King Shepherd as it lifted its massive head from the floor.

***

Reaper held back a few yards from the others and covered the rear as his lead man Ivan advanced on the house. The four man Gerovit team snaked across the property and took up positions in the trees about fifty yards from the cabin. He had convinced Sheriff Hatch to stage his men at the junction of the dead end road near the highway. They were at least five miles away through the dense woods and wouldn't hear a sound from Reaper's team.

'The FBI' would take the lead and call in the locals only if needed. Hatch demanded that he be present and Reaper saw an opportunity.

"You say this man killed an officer?" Reaper asked as they waited back in the trees.

"My father," Hatch said.

Hatch couldn't see the grin forming on Reaper's face in the half-moon light.

"Really. I see now why you are so eager to arrest him. If it were my father, I think I'd want revenge," Reaper said.

"Let's just say I won't be too upset if he catches a bullet during the arrest," Hatch said as he rocked the slide back a half inch and checked his pistol.

"That sounds more like a vigilante than a law man," Reaper said.

"Sometimes…up here…we need to be both," Hatch said.

Reaper nodded in agreement and withdrew a suppressor from his jacket. He slowly screwed it onto the barrel of his pistol as Hatch watched.

"I've always wanted to see one of those in action," Hatch said.

"Then tonight is your lucky night, Sheriff," Reaper said as he pointed the gun at Hatch's left eye and squeezed the trigger.

The whisper from the sub-sonic round blended in with the soft breeze as the sheriff's body crumpled to the ground. Not even the owls offered a hoot in protest.

Reaper jogged up to the next large walnut tree and watched as his man Ivan floated from one tree to the next like a wraith. He closed the distance to the dirt bike in under thirty seconds. Reaper watched with pride as the man he'd plucked from the ranks of the Spetnaz performed his field craft with perfection. He had hopes that one day Ivan would run the organization after he retired.

Reaper's breast buzzed as his satellite phone vibrated. He plucked the phone from his cargo pocket, and seeing Pavel's name, answered the poorly timed call.

"Speak quickly; we are making our approach."

"Barclay has betrayed us."

"Go on."

"He hired our Armenian *friend* to pay you a visit as soon as possible."

"How much is the contract?" Reaper asked.

"Two million."

Reaper was amused. The governor was obviously cleaning house in the run up to his candidacy.

"Where is the Armenian?"

"Don't worry. We called in a favor and took care of him. He won't be bothering us."

"Good. Does Barclay know?"

"No. What do you want me to do?" Pavel asked.

Reaper thought for a moment as he checked on Ivan's progress. He was nearly at the porch as he belly-crawled from the cover of a motorbike. Barclay had become a liability. His last few weeks were a wanderlust of errors that threatened to expose the group. Now Barclay had played his last hand. The earth was no longer big enough for them both. Once Barclay won the Presidency it would be all but impossible to stop him. Reaper accepted without hesitation the only outcome that guaranteed his survival.

"Kill him. Make it look natural."

"You don't want the honor?"

Reaper considered it for a moment. It would give him pleasure to look the smug politician in the eye as he took his last breath.

He could always visit Barclay and kill him after he got the journal, but time was precious. He had to ensure this whole mess was wrapped up as soon as possible and one thing he had learned in his line of work was to strike the target at the first opportunity. He had enough on his plate with the Von Hollens and he never backed out of an assignment.

Reaper knew there was another reason to see this through...Daniel Von Hollen. Reaper fingered the bullet scar on his hip as he thought back to their first encounter in a Denver hotel and regretted that he hadn't killed him on the spot. Tonight he would finish it.

"*Nyet.* Do we still have a man on his staff?"

"*Da.* I will call him immediately and give the order."

"Good. We'll be back tomorrow. I want to regroup in the morning and do a full debrief. This operation has suffered from too many mistakes. It's unacceptable."

"Yes, sir."

Reaper tucked the phone away and cursed under his breath at the thought of Barclay taking a contract out on him. He replaced the thought with one of Barclay slipping into darkness, and the corner of his mouth curled up in satisfaction.

Tom Adair

Reaper put a compact pair of night vision goggles to his eyes as Ivan crept up onto the porch and took a position to the left of the front window. If the Von Hollens were present, Ivan would give the signal and the team would advance on the cabin. There would be no prisoners. No escape. Tonight...it would end.

49

Sarah helped Melvin place the last of the human remains in the body bag. The team continued excavating but no weapon had been found.

Melvin looked around to see if they were alone. "What the hell is going on here Sarah?" he whispered.

"It's a bit complicated."

"Give me the Reader's Digest version."

"I think it's better if you wait to read about it in the paper."

Melvin wiped his mouth and exhaled deeply.

"How long have we known each other Sarah?"

"Long enough."

"My point. If I'm standing next to a hornet's nest, I deserve to know, don't I?"

Now it was Sarah looking around to make sure they were alone.

"Melvin…you trust me?"

"Of course."

"Then trust me when I tell you the less you know the better."

Melvin let out a deep sigh. "When this is over I expect the whole story."

"Deal," Sarah said before adding, "there is one more little favor I have to ask."

With very little protest, Melvin agreed to let Sarah collect the clothing and book it in separately from the remains. She had everything neatly arranged in large paper bags along the edge of the graves.

She slammed her door shut as she noted a new caravan of SUVs coming down the road in a cloud of dust. She set her camera down before heading towards Manny at a brisk pace.

Sheriff Westin leaned against his truck and seemed to pay little attention to the new arrivals at his crime scene. Manny didn't look as calm as he hiked his pants and smoothed out his dark hair. Sarah caught up to the group and was just about to ask who the visitors were when, to her horror, Governor Barlcay and several serious looking aides exited the lead vehicle.

Barclay extended his boney hand to Sheriff Westin and flashed his media polished smile.

"Sheriff Westin, how are you?"

"I couldn't be better," he said giving Vargas a wink.

Barclay made eye contact with each member of the sheriff's team as he sized up the group.

"So what brings you out to our sleepy county, Governor?"

Barclay put a soft hand on Westin's elbow and turned him away from the group.

"Can I have a word in private, Brian?"

Sarah watched Barclay place a hand on Westin's shoulder as they walked a few yards away.

***

"I need a favor from you on this one, Brian," Barclay said.

"I'm afraid I can't help you out Governor, this appears to be the scene of a double murder."

Barclay posed a quizzical look at the Sheriff.

"Dr. Russell tells me that these graves are over a century old. What possible concern is that to your agency?" Barclay said testing the sheriff.

"We haven't confirmed the age yet and until we get the evidence back to the laboratory we won't know for sure."

Barclay couldn't contain his amazement and smirked.

"I see. You want something from me, is that it? Fine, what can I offer you; perhaps a position heading the department of corrections?"

Not a muscle moved on Westin's stone-like expression.

Seeing this, Barclay wagged a finger and broke out into a wide smile.

"No, you've got your eye on the brass ring, don't you? After all, you're looking at the next President of the United States. All right, I'll play along. What will it take then…a cabinet position?"

Westin's expression turned to one of disgust as he shook his head and replied, "There is nothing you can offer me, Governor; I will make sure we investigate these murders to the fullest extent. Let the chips fall where they may."

278

Bloodlines

Barclay realized in that moment that the sheriff knew more than he had thought and changed tactics.

"Are you sure this is a fight you want?" he whispered.

Westin looked the Governor over from head to toe, "Frankly Governor, I don't think it will be much of a fight."

Barclay's eyes narrowed before lobbing a dismissive smirk at Westin.

"Mike…Major Gentry…will you join us please?" Barclay called out.

Westin knew well the two men who sauntered over. Mike Copeland was the state Attorney General. He didn't share the Governor's views on most issues or his party affiliation, but he was a dutiful AG. Major Cliff Gentry was a no nonsense, by-the-book state trooper on the Governor's staff.

"Mr. Attorney General, will you kindly inform Sheriff Westin to the situation he finds himself in," Barclay said.

Copeland looked sheepish and sounded apologetic as he read the state statutes provided from Dr. Russell.

"I'm sorry, Brian, you don't have a choice. The law is clear and I'm afraid if you try to block the state archaeologist from conducting their duty, I'll have no option but to instruct Major Gentry here to take you into custody."

"And believe me Brian, Major Gentry *does* have a jail cell to put you in," Barclay said with an icy tone.

Tilly Helton approached the group and tugged at the AG's sleeve. She had known Mike Copeland for years through her work at the Facility.

"Tilly? Can I help you?" Copeland said.

Tilly extended her cell phone to the AG, "There is someone that wants to talk to you, Mike."

Copeland gave her a quizzical look, but took the phone and listened for several minutes. His expression changed from confusion, to understanding, to relief.

"Yes, your honor, I understand completely. I will take care of it." Copeland said, and handed the phone back to Tilly.

Barclay noticed the look of pure astonishment on Copeland's face as he handed the phone back to Tilly.

"Who the hell was that?" Governor Barclay demanded.

Copeland looked at each man in the group and then back to Tilly.

"Mike?" Westin said.

Copeland looked back at Westin and gave a subtle wink. He made sure no one else could see it.

"That was Chief Justice Burger of the state Supreme Court," he paused for a moment to glance from Barclay to Westin. "He has issued an injunction against the state archaeologist and her office from interfering in this on-going murder investigation."

Copeland stood ramrod straight as he addressed Major Gentry like a drill instructor.

"Major Gentry, you are hereby commanded to remove from this scene all persons not affiliated with Arapahoe County law enforcement. Should *any person* resist your orders," he paused looking sideways at the Governor, "you are commanded to arrest them for obstruction of this court order and remand them to the United States Marshals Office for an appearance before Chief Justice Burger Monday morning."

He passed Tilly's phone over to Major Gentry after opening the attached document sent to the phone.

"This is outrageous!" Barclay wailed.

Copeland maintained his professional composure. The same was not true of Westin. The sheriff saddled up next to the Governor and whispered into his ear.

"By the way *Aaron*; that ill-advised stunt you sanctioned in my evidence room…you'll pay for that."

"Good luck proving anything, Brian. When I'm done with you, you'll be lucky to hold a job directing traffic at a construction site."

Barclay took a step back as Westin squared off in front of him. Barclay could smell the man's breath through his wicked smile.

"I have the video, Aaron. I promise you it will make for some great campaign videos."

Barclay's eyes widened as the veins covering his temples began to throb. He pursed his lips and they trembled as if holding back flood waters. Then a wave of calm flowed over his face erasing all signs of tension. Without a word, Barclay turned and calmly walked back to his SUV and climbed inside.

***

Bloodlines

Westin and Copeland shared a look of pure satisfaction before returning to the small group of investigators waiting ten yards away with Tilly. Copeland returned the phone to the older woman who wore a devilish expression.

"Okay, who's confused," Sarah said raising her hand.

Vargas joined her.

"How on earth did you manage that Tilly?" Copeland asked.

"Oh, that?" she said in her best southern drawl. "Well, as you know Mike, I'm not a lawyer. So after Dr. Russell arrived, I made a call to a friend and asked his *legal* opinion."

"You're friends with the chief justice?" Copeland asked.

"Me? Heaven's no. I called Judge Paul Whittier over in Golden. Do you know him?"

"Yes, I know Judge Whittier."

"Well Paul was just as confused as I was and I believe he was the one who called his good friend justice Burger for clarification. Apparently, they know each other from the Masonic lodge," she added, winking at Sarah.

"You don't say," Sarah said.

Tilly winked at Sarah again.

"Richards?" Westin said, "Get this scene wrapped up and the evidence back to the lab before somebody changes their mind and rescinds that court order."

"With pleasure, sir."

50

The King Shepherd crossed the floor and pointed at the wall adjacent to the corner of the window as if a pheasant was hidden behind it. Art had barely shifted in his chair when Boone snatched the thick rifle and thumbed the selector switch to semi-auto fire. His next move took Daniel and Art by complete surprise as he leveled the rifle and squeezed the trigger. The one hundred eighty grain bullet spat from the heavy barrel and cut through the window glass at nearly twenty-seven hundred feet per second.

Daniel never saw the man peek in the lower corner of the window before his head evaporated into a cloud of blood, bone, and buzz cut hair. Before the body thumped to the ground, a barrage of bullets began striking the cabin in deep echoing thuds.

Daniel dove for the light switch and Art collapsed to a prone position. The thick log walls stopped the rounds from penetrating, but soon the gunfire was redirected to the windows and thick cabin door.

Boone casually crossed the floor and peeked outside from the edge of the window. He thrust the heavy rifle out the window, flipped the selector switch to full auto, and emptied the magazine into the darkness. Daniel followed with a few rounds from his pistol as the older man reloaded.

Daniel watched in awe as the older man moved with the precision and purpose of a tier one operator with a dozen deployments under his belt. Without hesitation, Boone upended the heavy kitchen table and ordered Art to take cover. He then barked a command to his dog in Dutch before crossing the floor and heaving open the trap door leading down into the mine.

He looked up at Daniel, and with a hint of impatience said, "Let's go hunting."

"Stay down and out of sight," Daniel said pointing at Art.

Daniel holstered his pistol as he followed the older man down the ladder. At the bottom, Boone flipped a switch and a string of red lights glowed down the dark shaft.

Bloodlines

Boone paused and handed Daniel his rifle before grabbing its twin slung on a hook in the rock wall. Without a word, Boone racked a round in the chamber and tore off down the tunnel with Daniel on his heels.

They went about fifty yards before making a sharp left down another tunnel. They left the red lights in the distance as Daniel noticed the height of the tunnel shrinking. Ahead was a glimmer of moon light, and by the time they reached it, they were crawling up a gradual incline on hands and knees.

The entrance to the mine was partially blocked by a tangled bush that Boone parted down the middle with his rifle barrel. He scanned the darkened property and made several inaudible grunts as Daniel strained to look over his shoulder.

"Follow me, stay quiet, and watch my six," he said looking back at Daniel.

"I do it for a living," Daniel replied.

Boone crossed the darkness with the skill reminiscent of Daniel's former instructors. Like a shark sensing blood in the water, he closed the distance on the first man without even seeing him until he was a mere five yards away. The man was talking into a headset and firing controlled three round bursts into the cabin.

Boone rested his rifle against a large oak and slid his right sleeve up a few inches. He unwound a garrote from the leather band covering his wrist and took the ends in each hand. He struck with surprise, speed, and an overwhelming force of violence as the man's words were cut off from the headset. The man's rifle dropped to the ground with a slight clank that was masked by the continued gunfire on the cabin.

Daniel unhooked the man's radio and fastened the headset over his right ear. He listened as one of the voices called for a situation report in Russian. Daniel was about to give a hand signal to his partner but Boone was already closing the distance on the second man. Daniel wanted to advance on the other shooters but he had to cover his new partner.

The man's weapon was on semi-auto fire as he spat single bullets from the barrel and into the window. Daniel watched as Boone came within ten feet. Before he could close the distance, the man advanced to the next tree and fired three quick rounds at another window.

There was now another five feet between them. Daniel watched the older man reach up under the back of his shirt and draw out a black combat tomahawk. Even in the darkness, Daniel could see the resemblance to the one his father had carried in Vietnam.

Boone crouched and spun around the tree to the man's gun side. He closed half the distance before the killer caught the movement.

Boone was completely exposed as he advanced. The Russian killer spun his compact rifle around with lightning speed towards the advancing man.

The muzzle was an inch from crossing his chest when Boone smashed the blade of his tomahawk into the barrel and drove it to the side. He never broke stride as his body slammed the man into the thick walnut tree.

The killer grabbed Boone's right arm and tried to leverage it away from him. Boone corrected his stance, clasped the shaft below the blade head, and in one powerful move, drove the end spike between the man's eyes.

Daniel was so fixated on the skill of his host that he almost missed the Russian closing in on them from the left.

Daniel shifted left as the man advanced firing controlled bursts. The tree bark exploded all around Boone as he dropped and rolled on the ground.

Daniel anchored the heavy wooden stock into his shoulder, crouched and spun right around the tree, and sent three rounds into the man's chest at a mere twenty yards.

Boone gave a thankful nod before getting to his feet and scanning the area behind him. Daniel was scanning the darkness for the other shooters when a fragmentation grenade skipped across the ground and came to rest at their feet.

The last thing Daniel saw before diving behind the nearest tree was Boone lunging for the grenade.

51

Daniel heard two gunshots before the deafening explosion tore through the night air. He checked his body for signs of blood, then shouldered his weapon and spun around the tree. Out of the corner of his eye, he saw Hawkins Boone lying a distance away from him, on his left side. The man wasn't moving.

Daniel didn't stop to check him as he swung the muzzle back and forth ahead of him looking for the man who'd thrown the grenade.

Advancing ten yards, he found the mangled heap of torn flesh and shattered bone. Then he heard a groan.

Daniel turned and rushed back to his new friend. The older man was clasping his hand over his shoulder which had been peppered with shrapnel.

"*Jesus*, are you okay?" Daniel asked.

Boone clenched his teeth, grimaced, and nodded as Daniel helped him to his feet. *The old man is one tough son-of-a-bitch,* Daniel thought. Boone checked his rifle and wobbled a step. Daniel propped him against the tree seconds before a trio of bullets whistled past his head.

On instinct, Daniel turned left and angled away from Boone hoping to draw fire. The Russian was advancing from somewhere behind the cabin.

Daniel sent several rounds down range with metronomic rhythm. Seconds later, Boone was advancing on a convergent angle pinning the last man in an inescapable crossfire that cut him down as the action locked open on Daniel's empty rifle.

Not wanting to make the same mistake twice, the two men stood back to back behind a large tree as they peered into the darkness around them.

"Nice friends you have there," Boone said after catching his breath.

Daniel strained to hear any sound of danger in the darkness. Hearing none, he checked his friend's shoulder.

"Mom always warned us of stranger danger," he said flashing his white teeth.

Daniel propped his empty rifle against the tree and drew his tactical knife. He turned Boone away and cut away the bloody cloth over his shoulder. The wounds were not as bad as he had feared. Daniel was sure he could improvise a clotting agent from material in the cabin and stem the flow of blood until he could get medical aid.

"How on earth did you dodge that grenade?"

"I kicked it back to him," Boone said.

Daniel ducked under the opposite shoulder and helped his host towards the cabin. He froze about half-way to the front porch as a voice came over the headset he was still wearing.

"Bravo, Daniel."

Daniel recognized the heavy Slavic accent and sheltered Boone behind a woodpile. He grabbed the man's rifle and scanned the area.

"Why don't you join us?" the voice said.

"Us?"

"Art and I would love to sit and chat with you."

Daniel cursed under his breath as he checked the other Browning rifle. Two rounds left.

"Do you have any other magazines?" Daniel whispered.

"In the cabin."

Shit.

"Stay here, there's at least one tango in the cabin. If he gets the drop on me, I want you to grab a weapon off one of the dead guys and hide in the mine. Once he's gone, get to Denver and find Sarah Richards with the Arapahoe County Sheriff's Office. Help her find the key. Do you understand?"

Hawkins Boone nodded.

Daniel began to rise when Boone grabbed his arm.

"Men of honor never fail," he said.

Daniel smiled as he patted the man's arm.

Daniel approached the porch stairs with glacial speed, rifle up and swinging between the open door and windows. He expected to get cut down with each step and was surprised when he was able to take another. The lights were back on in the cabin, but Daniel could see little through the half-open door.

The front steps moaned with age as he took each one. He angled across the open doorway keeping the muzzle in front of him. Daniel winced at the sight of the dog crumpled in a heap on the floor. He didn't see any blood but he knew it was dead.

Daniel ran the length of the rifle along the door and swept it open as he stood at the jamb. As the door swung wide, his worst fears became reality. The black-haired Russian stood behind Art with a suppressed pistol. There wasn't enough of his head exposed to risk a snap shot.

"Hello Daniel, it's good to see you again."

"Is it?"

"It seems like only yesterday that we met in that hotel hallway. You gave me a little souvenir, remember?" the assassin asked.

"I remember you running away like a little girl," Daniel said.

Daniel could only see half the broad smile from behind Art's head.

"I can hear the anger in your voice, Daniel. You must want to kill me so bad you can taste it."

"Believe it or not, I've thought about it. A few years ago I might have settled for putting a round through that greasy head of yours, but you're actually worth more to me alive."

"Why is that?"

"Intelligence. Dead men can't talk. I suspect the guys at the agency will be overjoyed to dig into that mush you call a brain."

"No doubt. I think you may be over-estimating your position. We've been here before, you and I. I seem to remember something in your file about your inability to sacrifice a friend for the greater good. That hasn't changed, has it? I'll bet that August night in the Toro Boro still haunts you."

Daniel didn't let his shock show on his face. That mission, that failure, was classified at the highest levels of the military.

"You seem to be well informed, Mr…?"

"Nice try. That's not how this game is played, you know that."

"What do I call you then?"

"In a few moments, it won't matter."

"So what…you're just going to kill us? Why not take a sniper shot? That's your preference, isn't it?" Daniel asked.

"Truth be told, I wanted to meet you. I wanted to look into your eyes at the moment you lost this battle."

"So you're a psychopath, too. Good to know."

"Oh, come now Daniel. This is the way you prefer things, yes? Soldier to soldier."

"Art is not a soldier. Why don't you let him go and we can settle this with honor."

"Sure, sure… You just put your rifle down first…"

Daniel glanced around the room. A hundred tactical scenarios were racing through his mind. Had it been any other hostage he might have risked a snap shot, but not with Art. He couldn't take the chance. Not yet.

Daniel only had two rounds left and wasn't experienced enough with the heavy rifle to ensure the kind of accuracy he needed. If he tried to retreat, the killer would just shoot Art anyway. It was an impossible situation.

Daniel heard Art wince in pain as Reaper tightened his vice-like grip on Art's shoulder.

"You're out of options, Daniel. Put the rifle down or watch your uncle die."

"Don't…" Art said as Reaper pressed the muzzle into his ear.

"Okay, okay! Look…I'm putting it down," he said as he propped the rifle against the wall outside the door and stepped inside.

"Where is your friend?" Reaper asked.

"The grenade did him in," Daniel said.

"What a shame. Close the door and lock it please," Reaper said motioning with the gun.

Daniel stole a glance for Boone outside, but didn't see him before closing the door and throwing the latch. He surveyed the room for an improvised weapon or tactical advantage but found nothing of use. Nothing he could get to before the killer shot him, that is.

"I must say I'm impressed you were able to handle my men the way you did. They were some of my best. How did you do it?"

"They were louder than two elephants fucking on bubble wrap. It wasn't hard."

"I see," Reaper said grinning widely. "I can't tell you how much I'm going to enjoy killing you, Mr. Von Hollen."

"Him or me?" Art asked with a trace of humor.

"Both, I'm afraid."

"So what are you waiting for?" Art asked.

"First, I'd like to know what you're doing here?" Reaper asked.

"We thought it was a dude ranch," Daniel said.

"It must have something to do with the journal, yes? Where is the journal?"

Daniel glanced at Art's bag on the coffee table. He let his glance linger just long enough to ensure the assassin saw it too. Reaper moved towards the bag using Art as a shield.

"Get it out...slowly," he said to his hostage.

Art reached out and inched the leather bound book out of the bag.

"Open it."

Art did as he was told and Reaper glanced at the text while keeping Daniel in his peripheral vision.

"It's in code," Reaper said.

"Yes. We came here to break it," Daniel said.

"The old man," Reaper said.

"Yes," Daniel lied.

"And now I suppose you'll tell me the code key died with him?"

"Not exactly. There is a code key. Let Art go and I'll tell you where it is."

Reaper revealed a wicked grin. "How about I just shoot your uncle until you tell me. I'll start with the right foot..."

"Wait!" Daniel said. "I'll tell you."

"I'm waiting," Reaper said.

"The silver box...on the mantle; the code book is inside." Daniel said.

Reaper turned Art and pushed him face first into the wall.

"Move an inch, Arthur and I'll put you down. You too, Daniel...face the window; hands on the glass."

Daniel did as he was instructed but kept the killer in his sights using the reflection from the remaining glass shards.

Reaper inched backwards towards the mantle, keeping one eye on each man. The gun never wavered from Daniel.

Daniel watched as he crept closer to the mantle when his eye caught the faintest hint of movement to his left. Without moving his head, he shifted his sight towards the corner of the window and stared down the barrel of the Browning Automatic Rifle.

Daniel adjusted his focus and through the window caught the edge of a familiar face. Boone looked to have the rifle aligned just over Daniel's shoulder. The trajectory was a little too close for Daniel's comfort, but they were both thinking the same thing apparently. It was like working with one of his old teammates.

Daniel knew they would have only one shot and he calculated the time it would take to close in on the killer. Daniel allowed a slight bend in his knees as he focused on the killer moving towards the silver box. Reaper's steps were slow and shallow as he inched backwards but when he applied his weight to the soft board, he didn't stand a chance.

Daniel dropped his shoulder and went to a knee as Reaper's right leg crashed through the floor up to his thigh. Reaper fell back to his right and sent a suppressed round over Daniel's head as a much louder boom echoed through the room and window glass showered the floor. Daniel kept his eyes on Reaper as he dropped and saw the bullet strike the center of his chest. He hesitated for a split second until he saw the suppressed pistol begin to swing back his way.

Daniel dove forward and rolled past a chair as two more rounds zipped behind him and impacted the couch near Art. Daniel rolled up on his feet like a frog and lunged the last few feet at Reaper. He crashed into the Russian and heard him yell as his body was hyper-extended backwards. Daniel hoped his hip was dislocated.

He heard another suppressed round thud into the cabin wall as he struggled to gain control of the man's gun hand.

The man managed to land a devastating head butt to Daniel and he struggled to fight back the darkness clouding his head when he felt the impact of another body.

Art tried to grab the free arm but lost control and Reaper soon had his beefy hand clamped around Art's jugular. The man had the strength of a gorilla.

Daniel struggled as another head butt struck just below his eye. He drove two quick punches into the man's abdomen when his worst fears were realized. The assassin was wearing body armor.

Bloodlines

Taking a new course, Daniel slammed his fist into the man's groin but it only served to anger him more. His rage was fueled by a sudden adrenalin surge and he thrashed the man.

Daniel looked to Art and saw his face turning blue from lack of oxygen. He tried several more body blows but they were of no effect.

We are not going to die here! He yelled in his mind as he readjusted his grip on the gun hand. Daniel felt his grip slipping and from the corner of his eye he watched with dread as the muzzle turned towards him.

Time seemed to stand still as he watched the trigger finger flex and he waited for the bullet to spit from the muzzle towards him. He was just about to reach for his knife when a large boot stomped the gun hand onto the wooden floor.

The assassin screamed in pain as Boone ground his boot on the man's fingers until he released the gun. The man struggled a moment more until the muzzle from the Browning rifle pressed hard against his forehead.

"I may have only one shot here, Joe, but one's all I need." Boone said.

Art and Daniel dragged the man away from the box and slammed him face down onto the floor. Daniel made a quick search for a poison. He didn't want to lose this man like they had the other assassin at the Facility.

Art managed to find a roll of duct tape in the kitchen and they bound his hands and feet before securing a strip over his mouth. Only when their prisoner was searched and deemed safe did Daniel allow himself to relax.

"I thought I told you to go to the mine," Daniel said, breathing heavily.

"You did." Boone said.

"What if you'd been killed along with us…what then?"

"I guess I'd be dead."

Daniel rubbed his face in frustration as Boone knelt next to his dog and ran his fingers through the thick coat.

Art was sitting on his heels catching his breath, "What are we going to do with him?"

"You boys leave him to me," Boone said. He stood and walked to the end table, opened the drawer, and pulled out a fresh magazine for his rifle.

"You can't kill him," Daniel said.

"You don't have to watch."

Boone dropped the old magazine and slammed the fresh one into the well before charging the weapon. The clank of the metal slide seemed especially loud in the quiet room.

Daniel stepped in front of his host and put his hand up, "I can't let you."

"He killed my dog. Would have killed you and your uncle if it weren't for me."

"I know, and I'm grateful, but he'll be tried in a court of law."

"Yeah, well…tonight…tonight I'm holding court," he said as he brushed past Daniel.

He leveled the rifle at Reaper's head when Daniel called out, "And what of your obligation?"

"What obligation?"

Daniel came around him and stood facing the muzzle.

"The one John Henry entrusted to you. The obligation he swore to General Washington. You have a duty…your country is in danger." He inched the muzzle down towards the floor with his finger.

"This man can help us stop Barclay…put an end to this mystery once and for all."

Art got to his feet and joined his nephew in facing the older man. "You've done right by your family, Boone. Let us help you finish the job."

Hawkins Boone dropped his head and let out a long sigh. He looked tired. More tired than Daniel thought possible. He handed the rifle to Daniel and put his hands on his hips.

"What did you have in mind?"

Daniel thought for a moment until the corners of his mouth rose in a grin.

"How fast is that Oldsmobile out there?"

52

Art called Tilly to make arrangements to have his plane flown out to meet them and was pleasantly surprised to discover she had already sent it to Williamsburg after hearing of him being sighted there.

Thank God for Patty Anne, Art thought as he made a mental note to send a nice thank you gift. The plane was waiting for them at the regional airport about an hour and a half away.

Art filled Tilly in on the plan and listened intently as she told him about the dig. He gave some final instructions and hung up the phone before joining the other men hovering over the kitchen table.

Daniel and Boone were studying maps of the local terrain.

"This is a crazy plan, son," Boone said.

"No, it's perfect. I'll start out ahead of you two on point. That motorbike will make more noise than a grizzly in heat. If there are any cops around, they'll follow me, making it easier for you two to slip out undetected."

"There could be a dozen cops out there in the darkness," Boone said.

"I don't think so. If they were close, they would have heard the gunshots and be here by now. It's only a matter of time though. Somebody could have heard the gunfire and called 911. We may not have a lot of time."

"He's right," Art said. "I'm afraid the local sheriff is gunning for us. He and his deputies will be on edge."

"Say we get out of here, you expect us to drive all the way to Colorado?" Hawkins Boone asked.

Art filled them in on the arrival of the plane before adding, "We have a problem though."

"What?"

"What are we going to do with him?" Art said motioning to their prisoner. "If we leave him here, he'll just shoot or bribe his way out of jail."

"I guess we take him with us then," Daniel said.

"That's kidnapping, Daniel." Art said.

"We prefer to call it *rendition*."

"Whatever. His lawyer will use it for grounds to get a mistrial and set him free on bond. Then you can kiss him goodbye," Art said.

"What if there was another way?" Daniel asked.

"What did you have in mind?" Art said.

"You've already had one attempt on your life…" Daniel said.

Art smiled as Daniel spoke and the plan materialized in his head. His nephew never ceased to amaze him.

"So we tell the authorities we caught him at the Facility."

"It'll be his word against ours. I can even put another round through your office window, if you'd like Uncle Art."

"Not necessary," Art said holding up a hand.

"The best part is the local sheriff can save face after losing the last assassin."

"Genius."

"What about me?" Boone said.

Art and Daniel both exchanged glances. Art was about to say something when Reaper's satellite phone began to buzz on the table. Art glanced at the caller ID and hesitated for a second before answering in silence.

"Where are you?" Governor Barclay said.

Art recognized the voice but didn't know what to say.

"Have you got the journal?" Barclay snapped.

Art cupped his hand over the mouthpiece and took a deep breath before answering.

"We have your man."

"Who the hell is this?"

"You know who this is Aaron."

The line was silent on the other end and Art checked the display to make sure the call was still active.

"You don't have to speak, Aaron. I know what you've been up to and once the authorities get a chance to question this man I'm sure they'll have all the evidence they need to bury you."

"Where are you?"

"We'll be home soon enough."

There was silence on the line for several seconds and Art thought of hanging up just before Barclay spoke.

"Perhaps we can arrange a deal…a trade perhaps?"

Bloodlines

Art felt the bile rising in his gut. Barclay was just like every murderous thug he had ever pursued…he just happened to live in the Governor's mansion.

"Governor…you've got nothing I want, and once I get back to Colorado…you can run for President of the Canyon City Prison book club." Art punched the end call button and tossed the phone onto the sofa.

***

Sarah sat at the edge of the examination table resting her chin in her palms. She had brought most of the evidence back to the crime lab while a few technicians from the Facility team finished up at the dig site.

Sheriff Westin had ordered her to pull an all-nighter if necessary to find something they could hang on Barclay. Westin was in the investigations conference room reviewing the video detective Vargas had mysteriously acquired before the hard drive was wiped. Sarah knew it was no mystery. She remembered the computer technician taking a call from Vargas shortly after they had arrived at the computer lab. It didn't take a master detective to realize Vegas got an extra copy to use for blackmail or insurance. That was his M.O. *Hell, Marv might be one of his main sources of information,* Sarah thought.

The detectives were now briefing the sheriff on the double homicide and prostitution house as they weighed the possibility of serving an arrest warrant on the most senior elected official in the state.

She had searched and photographed all of the clothing from the grave before screening the soil samples they had collected. She managed to find two lead bullets, one from each soil sample around the men's shattered skulls. There was also a train ticket stub and pocket watch in one of the pockets.

She took high resolution photomicrographs then measured and weighed each one before e-mailing the specifications to Walter Haruki, the famed firearms examiner at the Facility. Walter enhanced his international notoriety the previous year by identifying the mysterious bullets that took the lives of several teenagers and the previous Governor.

Maybe he could use them to identify a possible murder weapon.

Daniel found Sheriff Hatch's body before throwing Reaper into the trunk of the Oldsmobile and slamming the lid. He took the police radio from the Sheriff's belt and handed it to Art.

"Monitor the channels. With any luck, I'll pull them in the opposite direction and you'll have a clear path to the airport. If I'm not there by oh-one hundred, take off without me."

"I'm not about to leave you stranded, Daniel."

"Believe me Art, I'll be along. Getting out of Kentucky will be a snap compared to some of the places I've been left behind."

"Well, just the same...let's plan on you making it there." Art said.

Daniel made a lazy salute as he fired up the motorbike and tore off down the dead-end mountain road.

"Don't worry, Art. He'll make it," Boone said as he placed the silver box on the seat between them.

"I'm not worried; Daniel is extremely resourceful."

Boone checked the mirrors and gauges before firing up the throaty V-8.

"Where on earth did you get this thing?" Art asked.

"Daddy got it in a poker game with a former rumrunner."

"You don't say?"

"Yep, aces and eights."

"The dead man's hand," Art said.

"Let's hope not," Boone said as he shifted the car into first and smashed the accelerator to the floorboard.

They were halfway to the highway when Art heard the panicked calls over the police radio. Daniel had broken a blockade and shot out the front tire on two police cruisers which were now trying to catch up on three wheels and a rim.

The local police were dispatching officers to aid in the pursuit and trying to raise Sheriff Hatch on the radio in Art's hand. It was only a matter of minutes before they sent someone looking for Hatch.

Art placed a hand on the silver box as they fishtailed through a turn and rattled over a pothole.

"Easy...explosives remember?" Art said.

"Don't you worry, I know these roads better than the men that built 'em."

Bloodlines

Art was about to respond with sarcasm when he saw the faintest of colors bouncing off the trees ahead. It took him a second to recognize the source as they grew in intensity around the next turn.

The red and blue strobe lights blazed through their windshield as the police cruiser rounded the corner fifty yards ahead. Boone killed his lights which prompted the police cruiser to hit his high beams.

Art guessed the cruiser was doing at least fifty based on the way the car bounced over the ruts in the road. The police car hogged the middle of the road barreling at them like a freight train.

Boone matched the trajectory and drove the accelerator pedal to the floor.

"What the *hell* are you doing?"

"Trust me. I know all these local cops. He'll move."

Art flexed his legs and pushed on the floor with his feet as if willing a brake pedal to materialize as he gripped the door handle.

"Boone..."

"He'll move."

"Booooone..." Art yelled just before Boone let out a barbaric cry of battle and choked the steering wheel until his fingers turned pale.

Ten feet from impact Art could see the fear in the young deputy's eyes as he jerked the steering wheel to the side.

Boone turned in the other direction and missed the back fender by an inch as the patrol car careened off the road and down into a small hay meadow.

Art jerked his head around. "Holy hell!" Art yelled.

Boone struggled to maintain his bearing on the road but after several skids managed to straighten the big Oldsmobile out.

Art looked back just in time to see the officer getting out of the car in the reflection of strobe lights.

"That was close," Art said. "How did you know he'd turn?"

Boone gave a sheepish smile towards Art, "I didn't."

Art let out a deep sigh as Boone patted the dashboard and praised the old car.

"They'll be sending more you know," Art said.

"How many cops you think they got in this county? By the time they figure out which way we've gone, we'll be at the airport," Boone said before he bounced onto the divided highway, traveled a half mile, and then shot off onto another unmarked dirt road.

"That brings us to another problem though," he said.

"What's that?" Art asked.

"What if this Sarah of yours can't find the key? How do you plan on getting into the box without destroying the contents?"

"Good point, maybe I should call her," he said dialing her cell phone.

"Hello?"

"Sarah, its Art."

"Sarah?"

"Yeah Art, I'm here. Listen, I tried…I really tried, but I couldn't find the key. I searched all the clothing and I screened the soil through quarter inch mesh…twice."

"Could it still be in the graves?"

"I wouldn't hold out much hope. Your team has been out there digging the past few hours and they would have called if they'd found something. I did manage to find two lead bullets so I sent the images and data to Walter."

"Well, that's something I guess. There wasn't anything else in the pockets?"

"There was a pocket watch, a train ticket stub, nothing else. I'm sorry, Art. I feel like I let you down," she said.

"Don't be silly, Sarah. It's possible the man who killed them took the key."

"It's a little strange he didn't take any of their other stuff, like the money," she said.

"Robbery wasn't the motive, remember?" Art said.

***

Sarah exhaled in frustration as she looked over the clothing and soil samples arranged in aluminum arson cans. So much work had been done. So much risk had been taken; and for what? She was about to ask Art a question when her eyes drifted up to the wall. There, sandwiched between glass and mat board were photos of the skater shoes Andy had framed for the lab tour. It was as if the lights were suddenly turned on in her mind.

"Sarah, are you still there?"

"Hold on a sec, Art," she said as she rolled her chair around to the other side of the table. She grabbed one of the paper evidence bags. She reached inside and pulled out the old leather boots, placing them on a sheet of brown butcher paper.

Sarah turned the boots over and examined the sole with a magnifying loop. She did a double take as she noticed a small seam along the edge of the heel.

"Sarah?"

"I think I've got something, Art," she said pinching the phone between her cheek and shoulder.

With gloved hands, she wiggled the heel back and forth until she felt a century worth of hardened clay soil give way. The heel slid forward and Sarah popped it from its metal rail. Taking a deep breath, she turned the heel over, and there shining as if it had just been polished, was the spiral shaped key with the serpent head. "Hell yeah!"

"You've got something?"

"I found it Art...I found the key!"

"Where?"

"It was in some kind of hidden compartment in the boot heel. I got the idea from..."

"Sarah, listen carefully," Art said cutting her off. "You need to get that key up to the facility. Daniel and I should be arriving in a few hours. Can you bring it up there?"

"Tonight?"

"Tomorrow is soon enough."

"What about booking it into evidence?"

"There's no time for that. No one else knows about the key, Sarah, and it's not like you're going to be using it in a trial."

He had a point.

"All right, I'll do it."

"Great."

"Where are you? It sounds like you're in a washing machine on full spin," Sarah said.

"It's a little hard to explain right now Sarah."

"Can I talk to Daniel?" Sarah asked.

Art tried to think of something to say that wouldn't alarm her and settled on a version of the truth.

"He's gone ahead to meet the plane. I'll have him call you in flight."

"Oh, okay. Hey Art?"

"Yeah?"

"We did good, huh?"

Art thought about it for a moment when he remembered something his old sergeant used to say.

That glorious moment when you feel bathed in the bright light is usually right before the train hits.

"Yeah, Sarah…"

53

Barclay sat at his desk; his face buried in both hands when Hammond came into the dimly lit office.

"Is everything all right, sir?" Hammond said.

Barclay looked up from his desk and stared over the bridge of his nose at his chief of security.

"That was Art Von Hollen."

"What…where is our man?"

"Captured," Barclay said as he realized the implications.

"Sir…if he talks…"

"You think I don't know that, Wes?" Barclay snapped.

"Of course…Sir. What would you like me to do?"

Barclay had been asking himself the same question for the last few minutes and he kept coming back to the last thing Art said to him on the phone. *Governor…you've got nothing I want.*

"Maybe there is…" he whispered, his eyes partially glazed over.

"Sir?"

Barclay snapped to as if coming out of a trance.

"Wes, I've got an assignment for you. I want you to get that red-haired CSI, the one that was at the dig. The one your man failed to scare off."

"Governor…she's a cop."

"I know she's a cop, *god dammit*." Barclay said as he stood and paced in front of the window. "Do you know what kind of *shit storm* we'll be in if our man talks?"

"Sir, I don't think he'll talk. He's got more to lose than we do."

"Are you willing to bet your life on that? Federal prison would be a vacation compared to the hell these men could bring down on us. We need her to trade for him…and we need to grab her tonight."

Hammond flinched at the sound of a knock at the office door.

"Yes?" the Governor called out. It was his personal assistant.

"Would you like me to pour your nightcap, sir?"

"Ah, yes thank you."

"Something from the private reserve, perhaps?"

"That would be fine," Barclay said.

He waited for her to cross the room out of ear shot before leaning into Hammond's ear to whisper, "Get it done…or *we're* done."

Hammond nodded and headed for the door. He passed the assistant without noticing the white powder being slipped into the Governor's drink.

***

Daniel was waiting at the bottom of the air stairs of the Gulfstream 150 when Art and Boone pulled up. Daniel noticed Art didn't hide his surprise.

"No police escort?"

"Let's not wait around to find out." Daniel said as he opened the trunk and hoisted their prisoner out with some help from Boone.

The sight of a man, head covered by a pillowcase, being dragged to a waiting plane, brought back a rush of memories for Daniel. He felt oddly at ease as if he had traveled back to another time and more dangerous place.

He led Reaper up the stairs and settled him into a captain's chair. He then wrapped his body on the chair with several passes of thick duct tape. Once the prisoner was secured, he turned his attention to Boone. The older man was standing in the doorway with a deer- in- the- headlights look.

"Is something wrong?"

"I've never been on one of these."

"It's just like riding in a car." Daniel said.

"Well…smoother than our ride to get here at least," Art said.

"It seems unnatural to me," Boone said.

"So is jumping out of a perfectly good aircraft but you do what you have to do," Daniel said.

Boone took a seat facing Reaper, buckled his seat belt, and drew it tight as a tourniquet.

Bloodlines

Fifteen minutes into their flight Daniel finally saw the color returning to Boone's fingers when he relaxed his death grip on the armrests as the plane leveled out.

The windows were pitch black with the night sky and Boone wouldn't be able to see the ground below.

Daniel grabbed a water bottle from the galley, snatched the pillowcase from the assassin's head, and tore the strip of tape from his mouth. Some facial hair came with it but the man didn't even flinch. Instead he looked around the cabin and nodded approvingly.

"You have a nice plane."

"I'm glad you like it," Art said as Daniel poured a swig of water down his throat.

"I have a much better plane," the assassin said.

"I'm sure that will come as a great comfort when you're sitting alone in your prison cell," Daniel said.

"I doubt I will see the inside of a cell."

"How do you figure that?" Daniel asked.

The man cast a condescending glare upon the three men as he smirked and shook his head.

"You people have no idea what danger you're in."

"From who...Barclay?" Daniel said.

The brief expression of disbelief was quickly tamped out and replaced with an evil grin.

"My people will come for me, and...for you. They will kill you, your families, your..."

The man's rant was replaced with a muffled scream as Boone leaned forward and flexed Reaper's index finger backwards until it snapped.

"Why don't you exercise your right to remain silent," Boone said.

Daniel and Art exchanged looks of surprise as Daniel replaced the duct tape and pillowcase over their prisoner.

He took a seat diagonal to Boone and let slip the faintest of smiles as he turned off his overhead light and stared out the window. Daniel had been threatened by men like this before; men who thought nothing of strapping bombs to children. The difference was that this man, this assassin, had proven he was capable of delivering on his threat.

He thought of Art and Tilly, but mostly, he thought of Sarah. There in the dim light of the cabin, against the low whine of the engines, Daniel made a solemn vow to heed the warning and ensure this man never hurt another person again.

54

Sarah waved to the off duty cop sitting in his car outside her house as she pulled into the driveway. Opening the door she was greeted by a spastic, whining dog. Ranger bolted into the back yard like a greyhound.

Sarah felt terrible she had left him alone so long and vowed not to test the limits of his bladder again. She considered installing a doggie door but brushed the thought away as she glanced at the mail slot on the front door.

I can't even keep rattlesnakes out...why give the crooks a bigger opening.

Sarah emptied her pockets onto the kitchen counter and caught sight of the spiral key. Holding it by the tip, she turned it slowly under the accent lighting over the breakfast bar. It was then she noticed the initials 'PR' stamped into the shaft just below the snake head.

Sarah turned up her nose at the sight of the snakehead as a shiver ran through her body. She set the key down as Ranger raked his claws against the door.

Letting him in, and despite feeling silly, Sarah dressed Ranger in his tactical vest.

Sarah focused on the one thing that always made her feel better; Daniel.

Although it had only been a week since their last date, Sarah felt like she hadn't seen him in months. So much had happened, so much had changed. Work as a CSI was punctuated by the ebbs and flows of stress, but this was different.

She was so *tired.*

Sarah decided to do something she rarely did alone. Walking over to the fridge, she cracked it open and pulled a bottle of beer from the door. She twisted off the cap and tossed it onto the counter before returning to the couch and propping her feet on the coffee table.

She couldn't help but relive the events of the past few days in her mind. Her heart rate spiked a little as she thought of the killings at the farmhouse, her encounter with the rattlesnake, and the trepidation she felt upon seeing Governor Barclay at her crime scene. She swallowed hard to get the beer down as she remembered the dirty old man at the barn and how he had stared at her. She could still smell his disgusting scent lingering on her clothes. It was worse than decomp.

Sarah flipped on the television with the hope of drowning the bad thoughts in a good late night movie. She would even settle for a wave of tacky infomercials.

She finally settled on a romantic comedy she didn't recognize, but was sure she'd seen before. Twenty minutes later Sarah fought a losing battle with her eyelids as she drifted off into a peaceful sleep on the couch.

Hearing the screaming on the television, Sarah opened her eyes. A young woman stumbled through the darkened woods, being chased by a man with a knife. The digital clock above the microwave read two in the morning.

Ranger was curled in a ball at her feet and she rubbed his coat as she leaned forward to stretch. Annoyed, Sarah watched as the woman in the B-rate movie tripped and was overtaken by the madman who stabbed her repeatedly.

You should have brought a Glock to that knife fight.

Sarah turned off the television, followed by the lights, before heading towards her bedroom.

After washing her face, she tossed her straight chestnut hair in the bathroom mirror, unsatisfied with her appearance. Tomorrow would be all business at the Facility, but that didn't mean she couldn't look good. She hadn't seen Daniel in a week.

A nice outfit would make up for the dark circles under her...*shit...a pimple!* Sarah cursed under her breath as she examined the tiny red bump like a coming plague. She snatched a bottle of acne gel from her cabinet and smothered it like a tick. Sarah stood back in the light and calculated she could hide it with a dab of cover up if it wasn't gone in the morning.

She regretted having an obsession with washing her face as it only served to wash away her fatigue. She needed to get to bed.

Instead, she thumbed through her closet for a professional yet eye-catching outfit. She tossed several options on the bed and mixed various pants and shirts to find an appealing combination. She remained uninspired. Ranger was no help either. He just stared at her, waiting for her to lay down. Her fashion show didn't even elicit a tail wag.

"I need to make a statement, buddy, can you help me out a little?" Sarah said.

Ranger lifted his head for a moment then rested it back on his paws.

Sarah stuck her tongue out at him and looked back at her choices.

"Oh?" she said as her eye caught the gift box Daniel had brought her. She threw open the lid and pulled the light blue Miguel Caballero designed shirt. The fit was snug but comfortable. Sarah quickly paired it with a pair of tan boot cut designer pants and custom cowboy boots. She added a leather belt with silver medallions and surveyed her appearance in the bathroom mirror.

"Not too shabby..."

Sarah was checking out her butt in the pants when Ranger came to his feet and stared down the hallway towards the living room. Sarah watched his tail straighten before she heard the rumblings of a growl tumble from his gut.

"What is it, Ranger?"

Ranger walked to the doorway and looked down the dark hallway.

As she heard his claws click down the hallway, she swiped her Glock from the nightstand and inched her way into the doorway. Ranger was nowhere to be seen.

"Ranger!" she hissed.

Nothing.

Sarah wrapped her weak hand over her gun hand and moved down the hallway at a combat ready position. At the end of the hallway she peeked into the living room and saw Ranger standing in front of the sliding glass door.

Sarah let out a deep breath she had been holding in and dropped the gun to her side.

"You need to go potty?"

Sarah crossed the darkened room and had her hand on the door handle when she froze at the sight of the blue light shining on the pole across the street.

55

Oh, shit!

Sarah tip-toed across the floor and peered out the front window towards the car parked across the street. It was empty.

Ranger began growling and Sarah rushed back to the sliding door in time to see movement in the back yard along the fence line. She flipped the lock and threw the door open as Ranger bolted from the deck. He tore off towards the rear of the house to her left.

She was about to step out onto the deck when a shadow emerged from the bushes and ran full steam towards her.

Panicked, Sarah forgot she was holding her Glock and instinctively slammed the sliding door shut. She managed to throw the lock with her thumb a half-second before the man crashed through the glass door and tackled her to the ground.

Sarah's lungs collapsed under the weight of what felt like an NFL linebacker just before her head slammed into the wood floor. The man was trying to grab her arms when something Daniel once told her flashed in her mind.

When the shit hits the fan…be the fan.

The man pinned her right arm down so she drove her left thumb into his eye. She followed the gouging by raking his face with her nails as the man dressed in black let out a scream and reeled back.

Sarah wasted no time in punching the man's exposed groin before he rolled partially off her.

She was no longer holding the Glock. She swept her arm through the darkness and over the hundreds of glass fragments littering the floor. In an instant the man was back on her and Sarah landed a palm strike to his nose. She held her breath and closed her eyes as a warm stream of blood showered over her. His left hand took hold of her hair and slammed her head back against the floor before punching her solar plexus.

Sarah coughed as she struggled to catch her breath. As the man got to his knees, he dragged her along by her hair. Sarah threw a punch but missed as he yanked her up onto her feet.

Bloodlines

She saw the man reaching for a gun on his hip when she slammed her heel into his foot. She twisted and rolled like a swing dancer to break his arm hold.

Ranger shot through the broken door and dug his teeth into the man's free arm. He yelled in pain and flailed his arm back and forth with Ranger holding on like a bronc rider.

Sarah dropped to her knees and groped through the darkness for her gun. The safety glass bit her hands as she swept the floor. She found the gun the moment Ranger was slammed into the wall, breaking his bite.

Unlike Sarah, Ranger landed on his feet, apparently unfazed by the beating he had taken. His bark activated the tactical strobe light on his vest, showering the man in a blinding light show. Ranger sprang back upon the man's gun arm and thrashed as the gun went off and an errant round put three holes into the floor at Sarah's feet.

She flinched as she shot twice towards the intruder, both rounds passing inches from his right side and impacting the wall behind him. Despite the sporadic flashes of light, Sarah could barely focus on the man as he thrashed around from the dog attack.

Making matters worse, the man swung Ranger back and forth in front of him causing Sarah to hesitate in taking another shot. The last thing she wanted was to hit Ranger.

There was no rhythm or predictability to Ranger's movement. He was like a piñata spinning in high wind during a massive lightning storm. Sarah pulled the trigger halfway back, waiting for the opportunity to send a round into his torso. She hoped he wasn't wearing a bullet proof vest.

Half-seconds seemed to last for hours as Sarah considered rushing the man and taking the shot at point blank range. She only hoped Ranger wouldn't bite her in all the confusion.

She readied herself to charge the man when a shotgun blast came down the hallway and struck Ranger.

He yelped as he released his bite and landed hard against the coffee table. Sarah didn't hesitate. She fired two quick rounds into the intruder's chest and the first intruder stumbled backwards and fell on his butt as Sarah spun to her left firing several more down the hallway in the direction of the shotgun blast.

She caught a glimpse of a second man retreating back into her bedroom just before the first intruder came to his knees and shot Sarah just above her left hip.

Time stopped. Sarah knew she had been hit but she didn't feel the pain. To her surprise, she wasn't afraid...she was pissed off.

Sarah settled the Trijicon front sight on the dark form and squeezed the trigger. She kept squeezing as she advanced and lost track of how many shots she fired. The man fell back onto the floor and Sarah could hear him coughing blood.

Sarah was on top of him a second later and sent a final round through his head as Ranger again latched onto his now flaccid arm.

For a split second the room was silent but that changed as Sarah heard the creak of a floorboard down the hallway.

Sarah dove behind the recliner chair as buckshot sailed through the air a micro-second ahead of the sound blast. She sprang up firing blindly down the hallway. Another Danielism flashed in her mind's eye; *Make your enemy advance through a wall of bullets.*

Ranger galloped down the hallway barking as the slide on Sarah's Glock locked to the rear. She reached for a spare magazine only to realize she didn't have one.

The next shotgun blast was followed by a high-pitched whimper.

"Ranger!" she screamed.

Every muscle tightened in her as she covered her mouth. She was out of ammo, exposed, and had no back up. For a second she panicked. Sarah shook the feeling and took a long deep breath. Then it hit her.

She looked across the room towards the kitchen and calculated the time it would take to cross the floor. *A second or two at most,* she thought. The danger would be in leaving her position and crossing in front of the open hallway. She'd be totally exposed.

But she knew there was no other choice. If she didn't move, she'd die.

Sarah gritted her teeth and sprang from her hiding place. The flashing strobe lights down the hallway made it difficult for her to see clearly but she caught a glimpse of movement down the hallway. She ignored the thought and focused on her objective. Passing in front of the hallway opening she thought she might make it; then she felt the buckshot rake her left shoulder.

Sarah winced as she spun and lost her footing, crashing into the dining room table. Ignoring the pain, Sarah upended the table and scrambled behind it for cover. Her shoulder was throbbing and it took all her strength to control her breathing. Each breath was labored and she fought to keep from gasping too loudly.

She couldn't hear the man coming but she knew he would be. Her only hope was that he would approach cautiously, not wanting to end up like his partner. The strobe light on Ranger's vest coughed in fits for a few seconds before ending and plunging the house once again into darkness.

She knew she had only seconds.

Looking to her left, Sarah was relieved her memory had been correct. The Remington tactical shotgun was propped against the wall right where she left it. She darted out on one knee and yanked the shotgun back to cover.

Sarah tightened her grasp around the pistol grip when a voice called out to her, "Sarah…you still here?"

She didn't recognize the voice.

"Saaaar-ah?" the voice sang, making her skin crawl.

Wanting to buy a little time she called back. "I see you brought a bigger snake with you this time…how's your friend doing?"

"About the same as your dog."

Mother…

"What do you want?" Sarah asked.

"You."

The voice was much closer now. Sarah thought he might be just inside the hallway about eight feet away.

"You're not my type." Sarah yelled.

"I know you're out of ammo, Sarah. I don't want to shoot you, but your boyfriend Daniel has a colleague of ours. We want to trade you for him; simple as that. Come out and I promise you won't be hurt. Why do you think my friend tried to grab you first?"

Sarah calculated the distance to the front door. For a split second she considered making a run for it, but she knew he'd cut her down half-way there. This was where she'd make her stand. There was no way she was going quietly. She had dealt with maniacs before and knew the only way to escape their wrath was to kill them.

She inched to the far side of the table on her knees and ran the shotgun barrel alongside the table leg.

"What do you say, Sarah?"

She was breathing heavy, but she focused all her strength on keeping it measured. Silence was her tactical advantage now. The man had to know she'd been hit. He also knew the cops had to be on the way with the amount of noise they'd made.

She'd run out the clock unless he exposed himself. Then she'd take him out.

Her heart pounded. Ten seconds passed, then twenty. After thirty seconds, Sarah considered the possibility he'd run off. Maybe he was smart enough to recognize a tactical disadvantage.

A trickle of relief began to wash over her when the shadow crossed the floor. Sarah spun around and saw the man shouldering his shotgun outside the large front porch window.

He had circled around the house!

Sarah saw him level his shotgun at her as she activated the tac-light, blinding him for a split second, as she leaned right.

The man jerked the trigger and shattered the window with rubber buckshot that bounced off the table where Sarah's head had been a half-second earlier.

Sarah wouldn't wait for another shot. She squeezed the trigger and watched as the man's throat exploded in a fountain of blood and tissue. She heard his body hit like a fallen tree against the house as she dashed across the floor to the window. Using the barrel, she cleared out a large section of broken glass and pointed the muzzle at his head.

There on the ground lay a monster spitting up mouthfuls of blood. He gasped and moved his lips. *Was he trying to say something?* Sarah didn't care to find out.

She welded her cheek to the stock and settled the front sight on his face. She was going to put him out of his misery when he did something that sent shudders of disgust rippling through her body.

He smiled.

Bloodlines

It was a grotesque smile. Dark red blood outlined his white teeth as he continued gurgling foamy blood like a mini-geyser. It was even bubbling up from his neck wound. Her finger touched the trigger but she didn't pull it back. She thought of Ranger. This man didn't deserve a quick death.

So she watched him lie there in agony until the light faded from his eyes and the last of the blood boiled up from inside his once beating heart.

Sarah heard the sirens in the distance and ran to check on Ranger. She stole a glance at the other man's lifeless body as she passed.

She hit the light to the hallway as she entered, and saw Ranger lying on his side in a pool of blood. His front left shoulder was shattered and the leg was attached by connective tissue but...*he was panting.*

"Ranger! Hold on buddy," Sarah said as she dashed to the bedroom closet. She yanked her hunting pack from the upper shelf and threw it on the bed. She dumped it out and grabbed the fanny pack sized first aid kit before sliding to her knees at his side.

She tore open a small pack of blood clotting agent and poured the granules over his wounds. She tore off her bullet-proof shirt and wrapped it around his shoulder using the sleeves to tie it closed. Ranger moaned in protest but didn't struggle as Sarah hoisted his body from the floor.

Sarah did her best to minimize the jarring motions as she ran to her truck. She laid him on the back seat and thundered the power stroke diesel engine to life. She backed the big truck out of the drive and thundered down the street. Two blocks away she saw the flash of red and blue lights in her rearview mirror.

56

August 11th; Steamboat Springs, Colorado

Art took a seat next to Daniel as they began their descent into the Steamboat Springs Airport. It was almost four in the morning but Daniel was wide awake. Art nodded towards Boone, "Looks like he finally fell asleep."

"Yeah, I promised I'd stay up." Daniel said in a whisper.

Art studied the man for a moment before whispering back. "He's an intriguing man, don't you think?"

Daniel had been thinking the same thing for the last few hours.

"Imagine his life, Art. Every day dedicated to protecting a box full of papers. Papers you've never even seen. No wife, no kids…waiting day in and day out for a visitor that may never come. Imagine his father and grandfather living their whole lives in that little cabin. I mean…what motivates someone to do that?"

"Faith," Art said.

"Faith?"

"Sure."

"In what?"

"Put yourself in their shoes. If you had been there, heard that none other than General Washington himself, had placed these secrets in your family's hands—you wouldn't have done it?"

Maybe, he thought.

"Did you get a hold of the sheriff?" Daniel asked changing the subject.

"He'll be waiting for us at the airport."

"And he's on board with our plan?"

"Are you kidding? He got a lot of grief from the feds over the last guy's death. Taking a high value killer into custody will tilt the balance sheet. He's a hundred and ten percent on board," Art said.

"Good."

"In other good news, Sarah will be up later today."

"Yep."

"I'm sure you're excited," Art said.

"I am."

Art crossed his legs and rested his chin on his thumb.

"You don't sound excited."

Daniel looked away from the darkened window and focused on his uncle.

"We've had some close calls the last few days," Daniel said.

"We have."

"Kind of makes you think," Daniel said.

"About what, Daniel?"

Daniel paused as he searched for the right words. He looked back at Boone slumped in his chair.

"I think it might be time for me to make some changes in my life."

"Good changes, or…"

Daniel raised his eyebrows, exhaled, and looked back out into the darkness.

***

Detective Manny Lopez was pissed.

This was the second time in a week he had responded to a crime scene at Sarah's house. Only this time, she was nowhere to be found.

He sent an alert call to her cell only to hear it chirping in the back bedroom. Two dead bodies, a pool of blood by the bedroom…no dog…no truck, and most importantly…no Sarah. Manny didn't like how the score sheet was adding up.

"Get some deputies out in the park there. Check the pavilion," Manny yelled to the deputy staring at the corpse on the front porch. Neighbors were peering out windows as a steady stream of patrol cars began circling the neighborhood, shining spotlights into every dark corner.

Manny's phone chirped an alert. It was Sheriff Westin.

"Give me an update, Manny."

"It doesn't look good, Sir," Manny briefed him on what little they knew.

"Do we have an ID on the shooters?"

"Normally, I would have left the wallets in place until the coroner arrived but given the circumstances…"

"Who?"

315

"One of them is Wes Hammond, sir."

"How do I know that name?"

"You met him early last night at the dig site. He's the head of Governor Barclay's security team."

Manny didn't hear a response. "Did you copy that sir?"

"That son-of-a-bitch! Did he actually think he could stop this investigation by killing one of our criminalists? I mean…what the *hell* did he hope to accomplish?"

Manny was just about to speak when he heard the thunder of Sarah's diesel truck rounding the corner. "Sir…I have to call you back. Sarah's truck is pulling up to the scene."

"Is she okay?"

"I don't know yet."

"Get back to me in five," Westin ordered.

"Roger that."

Manny bounced down the porch steps and met Sarah in the driveway. Sarah slid out of the truck, bloodstains visible on her shirt.

"Jesus, are you hit?"

"No, it's not my blood. I was wearing a bullet-proof shirt," she said looking down at her undershirt.

"What the *hell,* Sarah? I've been going out of my mind here. Where the hell have you been?"

"It's Ranger…he got shot," she said, tears welling up in her eyes.

Manny put an arm around her waist as he led her up the stairs to the house.

"Is he…"

"I don't know. I drove him to the emergency clinic and they rushed him inside. I wanted to call someone and I realized I didn't have my phone."

"You could have called me from the hospital."

"I don't have your number memorized, Manny…" she said raising her voice.

"Okay, okay…that's not important. I was just worried about you. We all were. The first deputy on scene went bat shit crazy on the radio."

Sarah paused at the top of the stairs to look at Hammond's body before going inside.

"He works for Barclay," she said as she plopped down on the couch.

"I know. He was at the dig scene."

Sarah didn't acknowledge the comment.

"What happened tonight?" Manny said as Detective Vargas came in the door, glanced around, and went into the kitchen. Sarah's hands were shaking and Manny took them in his to calm her down.

"It's the adrenalin," Vargas said as he came back and handed her a glass of water.

It took her several minutes to recount the events and when she finished, she buried her face in her hands. Manny rubbed his hand over her back but stopped suddenly, standing up to greet another officer.

"Lieutenant Manilow…what are you doing here?"

"This is an officer involved shooting…it's my responsibility to investigate," Manilow said in a low, even voice. His tone wasn't laced with the normal indignation.

"We haven't really gotten too deep into it yet, Lieutenant," Manny said.

"I was told that one of the suspects has been identified," Manilow said.

"Yes sir, the guy on the front porch," Manny said.

Manilow pursed his lips and strolled out to look over the body. He stood over it for several seconds looking at the man from different angles.

"This is the last thing I need right now," Sarah whispered to Manny.

"Just…let me handle this. Don't say a word, okay?" Manny whispered back a second before Manilow strolled back into the room.

"What's your assessment, Sal?" Manilow asked.

Sarah and Manny shared a confused glance. Aside from advice on how to treat an STD, no one ever consulted Vargas for his opinion. Vargas made a show of looking around the room before addressing the Lieutenant.

"Looks to me like two scumbags picked a fight with the wrong lab geek. They busted in here and she dumped them; simple as that. Personally, I think she should get a commendation," he said offering a wink to Sarah.

Sarah braced herself for an onslaught of quoted policies and critique of her judgment. To her surprise, they never came.

"Sounds good. Write it up and get it to me next week," he said. He then crossed the room and stood before Sarah.

"Are you going to be all right?"

"Yes, sir," she said, still a little confused.

"All right then, good work." he said before nodding to Manny and strolling out the front door. Sarah stood at the window and watched as Manilow climbed into his car and drove away from the scene.

She looked back at Vargas and then to Manny, "Okay, what the *hell* just happened?"

57

August 11th; Denver, Colorado
Sarah and Vargas sat in a pair of trendy, yet uncomfortable, chairs in a little waiting room outside the District Attorney's Office. Sheriff Westin and Manny had been in there almost two hours going over the case information and showing him the video surveillance tape from the farmhouse. It took the district attorney all but a minute to sign off on the search and arrest warrants once he had all the information. He wanted to give the state attorney general a heads up but Westin convinced him to hold off on the notification until they were at the Governor's mansion.

Despite policy, they didn't deploy the SWAT team and instead decided to knock and notify. Westin had the Denver Police meet them a block from the residence and review the warrants before descending on the mansion. They parked near the service entrance on Pennsylvania Street. It was ten minutes before eight in the morning. Manny, Vargas, and Sheriff Westin were in the lead car. Behind them two patrol cars followed by Andy Vaughn and Sarah in another.

"You look like shit, you know," Andy said.

"Thanks a lot; I kind of had a long night remember?"

"My point exactly."

"Yeah, well…"

"I can't believe Westin let you come to this Sarah," Andy said.

"I'm only here as an observer. He won't let me collect evidence."

"No offense, but I think it's a mistake. This is going to be the biggest arrest in state history and your presence here is going to be fodder for the defense. I can handle the search myself."

"I won't get in the way Andy. Anyway, I think I've earned it," she said as she rubbed her shoulder.

"It's not about that Sarah. I'm just thinking of the case."

"And you think *I'm not*?"

"No, of course not…that's…that's not what I meant."

"If our places were reversed, it would take the SWAT team to hold you back Andy."

"Maybe," he conceded.

"Look, we went over this. I'll wait in the car until the governor is transported and you do your preliminary stuff. Once you get to a comfortable point, call me on my cell and I'll come in. I just want to look around."

"Fine."

Sarah sighed, rolled her eyes and cracked her window an inch.

***

Westin unlocked his door but kept his hand off the handle.

"You two are clear on the plan?" Westin asked.

"Yes sir, you'll serve the warrants to the Governor along with Denver police and our deputies. Vegas and I will cover him with a coat and get him to the patrol car where he'll be transported back to the jail. Then we secure the residence and call in the criminalists." Manny said.

"Any last minute concerns?" Westin asked.

"I don't think his security will give us a problem," Vargas quipped.

Westin turned around and eyed the surly detective. "Vegas, I swear to God…"

"He'll be fine sir," Manny said giving his partner the evil eye in the rear view mirror.

"This one time Sal…keep it in check okay?"

"Hey…it's me," Vargas said holding up his hands.

"That's what I'm worried about," Westin said as he threw open the door.

Denver police opened the side gate with an electronic key card and parted as Westin brushed past them, warrants in hand. He pounded on the side door and waited for an aide to open the door.

"I'm Sheriff Westin, I have a search warrant for this residence. Where is the Governor?"

"Is this some kind of joke?" the aide said.

"Son, where is the Governor?"

"He's upstairs sleeping. He had a long night and the staff left instructions not to disturb him until nine. Maybe you could come back then?"

Westin pushed past the man, found the staircase to the second floor, and bounded up to the left with the aide and detectives following at his heels.

"Which room is his?" Westin ordered.

"Sheriff please, you can't just barge in here."

"We have an arrest warrant sir, either tell us which room he's in or I'll arrest you for obstruction," Manny said.

The aide pointed towards a set of wooden doors at the end of the hall.

"Is the First Lady in there, too?" Westin asked.

"She's in Aspen at a fundraiser," the aide said.

Westin marched down the hallway. The aide tried to follow but Manny stopped him with an outstretched hand. Westin knocked loudly and after receiving no answer pushed through the doors. The governor was under a heavy goose down comforter. Westin stood ramrod straight at the foot of the bed as Manny and Vargas came up behind him.

"Governor Barclay? Get up sir; we need to have a word with you."

Barclay didn't move.

"Governor," Westin said elevating his voice.

Westin looked back at Manny with a quizzical stare. Manny rounded his boss and leaned over the bed. He placed a hand on Barclay's shoulder and shook it back and forth.

"Mr. Governor?"

An alarm bell sounded in Westin's head as he threw back the covers and checked for a pulse.

"Vegas, call nine-one-one," Manny said as he started chest compressions.

***

Sarah and Andy sat listening to a morning talk radio program when an ambulance screamed around the corner from Eighth Avenue and through the service entrance gate.

"That can't be good," Andy said.

"Do you think he resisted arrest?"

321

"I have no idea," Andy said as he opened his cell and called Vargas. "Is everything okay in there?"

It took a moment for Vargas to answer.

"You two better get in here and bring your camera."

"Sarah, too?" Andy asked.

"Both of you, now."

Andy grabbed his camera bag as Sarah dug out their evidence collection kit before hurrying to the door. An aide was at the bottom of the stairs and directed them up to the second floor.

The two criminalists got to the bedroom as the paramedics hoisted Barclay's body onto a gurney. They started pushing it towards the doors. "Move!" the lead paramedic yelled.

Sarah and Andy parted as the paramedics blew past them like a runaway freight train.

"What the hell?" Andy said as Vargas approached them.

"He was unresponsive."

"You found him that way?" Sarah asked.

"No Richards, Manny held him down while the sheriff beat him with his nightstick...yes, we found him that way."

"Okay...I get it. I'm just trying to understand what happened."

"Sorry kitten, this whole thing just got way more complicated." Vargas said, putting a hand on her shoulder.

"Kitten? When we're done here, Vegas, I'm going to kick you square in the balls," Sarah said shrugging off his hand.

"Promise?"

"Andy, get in here and start taking some pictures. Look for anything out of the ordinary. I have to call the Lieutenant Governor and the Attorney General," Westin said as he stormed out of the room.

"So, are we thinking some kind of stroke or something?" Andy asked as Manny came to his side.

"I don't see any signs of a struggle, but keep your eyes open."

"Will do," Andy said as he cleared everyone out of the room. Sarah heard the ambulance pull out, sirens blaring, as she waited in the hallway with the two detectives. Manny sent the uniformed deputy to secure the entrance to the mansion.

"This seems fishy to me," Sarah whispered to Manny.

Bloodlines

"I hear you. Why don't you sneak a peek in some of these other rooms; just don't touch anything."

"No shit Sherlock!"

Sarah made a b-line to the bathroom. She knew that the bathroom was the best place to start looking for evidence of medical problems. The toilet and floor were clean and the towels looked untouched.

Using her knuckle, she opened the medicine cabinet and scanned the shelves for any prescription medication. Nothing. Except for one used tissue, the trash can was empty.

Sarah made a mental note to check the dumpster out back in case the staff threw out any evidence like towels caked with vomit. She passed through a door and walked into a private office.

The room was paneled in a dark cherry wood with red carpets and ornate Victorian furniture. She estimated the room to be at least twenty feet squared and circled the perimeter as she looked for evidence.

She stopped as she passed in front of a large wooden glass-door cabinet. Three rows of handguns were arranged along the red velvet lined back panel. Most of the guns looked old but they were in pristine condition. The vibration from her phone startled her as she dug it out of her cargo pants. It was Art.

"Art! Are you back?"

"We landed a little while ago and I just got into the office. Are you on your way up?"

"Not exactly."

"Sleeping in again, eh? When do you think you'll get on the road?"

Sarah filled him in on the events of the past ten hours when he interrupted her.

"He's dead?"

"I don't know. The paramedics rushed him out of here but Manny said he didn't have a pulse."

"My God."

"Art, I have to talk to Daniel, is he there?"

"Yes, he's standing right here, hold on," Art said. Sarah's voice cracked as she explained what happened to Ranger.

"Where is he?" Daniel asked.

"There's an emergency clinic near the house. He was in surgery for several hours. I talked to the doctor this morning and he said they had to amputate Ranger's leg."

"Shit," Daniel said.

"I'm so sorry, Daniel."

"Hey…this isn't your fault. He's a warrior, he'll pull through this. Text me the address to the clinic."

"You're coming down?"

"I made a promise to my buddy to look after him. Maybe I can make it back up here tonight or tomorrow. Are you still coming up?"

"I was planning to. Do you want me to wait for you?"

"No, I think Art needs you up here sooner rather than later. He wants to get into that box and you have the key."

"Okay, just promise to call me once you've talked to the doctor."

"Wilco, drive safe."

"I love you," Sarah said but Daniel had already passed the phone to Art.

Sarah heard Art exchange a few muffled words with Daniel before coming back on the line.

"I don't know, Sarah…given what you've been through maybe I should just send a courier for the key," Art said.

"Are you kidding? I can't do anything here and no one wants to get to the bottom of this more than I do. The son-of-a-bitch tried to kill me Art…twice!"

"Well, I don't think you should drive. Daniel is flying down there. Why don't you meet the plane at the airport when you're done. The pilot can have you back here safe and sound in less time than it takes to drive up."

Sarah was a little tired. More importantly, she was distracted. It might be nice to relax a little on the flight. She might even catch up on a little sleep.

"All right Art, I'll take you up on that," Sarah said.

"Good. Listen, Walter is here with me. He wants to talk to you."

Walter Haruki was the senior firearms examiner at the Facility and had been instrumental in the sniper killings the previous year.

"Sarah?"

"Hey Walter, what's up?"

"I've been going over those scanned images you sent and I've figured a few things out. The bullet is a lead ball with markings of a cloth patch so I'd say it's a muzzleloader."

"Do you think it's a flint lock or percussion cap ignition?" Sarah asked.

"No way to tell. If you see either, I'd take 'em," Walter said.

"I'm looking at one right now that is a percussion side lock," Sarah said.

"Now, they make modern muzzle loading pistols. Can you tell if it's old or new?"

"Hold on," Sarah said as she pulled a pair of latex gloves from her cargo pants and slid them on. She looked around to be sure she was alone before opening the cabinet and plucking the pistol from the peg it hung from.

"It looks old," she said, turning it in her hand.

"Are there any markings on the barrel?"

"It says Deringer Philadela on the barrel," Sarah said.

"Is Deringer with one 'R' or two?"

"One," Sarah said.

"What about the barrel, is it round or octagonal shaped?"

"Um, both I think. It looks octagonal, or at least it's flat on top but the bottom half is rounded."

"Okay, look at the muzzle…is it a large or small bore?" Walter asked.

"Looks bigger than my nine millimeter," Sarah said.

"See if you can find any documentation or a box for it," Walter said.

Sarah opened the lower cabinet doors and spotted a cigar-sized wooden box. She slid it out onto the floor and flipped open the brass hardware. The inside of the box was lined with green felt and contained a metal tool that looked like pliers with a cup on the end, some tin cloth patches, and… *"Shit,"* Sarah said.

"What's wrong?"

Sarah slid the pistol into the felt lining and it was a perfect fit.

"I'm pretty sure I found the box, but there's another space here for an additional pistol. Does that mean they were dueling pistols?"

"Maybe. Deringer sold sets of 'twin' pistols but, it's not a good sign." Walter said.

"I'll look around some more. Maybe it's in another room," Sarah said.

"Collectors usually keep them together. I'd wager that the missing one may be the one we're looking for," Walter said.

"Do you want me to take this one? Our warrant covers firearms."

"Definitely. Gun manufacturers sometimes tool a longer barrel and then cut it down for several pistols. The tool marks would still be unique after the final fitting but the two barrels may share enough unique tool marks to prove a close correspondence." Walter said.

"I'll have it up there in a few hours," Sarah said.

"Okay, see you then."

Sarah found Manny on the phone in the hallway. He held up a finger as he excused himself from the call and cupped his hand over the microphone.

"What's up?"

"I may have found the gun used on the bodies at the grave sites."

"You honestly think the killer would have kept it in the family?"

"It can't hurt to take a look?"

"Well, you can't participate in the investigation and search for evidence of the murders at the farmhouse, or the attack at your house, but no one has said anything about a century old double murder."

"Barclay couldn't have been involved so there should be no conflict of interest," Sarah said.

"That…and the fact that he's dead," Manny said.

"So, he *is* dead?"

"Nothing's official, but he didn't look good to me," Manny said.

"So what's new here?" Sarah asked.

"I give it thirty minutes before this place is crawling with state police, the CBI, and the media. It's going to turn into a major circus. Why don't you get out of here and head to the Facility."

"I have to wait for a ride from Andy."

Manny dug his keys out of his pocket.

"Here, take my car. Sal and I will be here all day. We'll get a ride back from someone. I'll keep you posted on what we find."

"I'll have someone from the lab pick your car up from the airport and drive it back here. I'm sure Andy will need the help."

58

August 11th; Centennial Airport
According to the pilot, Sarah had missed Daniel by thirty minutes and he wasn't answering his phone.

He did leave her a note on the plane saying he was looking forward to seeing her and that he would call her after visiting Ranger. He signed it with the words *I love you.* She kept the note in her shirt pocket.

Sarah spent the two hour flight listening for updates. The radio was exploding with news of the Governor's death; albeit from apparent natural causes. Colorado had lost its second Governor in a year and radio commentators were giving it wall to wall coverage. One radio host even floated a conspiracy theory, but it didn't gain any traction.

Art had an intern pick Sarah up at the Steamboat Springs airport and drive her straight to her town home on campus. Art provided luxurious town homes for every faculty member on campus. Sarah was the only non-faculty member to have a home and it was in the best location; over looking the lake and adjacent to the main trailheads leading into the mountains. She wished she used it more often. After dropping off her bags, she headed over to Art's office.

Sarah found Art and Tilly glued to the television in his office.

"Seems like we've been to this dance before," Sarah said.

"Sarah! You poor thing…come over here and give me a hug." Her embrace was warm and heartfelt. "I can't believe all you've been through. Is there any word on Ranger?"

"Nothing yet. Daniel should be calling later with an update."

"Can I get you something to drink, dear?" Tilly asked.

"I'm fine, thanks."

"I had the staff stock your fridge and put new sheets on the bed."

"I saw that, thanks Tilly."

Art had come up beside Tilly and took Sarah's hands in his.

"Sarah, you're going to be the death of me…you know that."

"What can I say, I'm a shit magnet."

"I'm just happy you're all right," he said. "I don't know what we'd do if anything happened to you." He put his arm around Tilly.

"I've been trained by the best," she said in her best James Bond accent.

Art smiled, and glanced down to the wooden box she was holding.

"Is that the gun?"

"Yep."

"And you brought the key?"

Sarah dug it out of her pocket and placed it in Art's open palm.

He turned it in his fingers as he held it up to the light of the window. "Good. Let's go; Walter is pacing his lab like an expectant father."

Art wasn't exaggerating. Walter was literally pacing back and forth near his comparison microscope. He saw Sarah coming through the door and rushed over to her.

"Excited, huh?" Sarah said.

"It's not every day you get to do a comparison on a century old pistol. There could be a scientific paper in this for me," Walter said.

"Whatever floats your boat."

Art grabbed Sarah by the elbow, "We'll be back in a bit, Walter."

"You're not staying?"

"We have something else to check on first. We'll be down in the Questioned Documents lab if you need to call us," Art said as he led Sarah from the room.

Sarah waited until they were in the hallway before speaking.

"Walter doesn't know about the box?" she asked.

"I thought it best to keep things quiet until we see what's inside."

They took the elevator down two floors and crossed through the administrative cubicles before entering the laboratory side of the floor. Art turned into the second lab on the right.

Dr. Keri Sanchez sat at a large light table in the center of the room as an older man blocked her from the silver box sitting in the chemical fume hood. Sarah learned that Art coaxed Dr. Sanchez from the Secret Service two years earlier and thought she might have a special interest in the contents from the nation's first president.

"Everyone playing nice in here?" Art asked.

"He won't even let me near it to take pictures, Art," Sanchez said.

Art chuckled.

"Sarah, may I introduce Mr. Hawkins Boone DeFrance; owner of the box in question." Art said extending his hand.

Sarah crossed the room and shook the man's hand. He shook hands like Daniel; firm and to the point.

"It's a pleasure."

"I must say, I've never seen so many pretty women in one building." Boone said.

Dr. Sanchez gave a forced smile as Boone motioned for her to come over to the fume hood. Her digital camera was fitted with a ring light flash and she began snapping photos of the silver box. Art laid the key on brown butcher paper lining the hood and Sanchez took several photos of that, too.

"So whose gonna open it?" Sanchez said after taking her last photo.

Art put his hand on the older man's shoulder, "I think it's only fitting if you do the honors, Boone."

Boone took a deep breath and picked up the key. Sarah thought she could see the slightest of tremors in the man's hand as he rested the tip in the lock opening. One second turned to two, then five, before Sarah spoke.

"I'm nervous, too."

Boone exhaled in a whoosh, "I didn't expect it to be this hard."

"You've been waiting for this moment your entire life." Art said.

"I used to think the same thing, but now I'm not so sure. I can't tell you how many nights I sat alone in that cabin staring at this box; wondering what was inside. Now I have the chance to finally open it and I'm scared."

"You've waited over sixty-five years…a few more minutes won't matter. Do you want to take a walk and talk about it?" Art asked.

Boone took another deep breath, exchanged looks with Sarah, and shook his head. "No, let's do this."

He slipped the spiral-shaped key into the lock and it turned along the way until it was fully seated.

"All right, turn it slowly," Art said as he activated the fan in the fume hood. "If you feel any resistance just stop; don't force it."

"Here goes nothing," Boone said. The key rotated a half-turn to the right when they heard a click and saw the lid raise a sixteenth of an inch. Boone expressed a look of trepidation with Art who gave him an encouraging nod in return.

Boone clasped both edges of the lid and rotated it upward a half inch at a time until it reached its zenith. He rested the lid against the back wall of the fume hood. The scientists peered over his shoulders. Art summed up the mood of the room with a single word.

"Amazing!"

59

A waft of stale air rose from the ornate box. To Sarah, it was like opening an old book. Dr. Sanchez snapped a photo, and then slipped on a pair of white cotton gloves.

Art was the first to speak. "This, ladies and gentlemen, is the Fidelity Medal Seaton described in his journal." Art cradled it in his fingers and laid it to the side of the silver box. Beneath it was a purple colored cloth patch in the shape of a heart. Sarah could see the word 'Merit' stitched into it along with scrolling vines.

"The Badge of Merit," Art said in wonderment as he too donned a pair of gloves and took it in his hands.

"What's that?" Sarah asked.

"It was an award given by General Washington to those who foiled the plot by General Benedict Arnold in taking West Point."

"So the man that owned this box helped stop that plot?" Sarah asked.

"Not according to the history books," Art said as he laid it upon the butcher paper for Dr. Sanchez to photograph.

"Seaton mentioned it in his journal, but my source tells me that only three of these were ever awarded and all three are accounted for. This appears to be a fourth…"

"What does that mean?" Sarah asked.

"I'm not sure," Art said. "I wish Daniel was here to see this."

Sarah was thinking the same thing at the moment but for different reasons.

Art handed Boone a pair of cotton gloves and the man held the heart-shaped patch in his hands like a newborn baby bird. Sarah noticed his eyes begin to well up and looked away out of respect.

"Look at this, Art," Dr. Sanchez said as she lifted a yellowed paper folded into four parts and laid it out on the light table. She activated the light under the table as she settled into her seat. Handling it by the corners, Dr. Sanchez opened each fold with deliberate delicacy. When it was completely open, they gazed upon the brown stained calligraphy.

Sarah's eyes were drawn to the signature at the bottom and she clasped her hand over her mouth. Art hadn't prepared them for what may lay inside the box.

"Art, the signature; is that who I think it is?" Dr. Sanchez said.

"I believe so, yes," he said as Sarah and Boone gathered around and tried to angle for a better look.

Sarah read the ending aloud, "With great respect, etc. George Washington."

"I knew it," Boone said as he nodded with satisfaction.

"I can't read that script. What does the letter say?" Boone asked.

Dr. Sanchez adjusted her reading glasses and followed each word with her finger as she read the letter aloud.

Ensign John Henry DeFrance, New York Militia,

No sum of treasure can compensate the services you have provided to the cause of liberty. In defiance of your station, and at great risk to your very life and honor, you have brought to light a conspiracy for which none of my loyal officers were aware. This plot was not just to bring about my assassination, or the capture of West Point. It was the first step in the establishment of a colonial monarchy that would rule the people by a new aristocracy. One that doused the very light of freedom we struggle to forge. The cause cannot bear the weight of such treason should it come to light in this time of sacrifice.

As I write this, the men who plotted my assassination have scattered through the colonies, but they may one day return. General Cornelius Barclay has betrayed the cause of liberty to quench his thirst for wealth and power. Were he not a man of such political standing I would see him hung, but alas, he has sheltered himself well within the establishment. I fear that too few would believe what you and I know to be true. It is enough that the plot has been derailed, but I fear that one day these wicked seeds sewn may rise again.

It is my sincerest hope that one day we may shed the prejudice, intolerance, and envy that make men slaves. That men may be free to pursue their own happiness without regard to tation or wealth. That one day we may gorge upon our own creations without levy or pass from those who govern from the art.

So it is with much regret and mental reservation that I must ask you to carry a heavy burden. It is a burden as great as that carried by Atlas. I must ask you to form an indissoluble bond of true brotherhood in the cause of all that is just, right, and true. Keep the evidence of these conspirators safe. Should this Phoenix arise from the ashes of treachery, I shall send for you. I fear that it is no longer safe for you to remain in the colonies. Go west to the land called Kentucky and govern yourself accordingly.

With Great Respect, etc.

George Washington

Art took the letter and read it again in silence. As he read, Sarah watched as his eyes welled up with tears until one finally trickled down his cheek.

"What does that mean?" she asked.

Art rubbed the back of his head with his fingertips.

"It appears that the conspiracy Washington feared never came to pass. Maybe he did get his revenge, or maybe the plotters gave up their attempts." Art said.

"So Seaton was killed because he discovered that some great, great relative of Governor Barclay plotted against George Washington?" Sarah asked.

"I'm sure people have been killed for less. Imagine how that might have played in the press. Barclay has several television ads touting his ties to the founding of the United States. If it came to light that his family actually aided the British, it could mean the difference in a close race," Art said.

Boone took the letter from Art's hand and moved his lips in silence as he read it for himself. Once finished, he laid it upon the light table and went back to the chemical fume hood. He stared into the empty silver box and shook his head.

"What are you thinking?" Art asked as he came up behind him.

"I'm just thinking about the letter."

Bloodlines

"I know. It's a major insight into the American Revolution. I suspect historians will open up an entirely new chapter of research into Cornelius Barclay."

Boone gave Art a dismissive shake of his head.

"No…not that one. The letter that brought my great grand-daddy out to the eastern plains of Colorado to meet Alison DeFrance."

***

Art led Sarah and Boone into the firearms lab. They found Walter Haruki hunched over his comparison microscope with a strange image on the monitor. Sarah set the silver box and the contents on Walter's desk before looking over his shoulder.

"Is that a bullet?"

Walter looked up from his scope and saw her looking at the monitor.

"Yeah, the one from the grave."

Boone looked at the antique pistol on the examination table.

"What is that white stuff plugging up the barrel?" he asked.

"Oh, I'm making a cast of the barrel." Walter said.

"Don't you have to fire a test shot to compare bullets?" Sarah asked.

"These bullets are used with a cloth patch which would prevent a lot of the striae from transferring to the bullet so I'm just looking at general rifling characteristics. Plus, I didn't want to cast a new bullet so I made a cast of the barrel instead."

"You have to cast a bullet to shoot it?"

"Yeah, this tool here from the box was custom made to fit these exact Deringers. It sounds strange I know, but that's how they made them back then. You didn't go down to the sporting goods store to buy your ammo; you made it yourself." Walter said.

"So what can you tell us…do you think it's the same gun?"

"I was just getting ready to pull the plug out and take a look. Sarah, can you grab that book off my desk and turn to the section on Deringers please? There's a table of general rifling characteristics you can read off to me."

Walter carefully extracted the white plug that perfectly replicated the interior rifling marks of the barrel.

"The bullet recovered from the grave is on the left. It weighed ninety-seven point fourteen grains which puts it in the forty-one caliber range."

"So the Deringer is a forty-one caliber?" Art asked.

"No, it's a forty-five but you would use a forty-one caliber ball with a cloth patch. It also has seven rifling grooves with a left twist," he said.

"You mean right twist," Sarah said.

Walter looked over his shoulder at her in surprise.

"No, this is a left twist Sarah."

"The table here says the Deringer has a right twist, not a left twist."

"Well, that can't be right. Let me see that."

Walter flipped through a few pages and then re-examined the casting.

"Could it be some printing mistake in the table?" Art asked.

"I don't think so, but this is only the second Deringer I've ever…"

Walter stopped mid-sentence as his eyes narrowed and the color flushed from his face. He slid his chair back to his desk and ran his fingers over the felt lining of the gun box Sarah had brought him from Barclay's mansion. "No," he whispered.

"What is it, Walter?" Art asked.

Walter looked at Art, mouth agape in disbelief and slid his chair across the floor to a file cabinet. He opened two drawers before his fingers found the file he was searching for.

"Walter…what are you looking for?" Art asked stepping closer to see the file.

"It can't be…I mean, I'm sure it's a coincidence," he said as he brought the file back to the examination table. He laid out several large format photographs of a Deringer pistol and began reading through his notes.

Walter began taking measurements with his calipers and soon the pace of his back and forth examination between the pistol and the photos quickened.

Sarah took one of the photos in her hand and said, "Hey, it looks just like the one here. Was this a popular model?"

Walter pushed past her and opened his desk drawer. He pulled out a small glass vial containing another barrel cast which he opened and laid upon the table before taking several measurements.

"This is an old case of yours, isn't it, Walter?" Art asked.

"Yes, from my days at the FBI."

Sarah looked at the photo of the Deringer and held it side by side with the real one.

"They look very similar, even the checkering on the grip looks the same. What's this placard in the photo referring to Walter? It says 'JWB Deringer'. Was that a particular model?" Sarah asked.

Walter didn't answer for several seconds. Checking one last measurement in his notes from the case file he laid the calipers down and pinched the bridge of his nose.

He rubbed the stubble on his chin as he looked from Sarah to Art to Boone.

"JWB stands for John Wilkes Booth."

60

"You're saying that this is the gun used to kill President Lincoln?" Sarah asked.

"No, *this* is the gun used to kill Lincoln," Walter said waving the photograph. "I examined it in the FBI lab in nineteen ninety-seven as a favor to the National Parks Service."

"So…what then, this is a copy?" Sarah asked.

"The twin," Art said.

"Perhaps," Walter said. "It's not something I'd want to take to court, but these guns were hand-made not mass produced. Your box here is for a pair of Deringer pistols. I just assumed the missing one was used to kill those men you found out in Arapahoe County. What if this gun," Walter said grasping the pistol in his hand, "*was* the one used to kill those two men?"

"Wait…hold on. That would mean that Barclay's family was involved in the Lincoln assassination? I'm not buying that. Some historian would have found a clue or something before now." Sarah said.

"Well, now…some historians believed that the Booth Deringer may have been part of a set. They were commonly paired that way back then. No one ever found another one with Booth's possessions so the theory never gained any traction."

"Wasn't Booth an actor, or something? How would he be related to Barclay?"

"Augustus," Boone spoke up.

"What?" Sarah asked.

"Of course," Art said snapping his fingers. "The letter."

"What letter?" Walter and Sarah asked at the same time.

"The letter that brought his great grandfather out to Colorado," Art said motioning to Boone. "You said the woman writing the letter described a handsome young actor that was all fired up and stormed out of the house during their meeting. What if he grabbed the pistol on his way out the door?" Art said.

"If that's true, this could be one of the most significant findings in American history," Sarah said.

Bloodlines

"No," Boone said. One by one he snatched the pistol, barrel cast, and fired bullet and placed them in the silver box on Walter's desk. Closing the lid he turned the key, locked it, and slid the key into his pocket.

"Um, that gun is evidence," Sarah said.

"Not anymore," he said.

"Boone..." Art said before being cut off.

"No, sir. This secret stays with me."

"I think you're over-reacting just a bit," Art said. "It's over, Boone. It's been over for a hundred and fifty years. One could argue it was over the day we beat the British."

Boone fixed a look of disbelief on Art as he shook his head from side to side.

"No. This secret is toxic. Your friend Seaton, Daniel, Sarah here, you...me...all of us put in peril over a secret of power and influence." He said as he pointed to everyone in the room.

"But, Barclay is dead," Sarah said.

"His bloodline ain't."

"Bloodline? I doubt very much his children will pose a threat to anyone," Art said.

"You don't, huh? You of all people should recognize the lengths to which a son will avenge his father, or have you forgotten about the other night?"

Art sighed.

"What do you think will happen if this story goes public and others start poking around like your friend, Seaton? There ain't no telling how many others are involved in this conspiracy and what they'll do to stop it from coming out. Are you willing to go all the way with these folks because a small team of Russian assassins may be the least of your worries."

"What are you proposing?" Art asked.

"I take the box."

"You're just going to go into hiding again...then what?" Art asked.

Boone thought about it for a minute as he rolled the idea around in his head a moment.

"You're right."

"Good, I'm glad..."

"I'm done hiding. I know who these jokers are now and what's at stake," Boone said.

"So…"

"I'm going after them."

"That's crazy," Sarah said.

Art held out a hand to quiet her. "Boone…the information in that box concerns all Americans. Have you considered that?"

"Art…this is between my family and theirs. It don't concern you or anyone else."

"Boone…" Art said before he was cut off.

"No. I appreciate everything you've done Art but…it's my problem now."

Art sat on the edge of the examination table and crossed his arms. "You're not a young man anymore Boone."

Boone huffed and smiled. "True enough but, there is another DeFrance. I think it's time I teach him to hunt."

61

Sarah had been waiting two days for Daniel to return to the Facility. She was reading a biography of George Washington when a soft knock came at her door. Sarah froze. This moment had been played out a million times in her mind but she wasn't prepared for the onslaught of emotion welling up inside her.

She closed the book, slid her feet into her slippers, and shuffled across the wooden floor. She stopped for a split-second at the mirror in the foyer and let her Chestnut hair out of the ponytail. Daniel liked it down. She grasped the handle and took a deep breath before throwing the door open.

The sight of him took her breath away. He leaned against the door jamb and flashed his pearly white teeth in a broad smile.

"Hey beautiful," he said.

"Hey there handsome."

Sarah ran the tips of her fingers through his wavy black hair as she gazed into his deep brown eyes. Daniel grabbed her hips and drew her close until their lips reunited. The first kiss was normal; even timid, but then it changed. Maybe it was just the time apart; or maybe it was her brush with death but, after a moment, Sarah was overtaken with lust. She felt Daniel's body tighten and the kissing became more passionate.

Daniel lifted her up and she wrapped her legs around his waist as he carried her over the threshold and kicked the door shut. The next hour was a blur of bare skin, brown eyes, and bed sheets. It was like their first time all over again she thought. She was exhausted when they finished and collapsed her head on his chest. She laid there until her breathing was steady.

"I'm so glad you're home safe," she said dragging her fingers over his chest hair in little circles.

"From what I've heard…you were in a lot more danger than I was."

She didn't know why but she smiled. "Naw. Nothing my fury little soldier and I couldn't handle. How is he by the way?"

"Ranger? The vet said it will take time to adjust to the prosthetic limb but he should be chasing down rabbits in a few weeks."

"A prosthetic limb?" Sarah asked, looking surprised.

"It's cutting edge stuff. It looks bionic or something. Once the doc heard about his military service he did the surgery for free and the CSU Vet School provided the prosthetic."

"You brought him back up here then?"

"Art insisted that he stay at the main house. Tilly was feeding him choice cuts of elk loin when I left."

"I know I shouldn't but, I feel responsible. Do you think he hates me?"

Daniel put a finger under her chin and turned her to look up at him.

"Why would you think that?"

"You know…"

"Sarah, he lost his leg…not his heart."

"I know but…he made it through so much over there…in war…and then to come back here…"

Daniel cut her off. "Sarah, a soldier doesn't always choose his battlefield but he always shows up ready to fight. Ranger would do it all again without hesitation, believe me."

Sarah looked deep into his eyes and brushed his cheek with the back of her hand.

"What about you?" she asked.

"What?"

"Would you go back…if they called?"

"They won't call."

"That's not an answer," she said.

Daniel offered a reassuring smile. "I'm done fighting."

Sarah didn't know why but she felt her eyes begin to well up with tears. She fought them back before they spilled onto her cheeks.

"Hey…" he said.

"I just don't want to lose you," she said.

"You won't," he said wiping a tear from her cheek.

"That's good to hear," she said as she lay back against his chest. "Hey, are you hungry?"

"I'm starving," he said.

Bloodlines

Sarah spent the rest of the afternoon preparing elk roast with rosemary potatoes, asparagus, and homemade biscuits; his favorite. She even made a dark gingerbread with lemon curd for dessert. Daniel built a roaring fire and filled in additional detail of his adventure with Art while she cooked. When he was finished, it was her turn to tell him about the letters in the silver box.

"Oh, I almost forgot. I have something for you," Sarah said.

Sarah grabbed a small box from the kitchen counter and handed it to him with a smile.

Daniel looked confused. "What is it?"

"Open it and find out silly."

Daniel untied the thin pale blue bow and pried open the palm-sized wooden box. Lying upon padded batting was the small oval medallion featuring an apple. It was polished to a high luster and glistened in the fire light.

"Is this?"

"Yep. Boone wanted to be here to give it to you personally, but he left yesterday."

"I can't take this. It should be in a museum or something."

"He thought you'd say that. He told me that there was no one who deserved it more than you did. Do you see the inscription on it?"

"Amor Patriae Vincit," Daniel read aloud.

"It means the love of country conquers. He made me memorize it. He said you'd understand what it meant."

Daniel nodded slightly and placed the medallion back in the box. Sarah caught the slightest hint of sorrow in his expression.

"You don't look happy," Sarah said.

"No, I'm fine. It's appreciated."

"You can put it with all those other medals you keep hidden in your gun safe," she said trying to get him to smile.

It worked, a little.

"He sure is an interesting guy," Sarah said.

"Yeah…" Daniel said tapping his finger on the small box.

"I can't imagine spending your whole life protecting something that's a mystery to you. I mean, he was willing to lay down his life for a promise, a pledge, for a secret in a silver box." Sarah said.

"Love of country," he whispered.

343

Sarah eyed him carefully. He was sweating and rubbing his hands together.

"Daniel...you're turning white as a sheet. Are you all right?"

Daniel cleared his throat, not once, but twice before coming around the counter to face her.

"Um, I actually have something for you, too."

"You didn't have to get me anything. Is it expensive? Just kidding," she said laughing.

Daniel looked back and forth between her green eyes. His expression was so serious, she thought.

"What is it?"

"You know what I said before...about not fighting anymore."

"Yeah."

"Well, that wasn't entirely true. There is one thing I'm willing to fight for."

"Daniel," she said blushing and rubbing his arm.

"These last few days...I've been asking myself a lot of questions."

"Like what?" she asked. Sarah watched for several seconds as he seemed to search for the right words.

"You know for most of my life I've been a professional soldier. The mission, the objectives, they all came from someone else. I measured my self-worth, my purpose, by the mission and the men around me. Now...now I'm in charge. So I've been asking myself what is my 'silver box'? What would I commit a life of selfless devotion to without any promise of reward or outcome?"

Sarah took his hand in hers. "Come up with any answers?"

Daniel squeezed her hand before letting go. He dug into his pocket and pulled out a small black jewelry box. Sarah clasped a hand over her mouth as Daniel knelt down on one knee and opened it. She felt a sudden wave of nausea as she steadied herself against the counter.

"Sarah, will you..."

"Oh, Daniel...yes!"

The End

Bloodlines

Also by Tom Adair

Fiction
The Scent of Fear

Non-fiction
Planning Your Career in Forensics

From investigating the shootings at Columbine High School to locating gravesites in the remote back country of the Rockies, Tom Adair has lived a life most crime authors only write about.

An internationally recognized forensic scientist, he has a Bachelor's degree in Anthropology and a Master's degree in Entomology. He has served as the president of the Association for Crime Scene Reconstruction, Rocky Mountain Association of Bloodstain Pattern Analysts, and the Rocky Mountain Division of the International Association for Identification. While in law enforcement he was board certified as a senior crime scene analyst, was one of only 40 board-certified bloodstain pattern analysts and one of 80 board-certified footwear examiners worldwide.

In addition to writing over 60 scientific papers, he has served as the editor of an international peer-reviewed science journal. Over his 15 year career he has been interviewed by and consulted for television, text books, novels, magazines, and newspaper articles as well as documentaries on the Discovery Channel and National Geographic. He continues to teach and conduct research in the forensic sciences. When he's not writing he enjoys hunting, hiking, fishing, and camping in Colorado's back country with his wife and chocolate lab.

authortomadair.com